Fall from Grace

Fall from Grace

An Inspector McLevy Mystery

DAVID ASHTON

First published in Great Britain in 2007 by
Polygon, an imprint of Birlinn Ltd
West Newington House
10 Newington Road
Edinburgh EH9 1QS

www.birlinn.co.uk

ISBN 10: 1 84697 007 5
ISBN 13: 978 1 84697 007 8

The publishers acknowledge subsidy from

 Scottish
Arts Council

towards the publication of this volume.

British Library Cataloguing-in-Publication Data
A catalogue record for this book is available
on request from the British Library.

Typeset in Great Britain by Antony Gray
Printed and bound by Creative Print and Design,
Ebbw Vale, Wales

TO
LISA and MADELEINE

1

To die the death, for naught long time may last;
The summer's beauty yields to winter's blast.

THOMAS SACKVILLE, *The Mirror for Magistrates*

Inspector James McLevy looked at his shadowy image in the glass of the window.

'You are a miserable bugger,' he thus addressed the standing figure.

Past and through the ghostly outlines of his face, he viewed the city of Edinburgh stretching out below him, the various lights reflecting up into the night sky.

For a moment he thought to see a shooting star far away in the distance but decided it was a firework left over from Bonfire Night.

Of late he had taken to prowling the bookstalls of Leith marketplace, randomly buying anything that caught his eye. His latest haul included some stories by Edgar Allan Poe and a tattered book of Arab legends. Poe had little to offer on shooting stars but the wise men of the East were of the opinion that these manifestations were firebrands hurled by the angels to keep out the wild spirits of nature, which seek to climb the constellations and peek into heaven.

No danger of McLevy climbing any constellation, he didn't have the puff.

The inspector crossed to the coal fire where on one side of the hearth a black encrusted tin coffee pot had its domain, lifted the thing up and shook it gloomily.

Dry as a bone. And his fourth cup of coffee, some of the grains of which were still lodged in his teeth, had produced no discernible effect on his depression of spirits.

As he clattered the pot back down, there was a stirring on the other side of the hearth.

Bathsheba opened one yellow eye to gaze at this intruder upon her slumber; a regular visitor of the evening, she would scratch at the window for entry, insinuate her elegant presence, lap up some milk from the saucer, curl up and sleep for a time, then slide back off into the night.

McLevy envied her that. He was stuck. She was on the move, a black cat that had crossed his path.

'Whit luck have you ever brought me, eh?' he demanded fiercely.

The cat went back to sleep and McLevy walked back to look down at a small rickety table where the plate from his supper had been shoved aside and its place taken by a thick ledger of sorts with red covers which lay open, the white page staring up at him in mute accusation.

To avoid this silent indictment, McLevy concentrated his gaze upon the scrapings of his meal; maiden's hair and dribbly beards, the coarse sinews of the meat boiled into pliant submission and the water then used to cook the curly kale as vegetable accompaniment.

It was a speciality of his landlady, Mrs MacPherson, who would hand the steaming mixture over to him at the door as if it was some sort of Dundonian ambrosia.

She did, indeed, hail from Bonny Dundee. He had many memories of that city, few of them happy and, in fact, he suspected that these dark submerged hauntings might be more than a contributory factor towards his present malaise.

That and a woman with gypsy eyes.

The page still gleamed white; he sighed, sat down and picked up a short stubby pencil.

Other diarists might have quills and parchment; he had a blunt pencil and an old ledger, which was a relic from a past case of embezzlement

He was in the habit of jotting down whatever came into his head most evenings; nothing that would change the fate of

8

humanity but it would preserve a record of his intuitions and thoughts, perhaps even philosophical musings.

One day he might publish such jottings of sagacity and be hailed as a fountain of wisdom. More likely he would be laughed out of the Leith police station so best keep it confidential for the nonce.

In fact he had kept it so confidential this night, he had so far not written a word.

Time to unburden, but how to begin?

He had read in the Arab book the idea that man was a mixture of the materiality that made up the universe.

It was either that or the maiden's hair and dribbly beards.

The inspector made his choice, tongue sticking out from the side of his mouth, head bent close to the paper.

It could be his near eyesight was failing, but he wrote anyway. Always the same heading, only the date changed.

The Diary of James McLevy, 7 November 1880

Of all the elements, fire is the least forgiving. Examine hell for instance. Or take Icarus, flying like an angel till the flame of the sun melted the wax from his wings and sent him plunging through the air, which likewise didn't give a damn, in a downward dive till he hit the ocean and sank like a stone. Water isn't all that merciful either.

Come to think of it, earth is the only one of four that gives a body half a chance. The blessed earth. We trample it beneath our boots and gouge it like a butcher a dead animal or a surgeon his cadaver, yet the earth does its level best to forgive us. Our sins.

A case that began almost a year ago has come to its natural end, and tomorrow will see the lid closed.

As is often with my pursuits, at times I was like a whirling Dervish, and at others, a mere bystander as Fate rolled out the dice.

The result of that throw was to witness a disaster in which all four elements played their parts. The reluctant earth, savage

9

fire, howling wind and ice-cold water.

Be that as it may, I shall attend the closing. The lady of the house will be concomitant. There's always a woman to hand. And the devil's never far away either.

As long as folk steer the middle course, we may all rest easy but that rarely happens. Someone somewhere, high or low, tries to bend occasion to their will without success and then, to gratify a hunger they barely comprehend, takes a wee step sideways, a deviation, and imperceptibly puts in motion events that set the gates of hell quivering with anticipation.

To strive beyond yourself is human aspiration and yet it is also an item on Satan's breakfast table. Right next to the boiled egg.

I should stop now. I fear my thought is moving in a direction that might well land me in the asylum.

But why does the vision of Icarus still hold in my mind?

Man strains every muscle to rise and embrace that which cradles the seed of his own destruction.

An unearthly yowl broke into this meditation; Bathsheba was at the window ready to embark upon her midnight prowl.

McLevy, with a sudden burst of energy, leapt up, pulled up the sill to let her depart and then leant his head out to follow her progress.

He watched as she padded along the damp slates and then slipped out of sight.

A strange cheerfulness unexpectedly possessed him, as if he had left his gloom upon the page.

James McLevy, inspector of police, would attack his next investigation with appropriate ferocity.

Crime was like the blood in his veins.

He looked out once more over his city. Edinburgh. And somewhere, towards the sea, the parish of Leith. His patch, where he was King of the Castle.

The cold November air stung at McLevy's face as he let out a whoop of laughter that echoed in the still night.

2

Mary Rough looked grimly into the flame of the oil lamp as she listened to her son thrashing around in the recesses of the warehouse.

Noise enough to wake the dead, or, more to her concern, a distant night watchman walking the Leith docks. It had been a big mistake to let that boy near whisky but his nerves needed steadying, the great gowk, and a rinse of kill-me-deadly was all that would do the trick.

Unfortunately, it also gave Daniel Rough the illusion that he was ruler of the world, and, in addition, as is so often the result of whisky, brought out the cantankerous side of his nature.

Not that it needed much bringing out. He would take issue with his own shadow, but, in drink, Daniel would beat that shadow to the ground and stamp it to death with his big hobnailed boot. Many was the time Mary had witnessed him crashing his foot down with enough force to raise sparks from stone, as he tried to destroy the fiend below.

There are seven kinds of beastly drunk: Swine, who sleeps and pukes, Sheep, who cannot speak, Martin, who drinks himself back sober, Goat, who is lascivious, Fox, who is crafty, Ape, who leaps and sings, and Lion who is quarrelsome. Daniel was a combination of Ape and Lion.

It was Mary's own fault. She had spoiled him as a wee boy because of his infirmity and now, as a huge man, he still bore the imprint of that indulgence.

His hulking form emerged from the shadows as he dragged out some large freight cases, still marked with the name of the ship, the *Dorabella*, which he began to pile up in the middle of the floor, whilst singing jaggedly under his breath,

'Wee Willie Winkie, rins through the town,
Up stairs and doon stairs, in his nicht gown.'

It is doubtful if Daniel knew that in some Jacobite songs, Willie Winkie was supposedly the nickname of William III, but he crashed a last wooden crate into position to compensate for any lack of learning, and let out a bellow which echoed on and on in the emptiness of the building.

'Mammy. I have it all in hand! Bring me my tools of trade!'

'Can ye no' be quiet?' she admonished. 'D'ye want the world tae know?'

A wild laugh came in response. The whisky may have calmed his nerves for a while, but now they were breaking loose again. It was always so when he came to this point, for he both loved and feared the fire.

It was a large warehouse, piled high with packing cases. All wooden. All grist to the mill. The ceiling was high and vaulted, a good updraught and plenty of gaps in the walls for the wind to whistle in and fan the flames.

Mary noted all this with a keen eye as she crossed towards him, carrying the lamp in one hand and a large sack, which she bore lightly enough, in the other.

The light from the lamp caught Daniel's shadow and threw it in grotesque against the assembled pile, as he capered round it, dragging his twisted right foot behind like a horse would haul a ploughshare through stony earth.

His infirmity. It had twisted his nature as well.

Daniel snatched at the sack and emptied it out, shaking a thick mass of wood shavings on to the floor, and then scraped them round the heaped cases with his warped, misshapen foot, giggling like an uncontrollable child.

'What's sae funny?' asked Mary, who was growing increasingly nervous, the sooner they were out of this place the better; she had a bad feeling which was getting worse by the second. Not helped by the fact that she had failed to move her bowels all day and was dying to sit on a midnight cackie-pot.

Daniel bent over and blew playfully at some shavings to propel them like a snowdrift towards the bottom of his created edifice. Then he straightened up and recited a fragment of what was swirling through his mind.

'I says tae the joiner fellow, "Can I have these shavings kind sir?" Says he, "Whit for?" Says I, "They start a fine fire." '

He laughed at that then a following thought, not so pleasant struck him. 'The auld bugger even wanted payment, is there nae charity in this thieving bastard world?'

His face suddenly contorted in anger and he produced a heavy hammer from the inside depths of his jacket to bring it crashing down repeatedly on the lid of one of the cases.

'So, I gave him this blow, then I gave him another!'

'Ye're a liar,' said Mary. 'Ye gave him the payment.'

Daniel ignored this shaft of mother-wit and dashed his hammer down on the dislodged lid, breaking it into pieces which he added to the accumulation.

'Ye don't need all that,' she remonstrated, 'the place is dry as a bone. Go up like the flames o' hell.'

Again he paid no attention and, his manic burst of energy far from exhausted, shoved the hammer back into his pocket then delved into the contents of the broken case, emerging with a small square box which he opened up and sniffed, in apparent ecstasy.

'Stinko D'Oros, ripe and ready.'

'Don't touch the merchandise!' came the sharp warning but Daniel, in response, bawled out like a market trader.

'Best quality, dozen in the box!'

'Quieten down, for the love of Christ!'

He bowed his head in seeming contrition, meekly closed the lid, handed the box over to Mary's keeping, and then signalled for the lamp.

'I'll do it,' said Mary.

'Give it me.'

'You're no' in control.'

'Give it me!!'

There was a drunken evil glare in his eye that frightened her. Mother or not, she sometimes wondered if, one sweet day, her darling son would split the maternal skull with his big fine hammer.

She handed over the lamp and he snuffed out the wick, leaving them both in complete darkness. Then he swung the vessel round to release the oil, which spattered over the heap of shavings and wood; laughing wildly as some of the fluid landed and slid like mucus all down his front.

'A wee lick here, a wee lick there, ach the whole damn thing!'

There was a crash of breaking metal and glass as he hurled the lamp to shatter on the sharp edge of the crates.

'Watch your body now!' Mary called out in the pitch-black surrounding her, an edge of panic in her tone. She had a superstitious terror of the dark, and always slept with a candle by the bed lest night-demons came to steal her soul for his Satanic Majesty.

Daniel fumbled in his pocket for a lucifer, which was struck up to illuminate his sweaty distorted face, eyes bulging in the sudden light.

'This place will fire like a tinder-box,' she warned, moving back to safe distance while she could still see.

'And I'm just the boy tae do it,' said Daniel with pride. But as he moved towards the pile, his boot crunched on a shard of glass and he staggered slightly.

'For Christ's good sake guard yerself!' Mary hissed, shoving the box that he had given her inside the deep pocket of her old coat, a souvenir from the time when she had once been a shop-lifter of high repute.

'Ach, it's my bad foot Mammy,' came the derisive, muffled response.

Daniel bent over, cupping the lucifer in hand, now it was time, now would see his fear go up in smoke. He crooned some more of the song, giving the words a sinister lilt.

'Tirling at the window, crying at the lock,
Are the weans in their bed, for now it's ten o'clock?'

For a moment time stood still, then tragedy which had been biding its occasion in the shadows, made a dire and purposeful entrance.

As Daniel dropped the lucifer on the shavings, they flared into life, leaping up like a tiger from ambush and found a sympathetic response from the oil spilled on his trousers and coat. He howled in pain, lost his footing and fell forward on to a blaze of his own creation as the rest of the dry tinder exultantly joined the conflagration.

In a matter of seconds, a wall of flame had formed a barrier between the horrified Mary and her combustible son.

She could hear his screams and reached out her arms helplessly to call his name as he burned like a pillar of fire.

But he led no tribe towards the Promised Land. The fear that had always haunted him had been well founded. The fire had claimed him, embraced him like a loving father and was teaching its child the secrets of white heat.

His shrieks of agony rang in Mary's ears as the flames leapt towards her, seeking another convert to the cause.

3

Like pilgrims to th'appointed place we tend;
The world's an inn, and death the journey's end.

JOHN DRYDEN, *Palamon and Arcite*

Dean Village, 8 November 1880

Margaret Bouch watched on, as her husband's coffin was lowered into the ground. The ropes held and it went smoothly enough into the appointed slot. She blinked a little as the icy, slanting November rain which had swept across Dean Cemetery from the moment the pitifully small cortège had entered the gates, stung her face through the black veil in retribution for tears unshed.

She recollected that as a child, funerals had always provoked in her a perverse desire to cock a snoot, to whirl a mad cartwheel, heels in the air, petticoats a'flying, to scandalise the moon faces of the mourners with flesh and bone.

What if she did so now, she pondered to herself?

What if she ripped the dripping bonnet from her recently widowed head, flipped it neatly to join the lumps of earth already falling on the coffin lid as the ropes were hauled out of the grave, and called aloud, 'I'll dance the hornpipe with the sailor boys tonight, how does that recommend itself unto you, Sir Thomas, my darling one?'

Perhaps not, was her decision. Save it for another day.

Margaret looked across to where their three children, all grown now, huddled together under a weeping umbrella.

Her son's pale face was set in stone and manly forbearance.

Everyone thought him an absolute brick, and who was she to disagree? He had accompanied them every day to the Court of Inquiry and they had both watched as his father's proud façade cracked like the very bridge itself.

Every day she had observed Sir Thomas ignore her and lean more and more heavily upon the filial arm as the clouds of shame and disgrace gathered above his head.

And then they had burst.

As she brought this to mind, another squall of rain hit her through the veil, the sudden violence driving some of the mourners back from the edge of the grave.

But Margaret Bouch stood firm. She was the widow after all. Widows don't give an inch.

The minister droned on, something about the Kingdom of Heaven and how to get there, surely better to quote from the Psalm? 'Praise the Lord upon earth: ye dragons, and all deeps; Fire and Hail, snow and vapours; Wind and storm, fulfilling his word.'

Praise the Lord indeed, was her unhallowed thought. He had shown no mercy that dreadful night towards the last year's end, nor, in Margaret's experience, had he ever demonstrated much inclination towards clemency upon earth.

The Reverend Jeremiah Sneddon of the Episcopalian Church of Scotland, a man in her opinion who more than lived up to his name, had insisted upon being bare-headed and his wispy white hair, plastered to his skull, left him to look like a monkey caught out in the rain.

Margaret had a quick glance round to make sure no one was aware of these profane contemplations but she was safe behind the veil. What a dreadful woman she was to be sure. Last night had she not drunk of strong whisky? And more than one glass. In the morning she had noticed her fingers tremble as she donned the widow's weeds.

She fumbled for her handkerchief, slyly raised her hand under the damp veil as if touching the cloth to her face, breathed out and sniffed. No. Not a trace. A faint redolence only of violets, from the lozenges sucked so assiduously after her toilette that very morning.

Toilette, Margaret reflected, now there's a respectable word, for was she not a respectable lady?

She felt as if her husband had been an iron band around her body and now, free of its constraint, she was shaking to pieces as the train roared overhead.

Margaret shivered. One of the newspapers had as its front page an artist's impression of the calamity, men, women and children falling into the bleak December sea like so many brittle leaves. Although almost a year ago, she could not rid her mind of that image.

And what of Sir Thomas, she wondered? What pictures were frozen inside the cold obstruction of his mind?

She had experienced an impersonal kind of compassion for the man despite the secrets he had concealed. A dutiful pity. But he had shut her from his life and locked her out like a poor beast in the rain. Year by year, the little wife had withered

17

and dwindled while he and his true love kissed and fondled to heart's content.

Now, Mistress Bouch was free. Free to destroy herself in any way she saw fit.

The minister closed his bible with a dull, righteous thud and Margaret became conscious that she was the focus of many eyes.

For a moment she was confused then remembered the protocol of interment. The widow knelt down, groped for a portion of the damp, sodden earth and cast it into the grave before her. The muddy mass landed on the polished oaken lid, stuck to one of the brass fittings, then slid slowly out of sight towards oblivion.

She hoped sincerely that would do the trick.

And it did. She watched the others follow suit, the rain herding in their thrown clods like a drover, and then the pall-bearers began to drift away. Just like her mind.

Margaret had felt such a welcome separation from reality since her lord and master had died and prayed most earnestly for its continuance.

In the meantime, all ceremonies were to be observed and she would play her part. They would all reconvene at the house in Bernard Street; a little too near the Leith docks for some, but Sir Thomas had it purchased as his base in Edinburgh because he liked to walk to the sea and gaze upon that which he planned to conquer.

Reconvene. She could just see it now. Tasteful funeral meats would be passed from hand to hand, malt whisky raised to lips, not the grieving widow's of course, and then after a respectful time the mourners would take their pious departure, surreptitiously scraping heels on the kerbing stone outside lest some oozing stigma had attached itself to their shoes along with the earth from the cemetery.

Margaret became aware that a man was standing before her muttering words of comfort she could scarcely hear such was the blessed separation.

A fellow engineer to her husband, bound by professional code to attend; a few of these, the family, and that was all Sir Thomas had to see him on his journey.

Not much of a show to be sure, but then the bridge builder had few intimates, certainly not her, no, few intimates, save the one.

She brought his face to mind.

Alan Telfer, his personal secretary, who scarcely bothered to conceal the look of cold disdain in his eyes if she dared to visit Edinburgh and disturb them at their work; this stupid interfering woman, this dowdy squashed creature who witnessed them with their heads together over the sacred drawings.

A fine combination.

But Mister Alan Telfer was missing from the scene due to the undisputed fact that he had, some time ago, blown out his brains.

Quel dommage. So regrettable.

A dreadful sight to be sure, she remembered.

She had borne witness to so many things.

In truth, there were two participants missing from the scene. Where, she wondered, was the other?

A gust of wind blasted the rain almost horizontally into the face of Reverend Sneddon, and the man of god moved hastily to follow the straggle of departing mourners towards the waiting carriages.

He left a space where piety had endured and through that frame, past the attendant gravediggers who stood patiently biding the time to begin their labour, Margaret saw a shrouded figure in the distance under a threadbare dripping tree.

The inspector. He had come after all. How like the man.

4

And take upon 's the mystery of things,
As if we were God's spies;

WILLIAM SHAKESPEARE, *King Lear*

Leith, December 1879
Murder is a dirty business. The corpse of the old man lay in a dismal
posture on the stone flags of the scullery floor where it had fallen, body
wrapped in a heavy outdoor coat, the blue serge still damp from last
night's rain.

An apologetic little dribble of blood led from the crushed head at
the foot of the stairs where the fellow had rested quietly enough until
assailed by the shriek of a hysterical kitchen maid who had arrived at the
crack of dawn, to help prepare breakfast.

Indeed some ham and a slab of liver, fresh bought that morning from
the butchers, were huddled together upon a plate near the sink where the
selfsame maid, who had entered from the side door, had dumped them
down before turning to discover the carnage lurking behind.

The liver also bore traces of blood though McLevy doubted if it would
receive the requisite cleansing.

He also doubted that even if treated so and fried up with some onions
and the ham, there would be much appetite in the house.

Nothing tempers the carnal like a cadaver.

Unless you are a policeman.

Constable Mulholland was upstairs exercising his Irish charm on
the maid who was a hefty specimen, and one of those glandular females
that the inspector avoided like the plague. Mulholland, however, was good
with glands.

McLevy was left with the dead butler.

The inspector had painstakingly scrutinised the floor slabs down to
the very cracks. Just under the man's skull he found fragments of flesh
and bone. Difficult to tell whether they had spilled out after his head

had been split and he had fallen, or if they were the result of the fall itself. But from the depth of the wound, he would have to assume a blow. A savage blow.

He then poked into the myriad moist crevices of the scullery but found nothing untoward.

A few cockroaches scuttled guiltily into hiding but they, undoubtedly, had an alibi. He remembered reading once in one of his books the fact that cockroaches were revered in Ancient Egypt. A mysterious bunch, the Egyptians.

It would seem as if entry had been forced by the jemmying open of one of the windows at the back garden, which provided access to the lower ground-floor level where the kitchen and scullery were based.

The question was, had the fellow been on his way in to commit the robbery when he encountered the butler, or had he already committed it and been on his way out? The inspector fervently hoped the latter. If nothing had been taken, then nothing could be traced, and that would shut off a fertile source of inquiry because in McLevy's experience the pawnshops in certain low areas of Leith were veritable mines of information. And he knew how to dig up the lode of crime therein, pick and shovel.

There were some scrapes down the stone steps which suggested that the old fellow may well have been struck at the top wee landing where the door led out into the hall and then fallen like a shot crow. Minute examination of these steps in turn had yielded nothing. The servant's skull had been cracked open, that was obvious enough, but the murder implement was nowhere to be seen. Nor was the murderer. Not a clue. What a pity.

He leant over and looked into the sightless eyes of the corpse; the old man's skin was stretched tightly over high cheekbones, the sockets above them deep and hollow, lips drawn back over the teeth as if the butler had sucked in death from a silver cup.

'I don't suppose, Archie,' he said, having been reliably informed that the man's name was Archibald Gourlay, 'I don't suppose ye might pass me a description of your assailant?'

No answer was forthcoming, but McLevy persisted.

'Anything that might help, no matter how small, rack your brains, sir.'

However the aforementioned brains had a chasm bashed into them, leaving the head looking like an indented round of cheese, and, with a sigh, the inspector brought the one-sided conversation to an end by pulling up gently a blanket which had been laid on the body to cover the bewildered frightened face, then made his way up the stairs to search out some live members of the household.

He emerged into the narrow gloomy hall, with a high, pale, consumptive ceiling, which did nothing to dispel the claustrophobia always induced in McLevy by the trappings of middle-class decorum. Queen Victoria would have been proud of this hallway; it was a testament to her glorious reign. The epitome of denied joy.

A little, grudging natural light came through the cold blue and green stained-glass window above the heavy street door, to be absorbed by the brown mottled walls. A dark knobbly umbrella stand was on sentry duty at the entrance, and halfway down the thin corridor jutted a small table, a wooden bare upright chair at each side, and a vase set on a white doily precisely in the middle of the table surface.

The edges of the lace doily were curled up slightly as if retracting from the general murk, and the vase, as far as he could see, was empty, unless it contained the ashes of some ancestor. Could be. It was a bilious pale yellow colour that might possibly indicate the funereal pallor of a long-dead relative.

McLevy hesitated. All the doors were closed and he had but a hazy notion of the geography of the house having been conducted straight to the murder scene.

He could hear the murmur of Mulholland's voice from somewhere off to the side and a smothered high-pitched response as the girl tried to gulp down her sobs and talk at the same time.

Aye, now he had the situation. The constable and maid were closeted in the small parlour and this door, against which he now pressed his ear, must be for the main drawing room.

There was no getting away from it, the inspector thought, he was a terrible nosy man. Jean Brash, the premier madam of the best bawdy-hoose in Edinburgh, the Just Land, had many times remarked that if you gave McLevy heaven, he would want hell along with it in case he missed out on something.

It was time he should visit Jean Brash. She made the best cup of coffee in Edinburgh. A Lebanese grinding.

Now, was that more sobbing that he heard through the panel? But not a high note, more like a low choked swallow of regret. On an impulse, he did not knock but silently turned the handle and slid into the chamber like a ghost.

5

> I had a dove and the sweet dove died;
> And I have thought it died of grieving:
> O, what could it grieve for? Its feet were tied,
> With a silken thread of my own hand's weaving.
>
> JOHN KEATS, *I had a dove and the sweet dove died*

A woman stood in the centre of the room, her head bowed, a stray shaft of greyish light from the dark curtained window catching at her figure like a child its mother's skirts.

McLevy observed the scene silently and, after a moment, she sensed his presence and lifted up a smooth white face unstained by tears, the skin almost translucent. Like a pearl.

The lady of the house. He had briefly glimpsed her as the secretary Alan Telfer had ushered him downstairs to make acquaintance with the corpse. Wife of Sir Thomas Bouch. Margaret, by name.

'Well Maggie,' he wondered to himself, 'your eyes are dry enough, but what haunts you this day?'

She was a petite woman, high cheekbones and above them the aforesaid eyes surprisingly dark and slanted, gypsy fashion, with dark eyebrows arching above like lightning conductors. A compact little body, contained and corseted, the feet deft and dainty.

McLevy was a great observer of women's feet and what covered their nakedness. These small boots, elastic-sided, peeping shyly out from below the dark severe hem of her dress, though in black leather to match her raven hair with its austere middle-parting, were surprisingly possessed of pointed toes.

Not snubbed in rectitude, but pointing. Straight as a die. At him. Now, there's a thing.

Nothing betrayed character like shoes. His own were solid and serviceable but that was a disguise like the rest of him and he lived in terror of the day that someone would rip the mask away and reveal him in the light.

When she spoke, her voice was musical enough but in a minor key. Muted. Nothing percussive.

'How may I help you, inspector?'

She seemed in no way perturbed that he had popped up in front of her with no word of warning. Nothing glandular here, and yet he sensed something, what was it? A vixen bites through her own flesh to escape the wire of the snare?

He must stop drinking so much coffee; it provoked his intuition to hallucinatory extremes.

Back to terra firma.

'I'm hoping that you can, Mistress Bouch.'

'It is my fervent wish. Fire away.'

McLevy nodded, but his mind was busy with the last two words. Perhaps her father had been a sharpshooter.

'Archibald Gourlay?' he ventured.

'The poor creature.'

'The corpse. What were his habits?'

'Habits?'

'Uhuh. They may have led him to his death, ye see. I need to know them. I need to know his life.'

'But surely – by accident, he chanced upon a thief. And suffered – death.'

'I'm not a great believer in accident.'

For a moment her eyes drifted away and McLevy glanced round the chamber. The walls were a drab olive green, hung with various photographs of bridges, ferry boats and trains mostly decked out in the claret and cream colours of the North British Railway Company.

Indeed, the whole aspect reminded him greatly of a waiting room in a railway station. Perhaps not surprising given Sir Thomas Bouch and his connections, but in the dark square masculine furniture which lined up against the walls like soldiers, there was not a trace to be found of femininity, not a frill to the antimacassar.

An empty space that people passed through. En route to another destination.

Margaret Bouch spoke slowly, her attention fixed inwardly, as if to hold some emotion at bay.

'Mister Gourlay had been butler here these past ten years. He managed this household to perfection.'

'Like a railway timetable?' McLevy asked, a wicked gleam lurking somewhere at the back of his eyes.

'Precisely so. He was a kind, gentle old man who lived to serve.'

'And died, no doubt, in the same capacity,' muttered the inspector. 'What of his desires?'

'Desires?'

'We all have them.'

McLevy's remark caused the woman to blink. He was somewhat amused by that; no doubt her acquaintance of policemen was slight, the occasional overbearing chief constable at official functions, and the inspector did not correspond to any known specification. No fixed abode.

'I never asked him,' she replied somewhat primly.

'That's the trouble wi' being a servant.' McLevy frowned as if personally affronted. 'Nobody ever asks you.'

He noted a flash of outrage in her eyes. Good.

'Let us therefore leave desires and return to habit,' he said. 'Of a Wednesday evening, what was his custom?'

'It was his night off. He would go and have a few drams with old friends. "A wee gab in the corner of the Old Ship," he would say. He loved to gossip.'

She essayed a passable imitation of an old man's voice and McLevy noted that also. A talent for mimicry was rare in a woman of this class and, more especially absent, was the willingness to display such a gift.

'The Old Ship?' he said. 'I know that tavern well, a good place for a wee dram.'

His tone was warm enough but his eyes were watchful. All friends together, eh? he thought to himself. The mistress and the servant.

25

'And he told you so? He confided that much in you?'

'Yes. But not the extent of his desires,' she replied dryly. 'Not what he wished for in his heart.'

'Peace and quiet, probably,' said the inspector, a trifle sententiously. 'Well, he's found it now.'

'Can murder bring you peace and quiet?'

She bit the words off somewhat tightly and McLevy was happy enough inside himself; getting the truth out of the respectable classes was a fiendish job, you had to catch them on the hip, or was it the hop?

'And when did he usually get back at night?'

'Late. And sometimes – slightly the worse for wear. I often heard the key scraping in the lock.'

Affection in the voice but the inspector had picked up on something else.

'Ye heard? Late at night? How so, if I may ask Mistress Bouch, to be alert so deep into the dark?'

'I sleep badly.'

'So do I,' said the inspector. 'I put it down to conscience.'

He smiled at her like a wolf in a nursery book illustration. Not chasing after Red Riding Hood or three smallish pigs; just a wolf in a green field, with all the time in the world. He often regarded himself so, and Margaret Bouch did not seem at all uncomfortable with this prospect.

Perhaps, she was part wolf herself, thought McLevy.

'So, did ye hear a scrape last night?' he continued. 'Or something else perchance?'

'I was not here, last night.'

The inspector raised his eyebrows the merest fraction and his mouth drooped slightly like a puzzled child; it was what Mulholland would recognise as McLevy's idiot look, and often drew response like a poultice.

'This is my husband's place of work, his office and study are set here on Bernard Street. The family home, his country retreat, is in Moffat.'

'That's border folk,' said McLevy. 'Sheep stealers and the like!'

He laughed loudly. She permitted herself a faint smile at this presumed witticism, but had Mulholland been on hand his long nose would have twitched in recognition that the inspector was up to his tricks.

'A fair distance.' McLevy's eyes widened at the thought. 'Back and forward all the time, eh?'

'Sir Thomas spends the week on the premises here and then at weekends, he does not. He returns.'

'To the bosom of his family?'

'That is correct,' she responded evenly.

'And you, Mistress Bouch?'

'I reside there. The Moffat house demands much of my attention.'

'But it didnae in former times, did it?'

'I beg your pardon?'

'Because, as you told me yourself, you'd lie awake in this place at night and listen to the key scraping in the lock.'

For a moment she did not answer and in the silence, a ship's horn from the Leith docks sounded in the distance like a lost soul.

'That is correct. In former times.'

'Yet, here you are today!'

McLevy beamed at her as if they had both reached a satisfactory conclusion to the exchange and Margaret Bouch shook her head as if it was spinning a little.

'I – I had some shopping to do in Edinburgh and took our carriage, we have a carriage you see, and arrived in the early morning to find this – catastrophe.'

That would mean, the inspector surmised, she had left Moffat before the break of dawn. Why such an hour? Was her arrival unannounced? Unexpected? What had she hoped to find, a house full of licentious women?

Under his scrutiny, Margaret Bouch suddenly pushed forward one of her dainty boots with the toe pointing up towards the ceiling. It was like a gesture of defiance.

'I dare say you would like to talk to my husband about all this, inspector.'

'I dare say I would.'

'Then, let me oblige you,' she said, walked to the study door, knocked sharply upon it then thrust it open.

6

And see ye not yon braid, braid road,
That lies across the lily leven?
That is the Path of Wickedness,
Though some call it the Road to Heaven.

BALLADS, Thomas the Rhymer

Dean Village, 8 November 1880

McLevy watched as Margaret Bouch picked her way down the curving cemetery path, her slight figure cutting through the rain like a shark's fin. Everyone else had quit the brow of the hill, save for three figures under a black umbrella observing her passage.

The Fates perhaps? Best keep eyes peeled for Atropos, the one who brandished the scissors for cutting the thread of life, or was that who was on the approach?

These eleven months ago, when she had opened the door to disclose her husband and his private secretary, the men had been bowed, heads together, over the drawings of the projected crossing for the Firth of Forth, the foundation stone of which had already been laid. It was an undertaking which would make Bouch's previous achievement, the Tay Bridge, seem mere child's play.

A panoramic photograph of that same bridge, upon the wall behind his desk, had towered above them all. Taken on a sunny day.

The images and conversation of the encounter raced through McLevy's mind as he watched the widow walk towards him; her figure flickered before his vision like a magic lantern show as a shaft of pale ruined sunlight broke through the clouds for a brief moment to light up the sheets of heavy, driven raindrops.

Sir Thomas Bouch had been bearded, his eyes wide set, face

impassive, the grey hair at the side of his head rising like cherub's wings. He had to his credit 300 designed miles of railway track and had built more bridges than any man of, or in, his age.

Flying high.

Alan Telfer shaved close, a thin face, pale eyes. In the Vatican he would have been private secretary to one of the Monsignors, carrying mysteries inside a scarlet sleeve.

There was also a military air to him, a straight back hinting at generations who had rushed into the cannon's mouth to die for king and country.

Here, his fanaticism had fixed itself upon one object only.

Both men had seemed oddly uninterested in the murder, as if it had happened in China.

They had been asleep, heard nothing, and would be grateful when this disturbance was over. There was much work to be done.

McLevy had been conscious of under-currents as deep and treacherous as the winter confluents of the River Tay itself.

Dark forces swirling over a bed of mud, sand and stone.

When Telfer had suggested that that the old man had in some way provoked the inconvenience of his own death by blundering in the worse for drink and grappling with the intruder instead of raising the alarm, Margaret Bouch drew in her breath as if struck to the core.

Seeing McLevy register this, the secretary, with a sideways flick of a glance and a faint dismissive smile, consigned such reactions to female irrationality and misplaced emotions. Her response had been a sudden gleam of hatred in the dark eyes, which then disappeared like lightning swallowed up in a storm.

Sir Thomas, on the other hand, had seemed to have no emotions at all. His whole being appeared to have withdrawn to a loftier plane, where great enterprises were being structured in the high reaches of his mind.

All grist to the mill.

A comical aspect had been unwittingly added to the situation when Mulholland joined the party; all five crammed within the small airless study.

The constable stood beside Margaret Bouch, nearly one foot and a half of height between them, and for a second there was a glint of humour in her eyes as she stared up at the lanky frame of Mulholland before she met McLevy's gaze and schooled her features back to dutiful serenity.

A blast of rain in his face brought McLevy back to the present moment. Perhaps he should walk up the cemetery path to meet the woman halfway. That's what a gentleman would do. But would a gentleman be lurking under a tree in the first place?

Better stand his ground.

Back to the grist.

The maid had contributed little save an ill-disguised desire to find further acquaintance with the constable in an unofficial setting, but Mulholland was somewhat sniffy about romance with kitchen maids.

When McLevy had asked the company if anything was missing from the house to support the idea of a possible burglary and also perhaps provide him with something more positive to go on than an uncommunicative corpse, Alan Telfer assured him that everything was in place.

It would seem that the investigation, hardly yet begun, was deadlocked. However, the inspector had remarked upon something.

Arranged on a long shelf running along the side of the study were the various awards and plaques that Sir Thomas had garnered during his so far meteoric career. Not at all a prideful display, the shelf somewhat tucked away in a recess, but the arrangement was disposed in orderly fashion and the inspector's sharp eye had noticed a gap in the assembly.

When he had brought it to the man's attention, Telfer was honour bound to agree. A silver candlestick, part of the gifts bestowed upon Sir Thomas when given the Freedom of the

Ancient Burgh of Dundee. It was missing. No longer to hand. An oversight on the secretary's part.

Had it by any chance been inscribed? Indeed so: '31st of May, 1878. To Sir Thomas Bouch from the grateful Burghers of Dundee.'

The inspector's first clue. He had not known then that it would lead him eventually to the mouth of hell.

A voice broke in on these ramblings.

'You might have joined us on the hill,' said the lady of the house.

Margaret was now standing in front of him and though garbed for deep mourning, was fashionably enough sculpted into her attire, the tiny waist, a dimension with which he had been granted some unexpected experience, accentuated by the sweep of her coat. She looked like a little doll, all dressed up for the funeral, bearing the weeds patiently enough but dying for a change of costume.

She would be the dancing lady to McLevy's hardy tin soldier, both perishing in the flames.

'I prefer to observe from distance,' he replied.

'From distance. How like the thing.'

She crooked her elbow and laid right hand upon her waist in an oddly provocative gesture. Behind the veil that hung from her daintily perched hat, the gypsy eyes looked him up, and looked him down. Behind the veil.

'Ye resemble a bee-keeper,' he remarked.

She laughed suddenly but there was a harsh edge, so much unspoken, she thought, so much water under the bridge. For instance, a moment in a room in Moffat when he had jammed his hat upon his head and ran for dear life.

Yet, why was he here, Margaret wondered?

Hope springs eternal.

With a swift incisive gesture, she threw back the veil to reveal her face, high cheekbones marble white amid the November gloom in a landscape of tombstones.

'And you look like . . .' she began.

---

some pig farmer's sons at the back of the barn, that he could more than hold his own.

His eyes glazed over as he dreamed of a divine consummation. He and his beloved like swans on the river; above them, blue skies and below, clear water.

However, into these sacred visions of the fragrant Emily, slid a depiction that, if not downright voluptuous, brought a definite tingle to the constable's loins.

She lay on the marital bed, a four-poster with dark velvet curtains and lashings of moonlight. Her nightgown was chaste enough, white as purity with frilly bits, but her lips were moist and parted, breath on the short side, the pupils of the eyes dilated with anticipation.

He was standing beside the plumped-up pillows, also in a nightgown, not quite as white, smiling down at her, any manifestation of desire well hidden by the burgeoning folds of flannel, but manly as a bull in the heat of summer.

Emily's bosom had found itself, perched above the level of the sheets. They were neat and starched but not the bosom. It was in motion trembling. Like the sea. Up and down. Up and down. A heavy swell.

There was a candle burning by the bed. He licked his forefinger and thumb, reached over, and put out the light.

Now they were free to wallow in the darkness.

Wallow? That couldn't be right, hogs did such in mud. No, wallow was out of the question. And there couldn't be darkness, not with the lashings of moonlight.

He shut his eyes tightly and brought his hands, palms together, up to touch his lips as if in meditation.

No. Wallow and darkness were not permissible; best concentrate on the moister, swelling aspects.

'What in god's name are you doing, constable?'

The young man spun round, eyes opened, face flushed, to meet the baleful scrutiny of his own and everyone else's appointed superior in Leith police station, Lieutenant Roach.

Margaret collected and arranged her impressions as if seeing him for the first time.

A heavy-set man with thick stubby arms; the hands small and strangely feminine possessed a grace of movement that contrasted with the rest of his constitution. The legs short, the feet small also, but planted firmly to the ground.

A somewhat comical assemblage until encountering the face. The lupine slate-grey eyes pierced a hole through to find the most secret, shameful thoughts, and behind the flesh of his cheeks, hard bone, chiselled by the east wind.

The mouth was curiously shaped, pouting almost. He wore a dark blue topcoat, collar turned up against the rain and a low-brimmed bowler, which sat somewhat uneasily on the wiry, pepper and salt hair.

His skin was parchment white, as if the sun had never troubled its surface.

'You look like an undertaker,' she concluded.

'I'm in the right place, then.'

A sudden blast of wind and rain swept in upon them and she seemed to lose her balance, toppling towards him.

His hands reached out to take her by the elbows, then arrested their motion. She regained her equilibrium close to his chest and lifted her face. The drips from the brim of his bowler fell on to her cheeks and chin. Her tongue reached out to savour one.

She let the liquid linger upon that fleshly organ, and then swallowed.

'I have come to say goodbye,' McLevy announced, his voice somewhat hoarse but he blamed it on the weather.

'Then say it.'

'Goodbye Mistress Bouch. The case is over.'

She laughed into the teeth of the wind, turned abruptly, pulled down her veil and marched off and back up the hill to where the Furies still stood and waited, under the umbrella.

McLevy felt an emptiness inside, but he could fill that up with coffee.

7

If with me you'd fondly stray
Over the hills and far away.
JOHN GAY, *The Beggar's*

Mulholland gazed with some admiration at his reflection in cracked mirror. It was a trifle distorted but beauty is foreve the eye of the beholder.

Love makes a fool of us all and the constable was i exception to that rule.

Therefore he gazed fondly at his own image.

Who could not fail but be impressed by the sincerity in his clear blue eyes, light brown hair neatly parted to the side, and skin like a milk cow?

Profile, now. He turned to observe same; a trifle sharp in feature but had his own Aunt Katie not often remarked that her nephew had the sideways apparition of a Roman emperor? Mind you, Mulholland wasn't so sure about that assertion. The ones he had witnessed in the Museum of Antiquities seemed to have badly broken noses and his own was straight as a Presbyterian pew.

There was also, of course, the Romanish aspect to be taken into consideration; to be sure he knew Aunt Katie was referring to the ancient empire rather than the Pope's Tiara, but still, it left an uneasy swampy feeling like a cloud of incense.

Back to the nose.

A bit long maybe, but was there not a saying amongst the vulgar sorts that a man with a long neb and big feet had much to offer in other departments?

Not that he would ever dream of boasting about the primal parts but he was satisfied from boyhood comparisons with

No one would want him leaning over their bedside, not unless they were dead.

The lieutenant's resemblance to a crocodile was nigh uncanny, hooded membrane eyes slightly bloodshot, a jaw full of large teeth that he often jerked from side to side, and a long snout, which at this moment he was twitching in Mulholland's direction.

'And where is Inspector McLevy, if I may be so bold?' Roach asked, his brooding gaze flitting round the room.

He had in truth been rather perturbed to open the door and find his constable in commune, apparently, with the occult. He knew Mulholland for a staunch Protestant, if Irish, and hoped the young man was not being religiously undermined by the wave of mesmerism, spiritualism, psychic phenomena and the like, sweeping the country. Had the Queen herself not been rumoured to have once taken part in a séance in order to contact her dearly beloved Albert?

In Roach's view the whole thing was nothing more than Catholicism in one of its many guises, such superstitious drivel concealing the sly tendrils of ultramontanism.

Therefore his eyes bore into Mulholland's searching out a shift in belief.

'The inspector,' replied the constable carefully, 'mentioned to me that he may be a little on the late side this morning. A personal matter, sir.'

'Indeed? It must have slipped his mind to inform me.'

'That's a mystery, sir. I know you are always foremost in his thoughts.'

What Mulholland did not add was that McLevy's aforesaid foremost thought was how to keep Roach from meddling in his investigations, but there was not a trace of this privy information on his candid countenance.

The wave of love and desire that had swept through his vibrant organic parts was placed in restrainers for the moment. He was back to pragmatic self because he needed to have the lieutenant firmly in his corner. Just behind Cupid.

Roach sniffed in disbelief at the constable's response and his eyes passed disdainfully over the station cubby-hole where the rank and file hung their uniforms and left spare boots strewn in disarray.

A smell of sweat hung in the air, mingling with the odours from the oft-used water closet next door.

The mirror, now mercifully free from the image of the love-sick Mulholland, was set into the wall by the door and intended for the inspection of both uniform and boots before the Leith constabulary launched themselves upon the grateful populace to protect the righteous and hammer down upon the criminal classes. It had a large crack running haphazardly down its full length with a spider's web of smaller cracks off to the one side. This side was also discoloured with what looked like a lime-green mould, and for anyone who was not in love as they gazed into the glass, the resultant image reflected was that of a personality lividly split in twain.

Roach looked upon this duality and repressed a shudder. The one was bad enough to regard; unlike most men he was not fond of his appearance.

God knows what Constable Ballantyne thought, the poor fellow being possessed of a birthmark, strawberry in colour that melted down half the span of his face.

Mulholland stood by patiently, and Roach remembered he had come in to complain.

'I emerged from my office,' he said querulously, 'to find the morning shift departed, Constable Ballantyne lost in admiration of the seagull droppings upon our window panes and Sergeant Murdoch apparently in deep contemplation at the station register but, in fact, resting fast asleep on the one elbow.'

'I don't know how he does that,' said Mulholland.

'The reward of inertia is inertia,' Roach snapped, misquoting perversely the dictum of Saint Augustine on patience. 'The place was empty. Empty of you, empty of McLevy, of direction, meaning, empty of life itself!'

This seemed a bit dramatic to Mulholland but Monday mornings can often appear so. Vacant of purpose.

'I'm sure it will fill up again, sir. Crime never sleeps. That's what the inspector always says.'

Roach grunted morosely at the proffered saw of consolation and seemed lost in gloom. He hunched over his clasped hands and moved them slowly back, then forward.

Perhaps, in that emptiness, he had seen existence stretching uselessly out before him like the Dead Sea.

Or perhaps the root of his despond had a more prosaic origin. Mulholland considered the facts before him.

The lieutenant had been playing a four ball on Musselburgh links this Saturday past. A President's Cup match against one of his own superiors, and the constable deduced that all might have not gone according to plan.

A toss up, in that case, whether to lance the wound or let the man suppurate in silence.

Ah well, Mulholland decided. Better out than in.

'How did the golf proceed at the weekend, sir?'

The floodgates of grievance burst asunder and spilled out a veritable deluge.

'I had a five-foot putt on the last green to win the match for myself and partner. Just as I was about to strike the ball, just at that moment, mind you, just then, not at any other moment, Sandy Grant, my own chief constable and a fellow mason to boot, *jingled* the coin in his pocket. A deliberate *jingle*!'

Mulholland bowed his head in sorrow and spoke.

'My Aunt Katie always says, "There's no limit to the darkness in man. To win the prize, he'd murder the world."'

This bucolic profundity lumbered past Roach, who was still seething with dejection.

The lieutenant seemed locked in a private misery of a memory too painful to further relate. His gaze was inward, lost in bleak contemplation.

Mulholland took a deep breath. Now or never.

He produced from his pocket a small jewellery box, opened

the lid and waved it gently under Roach's nose as if trying to bring the man back to consciousness with smelling salts.

'What do you think, sir?'

The lieutenant wrenched himself from the dreadful memory of a putt sailing beyond the hole and brought his investigative instincts to bear.

'It is a ring,' he said.

'An engagement ring, sir. Well bought. Hard earned.'

Mulholland delicately removed the circle from its setting and held it in fingers which had grasped many a criminal collar, but now offered up the object as if it were the Holy Grail.

Roach groaned under his breath. He had been rash enough, prompted mightily by Mrs Roach who had more than a passing interest in all this, to promise the constable some assistance in his suit for Emily Forbes.

He gazed gloomily at the golden hoop of potential matrimony; a hoop he had jumped through with initial enthusiasm and now would continue to do so, like an ageing lion a ring of fire, till the end of his days.

Mrs Roach, like many another female of a certain age and social standing, was obsessed by the memory of a romance she had never experienced and, as blood from a stone, would squeeze it vicariously from any promising situation.

This one was tailor-made. Young love.

'You were kind enough to suggest, sir,' Mulholland almost batted his eyelids in an attempt to portray bashful appreciation, an attempt which sat strangely on a face which though blessed with a clear skin, blue eyes and an open countenance, had seen more than its share of murder and mayhem, 'that, in the fullness of time, you might find your way towards approaching the father of my intended Emily, and, on my behalf, notwithstanding, and without troubling yourself in any way – '

'I shall speak to Robert Forbes,' Roach interrupted. 'But I vouch for nothing. He is an insurance adjuster and therefore not easily impressed.'

'I shall accept his valuation.'

Mulholland stood before his superior; arms aloft, holding the box up in one hand and ring in another, like some sort of religious icon.

'Put that miscellany out of sight,' Roach commanded and, as the constable replaced the ring and carefully secreted the box on his person, the lieutenant wondered how to introduce a note of reality into the conversation.

'Emily Forbes is a young woman. *Very* young.'

'I'm not in a tearing hurry, sir.'

'There may be other suitors.'

'I believe I have the inside track.'

'Then don't rush the fence.'

'It's the only way to get the horse over.'

A stubborn look had appeared on the constable's face and Roach sighed. He should have known better than bandy equine metaphors with an Irishman.

'I shall speak to Mister Forbes and see how the land lies for this galloping beast, but in the meantime – '

The lieutenant took a deep breath to indicate the importance of what was to follow.

'You will make no mention of my part in this to anyone, *especially* Inspector McLevy. He and romance do not walk hand in hand.'

Mulholland nodded but he could not keep hope from shining in his eyes and Roach felt duty bound to dull the expectation.

'You must keep in mind also, that Robert Forbes has attained a certain level of society, constable. Levels are . . . everything.'

The constable's hand clenched into a fist. This was undeniably true. He had experienced it from some of the young men at the musical soirées where he had first met Emily. Amused condescension. A barely concealed contempt for a social status of inverse proportion to his great height. Very low, indeed. Creeping on its belly, as far as these arrogant chancers were concerned.

Mulholland also took a deep breath.

'I shall try to rise above myself, sir.'

Roach decided to accept this flat statement at face value and signalled an end to the exchange by returning to his putting stroke and grievance.

'By rights I should have won that game. Sandy Grant did not play fair. He *jingled*. A fellow lodge member! And I lost the hole.'

'There's nae justice,' said a voice.

McLevy stood in the doorway. He had arrived silently and there was no telling how long he had been there.

Both others fell into a cold sweat.

Mulholland's hand closed protectively over the pocket where he'd put the ring and Roach prayed silently that the inspector had not overheard too much.

If McLevy knew that the lieutenant was acting as love's emissary, the future would contain more barbs than Cupid's quill could muster.

'Where have you been hiding, McLevy?' Roach demanded, trying to read his fate in the inspector's face, but the countenance in front of him was blank. The Sphinx would have supplied more indication.

'I attended a funeral,' came the eventual answer.

'Of your own making?'

'Not directly.'

'That's a nice change.'

For a moment McLevy darted a ruminative look towards his superior, then he turned to his constable.

'We have work before us, Mulholland,' he said.

'And what is that, sir?'

'The fire at the bonded warehouse.'

'I sniffed it on the wind this morning,' Roach interposed. 'But that is a concern primarily for the port authorities and official fire investigation.'

'Not any more.' McLevy shook himself as if in anticipation, and drops of water sprayed from his overcoat perilously near to Roach's highly polished shoes.

The lieutenant cut an immaculate figure as always.

The inspector, as usual, resembled a dog that had just run through a puddle.

'A report just in at the desk as I arrived. It seems that a body has been newly found amongst the debris,' said McLevy. 'That makes it our concern.'

'What kind of body?' asked Roach suspiciously.

The ghost of a smile touched McLevy's lips as he watched Mulholland struggle into his police cape and carefully place the helmet upon his head. With his great height and beanpole figure, it never failed to amuse the simpler side of his inspector.

'I havenae yet made acquaintance, sir,' he replied with due deference. 'But I am willing to wager that it is burnt to a crisp, and dead as a dodo.'

8

O Comforter, draw near,
Within my heart appear,
And kindle it, thy holy flame bestowing.
RICHARD LITTLEDALE, *Come down, O love divine*

The walls and ceiling of the warehouse were blackened by the fire but had stood firm. The wooden beams had absorbed, over the years, enough moisture from the sea and windswept rain, to render them proof against consuming flame.

The body had not been so lucky. It had lain under a pile of scorched debris, until discovered by the workmen brought in to sweep the site lest more combustion be lurking, ready to burst once more into destructive action.

Oliver Garvie looked down at the scrambled mess of something once human, and sighed.

'You'll forgive me if I don't come too near.'

He had met and escorted the policemen through the ruins of the fire leading them to an unsavoury tangle of flesh and bone, the scorched putrid matter peeling from the emerging skeleton. It was curled up in a foetal position, lying on its side, what was left of the face contorted, jaws open in a silent scream.

McLevy dropped to his knees and peered at the corpse, whistling a Jacobite tune under his breath,

'Charlie is my darling, the young Chevalier.'

The inspector was in his element, oblivious to the stench from the near carbonised flesh and the gruesome picture presented. He pored over the details of the body like a house-wife picking out a good piece of meat for the table.

Above him, Garvie and Mulholland eyed each other. It would seem that there was no love lost between them, and they made an odd contrast.

Oliver was very much the man of fashion and cut, even in this sad wreckage, an impeccable figure. His single-breasted frock coat was of a smooth dark material, fastened only with a top button to reveal the silk, silvery waistcoat below. To complete the upper body ensemble, a patterned cravat nestled at the neck of the fine-combed cotton shirt of such dazzling whiteness that might even match the hue from the imagined nightgown of Emily Forbes.

His hair was a glossy chestnut brown that fell in waves towards his left eye; the trousers were discreetly striped, hanging to the bottom of the heel of his boot, and all in all, especially taking into account the heavy sensual mouth which hinted at an aptitude for the boudoir, he presented a formidable proposition.

Through gritted teeth Mulholland would have to admit, given the fact the man's father owned a succession of butcher's shops, that Oliver Garvie exuded a certain *beefy* charm.

The constable on the other hand, was more of a *bony* proposition, only too conscious of the rough material of his police uniform the collar of which chafed against his long neck, and the fact that, however hard he pulled at them, his wrists dangled out from the sleeves as if he was some sort of half-witted farm boy.

There was also the matter of his helmet with its little metal nipple at the pinnacle. Given its positioning on his great stature, it looked, in the words of his Aunt Katie, 'like a pea on top of the Mountains of Mourne'.

All this had instantly flashed between them while McLevy whistled.

Garvie spoke down to the inspector, ignoring the tall figure beside him. His tone had the self-assured drawl of a man at ease in his class and social standing, though far from content with the situation in which he found himself.

'I've been here since first light. We found him not long ago. Buried, you see.'

Garvie dabbed at his brow with an immaculate white handkerchief, which he replaced with a flourish into the sleeve of his jacket so that it hung out as if the bold Oliver were a Restoration dandy.

Mulholland stepped past and his nose wrinkled as the stench of the corpse rose to meet him.

'It's a wonder you didn't smell him out,' he said.

'Twenty thousand pounds' worth of top-quality cigars creates quite a smokescreen,' Garvie observed wryly.

'Really? I don't use the things.'

'A decent cigar is the mark of a true gentleman.'

He smiled at Mulholland as if to take away any hint of disparagement in the remark, but the sting remained.

It is said that if stabbed by a bee, the best resource is to maintain a still quality in order that the insect may therefore withdraw its barb. If the spike breaks off, the bee will die. Allow it to retract the same and buzz about its business, then not only will it live on to serve Mother Nature, but you will suffer less pain.

That is what they say.

Mulholland's lack of motion however had less to do with

enlightened self-interest and more the demeanour of a man wondering where best to plant his large bony fist.

The inspector had part-registered this sniping exchange whilst, like the bee, going about his business.

Having examined the corpse from head to what were left of the feet, he had unearthed one worthy-of-note fact, moved off to find something else of equal interest, and judged it a propitious moment to bring all this nonsense to a halt.

Time for Mulholland to earn his corn.

'Constable, pass me your scientific opinion on these, if you'll be so gracious?'

He displayed the first find which he had teased out from under the body, a squat chunk of metal burnt black, with a hole from which some charred fragments of wood protruded.

'What's left of a hammer, I would say,' averred the constable.

'On the nail. And this?'

The inspector pointed towards an object that had also been buried in the debris, not far from the body.

Mulholland's nostrils flared at the prospect of displaying his deductive prowess as he moved away from the immaculate Oliver to examine the indicated field of study.

He squatted down, scrutinised, and then pronounced.

'The flames have fused it all together but, to my mind, this residue before us, is composed of glass and metal segments from an oil lamp.'

The inspector nodded a slow agreement and the constable, with the merest of glances back towards Garvie, raised his voice to make sure that every word was being registered by the cigar fanatic.

'The aforesaid pieces are near enough the corpus for us to draw certain conclusions.'

'Conclude away,' said McLevy whose mind was already moving in another direction.

Auld Clootie. A childhood name for the Prince of Darkness. Jean Scott who had raised him like her own son always warned him to beware the cloven hoof. The right foot of the corpse was

twisted and split, but he suspected that the fire had not caused such injury. Medical examination with luck would confirm this and he would therefore have a name with which to conjure.

'We have observed before entering the building, that the lock on the door was forced, possibly the hammer coming into play,' continued Mulholland, as if delivering a lecture to the hard of hearing and slow of wit, 'a clumsy botch of a job. It would seem the thief carried on this ill-conducted *modus operandi*, dropped the lamp, and inadvertently indulged in self-immolation.'

Oliver Garvie offered an elegant correction.

'Immolation tends to mean sacrifice, often accompanied by the sprinkling of water. The word you may seek is . . . incineration.'

A snort of laughter from McLevy brought a pink tinge to Mulholland's cheeks and the tips of his large ears glowed red. As the constable began to straighten up, the inspector addressed Garvie in loud cheery tones.

'Whatever the word, he set himself off into a fine wee funeral pyre. A stinking charry mess. Even unto the . . . bones of his feet.'

His laughter rang through the hushed quiet of the warehouse and a few of the workmen turned round to see what was so amusing about a dead body.

Oliver's features darkened, though when he spoke it was pleasantly enough, no need to descend to the other's level.

'Drollery aside, inspector. I would remind you that I have paid a considerable sum of money to import this cargo and you, the police, exist to protect respectable society.'

McLevy pursed his lips and nodded as if impressed by this judicious reprimand, then offered a response.

'Respectability aye strikes me as to resemble an overcoat. When you're cold you wear it all the time and when the heat takes you? It is left at home. On the peg.'

The mask of buffoonery was cast aside and, in its place, a cold implacable stare informed Garvie that the man before him was not impressed by rank or station.

But the importer, while possessed as his enemies might attest of many faults, did not lack nerve.

'I have suffered great loss and grievous financial damage,' he said evenly. 'All I seek is justice.'

For a moment McLevy looked intently into the face opposite and seemed to find something there, which brought a bleak smile to his face.

'That's my speciality,' he replied. 'High or low, rich or poor, I'll bring it down on you.'

This sounded more like a threat than a guarantee but Garvie held the inspector's gaze.

'What are your conclusions, so far?' he asked.

'Fire is the very devil.'

A response that held a wealth of implication, and, depending upon your conscience, could provoke a variety of reaction.

Oliver Garvie loved the gaming tables and could bluff with the best of them. He produced a rueful smile.

'It does tend to burn the fingers,' he said.

Mulholland had been watching this rally with close interest. Whether the inspector was taking the constable's side, was, as usual, difficult to fathom, but McLevy had a secret up his sleeve. After all this time, trailing the man in and out of scrapes that would try the patience of Saint Peter, from low disgusting taverns to the high treacherous reaches, he could recognise the signs. The inspector was up to something.

Then his attention shifted and his heart jumped. Could this be possible? And if so, was Fate dealing a card from above or below the deck?

9

Come into the garden, Maud,
For the black bat, night, has flown,
Come into the garden, Maud,
I am here at the gate alone;

ALFRED, LORD TENNYSON, *Maud*

A figure had appeared at the open door of the warehouse, silhouetted in the frame by the cold November light. The man wore a top hat, with a stout cane to hand and in his other he held a small case.

His whole being radiated a flinty moral probity, the unmistakable embodiment of Presbyterian rectitude.

Robert Forbes. Father of Emily. Here in official capacity no doubt as an insurance adjuster, but holding within that stiff demeanour the capacity to let Mulholland soar like an eagle with hopes high and an eye for the main chance, or crunch him under-foot like a snail.

The constable slithered up behind McLevy but just before he could whisper his tidings, Robert Forbes' voice rang out in the comparative silence of the warehouse.

'What are these men doing here?'

For a moment Mulholland thought Forbes referred to the inspector and himself and, despite the desperate dictates of love, bristled a little. They were policemen. There was a dead body. They belonged together like liver and bacon.

Then he realised that Forbes was aiming his remark at the workmen who were, in a somewhat desultory fashion, heaping some of the burnt timber up against the wall.

For the first time, Oliver Garvie appeared to lose a portion of composure.

'Mister Forbes. I had no idea, sir.'

'No idea of what, sir?'

'That you might come in person.'

Robert Forbes walked into the warehouse and moved towards them, the small black case held firmly in front of him like a buffer against the negligence of chance.

He had obviously registered the presence of the policemen but concentrated his gaze upon Garvie. When he spoke it was in low measured tones, but there was a nip of remonstrance in the air.

'These men must cease their labour at once,' he said.

Garvie waved over to the workmen who were only too glad to call a halt and await the outcome arising from the deliberation of their betters.

The insurance adjuster gave the floor of the warehouse a swift appraising glance then shook a stern head.

'Interfering with evidential artefacts can affect the outcome of a claim, Mister Garvie. I assume, since your policy is with the Providential, that you will be making such a demand?'

'Unfortunately, I fear that is so,' replied the bold Oliver, seeming to perspire a little.

'Then you would have done better to ensure that nothing was remotely disturbed until the arrival of an inspecting authority.'

'My thought entirely!' boomed McLevy.

Forbes favoured the inspector with the briefest of nods then fixed his gimlet-eyed stare once more upon Garvie who realised that some explanation might be in order.

'There was fear of a secondary fire and, of course, I wished to find out if any of my goods were recoverable, but it was hopeless.'

He raised his arms disconsolately, and then let them fall to his side.

'All gone. Up in smoke.'

'I understand your motive, sir,' said Forbes dryly, 'but the outcome is to be deplored. However the damage is already done, let us hope it is not irreparable.'

48

Although Mulholland was gloating inwardly at the apparent discomfiture of Oliver Garvie, he was also conscious of the fact that one day he might also be standing before Forbes to make a claim. Not a prospect to be relished, judging by the acerbic manner of the adjuster.

Perhaps Forbes would be easier over a daughter's hand, or perhaps, as the constable feared to be the more likely outcome, the man would be a damned sight harder.

Robert Forbes had remarked a small ledge where he might carefully lay his case and, while doing so, issued further instruction.

'If you would be so kind, Mister Garvie, to inform your workmen that nothing is to be further tampered with until I have finished examination, I should be obliged.'

'At once!' cried Garvie. 'I shall effect it so.'

'And, sir?'

This interjection stopped Garvie somewhat comically in mid-stride.

'I shall require you to deliver to my office all contracts, bills of landing and any other papers which appertain to, and confirm, the financial cost and certified quality of the imported cargo.'

'Rest assured,' was the firm reply, 'the matter will be dealt with, as soon as I have a moment.'

As Garvie strode off to do as he was bid, glad, by the look of it, to get out of range, Forbes opened his case.

It contained different-sized tweezers, and various other instruments for taking samples from the ashes.

There were also some sealed jars for storage, and a large magnifying glass wrapped in a white cloth, strapped into the lid of the case.

As he gazed down at the assembly, Forbes became aware of a presence at his elbow.

'Aye now, Robert,' said McLevy peering in also. 'I had no idea the adjusting was so scientific.'

In fact the inspector took good care to keep himself up to date with all the latest twists and turns of forensic

49

investigation from published science papers to the various tomes he found in the medical bookshops, but preferred to hide his analytic light under a bushel. The simpler folk thought him, the better.

'All part of the process,' said Forbes who knew McLevy of old and was not remotely taken in. 'How are you, James?'

'Still upright.'

Forbes nodded solemnly. 'I can see that.'

'How about yourself?' asked the inspector.

'I live to serve.'

This brief assertion made, he frowned as for the first time his eyes fell upon the charred cadaver.

'Is that a body?'

'It is indeed,' said McLevy. 'But don't trouble yourself, I doubt he had a policy with your company.'

'That's good to hear.'

There was obviously some history and a measure of respect between the two men about which Mulholland, who was loitering on the periphery of this exchange, made a note to quiz the inspector further, when opportunity arose.

McLevy smiled, though his eyes, as always, were watchful.

'I had not realised you were still in the field, Robert. I thought you nowadays to be a worshipful commander from the confines of the office desk, like my own esteemed Lieutenant Roach. Let others do the dirty work, eh?'

The response was somewhat elliptical.

'Mister Garvie is highly regarded in business circles, a young man of entrepreneurial vigour, respected by his peers – '

Forbes broke off here as an audible sniff from Mulholland brought his attention momentarily to the constable. He waited but Mulholland had no more to offer, other than an attempt to resemble trustworthy son-in-law material, and pull his wrists back into his sleeves.

The adjuster therefore continued.

'But this will be a considerable claim. Best investigated by myself.'

'Ye don't trust your underlings, Robert?'

'I run the department, inspector. I'll take the accountability.'

'I'm sure you'll do a better job than any other man, sir,' Mulholland suddenly volunteered.

'That would be boastful. I'll do the best I can.'

During this exchange, the eyes of Forbes had kept flicking back to the tarry, blackened corpse that crouched like some sort of Caliban, near to their feet.

He registered McLevy's thoughtful gaze, and smiled somewhat thinly.

'What is your opinion of this unfortunate event, inspector?'

Mulholland, eager to display his previous forensic interpretations, butted in like a horned goat.

'It looks like a break-in and incidental arson, sir.'

'What do you think, James?' repeated Forbes as if the constable's words had vanished into the ether.

'It has that appearance, Robert,' said McLevy slowly. 'But appearances can be deceitful.'

And that was it for the nonce.

They left the adjuster to his appointed task and, having poked amid the burnt offerings to no more avail, departed with a warning from McLevy to all and sundry, that nothing of or near the corpse was to be disturbed in any way until the police waggon arrived to convey the body back to the station where it would lie upon the cold slab to await further examination. The remnants of the hammer and fused fragments would also be collected in an evidence bag after Forbes had examined them.

Both policemen were silent for very different reasons as they emerged from the warehouse on to Commercial Street to witness the old docks spreading out before them in an untidy tangle of ropes and tackle. Boats, all shapes and sizes, jostled each other as they lay at anchor, while now and then could be seen the stumpy figure of an old seaman, sucking inevitably at a clay pipe as he stood on the deck to survey his world.

For a moment the air was still, then a misty rain came

swirling in to make ghosts out of the larger steamers and sailing ships as they waited patiently in harbour.

At distance could be heard the noise of the steam navvie, a machine capable of doing the labour of eighty men, as it dug up and inwards, to aid the construction work on the walls of the Edinburgh Dock, due to be opened in the next year. This dock would dwarf all the other basins and advance Leith to a high position amongst the seaports of the United Kingdom.

The building stone itself was from the Craigmillar quarry not far from the capital, the masonry 900,000 cubic feet, the cost of the whole project estimated to be in excess of £400,000, and the whole fandangle fairly shrieked prosperity.

A new, vibrant prosperity.

McLevy, however, preferred the old docks, with their creaking timbers and skulking rats.

You always knew where you were with a rat.

More and more he was finding that in place of the street crime, the pimps, whores, delvers and skylighters who used to flow through Leith like the blood did his veins, he was now dealing with the perfidy of the respectable classes.

Sleekit pouches. Hidden and devious; like the pox behind a welcoming smile from a nymph of the pavé.

Doctor Jarvis, the police surgeon, would be summoned to the cold slab and, if it were after lunch, breathing claret fumes all over the corpse, would hopefully confirm what McLevy had already spotted. Till then, the inspector, as was his proven custom, would keep his powder dry.

Therefore he was silent.

Mulholland, however, was chewing the bitter cud of jealous indignation.

As he had marched over to Garvie to deliver the inspector's demands as regards the non-disarrangement of corpses and then turned to go, he had most definitely heard a snort of laughter behind his back. He treated the noise with the contempt it deserved for a moment, but then another snigger cracked his good intentions and he whipped round.

All the workmen had broad grins on their faces and Garvie wasn't even looking in his direction but seemed to be examining the back of his hand.

What had been going on? Why had the men been laughing? Why was Oliver Garvie admiring the half-moons of his nails?

'What a pompous ass!' he burst out.

'Don't be so hard on yourself,' said McLevy as he bent down to pick up a flat stone and send it skimming over the scummy placid waters of the old docks.

'Eh?'

The stone skipped a number of times and then sank into the depths of the sea.

'A sixer!' McLevy almost hopped in the air with childlike satisfaction. 'That's a good omen.'

'Omen?'

The inspector suddenly changed countenance and stuck his face fiercely into that of his constable.

'What's the matter between you and Garvie anyway? Like twa dogs slavering over a gammon bone.'

'My Emily is not a gammon bone,' replied Mulholland stiffly.

McLevy was now well aware of what was going on behind his back but he played daft.

'Emily Forbes?'

'You have seen us together, inspector.'

'Only some months ago, through the gates of the Just Land.'

'Indeed. A house of ill repute. And you, bawling out like a man possessed.'

'I was trying to attract your attention.'

'You terrified my Emily. And I had the devil's own job explaining what you were doing there.'

'I was drinking coffee wi' Jean Brash,' said McLevy, beginning to enjoy himself. 'So. Garvie. Oho. A rival, eh?'

'I believe he has paid court.'

'For God's sake,' roared McLevy changing to sudden fury. 'This is a criminal investigation not the pangs of jealous love!'

He shook his finger under the long straight nose of his constable.

'And you are not young Lochinvar! Get a hold on yourself.'

With that, he stomped off in the direction of the Tolbooth Wynd for his stomach had reminded him of a missed breakfast, and all these funerals and burnt bodies gave a man the most terrible appetite.

With a bit of luck, he would find at the Old Ship, his favourite tavern and the place where poor Archibald Gourlay had spent his last night on earth almost a year ago – and there's another dead body – a drappit egg or two. McLevy did not believe in heavy daytime provender and this produce of the hen poached in the gravy made from the fowl's own liver, would sustain his vital forces without a sluggish aftermath.

Mulholland on the other hand, now loping beside him he noticed from the corner of his eye, swore blind by sheep's head broth, but the constable was young enough to take such a hodgepodge in his stride.

'How comes it, sir,' said Mulholland, paying not the slightest heed to the previous wise advice, a mark of amatory obsession through the ages, 'that you and Robert Forbes are so well acquainted?'

'I told ye once before.'

'Tell me again. You were in a terrible fury at the time and I more concentrated on avoiding the spittle.'

The inspector stopped dead. Now and again, Mulholland could surprise him. The constable was correct. McLevy had been removed from a case because of the trifling matter of him trying to pin a murder on the next prime minister of Great Britain.

Prime ministers may start wars but they rarely admit to murder. It turned out that McLevy may have been slightly mistaken but, in any case, he had taken his bad temper out on his subordinate.

'I was not in a fury. And you were sookin' up to Lieutenant Roach at the time to gain his approval. Just the same as you are now. Sook, sook.'

However, the young man was not to be distracted.

'Tell me again, please.'

'Agghh!'

McLevy turned abruptly and marched towards the Tolbooth Wynd, noticing with a jaundiced eye that the work of dismantling the old wynds, the narrow closes, lanes and small cramped courts that had bred many a decent criminal, was proceeding apace.

'Robert Forbes was like me one time. In the field,' he muttered, eyes casting around for another flat stone. 'We had a few capers thegither.'

'I note that he addressed you as James?'

'I was that tae him and he was Robert to me. One swindle wi' bonded whisky, we broke it and then we danced a jig upon the tavern tables.'

'Difficult to imagine, sir.'

'He was in the ranks then. A changed man now, who looks not back whence he cameth.'

McLevy gave up on the stone. The Old Ship beckoned in the distance and he could smell the gravy. He almost broke into a trot, a rare event for him and Mulholland lengthened stride to keep pace.

'D'you want me to put in a word?' the inspector asked, puffing slightly.

'No thanks,' came the hasty response.

'Why not?'

'I already have sufficient representation.'

'Who might that be?'

McLevy's eyes were wide with innocence and Mulholland feared the worst.

'It is a confidential matter, sir.'

The inspector suddenly let out a whoop of laughter sending some seagulls that had been moping about on the quayside, screeching up into the damp, cold heavens.

'Ye're getting very snifty, Mulholland, too much genteelity has that effect. Now let's get on with this case and leave romance where it belongs – on the shelf!'

One of the provoked gulls settled on the cross spar of a sailing ship, shortly bound for Copenhagen with a cargo of jute yarn.

Jute held no interest for the seagull. It lifted a sharp yellow beak and through beady eyes, watched the figures of the two men as they disappeared out of the November chill into the warmth of the tavern.

Then a far-off skirl of birds brought its head spinning round. In the distance a fishing boat was coming towards the harbour, followed by a mixed flock of terns, razorbills and herring gulls. They were feeding on the scraps thrown from the boat by the men already at work, gutting the fish and throwing the slimy innards back into the sea. Often these same men would stick a hook on a line inside the guts they cast to the wind and then haul the bird in by its bloody mouth.

A cruel sport. But it is a cruel world.

The gull wheeled off into the sky, in the direction of the noisy squabbling flock.

Feeding time.

10

It was a miracle of rare device,
A sunny pleasure-dome with caves of ice.

SAMUEL TAYLOR COLERIDGE, *Kubla Khan*

Jean Brash looked out of the window of her bawdy-hoose, and was conscious of a melting uneasy feeling in her heart.

Below, she could see Hannah Semple, her strong right hand and keeper of the keys of the Just Land, hanging out some of the sheets on the line with one of the girls.

This afternoon the weather had lifted a little with a stiff breeze finding its way up the hill, and Hannah was a demon for airing the bed linen even in November. It was her belief that the clients appreciated a whiff of cleanliness before sinking into the debauchery of their choice.

Jean had no strong opinion on this; in her experience, some liked to be enveloped in the musky odour of sin and any hint of otherwise set them looking anxiously around in case their lawful wife was somewhere in the vicinity.

Perhaps lying rigid under the bed, hands clasped prayerfully together, ready to slide out as if on wheels and confront the miscreant in the throes of his illicit libidinous pleasures.

The image amused her for a moment then the uneasy sea-sick undulations of emotion, tugging at her from under like drowning waves, brought Jean Brash to an inescapable, deep and undesired conclusion.

It would seem her affection had become fixed upon another. Her lover. Hopefully he had not noticed an older woman's infatuation; young men can often be trusted on that score. They rise and leave without a backward glance.

Yet she had set down the rules of engagement. It was to be purely for the enjoyment of the senses, concupiscence and champagne, fleshly abandon. All the easy virtues.

Something had changed however. It would seem she had lost part of herself to someone else. Now, in his absence, she felt herself incomplete, lacking hold, an emptiness in the breadbasket. Damnation.

Where was he now? What other trysts? She did not know and could not ask within the rules. The pair were to operate freely, and Jean was caught in a web of her own making.

Self-trammelled.

Once before in her life, she had suffered such a passage. A tainted oyster. She had swallowed it down, with a deal of relish. It had taken months to recover.

The comparison brought some much-needed humour to the situation. With luck it would pass.

As McLevy often said. 'You aye need luck.'

My God, if he knew that she was sick in love, he would spit out the coffee and die laughing.

He hadn't been round to scrounge a cup for a while, and she missed his perverse company. Possibly just as well, however, not be under that evil scrutiny.

Jean looked out of the corner of her eye and found her image peeking back from one of many mirrors that adorned her boudoir.

This was her refuge. On a recent whim, the curtains and hangings had been refurbished in a pale peach colour that contrasted delicately with the white sheets and pillows. This feminine aspect was also enhanced by filmy gauze, draped tastefully here and there, which, reflecting back and forward from one mirror to another, produced an illusion of changing shapes, a shifting world.

Hannah, who had preferred the former hue, a coral red more suited to the inner functions of the bawdy-hoose, acknowledged it with some irony as 'Yer fairy bower'.

So be it.

And here, her lover had not thus far penetrated. She would not allow it. Not that she'd been asked which rather piqued her. He seemed to have no interest in her personal details, only, as he often remarked, the pleasure of her company.

They met elsewhere in the attic rooms of a discreet house in McDonald Road, from which you might see in the far distance the grey tombstones of Rosebank cemetery, or watch the trains of the North British line puff their way from the east towards the docks, then back again.

Not that she ever saw the view. The curtains were always drawn, candles lit, shadows frenzied on the wall.

He rented those rooms and she wondered did he use them for other assignations?

The likeness shook her head in disapproval. A woman of her time and experience should know better.

There she stood, dressed up to the nines in the latest fashion, sheathed like a princess, the dress boned and tight-fitting, the cuirass bodice falling to the hips and flanks, moulding her long lean body like a second skin.

Red hair. Green eyes. Complexion still smooth, though at the corners of the eyes and the full mouth, some wrinkles threatened to gather.

Not enough yet for outright rebellion but gathering none the less.

She leant forward and gazed deeply into herself.

You'd never guess the things these eyes had looked upon from the time of a curtailed childhood when she had looked up and the shadow falling over her was that of a cruel and vicious animal.

Henry Preger. He had abused her and she had poisoned him eventually. But, not soon enough . . .

The image blinked to dispel such memory.

Jean threw back her head and flipped up the back of her dress, as she swung round. It trailed behind her like the closed tail of a bird; indeed the colour was peacock blue.

Some peacock, she thought as she marched restlessly around the room and then, on impulse, hurled herself on to the bed and closed her eyes.

They had met last night. No questions asked. Then he had left, late into the night. Business, he said. He had business on hand.

He had helped her into the waiting carriage and waved her goodbye, handkerchief fluttering.

Business on hand.

They had made another rendezvous for this very night but perhaps she would not go, perhaps she would punish him for not being at her beck and call.

Perhaps.

Outside in the garden, a bird chattered in alarm. A series of sharp cracks denoting a sensed danger.

'This is menial.'

Rachel Bryden's pale face was set in sulky lines, her hands were freezing and this was surely no occupation for a horizontal of her ability and class.

She had plied her trade in the Just Land for six months now and was highly regarded especially by the older clients who deluded themselves that her fair hair and soft skin, elegant body and oval countenance, might intimate a recently lost virginity, or, at the very least, purity that trembled on the verge of translation.

Her speciality was surrender. Then she brought blood to the surface and afterwards, as the client lay spent, her busy little mind calculated how far to compromise and following on, to corrupt.

'Menial,' she said once more.

Hannah Semple made no answer. Her mouth was full of clothes pegs.

'Do we not have maids?'

The older woman spat out a peg and stuck up the corner of a sheet.

'Aye,' she said. 'And you're one. Watch wi' that counterpane, you could be jiggin' on it the night.'

She laughed raucously, her squat purposeful figure surprisingly agile amongst the flapping sheets.

Rachel thought to let the material fall and get dirtied on the ground, just out of spite, just to let the old bitch see that her delicate fingers were not made for such a mundane pastime, but she hesitated.

The other girls had warned her that Hannah was not to be crossed, so she had listened and obeyed. Surrendered even. But behind her composed, poised features, behind the passive creature she presented to the world, Rachel was wilful and hot-blooded. Only one other knew of her secret, and he would never tell. She would not stay here long. They had big plans. Big plans.

The thought of it and the dangerous game involved, sent a shiver through her. Then fired the blood.

'Can we not send out to laundry?' she asked, unable to let the subject die.

'I like to keep my hands busy.'

'I have better uses for mine.'

'Uhuh?'

The old woman turned to meet the cool gaze. There was a measure of provocation in the air, but hard to nail down.

She had been observing this girl for a time now and still had not fathomed her out.

Hannah Semple knew that she was ugly. Pug-nosed, flat-featured, pock-marked and her teeth were nothing to write home about either. She barely rose to beyond five feet in height and Rachel was a good deal above, the long neck and pale blue evasive eyes hinting at a refinement the other would never possess.

But Rachel was also a harlot. An employee who was paid good money for wicked deeds . . . a franchised whore of the Just Land. That placed her under Hannah's jurisdiction; ugly or not.

She smiled, but her eyes held no humour.

'Listen girlie, just because the mistress has a soft spot for you doesnae mean I concur.'

Rachel cast down her eyes demurely.

'I am sure the mistress knows best,' she murmured.

Indeed it was true that Jean Brash indulged Rachel, claiming that she brought a different class of service that raised the tone and clientele in equal measure, but Hannah wasn't sure if that was the only reason the girl had become such a favourite.

It puzzled Hannah but she was buggered if she would pay it too much mind.

She pointed to the wicker basket they had lugged out between them, still part filled with sheets.

'Finish that. Peg them up and not another word out of you.'

'What if I don't?'

'You'll be sorry.'

'And who will make me so?'

Rachel jerked her head back as an explosive movement from Hannah brought forth a cut-throat razor which unfolded in mid-air to lay its keen edge against the taut skin of the girl's slender neck.

It was Hannah's proud assertion that rarely she unveiled that razor without drawing blood. Nothing in her face contradicted the possibility at this moment.

She pulled Rachel down by the bodice so that their faces were level and shifted the blade so that the tip rested high on the girl's face just beside the eye.

'Don't get cheeky,' she said softly.

'You wouldnae dare,' gasped the other.

'Why would I not?'

'Because I'm valuable merchandise!'

Hannah suddenly released her hold and roared with laughter at the retort. She packed away her razor while Rachel tried to still the trembling in her legs and keep the fear inside from showing on her face.

'That's the style girlie,' the older woman remarked amiably. 'Stand up for yourself, that's good. But the other thing is . . .' and thereupon she dropped all of her pegs back into the basket, 'do as you're told by me.'

For a moment their eyes met, then Rachel nodded her head in acceptance. Let the old bitch think she'd won.

'Now hang up the rest. On your own. By yourself. I put my trust in you to accomplish that task.'

With these sardonically delivered words, Hannah turned and made for the back door of the house without waiting to see if they would be obeyed.

As she turned the handle to enter in the house, Rachel's voice sounded behind her.

'What if I tell Mistress Brash about this?'

Hannah swivelled round.

Rachel was already hanging up the sheet, back presented, the remark thrown over her shoulder.

'I shall inform her myself, girlie,' said Hannah.

And she did.

Jean had opened her eyes to find that, rather than a lover looming over her bed, the dumpy purposeful form of her second in command stood there like Banquo's ghost.

'I knocked. Ye didnae answer.'

'I didnae hear,' muttered Jean.

'That's not like you.'

'I was sleeping.'

'That's not like you either.'

'I'll try to assemble myself into something you recognise.'

This snippy rejoinder provoked a grunt of amusement from Hannah and then she related the incident of the razor.

While she did so, Jean, for some reason, refused to move, and lay prone upon the bed much in the manner of her previously imagined wife under it.

'Was that not a wee bit harsh?' she pronounced, looking up at Hannah and the peach surroundings.

'Ye have to keep order.'

Both women were inclined to leave it there. Jean was aware that Hannah disapproved of her partiality for the tall figure of Rachel and it, to an extent, perplexed the mistress herself. Jean had experienced a few encounters with her own sex as she rose through the ranks, but she pinned her colours, for the most part, to the priapic mast.

And yet something about Rachel Bryden weakened her resolve to keep a professional detachment. Not good, and it went straight against the grain of her experience. This was the third and best-equipped brothel she had ever owned, a well-oiled machine of sliding sheets and compliant limbs.

But it had its own commandments. And one of them was that she never played favourites amongst the girls.

In the first bawdy-hoose, the Happy Land, which she had part-owned with Henry Preger until he had obligingly died, she had witnessed a savage knife fight between two of the whores over his malign patronage. One of the magpies had her face cut to ribbons and it was a point well made to Hannah at the washing line. Don't damage the merchandise.

On her ownsome, once Preger had died in spite of himself, Jean had then managed the Holy Land, moving from tarry-breeks, stokers and dock workers, to randy young apprentices, the lower professional classes and the occasional man of the church. All denominations welcome.

This present establishment was her pride and joy. The Just Land. It was set discreetly in a respectable district, upon the high reaches of Leith, and catered for the ruling classes, judges, bishops, heads of government and local council. Bastions of respectability. Linked by a lustful bent. And there was no depravity that Jean could not deliver.

If, like a previous provost of the city, you desired to be dressed in swaddling clothes, then talcum-powdered, and pampered like a baby with three heavy-breasted milk nurses to hand, that could be magicked up directly.

If, at the other end of the scale, you wished to be sprawled out upon the Berkley Horse and scourged like our Saviour, then Francine the Frenchwoman would lay it on with cold intent and no little artistry.

If, however, you were a flagellomaniac, this was not the house for you.

Pain supplied but not accepted; that was the motto.

This was the Just Land. Run like a ship of state.

But now, everything was sliding. This was Hannah's observation as she looked down at her mistress. There was a man somewhere, gumming up the works. A sticky-fingered man, she could smell him on the breeze.

Jean had taken to leaving of an evening, coming back late into the night, leaving for destinations unknown to Hannah and returning from same, driven in her coach by the giant Angus Dalrymple who was as close-mouthed as a healthy oyster.

No use asking him and even less use asking Jean who regarded her personal life as a private affair. But in Hannah's view there was no such thing as privacy. To be a bawdy-hoose keeper was to accept the twin requisitions of supply and demand.

And the girls were getting restless in their commander's continued absence. Lippy. Discipline was slipping. Hannah hated to admit a limitation of her iron hand but the place needed the calm authority of Jean Brash, and without that stillness at the centre, things began to drop from the periphery like pots off a tinker's cart.

'Are ye going out tonight, mistress?' she asked.

Jean's mind had a picture from the previous night of her lover, waving goodbye then turning to stride off down the street. She had craned her neck out of the carriage to see if he looked back.

Not even once. But nothing in the rules said you had to look back.

'I don't yet know,' she answered Hannah.

'The girls would appreciate your presence.'

'Surely you can keep them in line?'

'It's not the same,' answered Hannah.

And so they left it there.

11

Heat not a furnace for your foe so hot
That it do singe yourself.

WILLIAM SHAKESPEARE, *Henry VIII*

Leith, 1836

The big boy had plenty of time. His opponent was doubled up in pain, nose bloody, crouched over, unable to move any further. The other boys behind yelped and howled like a pack of wild dogs that could sense the kill.

'Say it.' The big boy licked his lips. This was the best bit, the moment before he put his hard Protestant fist into the wee porker's belly, the silence that invited the blow, the pure release of a long hatred. 'Say it. I kiss the Pope's arse, on my knees, his big fat arse. Say it!'

No response came from the crumpled form. The big boy had been hammering with his fist and boots for near the length of the narrow passage that led to the wee porker's wynd. If he'd got through there he'd be safe but they'd bottled up both ends and let the big boy loose. The porker had made no attempt to fight just taken the blows one after the other, hunched over like a dumb animal

'I'll give ye one more chance. Say it. I piss in Holy Water and drink it every day. Say it!'

Nothing. Ah well. Work to be done.

'Scour him good, Herkie. Break his bones!'

This shout from the pack brought his head round to glare them all to silence. It was his show.

He swaggered forward and savoured the moment. Not a sound except for the laboured breathing of his blood-anointed target.

Where to begin? The other had covered up, crouched, body bent, arms over his head, turned to the wall, protecting all the vital parts.

Of course he could start with the kidneys. Always a safe bet, some hard punches there would bring the quarry round but his hands were sore, plus he wasn't in a kidney mood. And he had a secret weapon.

He flexed his feet inside the heavy boots. Each leather toe was capped with a lead plate. His father worked in a foundry and had fitted them himself.

Taking aim carefully, he launched a kick at the other's leg, just above the ankle, crunching into the bone. A cry of pain. Another kick, then one more for luck.

In agony, the small boy turned round to clutch at his legs and Herkie grabbed his hair, pulling him upright so that he could look into the white face, contorted in pain but the eyes curiously blank, slate-grey, staring into his.

He put four punches into the belly. That was what he liked best. Other folk preferred the face but he was a belly man. One, two, three, four. The grey eyes did not change but suddenly a jet of bile shot out of the boy's mouth all over his assailant.

Herkie reeled back.

'That's no' fair. Aw, look at this, my Mammy'll kill me!'

His clothes were spattered with the yellow discharge and the sight provoked some hastily suppressed giggles from the watching pack.

He turned back and aimed a wild kick at the other who had by this time fallen on his hands and knees. The kick missed by a mile.

'Ye dirty wee Pape. Dirty wee swine. Yer mother cut her own throat and bled all over her knickers. A'body knows that. Catholic bitch. C'mon boys!'

In righteous indignation, he led the pack way towards the other exit of the passage but as they reached it, a voice stopped them.

'I'm no' done yet.'

They turned to see the fallen boy had somehow pulled himself upright and was standing with his small hands held in front of him in the parody of a pugilist's stance.

'No' done,' he said.

For a moment there was a flash of primitive fear on Herkie's face, then, realising that the eyes of the pack were upon him, his anger rose and he prepared to move back towards the swaying figure.

'Jamie? Jamie, is that you?' called a voice and they all took to their heels as a female figure approached from the wynd.

Jean Scott took the scene in at a glance, scooped the boy protectively into her ample stomach and shouted after the disappearing pack.

'If I catch ye, I'll leather your backsides ye spawn o' Satan!'

She held the boy tight and sighed. This had happened before and would happen again. He was an outcast.

Jean pulled him away from her and tutted to herself.

'Look at the mess of your face,' she scolded as if it was all his fault, whipped out a hankie, spat in it, and began to wipe the blood from his skin. His slate-grey eyes gazed at her and it broke her heart, but she had to be practical, tears got you nowhere.

'I never win a fight,' he said.

'That's because you're the smallest, they're all older than you and there's a whole gang!'

'I never win.'

'That Dunbar boy is an evil swine, he'll come tae a bad end you mark my words!'

She finished cleaning him up, grasped him firmly by the hand and he limped beside her as they walked back through the wynd towards the entrance to their close.

One of the windows above opened and a woman leaned out.

'Is he a' right, Jean?'

'He's fine.'

'I heard the rammy but I wasnae certain. These rascals are aye up tae something, eh?'

'Uhuh.'

The window closed again and Jean became aware that the boy was looking up at her. Solemn-faced.

'What is it?'

'They said my mammy cut her throat. A'body knows.'

Jean sighed again. Would it never end?

'Your mammy was a good soul, son.'

'But it's true. I saw her.'

Indeed he had. Jean had lived across the hall from them and found him keeping vigil at the kitchen table while his mother lay in the bed recess like a rag doll.

God knows why the woman had done that but Maria McLevy was a Catholic and the workings of such a mind would always be a mystery from Jean's staunch Protestant viewpoint.

However, she had taken the boy in and now he was her life and she his family, their bond was stronger than blood.

'Your mother was a good soul,' she said quietly.

'I've been saving my pocket money,' he replied as if in answer. Jean smiled; his shifts of thought were commonplace to her by this time.

'Have ye now?'

'But I don't know if it's enough.'

'I'll make it up. What is it ye want to buy, the Edinburgh Castle maybe?'

He shook his head gravely.

'No. A pair o' tackety boots.'

'Big heavy boots? And why is that?'

He made no response but a look passed over his face, which many a criminal in years to come would recognise and then worry over.

'Will we get a size up, so's ye can grow into them?'

'The bigger the better,' said the boy.

'McLevy, if it's not too much of a burden, could you bring yourself back to earth?'

The inspector wrenched himself from memory; God knows

why such a recollection should have come into his mind and perhaps it was an offshoot of the personnel connected to the morning funeral, but then again McLevy's thoughts did tend to drift when his superior was summing up the salient facts of a case.

He looked at Lieutenant Roach and wondered if, like the crocodile, he ate his meat alive and kicking.

'Your servant aye, sir.'

'That provides great comfort,' muttered Roach.

The two of them plus Mulholland were ensconced in the lieutenant's office with various chief constables, a Masonic lodge or two, a man with his foot on a dead stag, and Queen Victoria, looking down from the walls.

There was also a picture of Roach in plus fours leaning upon his driver in front of the clubhouse of the Royal Musselburgh golf course. He had yet to hit the ball and perhaps never would.

'So,' resumed the lieutenant, 'it would seem that we have a break-in, an accident of fire, the sinner unrecognisable and burnt to hell which is where he was bound for in any case, an unfortunate loss of good cigars which will leave Sandy Grant nothing to stuff in his face for a while, but, other than that, all neat and tidy.'

'All neat and tidy,' said McLevy.

Something in his tone caused Roach's eyes to narrow in historical reflex but then he dismissed it from his mind; there was a lodge meeting later and he needed time to ponder how to disseminate the details of his own chief constable's perfidy on the putting green amongst his Masonic brothers without sounding like a bad loser.

He waved his hand and shuffled some papers.

'Go therefore and do something useful,' he commanded.

McLevy was out like a shot and that should have sent a warning signal flying Roach's way but the good lieutenant had his attention taken by the tall figure of Mulholland, looming over him like the Leaning Tower of Pisa.

'I shall speak to Robert Forbes when the time is appropriate, constable,' he said without looking up from his papers. 'Go away.'

Mulholland resisted the temptation to rattle the engagement ring in its box in his pocket, nodded somewhat jerkily and moved off with only one backward beseeching glance from the door, which was resolutely ignored.

And yet he did not leave. Completely.

'There's one thing I would like to venture, sir.'

The lieutenant froze at his desk. He had a horrible feeling that this would concern his wife.

'Mrs Roach has assured me that you will be my champion.'

'Champion?' repeated Roach in a somewhat strangled voice.

'But I told her not to worry. We are all pushing in the same direction. Shoulders to the wheel.'

There was just the slightest tinge of bumptiousness in the remark, love indeed recognises little but its own importance.

The lieutenant waved his hand in a circular motion, not trusting himself to speak, and, finally, the door closed

Roach sighed. Five feet. Somewhere close to the height of Napoleon. And he'd missed the damned putt.

He looked up at the wall to his sovereign and wondered if Victoria had ever considered a game of golf.

She would *never* jingle.

When Mulholland emerged, he found the inspector watching Constable Ballantyne trying to catch a winter bluebottle against the window glass with a tumbler, so that he could slide some paper underneath then release the insect into the November air.

'That boy is too kind to be a policeman,' McLevy muttered. 'You, however, will do fine.'

'Where are we going then?' asked Mulholland.

'What?'

'I know you by now and you've had something on your mind since you poked at that corpse. Not only that, the only time you're polite to Doctor Jarvis is when he has observed and ratified what you have already noticed.'

The inspector grunted acknowledgement of the remark.

'Our esteemed police surgeon confirmed what I had remarked about the burnt offering while you were using big words and being scientific. The corpse's left foot was twisted but not from an accident of fire. A birth defect.'

'I heard him say so.'

'And it rang no bells?'

'Not yet.'

Disappointment clouded McLevy's eyes, there were times when he was abruptly reminded that the young constable did not possess his encyclopaedic knowledge of the criminal flotsam and jetsam that flowed in the streets of Leith.

'One of our charges has such a twisted foot, the hammer is his preferred advantage, and in stature he would also fit the bill. Giant of a man. A nice big corpse.'

'Daniel Rough!'

The name had now clicked into Mulholland's mind and he screwed up his eyes in annoyance at having to be spoon-fed by the inspector. He'd never hear the end of it.

'Love might sharpen some o' the senses but it does bugger all for the brain,' remarked McLevy acidly. 'Bugger all.'

'Got it!' Ballantyne turned in triumph from the window with the large, fat fly, buzzing morosely inside the tumbler and confined by a sheet of paper to prevent escape.

'I hope that's no' a crime report you're using, that insect might defecate at any moment,' said McLevy.

'No, sir. Blank sheet. Wouldnae dream.'

With these words, Ballantyne hurried towards the station door to release his captive.

'Too kind by half,' muttered the inspector, noting that the young man's right shoulder was still hunched from an injury suffered from a jailbreak almost a year ago.

McLevy took some responsibility for the incident. The thought reminded him that even the greatest man might lapse on occasion, so he fixed Mulholland with a marginally more benign eye and inclined his head for contribution.

'Daniel Rough. I have him now,' said the constable. 'A wild man.'

'In drink, especial. He's sampled our hospitality, twice for violent affray and theft, but low-class stuff. And something else that may or may not have relevance.'

'What may that be?'

'Also in drink. He has a penchant for setting things alight.'

'A theftuous pyromaniac?'

'You may describe him so,' said McLevy. 'To his mother, Mary.'

12

Then bring my bath and strew my bed,
As each kind night returns,
I'll change a mistress till I'm dead,
And fate change me for worms.

JOHN WILMOT, EARL OF ROCHESTER, *Against Constancy*

Rachel Bryden gazed up at the corniced ceiling, smiled with almost perfect malice and threw her naked limbs into the shape of a star.

'Does she lie like this?' she asked.

Oliver Garvie pursed his lips thoughtfully.

'A touch more decorum,' he replied.

She adopted another pose that left even less to the imagination.

'This perhaps? How does that please you?'

For a moment he was tempted to tangle up with her once more, catch the quickness of her breath as she slid round him like a snake, a sinuous lustful snake, but then he slowly shook his head.

'We've indulged sufficient my dear, even for the keenest appetite. Best return to your gainful employment.'

She had prepared a sulk but his words brought her to

laughter, and she quit the bed to begin dressing, donning her boots in an admirably business-like fashion.

'That old bitch Hannah Semple stuck a razor to my throat this very day.'

He smiled. 'All the more reason not to be late.'

'I want revenge.'

'We shall have it.'

She shook the dress over her head then turned in order for him to lace her up.

'This is the very best game.'

'But a dangerous one,' he murmured.

Indeed he had a picture in his mind of a circus performer juggling with Chinese swords that flashed in the lights as they spun high then fell back towards the man with increasing speed, the blades sharp and unforgiving.

'A cool head. Hot blood can wait.'

She leant back against him and his arms squeezed her cruelly till she gasped agreement.

'We shall have all the fun in the world when the game is over,' he said, spinning her away to complete the transformation, by donning her outdoor coat. For a moment she had her back to him, and when she turned, he was looking at a respectable young woman of modest beauty.

'Will you see her again?' she asked demurely.

'Of that I have no doubt.'

'Why?'

'Part of the game.'

She laughed and his mind flashed back to the first time he had seen her in the Just Land.

He had accompanied a group of wealthy businessmen, one of whom he was cultivating in particular for some urgently needed investment, and sat to the side in an armchair as the champagne flowed, the magpies laughed, and the ties of matrimony loosened.

From his vantage point he watched a willowy young creature walk down the stairs from the rooms above, holding on to the arm of some old dotterel who had no doubt been duped into imagined vigour, walk the man to the door, tenderly see him out, then turn with a look of complete and cold disdain upon her face. Their eyes met and he smiled to see such sport.

She smiled also without the slightest trace of being disconcerted and, as big Annie Drummond who overflowed the piano stool but had fingers as delicate as the cream puffs she loved to devour, launched into a version of 'Going home with the milk in the morning', the creature walked back towards him and stood as if for his appraisal.

'No fool like an old fool,' he said.

Her pale blue eyes usually so evasive fixed upon him.

'I don't pay for love,' he continued.

'Then I'll supply you for nothing,' she replied.

The die was cast. Two souls twinned in selfish contemplation without a moral scruple between them. And all else followed on.

It was she who suggested that he pay court to Jean Brash who luckily had not been on hand that night to see him at the bawdy-hoose.

No, he would meet her under more respectable surroundings and Rachel knew exactly where that might be and the way and means to intrigue her mistress.

He was eager enough to accept the challenge. It kept the woman from seeing what was happening under her nose and gave Rachel a secret to nurse, an advantage to hold that was so necessary to her character.

And how could he refuse the dear girl? It was her very own secrets that fuelled the present exploit, a means of escape that was also very necessary. For both of them.

A train whistle sounded in the distance but the dead in Rosebank cemetery were not in the mood for travel.

'You had better leave,' he said.

Rachel gazed at him. He was still stark naked and she now clothed. His body was fleshy, like a butcher's boy, but sleek and oily to the touch.

She was the client and he the whore.

A thrill of power ran through her and she flicked at the nipple of his chest with her forefinger. His lips parted slightly but he seemed much at home in his natural state, unlike all the other men she'd ever known.

On impulse she ran her mouth up against his, tongue darting in and out like a snake then glanced down and giggled to see the result of her labours.

'Go and earn your corn,' he said, though his voice had thickened slightly. 'Not long now.'

'Not long now,' Rachel repeated.

The door shut. And she was gone.

Garvie pursed his full lips and blew out a little breath. A bead of sweat ran down from his hairline in defiance of the season.

'She'll be the death of me,' he muttered, then grinned suddenly, walked to the window and pulled back the curtains to gaze out at a sea mist that was beginning to cover the scene before him, spreading out from the direction of the docks. To confirm the fact, a fog-bell sounded faintly in the distance coming from the lighthouse at the end of the West Pier.

Everything was in hand. All papers and documentation for the claim had been sent for the considered judgement of the insurance adjuster.

Robert Forbes.

Twenty thousand pounds.

Oliver opened the window and shivered as the dank air made contact with his skin. What did he have to fear?

Everything was in hand.

Including Jean Brash.

Must remember to get the sheets changed, he thought; women can smell each other a mile off, not that Rachel minded, she was devoid of jealousy. Like himself.

Not like that dolt of a constable, green to the gills because Garvie had flirted a little with a compliant Emily Forbes at one of the musical soirées; basically a cattle market for eligible bachelors where hopeful daughters of even more hopeful parents displayed their cultural and other wares. All for sale.

Emily was a child. Not worth the pain.

Everything was in hand, yet two separate images clicked into his mind.

One, the black charred corpse.

And two, the moment when that police inspector had laid out the prospect of justice before him. The fellow's eyes for a moment resembled those of a wolf and Oliver had found the examination oddly disconcerting. Just as well he played the cards. A poker face is a useful acquisition.

McLevy had a reputation. No mercy, high or low. Best keep out of the man's way as much as possible.

Oliver Garvie gazed out once more. The outlines were getting blurred. Just how he liked it.

13

Ah, my little son, thou hast murdered thy mother!

SIR THOMAS MALORY, *Le Morte D'Arthur*

A howl like a soul in torment rang through the station, coming from the direction of the cold room, bringing Roach speeding out of his room and causing Constable Ballantyne to wince in sympathy.

'What in God's name is going on, constable?'

Ballantyne's mark of birth pulsed an even deeper red, a sure sign that the young man was suffering some shred of compassion. Roach, on the other hand, looked much the same as usual. Buttoned up against raw weather.

'I think it might be a mother's grief, sir.'

'Mothers?' said Roach. 'What have mothers to do with anything?'

Another howl sent him to the cold room door, which he cautiously opened to peer inside.

Three figures stood frozen, as if arranged in a tableau for a photograph or some painting by one of these French realists that were starting to infect the world with their hellish visions.

The Decay of Death, or some such dross.

Roach observed an old woman, both hands up to her head, mouth open. McLevy stood beside, eyes fixed upon her, not a shred of fellow feeling on his face, and Mulholland, on the other side of the cold slab, held the sheet in one hand as if he was about to perform some magic trick as opposed to uncovering a twisted, blackened corpse.

Mary Rough looked down at the body and the words finally found their way out of her rigid, clenched mouth.

'Oh, my poor wee lamb, oh my God, he's putrid burnt!'

Another heartrending wail caused Roach to flinch; he signalled at the inspector to come out and closed the door hurriedly.

McLevy gave Mulholland the nod to cover up the cadaver and scrutinised Mary as she put her head back into her hands and sobbed quietly.

Yet, when they had visited her in Horse Wynd, where she kept a single room in one of the closes, he had been struck by a certain evasiveness in her reaction to their queries.

I havenae seen him for days. A wild spark but a good boy. What has he done, now?

He's been playing with fire, Mary.

Burnt himself to a crisp, ma'am.

Oh, god grant not. Not my wee boy, not my darling son!

The flames make no allowance. Darling or not.

But, how could it be?

Maybe somebody tipped him the word. To do a chore.

Whit kind of chore?

Break into a tobacco warehouse, ma'am.

And maybe it wasn't the only chore. A wild spark, eh?

I don't follow, inspector.

Are you sure of that?

I am.

And is that all you have to say?

I know nothing, inspector.

You will come with us to the station cold room. And view the body.

God grant it's no' my wee boy. God grant it so.

But all God had granted was his usual, now you see it now you don't. Good and evil men were dying all over the world for no discernible reason. There's nae justice.

Mary took her hands away from her face to find McLevy's eyes drilling into hers. She may have been relying on some leeway as the broken-hearted mother but, from the looks of the inspector, there was little of that on offer.

'Fire is the very devil, eh Mary?' he said. 'And your son dined out on flames.'

'When he was a wee boy,' she sniffed plaintively, 'ye couldnae let him near the candles in the chapel. Aye jabbing away at them.'

Most of the problems in Ireland started in chapels as far as Mulholland was concerned.

'But this wasn't an enclosure for such jiggery pokery, ma'am. It was full of tobacco.'

'If he was in drink, he'd aye want a wee puff.'

'But not a warehouse. That's a *big* thing.'

McLevy smiled at her like a wolf inviting the rabbit for tea.

'A very big thing. And not his previous style.'

Mary's legs started to shake and she swayed as if to topple on to the crackling that remained of her son.

There was another sharp rap at the door; the unseen lieutenant was champing at the bit.

'Shall I fetch you a chair, ma'am?' offered Mulholland, eager to demonstrate his Protestant compassion.

The inspector stopped at the door to throw Mulholland a complicit look, before offering meagre condolence.

'Don't hold back on your sorrow, Mary. Mulholland here will keep you company.'

A low moan came in reply and he quit the scene.

Roach was hopping from one foot to the other as McLevy emerged, the lieutenant had his lodge meeting to attend and carefully rehearsed allusions to the stratagems employed in a chief constable's trouser pocket would come to nothing if he was late for the gathering.

'What is going on, McLevy?' he inquired with some asperity as Mary let out a further long bellow of grief from the other side of the door. 'I attend enough opera with Mrs Roach, I don't need it in the station.'

'We have identified the burnt felon,' replied McLevy, adopting a formal tone. 'One Daniel Rough. That is his mother you hear, mourning her son.'

'Entirely proper,' said Roach. 'Anything else?'

'Just . . . a wee thing.'

'Such as?'

'The crime does not fit the man.'

'Fit?'

'He was a low thief. These are high stakes.'

Roach received a whiff of where McLevy was heading and didn't like it one bit.

'What are you implying?'

'Me?'

McLevy spread his arms wide, the picture of injured innocence, and Roach glanced at his timepiece then cursed silently. Nip this in the bud.

'Oliver Garvie is a respected businessman whose father's meat pies are renowned throughout the city; and if, by any remote chance, there is anything awry with the events of the fire Robert Forbes will find it so, he is meticulous to a fault, is that not the case?'

'Indeed he is, sir. Grinds exceeding small.'

'Neat and tidy, inspector. Leave it that way.'

So saying, Roach thrust his hat upon his head and fairly hurtled out of the station, hauling open the outside door. A blast of cold air signalled his departure and Ballantyne shivered as the stream hit home.

'I doubt that fly'll no last,' he worried. 'Mebbye I should have just left it be.'

'Things never improve by neglect,' was the cryptic response. 'Go next door and be nice. It doesn't come natural to Mulholland.'

Ballantyne did as he was bidden and some moments later the tall figure of the constable came out to join his inspector.

Mulholland looked down from a great height and shook his head.

'You've a heart of stone, sir. That poor woman is grieving fit to burst.'

Having delivered that weighty remonstrance, the constable looked with a frown towards the door of Roach's office, which had been left ajar.

'Has the lieutenant gone?'

'Uhuh.'

'That's a great pity.'

'Why?'

'I – he – asked me to remind him about something.'

'And what was that?'

Mulholland spoke from on high.

'Nothing to concern you, sir. Matter of communication. In the nature of a go-between.'

'The function of the pander throughout the ages,' McLevy muttered.

Back to business.

He clapped his hands together loudly as if to bring Mulholland out of a spell and spoke incisively.

'I don't doubt Mary's grief to be genuine but I also know that she and Daniel were thick as thieves. She knew his every move.'

'But the man's dead, there ends the matter.'

'What if he was a hired hand?'

'Hired for what?'

'That's a good question.'

A silence followed. Then Mulholland leant over so that his face was, for once, level with McLevy's.

'Are you thinking . . . deliberate arson, sir? Oliver Garvie?'

'Don't raise your hopes, Mulholland.'

'But why would he do that? The cargo has to be genuine. Certified so.'

McLevy sighed and nodded slowly.

'Aye, I know. But while I still wonder, I shall continue to investigate.'

A murmur of voices indicated the advent of Mary and Ballantyne and McLevy spoke quickly before the door opened from the cold room.

'Take her home, Mary. Play sympathy, lather it on, but when she is least expecting, look for an opening. You are in love and therefore somewhat glaikit but I am sure you noted that Mary couldnae wait to get out of her place.'

'Of course I noted it,' said Mulholland who had not.

'You'd have thought the prospect of viewing her son's burnt offering on the cold slab might have rendered her a wee bit reluctant, but no, she was out of that room like a shot. What does that recommend to you?'

'There might be something in there she does not wish us to see,' replied the constable berating himself inwardly for having to be led by the nose like this.

'Exactly!' advised McLevy. 'So you look for an opening and if you find a thing, report to me at once. Any time. Night or day.'

'Where will you be?'

'On the case. Elsewhere.'

A nod between them.

'It's cruel,' said the constable. 'But I'll do it.'

'It's a cruel business,' replied McLevy as the cold room door opened, and Mary came forth holding Ballantyne's hankie to her swollen eyes; indeed, as has been remarked, the boy was far too kind to be a policeman.

There was a burst of noise in the station as the evening shift of the Leith constabulary came pouring out of the cubby-hole, ready to confront crime wherever it raised its ugly head.

The noise and horseplay stilled abruptly when they became aware of McLevy looking in their direction.

But the inspector's gaze was inward. Since this case had begun, he had the sense of an evil fortune, following him like a dark shadow.

Of late he had been reading his recent bookstall acquisition, one of Edgar Allan Poe's short stories, 'The Masque of the Red Death', and this had stirred up some morbid fancies.

A spectral figure bringing death and damnation to all it touched.

He sometimes felt a wee bit like that.

A spectral figure.

Who would it tap next upon the shoulder?

14

For those whom God to ruin has designed,
He fits for fate, and first destroys their mind.

JOHN DRYDEN, *The Hind and the Panther*

She sat in her late husband's study, raised the glass to her lips, and took a deep shuddering draught of whisky.

The fiery liquid coursed through her veins and Margaret Bouch threw back her head to quicken the descent.

Her family were downstairs in the kitchen where, but a year ago, poor old Archibald Gourlay had conceived an unexpected meeting with his Maker. They thought her to be ensconced in memories of sad regret and wilting graveside flowers but she hummed a tune under her breath, one dainty foot tapping in time.

One morning, early, long ago, when she could not sleep, one morning, early, an April morning when the advent of spring disquieted the blood, she had risen, the hour must have been six or so, the first streaks of dawn lacing their light into a grey sky, and made her way down to the docks.

Sir Thomas was left behind, he had become recently reliant

on sleeping draughts and lay like one dead which was a merciful release as she slipped out of the bed, donned her clothes and ran away to sea.

The world was still, a slight mist weaving its way in and out of the spars of the sailing ships, and for a moment she felt as though she were the only person alive, awake, as if the universe were hers to do with what she liked.

As if she owned her life.

And then the profound silence was broken by a raucous voice as if to mock that self-delusion.

A tarry-breeks, an old sailor whose finest dream would be of a rich widow with a farm, stumbled his way up the jetty towards his ship. His hat was askew, his feet bare, boots lost to a whore from the previous night, but he hopped and skipped like a free spirit and lifted his voice in song.

> 'Whit shall we do with a drunken sailor,
> Whit shall we do with a drunken sailor,
> Whit shall we do with a drunken sailor,
> Earl-aye in the morning?'

She had watched the man skip onwards until the mists claimed him, and then finally returned to Bernard Street to be later told by her allotted spouse that he had decided to relocate the family to a house in Moffat on the borders. The children were still young enough to enjoy the delights of the country-side, Thomas Bouch had decided. No mention made of what she might prefer. No. The deed was done. His new secretary, Alan Telfer, would take care of all the details.

She protested. What did she know of the country? She loved the city.

Thomas, not yet a Sir by a long shot, frowned slightly, then turned and walked back into his study to think his great thoughts.

The secretary smiled.

What she loved was of no concern.

But, not any more.

She carried the tune now. Under her breath for the moment, though not for long.

She took another hefty gulp of whisky and sang quietly to herself.

'Shave his belly with a rusty razor,
Shave his belly with a rusty razor,
Shave his belly with a rusty razor,
Earl-aye in the morning.'

Margaret was sitting in his armchair, leather, claret and cream insignia of the North British Railway which had now distanced itself from its former blue-eyed boy and his very efficient secretary who had most efficiently blown his brains apart in this very room while the portrait of Sir Thomas and one other present had looked down upon the act.

Two high stools, now bereft of the backsides of both men, huddled forlornly at the desk where some drawings lay, dusty, curling at the edges, abandoned.

She lifted her glass to the portrait of Sir Thomas, above her on the opposite wall. His eyes were not looking at her but then they never quite had, always found something more interesting a few feet to her side.

Where his secret was kept.

The glass was now empty and her mood swung to melancholy, transported back to a moment full of longing and shame, offer and rejection. One week past.

31 October 1880

Sir Thomas Bouch sat in the garden of Moffat house, his hair turned white, a mask of old age clamped upon his face. The living dead. Fifty-eight years old.

Margaret watched from the French windows as a leaf from one of the trees landed on this broken husk of a man, then, from his shoulder fell to the ground.

'He has lost his reason,' she said softly. 'After the Inquiry. After the verdict. No sanctuary.'

McLevy, who had been observing from behind her in the room, did not tender ritual condolence.

'Perhaps it's for the best,' he remarked.

'Do you have any experience of madness?' she asked almost idly.

'I've had my moments.'

'His, is a quiet insanity,' she murmured. 'His mind has . . . slipped. To the side. I hardly noticed it depart. He has found a more acceptable place to exist.'

'Reality can be a bugger.'

She laughed and turned to face him.

It had been like this from almost the moment they had met, as if the truth must be seen for what it was, a bringer of pain and retribution.

'I have never loved him, unfortunately. Not for a moment.'

'Why marry then?'

'My father admired him.'

'And you admired your father?'

'That sort of thing.'

Now it was his occasion to laugh, or a sound somewhat close to laughter, like an animal coughing up a bone.

The disturbance reached the ears of the man in the garden and Sir Thomas looked round. For a moment he gazed past his wife to the shadowy figure behind as if it might be death a' calling, then his eyes shifted and he turned away to resume contemplation of empty hospitable space.

'It was good of you to come.'

McLevy had looked past her to witness Sir Thomas stare in at them but Margaret did not follow his gaze. Her own was fixed upon him and he felt a sudden warmth creep up under his collar.

'I was due some period off. Oftentimes my lieutenant is glad to see the back of me and I also wanted to return you this.'

He produced from a canvas sack, a silver candlestick that he laid carefully on a side table.

'I came across it in the evidence room. I apologise, it should have been restored long since. The perpetrator has unfortunately vanished and that episode closed.'

She looked at the candlestick with no great affection.

'I had forgotten. There is a great deal to forget.'

He stuffed the canvas bag back into his coat pocket, muttering to himself as it refused to fit neatly.

Margaret smiled. For a moment, she thought that he looked like a little boy, but it is always a dangerous sign when a woman takes a man for his younger version.

'So, you've come?' she said.

'Indeed.'

'It is a long distance to venture.'

'Uhuh. Here and back. Very long.'

'You intend to go back this day?'

'The coach returns within the hour.'

'Then we don't have much time.'

'No.'

She suddenly smiled at some inner thought and a glint of mischief showed in her eyes.

'Are you married, Mister McLevy?'

'No.'

'Betrothed?'

'I certainly hope not.'

Her gypsy eyes measured him up and down, leaving the inspector to feel like a prize bull at the cattle fair.

'Your note mentioned that you had something to tell me?' he asked.

'Indeed I do.'

'I assume it is to do with the case?'

'Not at all.'

At her remark, he stepped back and raised his hand, palm upwards, as if about to take an oath in court.

She stepped forward so that they were out of sight from the garden, took that hand, and laid it lightly round her waist.

A simple enough gesture but within it the seeds of a passion that could destroy both of them.

What kind of women were they serving up these days?

But as McLevy thought so, he could feel the pull of an attraction that had been there from the moment they had met.

He stood like a statue, knowing what was right but mightily magnetised to the opposite proposition.

She moved in close so that his hand slipped further round her back, her face tilted up towards him.

He could smell her breath, violets and a strange peaty fragrance, the merest hint of alcohol perhaps?

Must get closer, investigate further, after all he was a policeman was he not? These things must be investigated.

A harsh screech from the garden broke the spell as a large black crow swung down from the naked branch of an oak tree, landed on the neglected grass of the lawn and hopped towards the chilled numb figure of Sir Thomas, sitting in the wooden chair as if composed of the same element.

The aftermath of heavy rain had left a puddle in a small depression in the earth, near to the man's feet and this was the crow's target.

It was thirsty. So it dipped its beak.

One week past. Offer and rejection. Margaret shivered, filled the glass again but sipped more cautiously this time. She knew the dangers of whisky. It promoted a certain careless quality to the limbs and inflamed other parts, especially the tongue. She still had a part to play of the sorrowful widow, sea-shanties notwithstanding.

The family would leave tomorrow, and then she would be free. Unlike James McLevy.

She remembered how the spell had been broken. That damned crow. The inspector stepped back, a look of almost comical terror on his face and had bolted from the room. Then he darted back in again to retrieve a forgotten hat, jammed it on his head and fled the scene.

It would have been funny, had it not been so painful.

Her heart was hammering in her chest with the humiliation of that rejection. As if it would jump into her mouth, as if it would jump the confines of her body.

That damned crow.

She had watched it fly off croaking in satisfaction as the outside door of the house slammed shut and the inspector no doubt shot up the high street towards the marketplace where the statue of a ram celebrated the town's reliance on the wool trade.

The ram, however, had no ears. It had arrived that way and the sculptor, according to legend, committed suicide because of that omission.

Like Alan Telfer. A suicide of omission.

Margaret had been witness to so many things.

After the inspector had scuttled off like a frightened rat, she had walked to the French windows and called her husband's name. He had best come in. It was cold out there.

Sir Thomas had risen, turned, and looked at her like a dumb animal, a thread of mucus finding its way from his nose down on to his shirt front.

A mute and suffering animal. Like herself. Something they could both share.

Thomas Bouch died the next morning from a heavy cold, which had plagued him for all of that month.

He had no will to resist death.

For the faults in design, he was entirely responsible.

For the faults in construction, he was principally responsible.

For the faults in maintenance, principally if not entirely responsible.

That was the final verdict of the Court of Inquiry.

And it killed him.

Rain, rattling on the window brought her once more back to the here and now. She rose from the armchair, walked to the window and pulled back the curtains. It was dark outside, the street lamps throwing light upon the hunched figures of the passers-by and the wheels of the carriages spraying devious spouts of water from the torrential downpour, which was lashing on to the cobblestones.

Margaret nursed the whisky glass against her body and looked out into the night.

At least at the cemetery, she had the last act. She had laughed in the inspector's face and left him to the wind and rain.

He desired her. She knew that. He was a coward to his own heart.

She would find another, a sailor perhaps.

Damn that crow.

15

The breezes and the sunshine,
And soft refreshing rain.

JANE MONTGOMERY CAMPBELL, *Hymn*

McLevy meanwhile was cursing himself and the precipitation as he trailed a certain quarry through the drenched and sodden streets of Leith.

After a most unsatisfactory meeting with Robert Forbes where the adjuster had not only confirmed the certification for warehouse cargo to be genuine but informed McLevy that the claim was already forwarded to head office with his stamp of approval, the inspector's efforts to hint at possible arson were met with a blank stare.

Where was the proof?

When McLevy promoted the identity of Daniel Rough and his incendiary inclinations, he was met with an even blanker stare. Setting fire to a building was one thing, setting fire to yourself was surely carrying the process to an extreme.

And where was the proof?

Forbes spoke mildly enough but the look in his eyes suggested that he thought the inspector's mind might need some adjusting never mind the claim.

McLevy had slunk down the stairs from the Providential Insurance office feeling like a fool, only to run into Mulholland's beloved Emily coming up the selfsame steps to visit her father. Her eyes had widened as she twitched her skirts aside and shrank against the wall as he grunted a good evening to slouch his way past.

The cheerless evening matched perfectly with his mood,

dank and clammy, with the rain beating down monotonously like a minister's sermon.

But then as he walked along Great Junction Street with a dampness spreading through his right sock to remind him that the hole in the boot needed mending, whom should he see? Unaffected by weather, debonair under umbrella, a long cigar raised to fleshy lips, none other than the bold boy, Oliver Garvie.

He sauntered along as if it were the height of summer, a pleasant smile on his face and the inspector, on an impulse, followed like some humble retainer who had to maintain a certain distance between himself and his liege lord.

A stray dog ran out from one of the alleys and began barking viciously at McLevy.

He did not care for dogs especially wee snippy ones that might cause a mark to turn and see the cause of such a racket but, no, Garvie turned into Bonnington Road and went on his merry way.

McLevy contented himself with a well-aimed stone to send the animal yelping into the darkness and followed on.

The road led past the Rosebank cemetery where Jean Scott was buried and he berated himself for not having visited her grave for a while to bring some flowers to the only woman he had ever put his trust in, and for a moment he was a wee boy looking up at her as she unwrapped a parcel and said . . .

'There ye are, James.'

And there they were. A pair of tackety boots, black and shiny. The toe-caps had a piece of metal underneath which gleamed in the light like a knife blade.

Jean watched on proudly as he eased his feet into them, carefully tied the long laces then walked around her living room, boots tapping on the wooden floor.

'Don't you scrape my furniture now,' she warned.

He shook his head solemnly and then stood completely still in the middle of the room, his eyes fixed on a distant reckoning.

Where the boy's mind travelled on such occasions, Jean had no way of knowing but she loved him anyway.

She loved him anyway.

The memory had warmed McLevy strangely and he began to recover his spirits.

When Garvie turned into McDonald Road and flipped the cigar into the gutter, his shadow darted forward, picked up the butt and sniffed. Good quality. How many slaves had died to produce a leaf so fragrant and so fine?

McLevy was acquainted with McDonald Road but it was not one of his haunts. A respectable enough and therefore to his mind uninteresting thoroughfare, the tall buildings housing a deal of rented accommodation.

Garvie approached the door of one of the buildings, skilfully avoided a heavy drip of water from the leaking roof-gutter above, produced a key, inserted same in lock, and vanished from view.

The inspector moved into a doorway opposite to shelter from the elements, and pondered the situation.

He knew for a fact that Garvie's domicile was in the New Town, what was the dashing Oliver doing with a key that fitted a lock that opened a door in Leith?

The inspector checked the front windows for any sign of illumination but none came. The house was dark and had a faintly neglected air as if it had been left out in the rain. A lodging home of sorts, he would wager, where articled clerks and bank apprentices removed their stiff collars with a sigh and dreamed of a polished wooden desk between them and the rest of the world.

A desk with their name upon it.

McLevy's stomach rumbled and he realised that he had, as usual, forgotten to replenish that particular cavity since the drappit egg at the Old Ship.

Which seemed years ago; in fact the whole day was like an eternity besieged by deluge and memory.

The street was deserted; anyone with any sense would be dry and cosy indoors like Oliver Garvie.

Yet, what was the bugger doing here?

At the warehouse when he had faced squarely on to the immaculate Oliver, he noticed that despite the swagger and confidence presented, a telltale little tic had pulsed at the side of the man's left eye. Of course it could have been tiredness, a mote of dust, but it also could have been a sign of something suppressed. Guilt, for instance.

And as much as McLevy sifted and analysed the material of criminality, evidence uncovered, a suspect past, the hard facts of implemented death, the grind of the streets, the cold slab and the interrogation room, he also put great store in these fragments of impression and thin slices of intuition that brought him home by a different path.

But where had all this brought him?

The downpour stopped suddenly and, in the silence, amidst the drips that continued to fall from the slates and drain pipes, he heard carriage wheels approaching from the opposite end of the road.

And there it was, drawn by two horses he recognised and driven by a giant figure he recognised also as Angus Dalrymple.

A decent blacksmith once, but now his twin daughters hammered out sin on the anvil of the Just Land while he was both coachman and guardian to Jean Brash.

Who stepped out of the coach, opened the door of the same house and slipped inside.

The carriage drove off. McLevy, if he had been able to see his own countenance, would have roared with laughter.

The mouth, half open, lower lip protruding like a fish, a look of puzzled disbelief slapped across his face.

But few of us can see ourselves.

He closed his mouth and, while his mind raced with questions, ignored the queasy feeling in his belly.

Jean also had a key to the place, eh? An assignation, a partnership, or both?

No hesitation, in like a whippet, so was this a long-standing practice?

She had once led a life of crime, never been caught, claimed to have mended her ways, that desperate necessity had been the root of her knocking lumps out of the law, but he knew her to have a network of informers on the street and once a thief, the habit sticks.

Had she returned to felonious activities?

Had she ever left them?

What in hell's name were she and Garvie up to?

And, most importantly, why was he standing here like some gowk in the street?

He launched himself across the road and hurtled down a narrow side alley which he had noted earlier, the ground under his feet treacherous and slippy, the faint light from a street lamp revealing that the side wall which enclosed the garden or back green, was too high for him to scale.

Part way down was a wooden door, rusty and firm-locked, but if he could just get his foot on the handle and lever himself up? He cursed Mulholland's absence; the constable's height was invaluable at moments like these but he would be lost in love's dream or sookin' up to the lieutenant – aghh!

Somehow, McLevy managed to get a hand on the rough surface at the top of the wall and haul himself up so that he sat astride.

Below him were what looked in the gloom like some sharp-thorned and inhospitable gorse bushes, no point in dropping to earth and anyway he had good vantage from here.

And, what was on offer?

Most of the curtains at the back of the house were drawn but there was one lighted window and standing framed as if for a photograph, was Oliver Garvie.

The man was looking sideways at something.

A woman moved into the frame. Jean Brash, bonnet and outdoor coat already removed, red hair flowing, fingers busy at the top of her gown. Garvie reached out a hand and moved the dress aside to display the top of one bare shoulder.

As he caressed that, she threw back her head to expose the throat.

McLevy's groin was killing him, the wall was wide and he was sitting atop like Humpty Dumpty.

The woman was desperate, no doubt about it, she grabbed at Garvie and hauled him in to nuzzle at the bottom of her neck.

Things went from bad to worse.

This was terrible. McLevy wanted to shout out, *that's quite sufficient!* But the words stuck in his gullet and anyway he was an investigator, an observer, an eye-witness.

Garvie stopped suddenly and moved to the window to mercifully blot out the sight of Jean Brash unbuttoned. The man looked through the glass and McLevy instinctively ducked down. When he glanced up again, the curtain was drawn and the play was over.

Two shadows flickered for a moment by candlelight, two silhouettes which fell to earth and disappeared from view.

That left McLevy on a damp wall, with only the night and an empty belly for company.

16

It was a lover and his lass,
With a hey, and a ho, and a hey nonino.

WILLIAM SHAKESPEARE, *As You Like It*

Lieutenant Roach was not a happy man. Indeed he rarely approached that blissful state and possibly would not have been familiar with the feeling, unless it was a moment from his golfing memory where he had skimmed his gutta-percha ball on to the water hazard of a small dam and watched in astonishment as, instead of sinking, the ball had skipped over the water like a spring lamb, touching the surface at least three times before coming to land on the green. At that

ked my fingers to the bone to get where I am,' said
y, 'there's few men with my energy or application!'
that's true.' A mild observation that did not placate
e bit.

sacrificed much and will again, what is so dearly
cannot be lightly thrown away.'

y bought?'

es suddenly rapped the knuckle of his hand upon the
o emphasise the words.

spect! Position!'

he lieutenant was getting out of his depth, this was the
t of morass McLevy would have revelled in, Roach had
ten observed that the angrier folk got, the happier the
nspector became.

He took a reluctant leaf from his subordinate's book, and
remained silent, with a slightly surprised look on his face as if
to say, *I know I'm missing something but I am unsure of what it might
be. Clarify my addled wits.*

Roach couldn't quite manage the stupid expression McLevy
produced on his face on such occasions, but he did his best.

It provoked an illogically fierce response.

'Emily is too young. She must be protected!'

'Protected? From the constable?'

'From life itself. She is my daughter!'

The father's eyes were burning from some internal combustion and Roach decided to opt for discretion, although he
could not quite keep a slight chill out of his voice.

'I shall convey these sentiments to Mister Mulholland.'

Forbes stood and nodded somewhat jerkily then made for
the door. He turned from there to have the last word.

'I have nothing against the man.'

'I can see that,' was the dry response. 'Good night, Mister
Forbes.'

'Good night, Lieutenant Roach.'

The heavy door closed with a dismissive thud and Roach was
left in far from splendid isolation. He flexed his jaw thoughtfully

second, Roach knew the strange trembling in his heart of
momentary joy.

But that was then, and this was now. A small side room
of the Freemason's Hall in George Street, where, the worshipful
meeting of the lodge over and the sowing of seeds amongst
his fellow members as regards the perfidious conduct of a
certain chief constable in the President's Cup carried out with
scrupulous nicety, he had decided to place the suit of Constable
Mulholland in front of Robert Forbes.

They were both still dressed in Masonic regalia, the silver
sashes adding a layer of formality to the occasion.

Forbes sat at the end of a long table and Roach, not wishing to
seem invasive of the man's territory, found himself at the other
extremity so that he was forced into speaking rather loudly, as if
selling wares at the market.

So far the insurance adjuster's face resembled that of a man
staring at a blocked water closet.

Roach took a deep breath and tried not to bawl down the
distance between them.

'The constable does not lack culture.'

'I've heard him sing.'

Mulholland had a reasonable tenor voice. He and Emily had
performed some duets together at a musical evening *chez*
Roach. The lieutenant hated these soirées but his wife was in
her element, weaving romance like a spider's web.

'His promotion prospects are . . . reasonable.'

'Seems diligent enough.'

'More than that.'

'Nothing wrong wi' steady.'

'No. But, it makes him sound rather dull.'

'Vanity is not welcome in my house.'

Roach was beginning to feel obscurely annoyed with his
petitioning role and the granite responses spearing up the
table towards him.

He found an unexpected dignity and firmness of tone;
perhaps it was the Masonic carvings in the surrounding wood

panelling which provided the support.

'Mister Forbes I am not quite sure how I ended up as advocate for the constable's case but here I am, and I require from you, like Solomon, a judgment.'

This comparison to the great Israelite, who, though initially a wise ruler, was brought low by idolatry and fleshly inclination, brought Forbes snapping to attention.

'A judgment?'

'As regards his honourable intentions towards your daughter – what are his prospects?'

The succinct question produced an equally concise reply.

'Poor. Emily is too young. She does not know her own mind. Or heart.'

Roach nodded. In a strange way, he was growing into the function he had reluctantly assumed.

'I would agree with that. But perhaps . . . in years to come?'

'It would be many years.'

'The young man may believe that your daughter is worth waiting for.'

'He may wait. But what of her?'

'She has, I am told, expressed some . . . fondness?'

The forefinger of Robert Forbes began to tap upon the table, indicating a mite of agitation within.

While the man tapped on, Roach observed him with a professional eye. A widower of some three years' standing and well enough presented. The eyebrows were somewhat tufty and the face though not exactly pudgy had some flesh to spare but his posture was erect and his hair carefully combed to conceal an incipient bald spot at the back.

A small man. But he carried himself like the church elder he was and the darting restless eyes missed nothing.

Light brown in colour, the eyes. Hazel almost. An odd contradiction to the surrounding rectitude.

He pronounced judgment.

'As regards . . . fondness?' The word sat strangely in his mouth, like a sour plum. 'Emily is prone, I am afraid, to whims.

I indulge her far too much m... day, another.'

Somewhere in the roo... joined the party.

Roach glanced around, b... Forbes and the long table.

'So you see little future, only ...

'I cannot tell the future,' Forbe... chair and showing unmistakable sign... discussion.

But Roach did not move and Forbe... setting up a further obstacle.

'Then there is position. In society. The con... way to go.'

'But, I would have thought that you of all peop...

The lieutenant had blurted out the words be... account of their effect and stopped abruptly a... stiffened in his seat.

'Aye? What of me?'

Roach was committed now, too late, the cat out of the ba... forgetting that though it was common knowledge Robert... Forbes had worked himself up from the ranks, the man himself obviously harboured some sensitivity about his origins, and the subject must be approached with delicacy.

Thank god it wasn't McLevy on hand, though Forbes had mentioned that the inspector had landed up at his office not long ago that night with some annoying inquiries and the lieutenant would catch hold of him tomorrow to ask his subordinate what he was up to this time.

Forbes was still waiting. Roach twitched his saurian jaw and tried a smile but crocodiles are more noted for their rending teeth.

'That you would understand the possibilities of rising to the heights from another . . . level, as it were.'

And there Roach ground to a halt as the face before him went a dangerous shade of puce.

from side to side; he and Mrs Roach had not been blessed with progeny and it no doubt part accounted for the energy with which she threw herself into the giddy affairs of the young.

The lack also deprived him of understanding the disquiet that must burn in a father's breast at the prospect of losing a daughter and gaining what he might consider to be a dead loss.

For a moment he felt a strange pain and emptiness as he allowed himself to wonder what it might have been like to be a progenitor.

If a boy, he would have gained a caddie. Not to be sniffed at. The older you get, the heavier the golf bag.

And if a girl? Two Mrs Roaches, cheerful and chirpy, always on the go, flitting to and fro. Always. Chirpy.

Perhaps the Almighty, in His wisdom, knew best.

17

Come sing now, sing; for I know you sing well,
I see ye have a singing face.

JOHN FLETCHER, *The Wild-Goose Chase*

The two thieves grinned nervously at each other as they waited in the darkness of the wynd. This should be easy, a drunk man and woman, easy pickings. However, though they were good at their trade, they had but recently arrived in Leith and so were still finding their feet.

That is they knew how to freeze a mark to the wall with one knife to the throat and cut his purse loose with the other blade, but geography and local rules of engagement were yet to be fully discovered.

They were about to receive a lesson.

Donnie Stevens and Jug Donleavy – hard men, well known in their native Paisley, but forced to quit the place owing to the inadvertent death of a fellow robber over an argument as to whose turn it was to buy the next round of rustie-nails, a large measure of cheap whisky that brought down the red mist like no other. So it had proved and the man had died. The inadvertent part being he had four brothers, evil bastards who would not listen to reason.

Donnie was a small rat-faced specimen with a vicious temper, it was he who had stuck the fellow robber; Jug was an amiable thickset thug whose ready smile had lulled many a victim off guard.

That smile and the fact that his ears stuck out like an elephant's gave him a gormless air but his favoured weapon was a length of lead piping which broke heads, noses and collar bones with a fine disregard.

The drunk woman was singing, a hellish caterwauling of Robert Burns' beautiful love song,

'Flow gently Sweet Afton, amang thy green braes,
Flow gently I'll sing ye, a song in thy praise;
My-yy Mary-eees a-a-sleep – '

Her voice cracked on the note and dissolved into maudlin tears as she staggered heavily in the narrow wynd, causing the beanpole drunk supporting her to stagger also and find himself unexpectedly on the point of Donnie's knife, the tip resting just under his chin.

'Not a move,' said the vindictive Donnie, 'or I'll cut ribbons out of ye.'

'He will that,' agreed Jug. 'Jist hand over yer wee poke of money, kind sir, and we can all go home. Safe and sound.'

As Jug laughed at that thought, Donnie dug the knife in for emphasis and the beanpole, his blue eyes wide with what Donnie took for fear, nodded gingerly and reached slowly into his inside jacket pocket.

But as he did so, he dropped the woman who landed on her backside with a howl of pain and split the knifeman's attention for a moment.

It was enough. What Mulholland produced from his pocket

second, Roach knew the strange trembling in his heart of momentary joy.

But that was then, and this was now. A small side room of the Freemason's Hall in George Street, where, the worshipful meeting of the lodge over and the sowing of seeds amongst his fellow members as regards the perfidious conduct of a certain chief constable in the President's Cup carried out with scrupulous nicety, he had decided to place the suit of Constable Mulholland in front of Robert Forbes.

They were both still dressed in Masonic regalia, the silver sashes adding a layer of formality to the occasion.

Forbes sat at the end of a long table and Roach, not wishing to seem invasive of the man's territory, found himself at the other extremity so that he was forced into speaking rather loudly, as if selling wares at the market.

So far the insurance adjuster's face resembled that of a man staring at a blocked water closet.

Roach took a deep breath and tried not to bawl down the distance between them.

'The constable does not lack culture.'

'I've heard him sing.'

Mulholland had a reasonable tenor voice. He and Emily had performed some duets together at a musical evening *chez* Roach. The lieutenant hated these soirées but his wife was in her element, weaving romance like a spider's web.

'His promotion prospects are . . . reasonable.'

'Seems diligent enough.'

'More than that.'

'Nothing wrong wi' steady.'

'No. But, it makes him sound rather dull.'

'Vanity is not welcome in my house.'

Roach was beginning to feel obscurely annoyed with his petitioning role and the granite responses spearing up the table towards him.

He found an unexpected dignity and firmness of tone; perhaps it was the Masonic carvings in the surrounding wood panelling which provided the support.

'Mister Forbes I am not quite sure how I ended up as advocate for the constable's case but here I am, and I require from you, like Solomon, a judgment.'

This comparison to the great Israelite, who, though initially a wise ruler, was brought low by idolatry and fleshly inclination, brought Forbes snapping to attention.

'A judgment?'

'As regards his honourable intentions towards your daughter – what are his prospects?'

The succinct question produced an equally concise reply.

'Poor. Emily is too young. She does not know her own mind. Or heart.'

Roach nodded. In a strange way, he was growing into the function he had reluctantly assumed.

'I would agree with that. But perhaps . . . in years to come?'

'It would be many years.'

'The young man may believe that your daughter is worth waiting for.'

'He may wait. But what of her?'

'She has, I am told, expressed some . . . fondness?'

The forefinger of Robert Forbes began to tap upon the table, indicating a mite of agitation within.

While the man tapped on, Roach observed him with a professional eye. A widower of some three years' standing and well enough presented. The eyebrows were somewhat tufty and the face though not exactly pudgy had some flesh to spare but his posture was erect and his hair carefully combed to conceal an incipient bald spot at the back.

A small man. But he carried himself like the church elder he was and the darting restless eyes missed nothing.

Light brown in colour, the eyes. Hazel almost. An odd contradiction to the surrounding rectitude.

He pronounced judgment.

'As regards . . . fondness?' The word sat strangely in his mouth, like a sour plum. 'Emily is prone, I am afraid, to whims.

I indulge her far too much myself. One day, it's one thing. One day, another.'

Somewhere in the room a floorboard creaked as if a ghost had joined the party.

Roach glanced around, but there was only himself, Robert Forbes and the long table.

'So you see little future, only a whim?'

'I cannot tell the future,' Forbes responded, shifting in his chair and showing unmistakable signs of wishing to curtail the discussion.

But Roach did not move and Forbes was provoked into setting up a further obstacle.

'Then there is position. In society. The constable has a long way to go.'

'But, I would have thought that you of all people – '

The lieutenant had blurted out the words before taking account of their effect and stopped abruptly as Forbes stiffened in his seat.

'Aye? What of me?'

Roach was committed now, too late, the cat out of the bag, forgetting that though it was common knowledge Robert Forbes had worked himself up from the ranks, the man himself obviously harboured some sensitivity about his origins, and the subject must be approached with delicacy.

Thank god it wasn't McLevy on hand, though Forbes had mentioned that the inspector had landed up at his office not long ago that night with some annoying inquiries and the lieutenant would catch hold of him tomorrow to ask his subordinate what he was up to this time.

Forbes was still waiting. Roach twitched his saurian jaw and tried a smile but crocodiles are more noted for their rending teeth.

'That you would understand the possibilities of rising to the heights from another . . . level, as it were.'

And there Roach ground to a halt as the face before him went a dangerous shade of puce.

'I have worked my fingers to the bone to get where I am,' said Forbes tightly, 'there's few men with my energy or application!'

'I'm sure that's true.' A mild observation that did not placate the man one bit.

'I have sacrificed much and will again, what is so dearly bought, cannot be lightly thrown away.'

'Dearly bought?'

Forbes suddenly rapped the knuckle of his hand upon the table to emphasise the words.

'Respect! Position!'

The lieutenant was getting out of his depth, this was the sort of morass McLevy would have revelled in, Roach had often observed that the angrier folk got, the happier the inspector became.

He took a reluctant leaf from his subordinate's book, and remained silent, with a slightly surprised look on his face as if to say, 'I know I'm missing something but I am unsure of what it might be. Clarify my addled wits.'

Roach couldn't quite manage the stupid expression McLevy produced on his face on such occasions, but he did his best.

It provoked an illogically fierce response.

'Emily is too young. She must be protected!'

'Protected? From the constable?'

'From life itself. She is my daughter!'

The father's eyes were burning from some internal combustion and Roach decided to opt for discretion, although he could not quite keep a slight chill out of his voice.

'I shall convey these sentiments to Mister Mulholland.'

Forbes stood and nodded somewhat jerkily then made for the door. He turned from there to have the last word.

'I have nothing against the man.'

'I can see that,' was the dry response. 'Good night, Mister Forbes.'

'Good night, Lieutenant Roach.'

The heavy door closed with a dismissive thud and Roach was left in far from splendid isolation. He flexed his jaw thoughtfully was not a purse but a large bony fist which he planted into the middle of Donnie's face, crunching back his nose and sending the man hurtling in reverse for at least three feet to land on his hands and knees, spitting blood with a terrible ringing in his ears.

Jug's mouth dropped open, this was their first plunder in Leith, and no one had prepared him for such violence.

He stepped forward, drawing out his lead piping but the beanpole simply walked up and kicked him in the groin.

Mulholland's Aunt Katie had always advised him thus, 'When in doubt, go for the crown jewels.'

Or as McLevy also counselled in the early days when a wee street keelie had laid the callow young constable low during a resisted arrest, 'Hit them first. And hit them hard.'

Jug joined Donnie in a groaning chorus on the ground and Mulholland cursed the fact that, having changed into civilian clothes to escort Mary Rough homewards, he had neither restrainers nor his lethal self-fashioned hornbeam truncheon to hand.

He moved in anyway, another couple of blows would do it, knock the wits out of them long enough for him to borrow a cart from somewhere and wheel them to the station.

This intention was somewhat forestalled however when Mary, in her befuddled state and the gloom of the wynd not helping one bit, took him to be in danger, threw her arms around his legs and clung on like a leech.

'I'll save ye, constable!' she bellowed.

That word alone was enough to send Donnie and Jug off as speedily as their crippled condition allowed, while Mulholland tried in vain to disentangle himself from Mary's vice-like grip of his kneecaps.

By the time he had achieved this, hauling her up to face him, the thieves were long gone.

'Jist as well I'm here, eh?' said Mary.

Mulholland sighed. Though he was not too downcast. He had noted the faces; they would meet again.

'Just as well, ma'am,' he replied politely.

Mary drew herself together in queenly manner.

'Ye can let me go now, constable. I'll sail under my own steam.'

And that she did. Not without the odd tack to the wind but kept her dignity and footing, through the narrow alleys, into one of the closes; even after some unsuccessful passes at the lock of her door with a bent key, Mary still achieved a ladylike decorum as she handed it to the constable.

'You do it so. My eyes betray me.'

He did as instructed. She walked into the single room where she lived her life, sat in a crooked chair, directed him to light a candle in case the bogeymen arrived to steal her Catholic soul and promptly fell asleep.

Mulholland lit the candle and looked down at her with obscure affection. She reminded him of the old women he had grown up with in Ireland; life had washed over them like a violent sea, leaving barnacles for eyes, strands of weed for hair, and wrinkled skins from the blasts of salt.

Yet they survived. Endured. And laughed.

As Mary had in the Old Ship. Mind you she had reason to be cheerful, it was Mulholland buying the drinks. For him weak beer, for her a hooker of the hard stuff.

She alternated between tears for her dead son and raucous mirth over some of the scrapes that had landed upon her in life.

She'd had to steal her own wedding dress from a department store, and the man she married, Andrew Rough, a skylighter of note, had fallen from a roof in the course of a burglary, landed in a waggon full of pigs heading for the slaughterhoose, and stank for years.

Tall tales from long ago. Andrew was departed like his son, the poor man had caught a wasting disease in the Perth Penitentiary and died skin and bones.

She had no fear to tell the constable of past crimes, because now she was as pure as the driven bloody snow.

Mary laughed once more though the pain was never far away and Mulholland also wondered if she was testing him out to see if he was after something, which he indeed was, but he gave no hint of such, smiled bashfully and not once put in a question about the fire.

Another thing learned from McLevy. Never ask the anticipated.

However he did have to tolerate many amused glances from the regulars of the tavern who knew him for a clean-living fellow and no doubt wondered what he was doing with such a disreputable old biddy.

When they were drinking in the curtained booth it was satisfactory enough but as it came time to leave, Mary had leant heavily upon him, announcing loudly to the assembly that he was a fine big specimen, and she'd wager that he was all in proportion.

Mulholland hurried her outside ignoring the open laughter at his back, and when the night air fermented the alcohol content in her blood, had no option but to stagger along with her, grit his teeth when she lifted her voice in song, and pray that he did not encounter anyone of note.

Robert Forbes, for instance. Or Emily. Or both.

But all he had encountered was a knife at his throat, a mere bagatelle.

Mary snorted in her sleep and Mulholland prepared, like her eyes, to betray the old woman.

The room was clean enough and bare of furnishings with a small bed stuck into the corner. The inventory included a chipped and battered chest of drawers which stood on three feet with a lump of stone stuck under to make a fourth, a recess where some tawdry clothes were hanging, an empty fireplace, a wee coalbunker and any amount of floorboards, cracked and creviced, that might provide a hiding spot were there a policeman in the house.

Which indeed there was.

When they had questioned Mary earlier he had noted the inspector's eyes sweep round the room appraisingly and Mulholland now did the same.

Where to begin?

McLevy had recommended, *when she is least expecting, look for an opening.*

The woman was asleep, unconscious, a less expectant state could hardly be envisaged.

Mary was too crafty to undo herself with a word. Yet, the inspector was sure that she was hiding something.

So, where was the constable to begin?

If, for instance, the expired mouse under Mary's bed had been alive with eyes to see, it would have witnessed the tall figure of a man swiftly, surely and always most neatly, sift through the pitiful contents of the chest of drawers, rifle the threadbare hanging clothes, tap the walls and boards for hollow spots, look below the mattress and sheets, then beneath the frame to find amid the dust, for folk with no carpets to sweep things under have to sweep it somewhere, a lifeless rodent body.

But a dead mouse cannot look for or at itself, and so the circle was complete. Apart from a mercifully empty chanty-pot, Mulholland had found nothing.

Little bubbles of saliva were forming at Mary's mouth where she blew out gently in her sleep; then she started and almost came awake.

Hypnos, however, once more received her in his arms, and, as Mulholland's head had whipped round in alarm at her stirring then watched her be claimed anew by the God of Sleep, his attention was taken by the fireplace.

The grate was empty but that was not his target.

The small coalbunker.

McLevy was a great man for extremities. It was his assertion that the hands and feet could tell you just about all you wanted to know.

Faces, however, were the very devil.

The constable had noted that as Mary tucked in with relish to her hookers of whisky, two of the nails on her right hand were crusted with a residue of black. The woman, despite her aptitude for knocking back John Barleycorn, maintained herself diligently enough. A habit from her former criminal days when a decent shoplifter always had to look respectable.

Despite the damp weather the fire had not been set, nor were there any ashes to be seen.

So, why the black crust?

The constable opened the bunker and gazed inside. Coal, to be sure, filled it halfway up; of the lowest quality, crumbling and powdery, just perfect for getting under the fingernails.

Which Mulholland was about to experience as he reached in and searched amongst the brittle fragments.

As his fingers probed further, he came across a sharp edge that was certainly not a lump of cheap coal.

Both hands in now, to lift it out into the light.

A smallish box. He blew the coal dust off it towards the fire grating, no point in making a mess.

A thin wooden box with a marking on it which stirred a vague memory, then when he opened it up and sniffed the contents, the memory sharpened.

A smile spread across his face.

A smile of triumph that promised retribution but took little account of the vagaries of Fate.

At that moment Mary awoke to see the constable and what he held in his hands.

She bowed her head, and Mulholland moved in for the kill.

18

Revenge is a kind of wild justice.

FRANCIS BACON, *Essay*

Leith, 1836

Herkie Dunbar tried to keep the fear at bay as he limped down the sharp cobbles, and turned into the alley that led to the wynd where he lived.

He was big for his age, raw-boned, hard-knuckled and king of the gang, but at this moment in mortal dread because of the following set of circumstances.

Along with the wild straggle of boys who terrorised all the smaller, younger children in the wynds, with particular attention paid to any pretty girl with fair hair who would be surrounded and spat upon until she was covered from head to foot with saliva and in hysterics, tears and spittle running down her face in equal measure, it was his custom to bathe every Saturday morning in the nudie, bare scud, under the hot summer sun, in Puddocky Burn, their name for the Water of Leith.

This water rose twenty miles away in the Pentland Firth, meandered through the countryside and then dipped sharply all the way down towards the Leith docks.

There was a secluded spot near to where Great Junction Street branched over the river, where the boys would throw off all their clothes and dare each other to feats of derring-do, Herkie taking particular pleasure in hurling others into the water and listening to their howls of fear as the fast-moving current almost dragged them to the bottom.

He was a good swimmer, naked body gleaming in the water like a fish as he held someone under until they begged for mercy and promised him anything he asked.

This usually involved ritual humiliation or even sexual favour for, as has been already noted, Herkie was big for his age.

Therefore, though he was king, he was not beloved by his subjects.

So when his boots disappeared, the gang did as well, leaving him searching alone by the riverbank.

He had left a neat pile of his clothes, the heavy boots on top in case of strong wind, but when he returned dripping and boisterous, they were gone.

One of the smaller boys was supposed to stand guard but he had become distracted, pitching a hail of stones at some swans upstream who were disputing the tenancy of the running water.

Herkie would have given him a good kicking but he did not have the implements.

No one had seen anything untoward; no one had noticed a figure, which had crept out from the reeds, made a lift, then back behind the rushes to hide like Moses in a basket.

Herkie had eventually given up the search and now was on his reluctant way homewards.

The sharp cobblestones hurt the boy's bare feet but that was nothing to the pain he would suffer when his father found out the loss.

Dirkie Dunbar was known as the Iron Man, part because of his skill shaping that metal in the foundry, part because of the heavy cutting edge of his fists and the cold implacable intent with which he crashed them down like a heavy hammer. He had three sons who lived in abject fear of his anger. Herkie was the youngest and his bowels were already loose at the prospect of those fists.

What could he tell his father?

Nothing that would make any difference.

The frightened boy could feel the bruises already.

And then he saw them. His boots. At the other end of the narrow alley, on the cobbles, neatly arranged with the toes pointing off as if waiting for him to slip them on and rampage his fill.

A pale shaft of sunlight shone into the passage and illuminated the leather, glinting off the metal toecaps as if guiding him to their side and Herkie was full of rejoicing not caring how they got there.

A gift from a Protestant God perhaps.

Or perhaps not.

As Herkie rushed forward to claim his prize, a figure stepped out and stood between him and his property.

He blinked in disbelief. It was the wee porker, the boy he had not long ago battered and kicked till he had spewed up all over him. A dirty Papish vomiter.

Then the penny dropped. The wee bastard, he must have stolen the boots.

What did not occur to Herkie was that the reason the boots were now on show might be part of a larger picture, no; his only thought was how come the wee porker knew where to make the theft? How come he knew?

Then the big boy remembered some time ago, he and some others had held the porker's head under the water till he was near drowned. He was feart o' the water, couldnae swim a stroke, they had dipped him up and down like a witch, that was great fun.

They had left him sprawled out on his face with the slime pouring out of his nose and mouth. Great fun.

But it had been by the Water of Leith and would explain why the porker had known the prime location.

The wee bastard.

'You stole my boots!' The big boy fairly howled.

The other's slate-grey eyes were unmoving.

'Ye can have them back.'

'I'll murder ye!'

'Ye can have them back.'

'Bring me.'

'Come and get so,' said Jamie McLevy.

Herkie was at least a head taller than his opposite, stronger, and older, a hard dirty fighter, but he was on his own and something in his opponent's stillness should have warned that the outcome might not be like past encounters.

He moved forward, bare toes gripping at the cobbles.

'Yer mammy cut her throat, they hung her on a hook like a pig and a' body laughed. Mad auld Papish bitch.'

The insult did not achieve the hoped-for loss of reason, cause the boy to run headlong for vengeance and give Herkie a chance to get his powerful arms wrapped round. Once he got to close quarters he could crush and gouge. The fight was his.

But no. The other was still out of reach; he had not budged an inch, neither back nor forward.

Herkie let out a howl and made his move, hurling himself towards his target but he should have looked down.

The right tackety boot of Jamie McLevy crashed in just below the knee-cap, paralysing the bigger boy to the spot with the most hellish pain as if his bone was splintered.

The other kneecap suffered the same fate from the same tackety boot.

He fell to the ground, mouth open, almost retching with agony. A foot came down on his outstretched hand, crunching the fingers to the stone beneath. The other hand went the same way. No favourites played.

The bigger boy might as well have been crucified.

He lifted his head and watched as the other solemnly unbuttoned himself and carefully urinated, first into one of Herkie's boots, then the other. No favourites.

'Ye can have them back,' said Jamie.

There was not a trace of feeling on his face. The eyes were blank, impersonal almost and all the more petrifying because of it.

Only a small boy but he carried a wilderness of anguish and the terrible fear that one day his mother's madness might infect and drown him if it had not already done so.

He walked out of the passage into the sunlight and was gone without a backward glance.

After a long time, Herkie Dunbar crawled painfully towards his boots and when he got there, sniffed cautiously.

Not too bad a smell, all that Holy Water must purify the pish, with a bit of luck he could rinse them out and no one would ever know.

That he had lost the fight.

When McLevy's eyes came back to focus, he found he was once more looking at the blank page of his diary. He had sat at the table with best intentions, then not written a word and instead slid off into memory.

The cemetery meeting with Margaret Bouch this very morning had no doubt triggered that particular recollection, because Dunbar, the grown man, had played a part in the history of Sir Thomas and his tragic fall.

More and more McLevy drifted in and out of the past these

days, a sign of age no doubt but in this case also, a wish to avoid some uncomfortable aspects of his present situation.

Aspects and images.

Margaret Bouch, her tongue outstretched to catch the falling drip. And swallow it down.

Jean Brash at the window, red hair against the white skin of her naked shoulders as Oliver Garvie delved in.

How long had McLevy sat on that wall looking at the finally closed curtain?

Not long. His backside had become too damp and he hoped the result would not be investigational haemorrhoids.

If an entanglement it was none of his business but what if there was more to it than that?

There was certainly not less. It was obviously a full-blooded affair, red in tooth and claw.

He reviewed the case so far, but was conscious that there was an element of avoidance in the process; two women, one close to hand, the other through a glass. McLevy did not delude himself that he was unaware of how love could rage.

He was by no means an innocent but had always taken his satisfaction in other cities, never close to hand.

And as regards love, he had never brought it home.

The prospect was terrifying. To lose yourself in another person. To lose yourself. Like madness.

Perhaps he would write of this later in his diary. A confidence, between himself and the page.

Meanwhile, back to the certainty of crime.

The night of the fire, the watchman had been absent and when he and Mulholland went a' visiting, the man's wife informed them that he had a fever. Sure enough the fellow lay in bed sweating and pallid but that could have been downright fear.

While Mulholland distracted the woman, McLevy ducked in to the scullery for a quick snoop, and spotted, shoved to the back of a shelf, a near-full bottle of whisky. Fine quality at that.

Medicinal, the wife said when challenged, and she aye bought fine quality.

Her clothes and the furnishings of the two cramped rooms, three children sleeping next door, would seem to contradict that but short of dragging the man from his sickbed and hauling him to the station, an act that though tempting might be hard to justify to his Lieutenant Roach should the accused collapse and die leaving his snottery offspring fatherless, McLevy had to leave it there.

He would be back though, he said, and fixed the trembling man with a baleful stare but the wife was unimpressed.

They had nothing to hide. Why pick on poor folk?

But she was wrong there; McLevy would pick on anybody plus, if they were that impoverished, how afford the whisky?

And the watchman's absence was very convenient. The inspector did not cleave to convenience. Or coincidence.

He wondered for a moment how Mulholland was faring with old Mary Rough. The constable had probably given up long ago and was standing underneath Emily Forbes' window serenading her like a smitten Sicilian.

The inspector moved towards the faint-glowing fireplace where his coffee pot stood on the hearth. As he poured out into his stone mug, he glanced in and frowned to see the network of cracks running along the interior; he'd be losing precious coffee to those cracks.

He'd arrived too late for supper so had to make do with his own bread, cheese and pickle. The bread was three days old, the cheese ten, and the pickle time out of mind.

This was his second cup of bituminous coffee, reduced to what looked like a black sludge. It would go well with the pickle.

McLevy looked around his room and sighed contentedly. Save for the books, it bore little trace of the person within and that was just how he liked it.

Two battered armchairs, one with a broken spring for guests who never arrived, a couple of thin stringy carpets that had seen better days and the spindly-legged table which served for meals and scribbling.

The whole place maintained clean as a whistle by his landlady, Mrs MacPherson.

Not a mirror, not a photograph to mar the looping whorls of brown flowers on the faded wallpaper.

Of late he had, to his surprise, become increasingly shipshape, not that it reflected in how he presented himself to the outside world, but in this room everything was kept in its place.

Even his beloved books were arranged in neat piles, the spines facing outwards for easy identification, stacked up against the brown wallpaper, some of the towers reaching up to almost waist height. He played a childlike game where he imagined them to be like columns of a temple and took great pleasure in favouring one then another in terms of how high they might aspire.

His reading was voracious, eclectic, and he relished the retention of obscure facts and strange turns of phrase from literature or poetry.

Such are the ways of the solitary man.

A scratching at the window intruded upon these reflections and an indignant yowl claimed his attention.

A visitor.

He walked over, reached across the table to raise the sash window and the black shape of Bathsheba ghosted in to make at once for two chipped saucers near to the fire containing, respectively, a recently poured ladle of milk and some leftover scraps of cheese and pickle.

The cat dived into the cheese, sniffed in suspicion at the pickle before dismissing it altogether, then moved over to lap with some rapidity at the milk.

It always struck McLevy that the intake of liquid on such an occasion was out of proportion to the lingual exertion involved, but he was not of the feline species.

He waited patiently until Bathsheba emptied the saucer and then watched her jump up to the hearth where McLevy had arranged an old torn red semmit, far enough from the meagre flames not to catch a spark but sufficiently near to absorb some warmth.

One of the armchairs, the one without the broken spring, was set before the ingle and McLevy sat down to regard the animal thoughtfully.

She would rest for about half an hour and then be on her way, over the rooftops to a world he could only wonder over, where yellow eyes gleamed in the night and various small birds and rodents found their own world abruptly terminated.

A time before Bathsheba had obviously been pregnant, some dirty old tom had pinned her to the slates. It had been her first litter but he had never seen trace of offspring and did not like to dwell upon their fate.

Now, she was returned her svelte queenly self.

'What kind of mother are you?' he suddenly demanded. 'Did ye drop the poor wee buggers off the roof?'

The cat yawned and buried her head into the fur near to her tail.

McLevy rested back his own cranium, noted a damp patch on the ceiling and frowned.

In the morning he would call on a banker who owed him a favour and who also knew more about the financial dealings in Edinburgh than any man alive. The information McLevy sought as regards Oliver Garvie would be confidential but the pastime the banker wished to keep hidden from the world was also a clandestine matter.

He closed his eyes and drifted.

Secrets everywhere.

19

I was a little stranger, which at my entrance into
the world was saluted and surrounded by
innumerable joys. My knowledge was divine.

THOMAS TRAHERNE, *Centuries of Meditations*

As Mulholland almost galloped through the damp streets, his
mind raced with the probabilities of glory. A golden future.

Emily in adoration trembling as the ring was fixed upon her
finger and the organ swelled. Mrs Roach tears in her eyes, the
lieutenant waggling the stripes of promotion discreetly by
his side, Robert Forbes beaming proudly at his newly adjusted
son-in-law, and McLevy, nose out of joint at a case cracked in
his absence, skulking at the back of the church, knowing that
time was not on his side and the younger man was coming
through.

On the rails. The old horse tiring, the thoroughbred
sweeping past with nary a backward glance, or maybe a small
compassionate flick of the eyes, then kick the turf, great clods
of earth spraying all over the lumbering beast behind, as it
headed towards the knackers yard!

From these thoughts, it is not difficult to observe that the
constable was getting a mite beyond himself.

This exhilaration prompted Mulholland to laugh aloud as
he forded the puddles of East Claremont Street, causing a
respectable couple coming towards him to quicken their pace
past, and a young nymph of the pavé, the girl could not have
been more than Emily's age, to sniff a potential joker on the
ran-dan and hiss quietly from one of the wynds,

'In here my mannie, warm and cosy, like a robin's nest.'

She must be new on the bones not to recognise him even in
his civilian clothes but Mulholland had no time to lay out the

dangers of the life she led, no time to fix her with a piercing glance so that she felt the weight of authority, not his lustful body, pressing upon her.

The constable waved a hand; palm outstretched like a holy saint warding off temptation, and strode on through the faint glimmering light of the street lamps.

The girl watched his figure disappearing into the gloom and sighed. A cold damp night, her feet soaking wet, and not a randie-boy in sight. Still, not long till the taverns emptied and she might yet make a catch.

She took out a small mirror and gazed at her face in reflection. No sign of the pox. But you could rarely tell from countenance who did or did not possess such.

Men cursed and called it *cuntbitten*, women suffered the same and called the raspberry-like scabs *grandgore*.

She'd had unprotected congress with a baker's apprentice the night before, no sheath to hand, and hoped the young man was clean-living.

But if he was so, what was he doing with her?

She giggled like a child at that. He had promised her a puggy bun, her favourite, a treacle sponge mixture inside a pastry case, on their next mounting and maybe he'd be her regular and after that, who knows?

So wished-for affection overcomes bitter experience to kindle hope in the human heart.

But she was also a practical girl and looked after the departed Mulholland with a sense of regret.

Thought she had a chance there, it's not often you see a man with such a smile on his face.

Not often.

The constable meanwhile was still bound for glory and the New Town, in the shape of Doune Terrace just below Moray Place where Oliver Garvie had his residence.

An elegant façade where rich folk could look down on the lowly worms crawling through the streets. Well we'd see about the worms, eh?

He had worked his way through the back roads and now was coming around Royal Terrace, close to his destiny, and as he walked along he suddenly skipped up into the air like a demented giraffe as his mind replayed that last exchange with Mary Rough.

The old woman, all mirth and merriment gone, levelled her gaze at Mulholland who cradled the wooden box in his hands. The constable had found a little stool to perch upon where he sat like some sort of giant insect, because he did not want to be towering over Mary.

No. Sympathy was the key.

A long silence. Then finally she spoke. Resigned.

'He was drunk that night. I went along tae try and keep control. Some hope, eh?'

So even now she denied complicity, just a loving mother with a rambunctious son. Well, he'd let her off with such for the moment.

That's what McLevy would have thought and it had some merit but Mulholland would soon fly above him. High into the clouds, with wings of gold. Higher and higher.

'What was the plan?' he asked softly.

'He was tae fire the place. Daniel said nobody would be there tae stop us. Guaranteed.'

'Guaranteed, eh?'

'That's whit he said.'

She fell silent again and Mulholland resisted the temptation to follow that line of questioning which could be revisited later. The absent watchman could wait. Gently does it, and always remember she was a Catholic. Faith is the key, even a ruptured disreputable faith like hers.

'The Lord loves a penitent, Mary,' he murmured.

'So, he does,' the old woman conceded.

She looked at the box he held as if it contained, like Pandora's, all of the inflictive evils.

'Daniel was molassed wi' drink. He ripped open a case, threw that thing at me. I didnae even know I had it till I got hame. I ran terrified. Whit I could see in my mind. My poor wee lamb.'

'So you hid the box away?'

'Aye. It was all I had left of him. The wee lamb.'

She bowed her head once more and though Mulholland knew the man's reputation as an unmitigated thug, he nodded as if he had personally witnessed Daniel gambolling in the fields, covered in a woolly fleece, bleating like a soul possessed.

'What happened to him? Your wee boy?'

Mary's eyes creased with pain. She was a wily old bird, a born survivor, and no doubt, in time, would try to wriggle off the hook, but at that moment her face held such a depth of suffering that Mulholland almost found it difficult to meet her gaze.

Almost.

'What transpired that night, Mary?' he repeated.

'Daniel, he – bent over tae light the shavings. Fell on his face. The oil must have splashed all over him. He went up like Bonfire Night.'

For a moment her lips twisted in grim humour and Mulholland judged it time to make his move. On to what really mattered, never mind the burnt lambkin.

'He was to fire the place, you said?'

'Aye.'

Deep breath now.

'Who put him up to it, Mary?'

'A fine gentleman.'

If Mulholland had breathed in any more, he would have bloated up like a bullfrog.

'Did you perhaps glimpse this gentleman?'

'No' really. I don't get out much.'

The constable deflated somewhat. Mary carried on regardless.

'Daniel met up with him. In private, room back o' Devlin's tavern.' A note of pride entered her voice. 'My son had been recommended.'

'This gentleman. Did he have a name?'

Mary gave him a sceptical look and Mulholland realised that in his eagerness to pursue and pounce, he had asked a profoundly stupid question. As if a man who was planning arson would leave his calling card.

'Did Daniel say what the man looked like, maybe?'

'A' he said was . . . fine and fleshy.'

'Fleshy? Like a butcher's boy?'

'I wouldnae know, I wasnae there.'

Mary's eyes had narrowed and Mulholland realised that she suspected he was trying to tie her into the event more tightly than she wished to be. Either she was as innocent as she pretended, or she was a willing accomplice to arson, but that could wait.

He pitched his voice to a more even, soothing note.

'Anything else? Did your wee boy notice anything else about this fine fleshy gentleman?'

Mary thought for a moment then nodded vigorously.

'Aye. Right enough. A hankie.'

'A hankie?'

'In his sleeve. Daniel thought it awfy class. "I'll dae that Mammy," he said. "I'll wear my hankie up my sleeve." But he never did.'

She choked back a sob, however Mulholland's mind retraced a moment in the warehouse when Garvie mopped at his brow and stuffed his handkerchief back so that it flounced out from just above the wrist.

Another nail in the coffin of proof.

'What about payment?'

'After the job was done.'

'Where?'

'Whit difference does it make?'

She was correct, the question superfluous even as he spoke it. Garvie now knew the man was dead and he wouldn't be hanging about the back room of Devlin's waving money at the passing trade.

Besides, Mulholland had something a deal more powerful up his own sleeve.

'Ach,' said Mary, out of the blue. 'When I saw his poor body, it knocked the stuffing out of me.'

She had shrunk back into herself, face crumpled, eyes bewildered and lost.

Mulholland smiled; he could afford compassion now or rather he could let his natural compassion emerge. For when the other farmyard boys wanted to hang a cat up by the tail and shoot arrows at it, was it not himself that persuaded them to give the animal at least ten yards of a start?

'Otherwise you'd have told me nothing. Eh, Mary?'

'Probably not,' she replied with a weary humour.

Their eyes met. Mulholland glanced down at the find from the coal-bunker, which now lay wedged between his bony knees. He lifted it up and offered it forth like a holy relic. A wafer on the Catholic tongue.

'So you could attest, on the Holy Book, this box of cigars here . . . it comes from the warehouse?'

'That I can swear,' said Mary piously.

The constable opened the box and sniffed again. The bitter acrid smell from within brought such joy that he felt another leap coming on.

But he resisted the temptation and continued to crouch on the stool like a praying mantis.

He sniffed once more then glanced up expectantly.

Mary nodded. 'Perks o' the job, Daniel said. He ca'd them Stinko D'Oros.'

'Indeed they are.' Mulholland closed the box with a snap. 'The cheapest, nastiest cigar on the market. Foul as a dead badger. Stinko D'Oros. My Aunt Katie used to smoke them before she turned to the pipe.'

'God help her now,' offered Mary.

Mulholland stood suddenly. He had what he wanted and he knew exactly what to do with it. This was his moment. All the lines of his life had converged like a railway terminus. Bound for glory.

No time to waste.

'Mary,' he said urgently, 'I have to get somewhere and I'm trusting you're not going to run out on me. Am I mistaken in that trust?'

'Where have I got tae go?' she replied with a bleak smile. 'And any-how, I want tae bury my son. Whit's left o' him.'

She sighed and shook her head like a weary animal.

'I'll take my licks.'

'And I'll put a strong word in for you at trial, see if I don't.'

He was already moving to the door, the cigar box stuffed into the poacher's pocket of his long black coat.

Mulholland turned to survey the old woman in the chair, every detail of the room etched into his mind. This was a moment he would never forget, a moment when his life had taken a decisive spin for the better.

'You've helped me something fine,' he declared grandly.
'What have I done?' asked Mary.
But the door had slammed and the constable was gone.

Now Mulholland crashed a heavy brass knocker upon another door in Doune Terrace. The knocker was in the shape of a fish with pouting lips that put the constable in mind of the man himself, though when the door opened, it was not Oliver Garvie but a uniformed supercilious old flunky who appeared, his lip curled slightly at the sight of the wild-eyed lanky figure looming in the half light.

'I'm a policeman,' said Mulholland. 'Where's the master of the house?'

The old fellow blinked. This was not a customary doorstep greeting.

'Mister Garvie is not at home,' he said carefully. 'His return is unspecified. I would suggest, sir, that you make your way back in the morning.'

'That's a grand suggestion,' said Mulholland, pushing past the fellow, 'but time and the hour waits for no man.'

The flunky gazed in dismay as the wet from the constable's large heavy shoes seeped on to the highly polished floorboards of the hall.

He had no option but to close the door and watch as Mulholland took tenancy of a chair in the hall beside an equally highly polished, delicately carved table, where business gentlemen were supposed to deposit their visiting cards in a silver tray.

The constable clenched his hands together tightly, his previous certainty and bravado somewhat mitigated by the surrounding rich furnishings and opulence. And this was only the hall; God knows what the rest of the place was like. No doubt the water closet had a chain of jewels.

'The matter is urgent,' he announced loudly, as much to encourage himself as to inform the old man, who was staring at him as if he were a creature from the zoo. 'It cannot attend tomorrow. I'll wait my hurry.'

'What if he doesnae come till late?' said the old fellow plaintively, knowing Garvie to be a night-owl and also that he could not get to bed while this weird intruder lurked in the hallway.

'I'll wait longer,' was the reply.

'Is the master expecting you?'

To this almost desperate question, Mulholland closed his hand round the engagement ring box hidden deep in his pocket, and, thus fortified, reverted to his candid, blue-eyed, wouldn't-harm-a-fly face.

'To be sure,' said the constable. 'I saw him only this very morning and our meeting has been on the cards since then. On the cards.'

20

Man, I can assure you, is a nasty creature.

JEAN-BAPTISTE MOLIÈRE, *Tartuffe*

Leith, December 1879

Hercules Dunbar looked at the silver candlestick and then up at the hard intent faces of the two policemen.

One minute he'd been like a pig in straw, five o'clock in the evening, the whole night standing by, two pliant whores in the shape of Big Nosed Kate and Sally Toms arching their backs over him blistering the sheets, and then the locked door to the private boudoir at the back of the Foul Anchor tavern splintered open from a hefty kick and all hell broke loose.

Kate threw an empty bottle of whisky at the tall policeman who avoided it neatly; she then launched herself, naked as a jay, to follow the trajectory of the missile but he sidestepped her as well and she hit the wall with a thud then crumpled to the floor.

Sally, meanwhile, who had been at the opposite end of Hercules and was therefore slower on the uptake, screamed ravishment and blue murder to the heavens, her naked bosom still part covered in Edinburgh Fog, a dessert of whipped cream, sugar and nuts, from an earlier frolic, quivering with fear and indignation. It was a bosom out of proportion to the rest of her slight structure, and all the more impressive for that fact. The policeman's eyes popped; the last Edinburgh Fog witnessed had been on a dish in a teahouse with a paper doily underneath and the young lady at that moment in his company bore little resemblance to either of these hellcats.

Hercules had taken the opportunity while the man was thus distracted to grab some clothes and squeeze himself out of the rear window of the tavern.

It was a long drop, and as he lay there winded, a pair of boots approached in the early evening murk, until they filled the frame of his vision. His hands were snatched behind his back and the restrainers put on.

He looked up.

Jamie McLevy.

Some things never change.

McLevy, now in the interrogation room of the Leith station, in turn looked down at Hercules Dunbar. The man still had the raw-boned frame of his youth but dissipation and hard living had scored lines into the face and hollowed out the outlines of his body.

Yet the fellow was not without feral humour. What he lacked was a moral compass.

It's too late now, as Confucius had remarked in one of his books.

'Well Herkie,' said the inspector, 'you left a trail a mile wide.'

'Is that so?' Dunbar grinned defiantly. 'Jist as well. Ye'd never have found it else.'

The policemen had trawled round the half-uncles, the local name for the small pawnshops in the wynds and closes of Leith, until striking gold or rather silver at Ned Hamilton's lair in Vinegar Close. While Ned had denied any knowledge of stolen goods or the like, his eyes kept flicking to an empty tea chest wedged against the back wall.

McLevy simply walked up and booted it aside to reveal a locked box cut into the brickwork behind where Ned kept his real stash in the hidey-hole.

Hamilton tried to claim rights of property but when McLevy threatened to pick the box up bodily and throw it through the window of the shop out into the street, the man produced a key, opened it up and amongst the tangle of cheap jewellery, garish bangles, rubies of glass, watches and fob chains, was what they sought.

A silver candlestick, luckily not yet melted down, still inscribed to Sir Thomas Bouch, who most certainly had not dropped by Vinegar Close to pawn the object.

The threat of being hauled up before the judge as a fence and resetter of theftuous plunder squeezed out a name from Ned's unwilling lips, and then it was merely a matter of sifting through the low taverns of Leith until they found out where Dunbar had holed up to spend his ill-gotten gains.

Ill-gotten, indeed and much good it had done him, two ascendant whores and an Edinburgh Fog.

All present regarded the silver tribute from Dundee, as outside the interrogation room Constable Ballantyne sat quietly at his post and dreamed of being a hero.

'You pawned that candlestick,' McLevy said quietly enough.

'I found it in the street,' came the ready response.

'That was lucky,' offered Mulholland mildly, taking his tone from the inspector.

'Luck is often on my side.'

'Good. You'll need it,' McLevy smiled, his wolf-grey eyes fixed upon the prey. 'The charge is murder. The judge will be waiting. Judge MacGregor. His family own a hemp company. Hangman's rope is made of such.'

'Murder?' Dunbar's jaw dropped and his face expressed what seemed like honest amazement. 'I dinnae do murder.'

'You broke into the house of Sir Thomas Bouch in Bernard Street, a night previous. You stole that silver. An old servant tried to stop you in your tracks.'

'You killed him where he stood. Smashed his head. Probably with that candlestick,' Mulholland chimed in helpfully though he knew unfortunately the silver stand had been given a good wipe and no trace of death remained.

'I never touched him!' Dunbar realised his mistake and tried to retract at once. 'I wisnae there. Ye cannae kill a man if you're no' there. That's impossible.'

'Kate and Sally don't think so,' replied the inspector evenly. 'Ye boasted your prowess of thievery to them. And they were only too pleased to pass it on.'

'They're good girls, they wouldnae do that.'

'Oh yes they would,' Mulholland shook his head benignly. 'Especially after we put a charge of accessory before them.'

McLevy smiled grimly. 'It's amazing how murder can leave you dancing on your lonesome, Herkie.'

A wild desperate light came into Dunbar's eyes though, had he but realised, Kate and Sally, even under threat, had stuck to the code of the Fraternity and refused to betray the man they had straddled to such good effect.

McLevy was relying on the proven fact that there was not a criminal born whose tongue would not loosen with whisky and lewd cavorting.

It was a bluff, but by the look on Dunbar's face, thought Mulholland, the bluff would not be called.

'And then there's the matter of the footprint,' said the inspector.

The constable blinked. Footprint?

'In the garden. Where you jemmied at the window. Your left boot sunk a deep mark. Mulholland here took a cast and I'll wager, we'll match you up to perfection.'

At McLevy's words Dunbar glanced down with some dismay at his treacherous foot sinister, then up at Mulholland who, behind a knowing smile, concealed the fact that the heavy overnight rain had obliterated any imprints below the window to a unidentifiable sludge.

Another bluff. Life is full of them.

'Dancing on that rope, eh Herkie?'

The inspector let out a roar of laughter. He had switched to outright provocation, this was his technique of interrogation, always switch the ground, never leave a certainty beneath the feet, not unlike the hangman.

Dunbar lunged forward in the chair where he had been deposited, hands still manacled behind.

There were two chairs and one bare table in the interrogation room.

The walls were a dirty white with various smears of what might well have been some bodily discharge; McLevy had locked the door and pocketed the key.

It was a long narrow space with no windows, claustrophobic, insulated, like being confined within the pod of a vegetable; tailor-made for confession.

'If I wasnae cuffed, we'd see who the man was here!'

This howled threat brought a response.

McLevy stepped behind Dunbar and unlocked the manacles.

'There ye are, my mannie,' he said. 'How's that?'

Dunbar rubbed at his chafed wrists. Now that he was free, he was curiously bereft of action. McLevy stood in front of him, arms hanging slack by his side, Mulholland was to the side, lounging back against the wall but not quite touching the surface.

'Two against one, eh?' Dunbar's throat was dry and what was meant to sound like a jeer came out in a wheeze.

'Not at all.' McLevy spread his hands as if to show that he carried no weapon. 'The constable is merely an observer, and will do what I command him. He is far below me in rank and must perform accordingly.'

Then turning to the aforesaid constable, McLevy pointed an index finger as if addressing a dog and ordered.

'Stay there!'

Dunbar laughed and Mulholland's backbone stiffened. No doubt the inspector was up to something as usual, but sometimes he came too near the knuckle.

'So I'll make a wee bargain with you, Herkie.' The lupine eyes gleamed in a friendly fashion. 'If you can lay me out upon the ground, I'll promise you a good hour's start from this station before we hunt you down, but if I prevail, you'll tell me the truth of last night.'

Although Mulholland's face remained impassive, he whistled silently to himself inside. This was a new one, and a wild assurance, even for McLevy. There was a history here of sorts, you could almost smell the blood of the past.

'Whit have I got tae lose, eh?' said Dunbar, the wildness in his eyes matched by a savage grin.

'Only a tooth or two,' was the serene response.

And so they began, not for the first time, to engage in warfare.

Had it been in water Hercules might have stood a chance; the inspector feared that element, a primitive terror of being dragged under in an embrace that filled the lungs, washed out the eyes then swallowed you into a gaping mouth like a mother animal gulping down her own young. Like his own mother drowning him in her madness.

But it was earth. And McLevy loved the earth.

Dunbar stood up and flexed his fingers then suddenly made a rush, head down, intending to pin his opponent against the table and get to work at close quarters.

But the inspector was no longer where he had been, an attribute Mulholland had noticed before in that for someone of such stocky build, he could skip like a mountain goat.

Which he did, to the side and then as Dunbar crashed into the sharp edge of the table, McLevy erupted into a fury of cold violence that made the constable quite content with his role of observer.

Stay put. As commanded. It was the inspector's show.

McLevy lifted up the fellow by the scruff of the neck and planted four ferocious punches into the belly. At each one, the man doubled over and each time he was hauled back to face the music.

On the fourth, the inspector let him hang there, hunched over, paralysed by the most profound pain.

As the fury drained from McLevy's eyes, Mulholland stepped up and slid the man's chair under him so that he collapsed back, still doubled over but at least with something to rest his backside upon.

McLevy perched himself on the edge of the table and waited, his hands primly folded like a priest about to hear a penitent.

There was room enough for Mulholland so he perched upon the edge as well, though while the inspector's surprisingly small feet swung in the air, the constable's were planted squarely upon the floor.

The silver candlestick was placed between them as if for the enactment of some ritual.

McLevy sung a song under his breath to keep time with his feet.

> 'Charlie is my darling, my darling, my darling.
> Charlie is my darling, the young Chevalier.'

A Jacobite air, seditious in origin. Mulholland was not tempted to harmonise.

Finally Dunbar raised his head to see this strange pair then slowly, painfully, straightened up.

Give the man his due; he kept to his side of the bargain.

'The bastards owed me,' he said.

'Elucidate,' replied James McLevy.

The story Dunbar told was a long and rambling one full of grievances, imagined or otherwise, betrayal, treachery, the loss of a dear friend, bad practice, and most heinously, the contemptible treatment of a faithful employee. The list was apparently endless but might be summed up thus.

This, of course, was Dunbar's version.

Like his father before him, he had become an expert in the forging of iron but work in Edinburgh being scarce had quit the city to be employed at the Wormit Foundry in Dundee, eventually working his way up to the job of foreman moulder in charge of all under the roof save the turners whose craft was beyond mortal comprehension.

In that foundry, while the smoke rose and the sparks flew day and night, the fires glowing like volcanic lava in the dark, they had constructed the High Girders, then the cast-iron columns strutted and cross-braced, bolted vertically through flanges which would support these girders to a span of near 250 feet, thirteen of them, that would knit a strand of iron from pier to pier, shore to shore, to form the central structure of a series of black rainbows from the trap rocks of Wormit to the sandy shelves of Magdalen Green.

To span the river below, in all its moods.

The Tay Bridge.

Two and a quarter miles long.

A lattice-grid of cast and wrought iron. Like a spider's web across the River Tay.

The result and solution to a war between two railway companies, separated by the river. The North British on one side, the Caledonian on the other.

These two enemies had fought for untold years over Scotland like dogs over a bone.

And to put the matter simply, in order for the North British to prevail, it would have to run its trains straight through from Edinburgh to Dundee and onwards.

Before the bridge, a journey of forty-six miles took an inexorable three hours twelve minutes and that was the fast train. It involved starting from Waverley station at 6.25 a.m. in a freezing carriage with two smelly fish trucks in the rear, then a ferry from Granton where the fish smell got worse, another train from Bruntisland to Tayport on the south side of the Tay estuary, yet another boat across to Broughty Ferry, and a third train which limped into Dundee carrying the miserable, hungry, disconsolate passengers to their journey's end.

And if the weather was disagreeable, as it often was, then the journey was longer than the descent into hell.

Of course the Caledonian fought the bridge tooth and nail but, at last, after a conflict that almost bankrupted both companies, the North British proved more than equal to its opponent in negotiating the treacherous sands and eddies of disturbed capitalism, and won the day.

The money was raised, Parliament nodded, Royal Assent was given and then, as the song would say,

'Way hay and up she rises,
Earl-aye in the morning.'

Designed by the great Victorian engineer, Sir Thomas Bouch, dubbed so at Windsor Castle by the Queen who had herself on the North British engine, 'Netherby', in fine weather with the waters below lit by the evening sun like a picture postcard, crossed the completed bridge in the late June of 1879, and pronounced to all and sundry that she was pleased to confer upon the originator of this grand edifice, a knighthood.

The Tay Bridge.

It had been his dream for twenty years.

Sir Thomas had the most profound faith in himself. It had never occurred to him to think otherwise.

But that bugger of a bridge took six years to build, ten million bricks, two million rivets, eighty-seven thousand cubic feet of timber, fifteen thousand casks of cement and employed over the years six hundred men, nearly all of whom were paid the princely sum of eight pence an hour.

What of these men? They broke their bones and gave their lives to build a monster of iron and stone, which had neither mercy nor compassion for the insects that swarmed over its great body like termites building a tower to the heavens.

The bridge, like a savage god, crushed them as they strove to give it life and form.

Christ Jesus knows how many were badly injured, but for sure twenty men died, the wind picking them off a girder-span and hurling the body eighty feet down to the waters below, the impact splitting them apart like rotten apples. Or, as a cylinder collapsed, two men sucked into the mud and held in its treacherous embrace till they were drowned like rats.

An August explosion killed six more, a digging gang on Pier 54, down in the depths, an air bell above, the pumps sucking out the water, then the blast turned their bones to sawdust and cruciformed their limbs.

The cause of the explosion was never found.

Meanwhile Thomas Bouch sat at his desk and thought his great thoughts.

As a result of these deaths, the wages were raised from eight to ten pence.

Some of this McLevy gleaned from Dunbar's own words, some he discovered later, most of the stories and facts were, after all, in the public domain.

Most, but not all. Not by a long shot.

And Dunbar had lost his best friend, Tommy Loughran, a nice wee man for a riveter, not three years before, to a wild February storm. Spans twelve and thirteen of the high girders had not yet been made secure to the main structure and down they went, taking Tommy with them. He left a wife heavy with child and two others hanging round her skirts.

This was not unusual; the life of a working man is cheap. And after all, who was at fault? Surely Nature must take the blame. According to official version, the howling gale battered upon the unsecured girders for three hours till they lost their state of equilibrium on the lifting apparatus and toppled like the Giant's beanstalk after Jack got to work with the axe.

So Tommy Loughran died for the greater good of the powers that be and would receive his reward in glory helping Saint Peter instal rivets to fortify the heavenly gates.

And yet McLevy sensed in Dunbar as regards his friend's death, a

129

personal guilt as if something was gnawing away at him inside. It would not be an issue of morality, the man possessed no such thing, therefore what was causing unease in a psyche not inclined towards the fine-tuning of conscience?

As if to confirm his somewhat coarse disposition, the fellow hawked up a wodge of phlegm from his lungs and spat it out on to the floor of the interrogation room where it bounced like a rubber ball.

'The bastards owed me,' he repeated.

'For what?' asked Mulholland.

'Whit I did. Whit I did not. The blind eye.'

McLevy was silent thus far, his eyes fixed upon Dunbar as if trying to see behind the mask the man presented, so the constable was honour bound to continue.

'The blind eye?'

'Whit I turned.'

'To what?'

Dunbar laughed harshly. He was beginning to enjoy himself with Mulholland but, in so doing, ignored McLevy at his peril. His aching belly could have reminded him of this but physical pain was so much part of his life that he kept it at distance and bore it like an animal.

'Ye ever hear o' Beaumont Egg?'

'I have not,' replied Mulholland after a moment of thought.

'Then ye can remain an ignorant Irish pig!'

Mulholland flushed red and Dunbar tensed himself but now it was McLevy's turn.

'So that is why you stole. They owed you.'

'They did. And threw me off the job for no reason.'

'How so?'

'That bastard Alan Telfer!'

'The right hand of Sir Thomas?'

'A minion! He sneaked in. I was the foreman, no bugger knew as much of the iron-moulding as me. But as soon as that bridge was built, he threw me out.'

'There must have been a reason?'

'He sneaked in the foundry. Witnessed me. I had drink taken.'

'That's a surprise,' was the dry response.

130

'It was my birthday!' Dunbar said defensively.

Now it was Mulholland's occasion for silence as he watched McLevy manipulate the exchange so that the other was forever on the back foot. Yet the inspector somehow gave the impression that he and Dunbar were working towards a common end, uncovering the truth together as it were, though that would change at some point, the constable would have wagered his carefully tended Protestant soul upon it.

'So,' McLevy mused thoughtfully, 'to assuage your hurt feelings and empty pockets, you removed from the possession of your former employers, that which you believed rightfully belonged to yourself as compensation for unfair dismissal?'

Dunbar had momentary difficulty in following this somewhat convoluted reasoning, but got there eventually and near nodded his head off in agreement.

'That is correct. The bastards!'

McLevy smiled and also nodded, all friends together, but then leant back again, folded his hands together, this time more resembling a Buddha than a priest, and waited.

Hercules felt obscurely summoned to contribute more.

'And it wasnae the first time,' he affirmed.

Mulholland's long nose twitched in apparent bewilderment.

'It wasn't the first time you had broken into the place?'

'No. Not at all.'

'Not at all you had? Or not at all you had not?'

'For the love of Christ,' Dunbar muttered indignantly. 'Not at all I hadnae.'

He shook his head at McLevy as if to say, 'How do you endure this great gowk?' and received a complicit headshake in reply, yet the two policemen were playing him like a hooked fish.

Hercules felt an ill-founded sense of well-being; he and the inspector might be sworn enemies but there was respect to be paid on each side.

Unlike this dozie from the bogs of Ireland.

He ignored Mulholland altogether and addressed McLevy as close to an equal.

'It wasnae the first time I had asked for my due. I banged upon their door.'

'And when would that be?' asked his almost equal.

'Not long since. A Sabbath day. Sir Thomas wasnae on the premises.' Dunbar puffed up importantly as if he had hammered on the portal like a creditor. 'I was taken to Alan Telfer and there I made my just demand.'

'What was his response?'

Dunbar's face darkened with chagrin.

'The bastard laughed at me.'

'He was a brave man,' McLevy observed, a tinge of admiration to his tone as if he believed Dunbar a fellow to be reckoned. 'Or a foolish one, eh?'

'He threatened me wi' the police.'

'Well that's where you've ended up, right enough.'

This comment from Mulholland was treated by the other two with the contempt it deserved, and then McLevy hopped off the table to drag over the second chair so that he and Dunbar sat together like two old men on a park bench.

'Surely he could have just shown you to the door like a gentleman, why threaten you, Herkie?'

'Because I threatened him,' the man boasted.

'With what?'

For a moment Dunbar almost blurted out what was in his mind, but then his instinctive feral cunning kicked in and he closed his eyes, shaking his head, a self-important smile on his face to indicate the depth of the secrets he held.

Perhaps it had something to do with this mysterious Beaumont Egg the man had mentioned to tantalise Mulholland, or perhaps Dunbar was giving himself airs to cover the fact that he had gone cap in hand to be treated like a doorstep beggar, but it was time now for the subject of murder.

'So you had your vengeance, eh?'

'I did indeed.'

'While they were snoring, the Great Man and his secretary – '

Here, Dunbar suddenly let out a loud snigger. 'Aye, like dirty pigs.'

The man had a sly look upon his face but McLevy did not wish to pursue this divergence from the main narrative.

'While they were snoring,' he continued, 'you made a fool of them, robbed them blind.'

'Whit was my due,' asserted Dunbar complacently, not realising that he was in the process of tying a noose around his own neck.

McLevy leant forward from his chair, faced away from Dunbar and made a little movement with his hand like a man feeding bread to the ducks.

He spoke softly almost in a whisper, as if they were both witnessing the scene.

'You went into the study and looked around, what could you take to make up for the wrongs committed? And there was the candlestick, what better? Inscribed to Sir Thomas who gets all the credit for your labour, the crime fits the insult, eh?'

Dunbar nodded his appreciation of McLevy's grasp of the subtle undercurrents to this event while Mulholland, who would be an important witness at trial, trained his large pink ears towards the two men, side by side, all friends together.

McLevy carried on with his reconstruction in a soft mesmeric tone, which his superior Lieutenant Roach would have found hard to recognise and alarming to witness, like a wolf lying down with lambs.

'Out you came, into the hall, quiet as a mouse, and there in front of you was Archibald Gourlay, the butler, another quiet man. Face to face. In from the street while you were busy about your righteous task, a wee bit shaky on his feet, whisky on his breath, the drink is a terrible thing, eh Herkie?'

For a moment Hercules Dunbar hesitated, and then nodded assent.

'He was puggled, right enough.'

'A terrible thing, the drink.' The inspector bowed his head in the sorrow of wisdom.

Mulholland also bowed his head but it was to hide the light of triumph in his eyes. They had him now.

Or had they?

McLevy continued, his voice quiet and reassuring, as if impending death was to be a pleasant surprise.

'And of course a man as strong as you would not dream of doing harm to a man as old as that, no. Not smash his head with a candlestick as the constable was daft enough to suggest but perhaps, by accident, you wished to escape, he stood in your way, you gave him a wee gentle push, is that the way of it?'

'Aye,' said Dunbar slowly. 'Jist a wee push.'

'And down he fell?'

'Over his own feet.'

'A terrible thing, the drink. A man of his age should know better, eh?'

'Dangerous, right enough.'

McLevy and Dunbar nodded together, wise beyond their years, and Mulholland tried not to catch the suspect's eye lest it break the spell.

'So, one minute he was there before ye, and the next?'

McLevy held up his hands palms outward as if to ward off unwarranted accusation.

'Out of sight. Down the stairs. Arse over elbow.'

He laughed heartily as though no harm had been done, a comical event, like Humpty Dumpty falling, like the old man who would not say his prayers; Dunbar laughed also but then a strange look came into his eyes.

'Not down the stairs,' he said slowly. 'I left him in the hall. On his arse right enough. But . . . in the hall. It was me went doon the stairs. I ran like hell. Then, out the window.'

The inspector's eyes narrowed; either the man had realised he was about to hang himself or the invented structure did not fit what had actually taken place.

He kept his tone pleasant, try again.

'Well that's a puzzle Herkie, because I found him at the bottom of the steps.'

He forbore to add, 'With his head split open, because you crashed something into it, you murderous evil snaffler.'

Try again. One step at a time. Tie him in with a silken cord, the rope can arrive later.

'Maybe what transpired. He followed you. On the stairs. Grabbed at you. Called out. Made a big noise. You shoved free, a wee push. Down he fell into the scullery. You left him there. Sitting. On his backside. Like you said, eh?'

Dunbar shook his head promptly and McLevy knew he had lost the man.

'No. He didnae say a word. Ever. Jist sat doon wi' a bump. I left him sitting. In the hallway. Looking at me. His mouth was open. But he didnae say a word.'

'What about his head?' asked an exasperated Mulholland who also knew that their hard work was all in vain and as his Aunt Katie would have said, 'You can lead a horse to clear water but what if the creature is devoid of thirst?'

'It was fine,' came the stolid reply.

'Not a great big wound in it, then? Full of the joys of spring, was he?'

This irony from the constable was wasted on Dunbar.

'He was fine,' was the answer.

'Fine?'

McLevy suddenly stood and kicked away the chair so that it skittered across the room to crash into the wall, much in the manner of Big Nosed Kate.

'Fine?' he roared.

Mulholland jumped off the table so that he was on the other side of the suspect, who had begun to realise that perhaps everything wasn't so fine after all.

'Full of the joys of spring, eh?' the constable repeated.

'No' exactly,' responded Hercules who was beginning to relish this despite the tremor of fear in his guts.

'Looking at you, was he?' McLevy came in from the angle, a savage glint in his eye.

'Right enough.'

'So he would know your features? Face to face, you said.'

'I didnae say that, you did.'

'You did not contradict me. Face to face!'

Dunbar judged it a wiser course to stay silent. The constable wasn't quite sure where the inspector was heading so he contented himself with looming menacingly.

'So, he would know you from before?'

'Before?'

'When you banged upon the door to claim your miserable just demands, you were taken to Alan Telfer, you claim. Who answered the door? Who looked at you? Who led you through the house to meet the secretary?'

'The auld man,' Dunbar finally muttered.

'Archibald Gourlay was his name,' said McLevy. 'The butler, a man about his lawful pursuits.'

'And he would recognise you!' Mulholland had caught on to the line of question and they would try to keep the man bouncing between them till he betrayed himself.

'It was dark in that hall,' was the defiant response.

'Darkness be buggered!' bawled McLevy. 'He would know you from before, rouse the household and inform Alan Telfer, that the man who'd come to visit previous was the man who'd robbed the house, right left and centre.'

'You couldn't let that happen,' Mulholland interjected.

'One old man could put you in the jail, one man only, and to save your worthless soul, you smashed him down,' the inspector accused.

'With the candlestick,' cried Mulholland in triumph. 'I was right all along!'

'I didnae use such,' Dunbar asserted indignantly.

'Then what did you use?' demanded McLevy.

'Nothing.'

'Nothing?'

'I never laid hand on him.'

'You're a liar!'

McLevy hauled Dunbar off the chair and upward so that their noses almost touched.

'Ye broke his skull.'

'I did not.'

'Ye did so.'

'Didnae.'

'I'll pee in your boots.'

'Go ahead.'

'Your gang's no' here, now.'

'I should hae drowned you when I had the chance.'

'And I should have kicked you harder!'

Mulholland sighed. This was getting them nowhere for the harder McLevy hammered in, the more stubborn became the denials; either the man had lied himself into a corner or the truth lay in a different version of events.

Furthermore the constable was due time off this evening and hoped to attend a choir practice at church, where he would combine hymns of worship with hopeful glances in the direction of some well-brought-up young ladies who lifted their voices and bodices to God; thrilled by the organ's swelling thunder, a becoming flush upon their faces and discernible pulse beating in their throats, they were ripe for a spiritual plucking.

Presbyterian veneration might never spill over into gay abandon but it had its moments.

Finally McLevy, with an exclamation of disgust, hurled Dunbar back into his chair.

'Ye can stew in the cells all night and we'll see how smart you are in the morning,' he growled running his hands through his hair which was now standing up on end with sheer frustration.

'The story'll be the same,' muttered Dunbar. 'I left him living.'

'And I found him dead!'

'Maybe something happened in between?' suggested Mulholland somewhat unwisely, his mind having wandered to the daughter of the manse, a fair-haired buxom blue-eyed warbler whose efforts to hit the high notes rendered the confines of her corset somewhat inadequate at times.

'Nothing happened in between,' snapped McLevy, glowering at the constable before directing a last malevolent look towards Dunbar.

'You murdered the man. Pure and simple.'

'But whit if I didnae?' Dunbar retorted, having found some kind of courage at the prospect of the cells; at least he wouldn't have this bastard haunting him and anything could happen in the inspector's absence.

'Whit if I didnae?' he repeated.

McLevy made no response and Dunbar's words danced in the air like a melody out of tune.

21

Yet still between his Darknesss and his Brightness
There passed a mutual glance of great politeness.

LORD BYRON, The Vision of Judgment

*The inspector closed the door of Bernard Street, the house now lacking a
butler, and recalled his last, by no means memorable, rejoinder to Alan
Telfer.*

'I'll see myself out.'

*The secretary had inclined his head, a shaft of light from under the
study door indicating that Sir Thomas was still hard at work on his
design for the Forth Bridge, for which he planned spans of sixteen
hundred feet in length, the structure itself like an iron bird of prey
swooping one hundred feet above the water.*

*The Great Man had already answered, admittedly in monosyllables,
previous inquiries about the night in question, and was not to be disturbed by further demands.*

*The inspector had been happy enough to accept that; he found Sir
Thomas almost impenetrable, and suspected that the man was patho-
logically shy and withdrawn, though that could also be the sign of
overweening arrogance, internalised to the point where he and God
might well be interchangeable.*

McLevy knew the feeling well.

*That left him with Alan Telfer who, while responding with scrupulous
civility, managed to subtly convey this was a complete waste of time for
both men.*

*As regards the night of the murder, the secretary could add nothing
more save the reiteration that having worked late into the night, he and
Sir Thomas had retired to their respective quarters, Sir Thomas the
master bedroom, and himself a small attic room which he occupied when
the volume of work and lateness of the hour made it impractical for him
to return to his lodgings on the other side of the city.*

Both men been roused from their beds in the early morning by the

138

maid, who had now also departed their employ, screaming like a banshee. They had subsequently witnessed the dead body of the butler, Archibald Gourlay, had contacted the relevant authorities and McLevy knew the rest.

Sir Thomas, McLevy recalled, had a faint Northern accent courtesy of his native Cumberland, but the secretary's was untraceable, the words clipped, precise, contained, the face cold and smooth, eyes blue and lidded, the mouth thin. There was a reptilian quality to Alan Telfer and the inspector would not have been surprised if the man's tongue were two feet long and slightly forked.

When McLevy sprung the name of Dunbar upon the scene, the secretary indeed remembered the man's Sabbath intrusion.

He confirmed the relevant facts but from an icily opposite point of view.

The man had been sacked deservedly for being drunk and incapable at the workplace, a condition all the more heinous because of his position of responsibility.

Luckily, it being a Sunday when Dunbar hammered upon the door, Sir Thomas had been at the family house in Moffat when the fellow blundered in with his foolish demands; had he by chance disturbed the Great Man at his desk, Telfer would have called the police at once.

'But you threatened the law upon him, did you not?' asked McLevy, as they stood in the main salon which so much resembled the waiting room of a railway station, the room where the inspector had first set his eyes upon Margaret Bouch, the dainty wife of Sir Thomas.

'Eventually,' was Telfer's calm rejoinder.

'Why?'

'He would not leave.'

'But then he did?'

'Eventually. People do leave, eventually.'

A thin smile indicated that McLevy might well be included in this comprehensive statement.

'Uhuh?' replied the inspector, unmoved. 'So you faced him down?'

'In a manner of speaking.'

'Were you not afraid for yourself? Hercules Dunbar is a violent man.'

'Brute force has little effect upon me,' Telfer said dismissively. Then the secretary frowned as the import of McLevy's questions rattled up a conclusion in his mind.

'Is this man Dunbar connected to the burglary?'

'Could be.'

'And the murder?'

'Could be.'

The atmosphere between them changed somewhat, nothing the inspector could put his finger on, but the air suddenly crackled as if some alarm had been sounded.

Or was it just too much coffee? A grateful Mulholland, having been given the rest of the night off, had insisted on treating his inspector to a large mug of the stuff in the Old Ship, the tavern being one of the few where a man might partake of something other than a snifter of alcohol.

Whatever. Both men were now on the alert.

'Dunbar threatened you in turn, did he not?' asked McLevy, his eyes fixed directly upon Telfer.

'He ranted and raved. An empty vessel.'

'No doubt. But what was the nature of his menace?'

'I don't really remember. It was mere . . . bluster.'

'Bluster?' McLevy laughed suddenly. 'I know it well. But what kind of bluster?'

'It all passed me by,' was the uninformative answer.

'Have you ever heard of Beaumont Egg?' asked the inspector, echoing Dunbar's words.

For a moment the secretary was perfectly still, head bowed, as if considering inwardly.

But what was he considering?

Finally Telfer lifted the bland aforementioned visage and pursed his lips thoughtfully.

'I have heard the term,' he murmured. 'But I am afraid I cannot exactly recall the meaning.'

'I'll find it out,' said McLevy. 'Eventually.'

Another echo of a spoken word and the secretary inclined his head as if to acknowledge the fact. He gazed at McLevy's impassive countenance if not with a new respect, then at least with recognition that the man was not as bovine in thought as he appeared in body.

In acknowledgement of this, Telfer creased up his eyes in further thought.

'I believe . . . it may be a mastic of sorts, a mixture of iron filings but . . . please do not quote me as authority.'

He smiled though the eyes were lidded and watchful.

'It is possibly used in the foundry trade but I am not familiar with such elemental matters, Sir Thomas and I involve ourselves with . . . higher concerns.'

Another glance back at the closed door of the study indicated that unless McLevy had more to say, the exchange was curtailed.

But McLevy did have more to say.

'Hercules Dunbar mentioned such. He also spoke of a blind eye.'

'Blind eye?'

'Being turned.'

The secretary sighed somewhat elaborately, possibly revising his earlier good opinion of the policeman, though McLevy had noticed the fraction of a hesitation before the exhalation of modified impatience.

'Turned to what, may I ask?'

'He would not say.'

Telfer had long white fingers; he placed them together as if to form a church and raised them to the tip of his chin. A Cardinal dismissal.

'I am sorry, inspector, but my time is valuable and my labours many. I doubt if I can help you further.'

So saying he signalled discreetly towards the door that led out into the hall and thence to the street.

The inspector did not budge however.

'It is my surmise that Dunbar was hinting at some malpractice of sorts, did he mention anything of this to you?' he asked bluntly.

'He did not,' was the clipped response.

'But if he had,' persisted McLevy. 'Would it have struck a chord?'

Alan Telfer stiffened slightly and, for the first time, an edge of anger entered his voice.

'What is your implication here, sir?'

McLevy was all innocence and honesty.

'I am merely trying to tease out what Dunbar may have meant. It puzzles me.'

'If I might suggest, inspector, you would be better employed charging the man with larceny and homicide rather than giving credence to his ignorant allegations.'

The inspector nodded humbly enough but still he stood there like a cow looking over a dyke and this dumb obduracy seemed to provoke Alan Telfer further.

'The world is full of small men who envy the giants that walk amongst them. They would wish to besmirch their achievements and bring these sublime creators down to their own disgusting cretinous level!'

The words were hissed out and indeed McLevy expected the snakelike tongue to flicker forth at any moment.

'Sir Thomas is such a giant. It is my privilege to guard him against the jealousy of small minds and the slander of those who cannot bear his genius.'

A hooded darting look left McLevy in no doubt that he was to be numbered amongst the envious pigmies.

Then as suddenly as the storm had blown up, it vanished and Alan Telfer returned to habitual urbanity.

'I would advise, sir, that you take anything Hercules Dunbar alleges with the proverbial pinch of salt. He is a drunkard, a thief and a murderer.'

'The murder has yet to be proved,' said McLevy.

A twist of humour came to the thin lips.

'Then prove it, inspector. That is your profession.'

In the silence that followed this suggestion, Sir Thomas Bouch's voice sounded from behind the closed door.

'Alan? Where are the designs for the south section?'

Telfer's head went up and for a moment he looked like a dog being called by his master, then he smiled courteously enough at McLevy and gestured once more at the door that led to the hallway and the outside world.

Which is when the inspector remarked, 'I'll find my own way out.'

And that is just what the inspector did.

22

The heart is a small thing, but desireth great matters.
It is not sufficient for a kite's dinner, yet
the whole world is not sufficient for it.

FRANCIS QUARLES, Emblems

Now he stood in Bernard Street and shivered. Though it was a still night, the cold sea air carried enough salt crystals to sting the skin.

McLevy resolved to walk down to the Leith docks; perhaps he would hazard another mug of coffee at the Old Ship, and while he thus perambulated let some random intuitions flow through his mind.

So, he walked.

That house was full of secrets; they ran to and fro like rats beneath the floorboards.

Telfer had evinced a weird passion in the defence of Sir Thomas, as if they shared the grandeur of creation together, as if he were the keeper of the flame.

Guardian of the other's soul and reputation.

Like a faithful dog snarling to protect its master.

Against what?

The jealousy of small minds or something more substantially material?

And how far would Telfer proceed to shield Sir Thomas?

What about the blind eye?

Was it not Admiral Nelson who had first turned such a thing at the battle of Copenhagen?

McLevy shook his head at this collection of dog-eared insights and moved towards the practical.

In the morning he would squeeze the truth from Hercules Dunbar if he had to stretch him on the rack.

But what of the inspector's own secret? While he was engaged with Telfer, was a part of his attention not casting round for other movement in the house?

Dainty feet a' tapping.

The dancing lady to his hardy tin soldier.

And was that perhaps the reason he had divested himself of Mulholland, not that the constable needed much divesting; was it in order that should a meeting contrive itself with the lady of the house, the inspector could embrace the principle, two is company but three are one too many?

As he neared the docks, McLevy reflected, perhaps with some relief, that, of course, she would be back in Moffat by now. On the borders. Stealing sheep.

The image of Margaret Bouch in her plaidie, sneaking up on an unsuspecting lamb provoked him to a harsh cough of laughter that echoed in the silence, causing the woman who was sitting on one of the iron bollards of the Inner Harbour to swivel round.

The sky was clear, the stars were out and a crescent moon smiled aslant in the cold, salty night.

The stray beam of a nearby street lamp caught the high cheekbones and, even at this distance, he could discern the gypsy eyes weighing him up like a slaughterhoose attendant would an Aberdeen Angus.

'Whit are you doing here?' he blurted out.

Margaret Bouch laughed, a silvery sound like manacles clinking in a holding cell.

'I'm looking at the ships, inspector. Surely that is not against the law?'

He muttered something under his breath then trudged over to glower down at her.

'This is no place for a respectable woman.'

'Perhaps I am not respectable.'

Her small, gloved hands lay quietly in her lap, the dark outdoor coat was wrapped round her like a soft fur and for some reason he was put in mind of Bathsheba, the cat.

McLevy cast a quick wary glance to left and right, but this part of the harbour area was uninhabited, possibly because the taverns were situated further along the old quayside at the Shore and the graving docks behind them had no ships laid up at present.

He sat on another bollard close by hers, leant forward, clasped his hands together and puffed out a breath that took the form of smoke in the cold night.

'Where's your bonnet?' he asked suddenly.

She reached down beside her, picked up the hat she had discarded to feel the air on her skin, shook it at him as if it were a tambourine, and then replaced it on the ground.

That took care of that, then.

'I've just left your house,' he said.

'It is not mine,' she replied dryly. 'And you are welcome to it.'

They both looked over towards the Old Docks where the small lights on the various masts glowed like Jack o' lanterns, flitting in and out of sight as the ships rocked gently in the waves.

A few creaks and plashes occasionally disturbed the silence but, for the most part, it was as if the whole scene were an artist's rendition.

Two figures in a world that held its breath.

'I may have my hands on the killer of your butler,' remarked McLevy in the stillness.

'I am pleased to hear that.'

'The candlestick stolen from your husband might well be the weapon of destruction.' McLevy smacked his lips together as if tasting the crime. 'Though that is still a matter of debate. It might have just been a push, a thin skull and a sharp edge. Fragments of blood and bone on the stairs but the candlestick was wiped clean. Pity that.'

She made no answer and he warmed further to the theme.

'But even if the implement were covered in blood, we cannot yet compare or identify the type. Science has not advanced thus far. But it will. One day. I have no doubt.'

'Must we talk of murder?' she remarked quietly.

Without that subject the inspector seemed a trifle lost for words. He shuffled his feet together like a little boy and whistled tunelessly under his breath.

Margaret shot him a look and he stopped whistling.

'I thought you were in Moffat?' he muttered, somewhat aggrieved.

It would seem as if the nuances of the night were somewhat beyond McLevy's ken. Will o' the wisps, crescent moons, mysterious women on iron bollards, all wasted on a man whose only concerns seemed to be geography and homicide.

'I have had to remain here in order to recruit some domestic staff for

Sir Thomas,' Margaret replied evenly. 'And I have been helping Mister Gourlay's family with the funeral arrangements.'

'See now? We're back to murder!' he responded with a gleam in his eye.

She shook her head though there was an unwilling smile, tugging at the corner of her mouth.

'Are you expert in funerals then?' he asked.

'My parents died in quick succession,' she replied crisply. 'One acquires a facility.'

'I'll do my own, thank you,' was his riposte.

But all this time the inspector had been glancing over at her from below his brows, while she favoured him with her profile, staring straight ahead.

Somewhere in the sky above, a seagull emitted a series of melancholic, high-pitched calls. They echoed then faded in the stillness, leaving only the muffled sound of the ships creaking and swaying with the swell of the sea.

Margaret's gypsy eyes were fixed far beyond the horizon and McLevy shifted uneasily as if he sensed her drifting away with the waves.

'How've you found yourself here?' he asked quietly.

'Do you mean in this world, or the Leith docks?'

'The docks.'

'I was on my way back from the Gourlay family, I did not wish to return directly to Bernard Street. I often come to this place.'

'It is dangerous,' he warned.

'I have never found it so.'

'You might be mistaken for a lady of the night.'

'I like the night-time,' was the cryptic response.

She sat there like a graven image but McLevy thought he could sense a compulsive yearning to be free, to break all bonds. It might be he felt this because he possessed the same. Buried deep. Just beside the madness.

'When I was a little girl,' she murmured, 'I dreamt of being a pirate.'

'A pirate?'

'Yes. A sword between my teeth.'

'I had you down for a sheep stealer.'

'Nothing on land.'

The inspector pondered this for he loved the earth.

'I don't like the sea,' he muttered.

'Why not?'

'It's too deep.'

Margaret laughed once more and wondered why she felt so comfortable in his presence. The thought came to her that perhaps they might have known each other in a previous existence. Ancient Egypt seemed to be a popular venue and she tried to imagine herself decked out in the robes of a temple princess. But what of McLevy?

'Were there policemen in Antiquity?' she asked.

'I expect so. Man was born criminal.'

'Criminal?'

'I am as great a wrongdoer as any such I catch.'

This change of subject intrigued her.

'It is your contention, then, that we are born to guilt?'

'That is my contention.'

'I might take issue with you there.'

McLevy waited for her to elaborate on that issue, but she smiled then lifted her face up towards the moon. As she did so, the hand nearest to him swung free and hung down by her side. It occurred to the inspector that if he touched across it would be his to grasp; but it also occurred that she was married and respectable was she not? Out of reach.

'Do you have offspring?'

This somewhat brutal inquiry jolted Margaret from the alternate reality of moonlit piracy, Egypt and original sin, causing her to blink a moment before response.

'Three. Two girls. One boy.'

'Three? You don't look it.'

'It was long ago,' she retorted dryly. 'They are grown now, out of my hands.'

'Do you love them?'

'They respect me,' was the elliptical response.

'What about their father?'

The inspector may well have meant, 'Do you love him?' but Margaret chose to answer the other possibility.

'They respect him also,' she replied.

However the mood was broken now; the crescent moon reflected itself on the water in vain, sewage broke the surface and rats lurked in the shadows, tails entwined.

'Tell me about your killer,' she asked, pulling the hand back into her lap and turning to face him.

So the inspector did and she paid heed.

Of course Margaret Bouch knew nothing of Hercules Dunbar, he would have been an anonymous face in the crowd of workmen when she sat on the train making the first official crossing in September 1877.

The Tay Bridge.

Completed near to time, dead riveters notwithstanding.

Her husband of course had been at the front with the other dignitaries while she had sat with the ladies. While some of the delicate creatures paled at the enclosed roar and the sinister shadows of the iron lattice whipping past the carriage windows, Margaret had looked down at the russet colours of autumn which bedecked the fields on each side of the expanse of water, and wondered what it would be like to launch oneself into the air to land like a graceful leaf amongst the yachts, wherries and fishing boats which filled the river below.

The band played, but no one had danced in her carriage as they arrived at the other side; the crowds beneath watching as the train moved along the bridge like a giant shiny insect.

The sun shone. It was a beautiful day. Surely God was on the board of the North British Railway.

Thomas Bouch was the hero of the hour. He had travelled on the foot-plate of the engine, holding tightly to his hat and smiling awkwardly at the cheering throng.

When asked to say a few words, he had said very few.

And after lunch, they all went home.

To Bernard Street.

As McLevy described the possible circumstance of theft and murder, Margaret listened impassively. He made no mention of Beaumont Egg, what would a dainty woman know of such a thing, but when he portrayed his meeting with Alan Telfer, a somewhat coloured version it must be said, where his doughty investigative worth encountered evasive condescension, the bollard woman looked as if she would like to spit on the ground.

'I would not believe a word the man says,' she exclaimed, looking away. 'He is despicable!'

'How so?' probed the inspector.

For a moment it appeared as if Margaret would let loose a torrent from the fury of frustration she felt within, but then she bit down hard on her lip.

'He is unhealthy,' was all she added.

That would seem to be that, then.

'Does he have the pox?' McLevy asked in apparent hope.

She laughed at the remark and, as he had anticipated, the shift in emotion spilled out into more words.

'His ... influence is unhealthy. He separates Sir Thomas from the real world.'

'Perhaps your husband desires that?'

Her lips thinned.

'It is unhealthy,' she pronounced flatly.

McLevy had a knack with women. Despite his seeming adherence to all things masculine in the patriarchal society of their glorious queen, he had an instinct for the broken glass of fractured pain that took up more than its fair share of the feminine psyche.

Every morning a woman rises, and then bathes in the Lake of Disappointment.

That was his insight.

However, he wasn't above abusing that intuition.

So he slid the question in gently, but with a hunter's gleam in the eye.

'What form does this ... infection take?'

However Margaret Bouch had pirate blood and she could recognise the advent of a grappling iron.

She turned once more to face him.

'It's time I went home,' she said.

McLevy stood abruptly as she rose and donned her hat.

'I shall escort you.'

'There's no need.'

'It is my duty.'

She nodded somewhat curtly. They began walking down the Shore, a discernible distance between their bodies and a feeling of obscure irritation on both sides.

'Ye don't seem all that interested,' grunted the inspector.

'In what, may I ask?'

'In your poor auld butler and who stove in his head.'

There was enough truth in this dour assertion to bring a flush to Margaret's face and she was glad that the dark hid the reaction. Indeed as soon as she had seen McLevy her thoughts had been not of death but life. Though why should she be ashamed of that?

'I have helped his family.'

'With the funeral. Ye told me.'

'It is not my function to solve criminality, it is yours.'

'That's what Alan Telfer informed me.'

Being twinned with the secretary irritated her even further and Margaret almost hissed through her teeth in annoyance.

In stiff silence they walked onwards, there was no crooked elbow, no dainty gloved hand slipping into the provided space to tighten on a muscle at a pretended loss of footing.

Any intimacy was long gone and they would have strode thus in a frozen mutual disdain all the way home, had it not been for an unexpected event.

A giant of a man stepped out from the shadows and confronted them.

Patrick Scullion: a bad sailor, just thrown off his ship for insubordination and general malingering. He had been drowning his sorrows in a low dive of a tavern and was in a most foul temper at what he regarded as the dirty tricks of a dirty life.

This was a soft mark, he thought. A respectable couple out of place in such an isolated, run-down area of the harbourage, the woman tiny, and the man no great menace of a figure with a low-brimmed bowler, bulky and slow moving.

Easy meat for a giant.

He let out a roar and the whisky fumes from his rancid mouth caused Margaret to flinch back, which he mistook for fear whereas it was merely the result of a keen sense of smell.

Patrick reached out and with one huge hand took the man by the lapels of his coat.

'I'll have yer money, my darlin' gentry,' he growled. 'Or that pretty little wife will see your face crushed and broken and the blood like a fountain.'

This threat provoked a strange response.

'She is not my wife,' said the bulky man.

At that moment the crescent moon, perhaps not wishing to be called as witness in court, hid behind a cloud.

As the light changed and the giant's eyes took a moment to readjust, two things happened.

Margaret put up a hand as if to steady her bonnet and McLevy exploded into savage action.

Hit them first and hit them hard.

The inspector's boot thudded in between Patrick's legs like a Bolt of Retribution and almost in the same movement, as the man keeled over in the most profound agony, McLevy turned away as if to shield himself from a retaliatory blow and swept back his elbow into the man's face.

Patrick was then brought up to the straight and narrow by the same elbow once more smashing upwards, jerking his head back so that he looked for a moment into the slate-grey expressionless eyes before another hammer blow, this time with the fist into a belly full of cheap whisky, brought him retching on to his hands and knees.

McLevy whipped out a set of handcuffs, quickly and efficiently manacled the giant's hands behind his back, and then stood away to scrutinise his handiwork.

When he looked over at Margaret, her mouth was slightly parted, and for a moment the tip of a tongue passed lightly over her lips.

'You are a man of violence,' she observed.

'It's never far away,' was the reply.

She smiled and cast her eyes over the groaning ogre, apparently unperturbed at what she had witnessed.

'I am reminded of a saying from Ephesians, "We are all children of Wrath."'

'Uhuh,' said McLevy. 'We get it from God.'

Margaret laughed then turned to walk away at pace, leaving him caught between the devil and the deep blue sea.

'I cannot haul this behemoth and keep up with you,' he protested.

She swivelled and for a moment rested her heel on the ground so that one toe pointed up into the air.

'I am perfectly capable of my own safe conduct.'

Margaret put her hand up to the bonnet once more and drew out a lethal-looking hatpin, at least five inches long.

'This would have gone into his eye,' she declared.

'What about the other eye?'

She made a fencing motion with the hatpin to indicate a skewering of the second orb, replaced the implement with a flourish in her bonnet, and then marched off towards home and hearth.

As she did so, the moon appeared through the clouds directly in front of her vision. She lifted her head to the sky and emitted a soft howl.

Like a wolf. And then she was gone.

McLevy also lifted his head, but he did not howl for fear of enchantment.

He was even less enchanted when he lugged the giant sailor into the station a half-hour later, only to find that there had been a breakout from the cells.

This was not good.

Lieutenant Roach had been summoned from a Handel concert, which was no great loss to him since the number of notes made his head dizzy, and lurked remonstratively at the station desk along with a strangely, but a little late in the day, alert Sergeant Murdoch.

Mulholland, having worshipped in song God and the buxom blue-eyed daughter of the manse, had been intercepted on his way home and already taken out a body of men to scour the streets.

The circumstances, with which the good lieutenant was eager to acquaint his inspector, were as follows.

Constable Ballantyne, the station being quiet, had visited the cells to give Hercules Dunbar his supper, a tin can of kale broth to be passed through the bars.

He found the man convulsed upon the floor, slavering, apparently in the grip of some noxious seizure.

A kind heart can get ripped to pieces in this harsh world.

Ballantyne quickly unlocked the cell door and leant over the poor suffering soul. The man was face down on the floor but as the constable turned him over as gently as possible, the fellow made a miraculous recovery and hauled the young man over so violently that his shoulder snapped, then crashed four or five blows into him.

While Ballantyne lay semi-conscious, a piece of torn blanket was stuffed in his mouth and another savage blow rendered him sufficiently comatose to take no further part in proceedings.

Which were that Hercules Dunbar, taking advantage of the fact that the night shift had just changed over so the station was empty except for Sergeant Murdoch dozing over the evening newspaper, slipped away and vanished into the darkness of night.

Mulholland, who had assumed the mantle of the man of the moment as Roach took great pleasure in telling the aggrieved inspector, was directing pursuit through the nooks and crannies of Leith and would no doubt return triumphant.

The inspector wasn't so sure about that; Dunbar would now be forewarned and not easily taken. If the bugger had any sense, and he wasn't entirely bereft, he would get out of the city as fast as his legs could take him.

Nor would he be festooned with harlots.

McLevy had the two thieves slammed behind bars, and then drew a deep breath.

'Where's Ballantyne?' he asked.

'In my office,' replied Roach. 'His shoulder has been severely dislocated. I have sent for Doctor Jarvis.'

'He'll be at his club, knee deep in claret,' grunted the inspector. 'I'll do it.'

'Are you qualified?' Roach enquired.

'I've broken enough bones in my time,' was the uncompromising response.

Now it was the lieutenant's turn to grunt. The two men looked at each other, neither wishing to state the obvious fact that this was a dreadful smack in the lugs and a loss of honour; once the word got round, especially to Haymarket station, the Edinburgh City police would be laughing till the tears ran down their ugly faces.

And the blame could only be laid at the one door. Even if the prisoner was hanging from a homemade gallows, or had cut his throat with a rusty spike, you never went into a cell alone.

'It might transpire that Ballantyne is not fitted for a life in the force,' remarked Roach soberly.

'We can keep him in the station,' McLevy muttered.

'That's what we have already tried. And see the result.'

'He'll learn. Experience teaches the unwary.'

'I have never,' the lieutenant rejoined grimly, 'in my life, ever come across evidence to support that assertion.'

On that nihilistic note, they turned as one for a change, and headed toward the lieutenant's lair.

Ballantyne was nursing his bad shoulder as they entered, the birthmark side of his face turned away to hide his shame and embarrassment.

The inspector took a passably white handkerchief from his pocket and twirled it round so that it formed into the shape of a twist of rope.

'Bite down on this,' he said gruffly.

The constable accepted the offering without a word and, as he had sunk his teeth unwillingly into the dirty shred of blanket, did the same with trust to the handkerchief.

McLevy stood behind the young man where he sat, took firm hold of the shoulder and then suddenly jerked it back into position.

A muffled yelp of pain followed the action but the bone was now back in its socket though Ballantyne carried that shoulder high till the end of his days.

The inspector held forth his hand and Ballantyne looked blankly at him before remembering the hankie in his mouth which he removed, shook out, thought to wipe it dry upon his trousers, changed his mind, thought to wipe it on his tunic, changed his mind again and, in dire frustration and pain, clenched tight his eyes then offered the cloth up blindly, like a hostage to fortune.

As McLevy retrieved the handkerchief, Roach shook his head gloomily; his crown of thorns had just acquired another barb. The chief constable, Sandy Grant, would see this as an opportunity to wield authority.

A deep bunker of condemnation awaited the errant driver, the ball already in the air.

Ballantyne finally opened his eyes.

'I've let ye down, have I not sir?'

He had addressed this remark to McLevy but it was Roach who answered.

'I am afraid, constable, that cannot be denied, or ignored.'

For a moment the young man's lip quivered, but then he pulled himself together and tried to disregard the jagging pain from his previously displaced, now rejointed, limb.

'I'll clear out my desk if that is your wish, sir.'

Again he spoke to McLevy who slowly shook his head.

'I've looked at your desk,' he said. 'There's nothing in it but dead flies and broken pen nibs.'

The inspector glanced over at his lieutenant who sighed then nodded reluctant assent to the unspoken request.

'Away ye go home, Ballantyne,' McLevy pronounced sombrely. 'You've suffered sufficient for the day.'

The constable rose and made his way gingerly towards the door but, on reaching it, was struck by a sudden and unwelcome memory.

'Jist before he hit a last time, Dunbar – he spat something in my ear.'

'Surely not saliva?'

To this question delivered with finicky distaste by Lieutenant Roach, the young man shook his head.

'No. It was words. He said. Dunbar. He said. "Tell McLevy, I'll see him in hell." It was words.'

The door closed and the constable was gone. Roach looked up at the portrait of Queen Victoria and wondered if she had really attended a séance to search out ectoplasmic evidence of her beloved Albert.

McLevy indulged in no such displaced activity. Dunbar's words rang true.

For one or the other, hell was on the cards.

23

The stag in limpid currents with surprise,
Sees crystal branches on his forehead rise.

AMBROSE PHILIPS, *A Winter-Piece*

When Mulholland was a young buck, the grand game to play had been Nettle Little Nelly. All the boys would sit round in a solemn circle and an empty bottle with a feather stuck in its neck was carefully spun. The unfortunate to whom that feather pointed when the bottle stopped, was the designated Nelly and would be taken to a slope then hurled down the bank into a huge patch of stinging nettles.

It was then the unfortunate's task to ascend the slope and either break his way through the ring of boys above or drag someone off the rim and throw the other down in exchange of place.

This rarely happened due to the advantage of terrain and so the victim of this merry ritual would eventually collapse, legs, arms, hands and face covered in painful blisters from being repeatedly propelled back into the hurtful inferno below.

He would then either, as forfeit, have to eat dried cow dung or kiss the ugliest girl in the village.

Simple country pastimes.

Mulholland, being the tallest, was the self-appointed spinner of the bottle and had perfected the art to such a degree that the feather always pointed in another direction.

Never at himself.

He often felt sorry for the victim.

But not this time.

He looked across at Oliver Garvie who had just lit up a representative of what would be the very bone of contention, to blow a trail of high-grade smoke across the room towards the glowing fire. It mingled with the hot fumes of some equally high-grade coal then wafted up the chimney.

The constable had refused the offer of coffee, a smoke, a place to park his backside or any other blandishments and stayed standing, maintaining a watchful silence while the other had made himself at home.

Mulholland had a vision of the bold Oliver, naked as an ape, flying through the air toward a clump of nettles.

The man had evinced no surprise on whistling his way in through the front door to find the grim figure of Mulholland crouching in the hall like some sort of *tricoteuse* under the guillotine waiting for a head to fall. After dismissing the old retainer, who went off to have his hot toddy, Garvie most cordially invited the constable into his study and sat in a large burgundy-coloured leather armchair, feet splayed out, body satiated, a smile on the full lips, the very embodiment of languid ease. Soon change that, thought the constable.

The opulent red velvet curtains had been pulled shut; the wallpaper was also of a burgundy hue and the leather binding of the many books upon the high shelves shone with a self-satisfied air.

A large painting above Oliver's head distracted Mulholland for a moment, it being a goddess or nymph of classical out-lines; his betting would be a goddess, nymphs being on the slender side and this was a hefty specimen. Furthermore there was much of her to be seen, the only covering being some wispy bits of chiffon, as she reached up to a branch where Cupid, by the looks of it, was dangling out a red apple.

The son of Venus had a crafty smile on his face and Mul-holland was troubled by the notion that someone he was counting on might have other irons in the fire.

He wrenched himself away from the sight, also realising that he was postponing the prosecution of a suspect because his motives were not purely for the sake of justice and that McLevy would be hopping mad when he learned of this action.

But that was the inspector's hard luck.

All is fair in love and war.

Oliver blew out a smoke ring and watched it waver in the air before disintegrating.

Mulholland took a deep breath and thus began, going for the jugular.

'Cheap cigars masquerading as finest leaf and you collect a vast sum for a very small outlay. Good business, Mister Garvie.'

For a moment Oliver was stock still at this blunt accusation, then he roared with laughter.

'And how am I supposed to have accomplished all this, constable?' he replied in apparent good humour.

Another deep breath and this time it was Mulholland jumping off the edge of the cliff.

'You hired Daniel Rough to fire up the warehouse, probably bribed the watchman to cry off sick, we'll question him again. The crates were solid enough, the contents false, and the fire knows no difference. A clever plan, but it got a wee bit spoiled when your hireling . . . incinerated as you were so kind to point out to me.'

Garvie blinked as if he was having difficulty following this accusatory harangue.

'Daniel Rough? I don't know of such a person,' he replied lazily, lifting his cigar for another puff.

'Back of Devlin's tavern. That's where you gave him the nod.'

This time Garvie blinked for a different reason, then he frowned as if trying hard to follow the train of thought.

'And this is the fellow who was incinerated, eh?'

'Up in flames. As you are now.'

Mulholland hauled the cigar box out of his deep pocket, flipped back the lid and stuck it under Garvie's nose.

Oliver sniffed and pulled a face.

'Dear me. Poisonous weed, eh?'

'Stinko D'Oros. Cheap and nasty. I have a witness who will swear that the warehouse was full of these things and that this was a part of the cargo from the ship *Dorabella*.'

were, more in sorrow than in anger, which imbued the words with a sobering formality.

'It is not possible my friend. And if I am to be slandered with this accusation, then so must he. With, at worst, collusion and, at best, downright incompetence. Throw the mud and it will stick to both.'

Again Mulholland made no answer. He was wedged in a cleft stick of his own making.

Garvie turned away from him, looked into the glowing coals and added another load from the ornate brass scuttle; he picked up a heavy iron poker and thrust it in so that the flames leapt upwards; fire was a natural element that would burn anybody. It made no distinction.

'If I am to be accused then so is he,' Oliver said softly. 'His reputation ruined and that of his daughter in society quite shamefully defiled.'

He turned back to face the constable, poker hanging loosely in his hand.

'Are you willing to put Emily through such an ordeal in order to satisfy what I regret to describe as your own petty jealousy?'

The words were said almost under his breath but Mulholland flushed as they struck home.

'I will do my job,' he finally retorted.

Garvie nodded as if they had reached agreement.

'Then do it,' he replied, gathering energy as he spoke. 'Go to the house of Robert Forbes, lay before him your suspicions, evaluate his response and then?' Oliver shook his head as if the enormity of what Mulholland contemplated was beyond belief. 'Charge two innocent men if that is your decision, but for Emily's sake and your own, talk first with Robert Forbes.'

Mulholland made an impulsive movement as if to leave then hesitated.

It provoked a wry smile from the other who knew what was passing through the constable's mind.

'Don't perturb yourself, I shall be here whenever you return,

'A witness,' murmured Garvie, so far unruffled. 'And who might that be?'

'Reliable enough. Mother of Daniel. A fine upstanding woman.' But Mulholland though he strove for firm and measured tone, was suddenly seeing Mary Rough's far from impressive figure in the witness box, with a defence advocate tearing into her.

'And how, if I may ask, did she acquire these Stinkos as you call them?'

'She was there at the time,' muttered the constable.

'While the son was engaged in firing the place?'

'That is correct.'

'To hold his hand no doubt.'

Mulholland had no answer to offer save shoving the cigar box back into his pocket in case Garvie tried to steal the vital evidence.

The constable wondered if he should throw in the handkerchief stuffed up the sleeve of the man at Devlin's, but, in fact, Garvie was not sporting it in such a fashion at this moment and somehow what had appeared another nail in the coffin of proof at Mary Rough's humble dwelling, lacked evidential penetration in these surroundings.

Oliver stubbed out his own cigar and chuckled to himself as if mightily amused.

'Forgive me. A box of cheap cigars and the word of a thieving old woman. I don't see that unleashing the full weight of the law upon my sinful head. Do you?'

'The whole investigation will begin again,' the constable replied sternly, sticking to his guns. 'Piece by piece. All your affairs gone into. Piece by piece.'

'I have nothing to hide.'

'Then you have nothing to fear.'

Garvie rubbed his fingers together to rid them of the shreds of tobacco, then levered himself out of the chair with a certain animal grace and began to walk around the room much in the manner of an advocate.

'And what is my motive in all this?' he flung over his shoulder as he admired the voluptuous goddess who still had not attained and therefore munched upon the apple of love.

'Greed,' came the response.

'I have plenty of money. Unlike so many.'

There was a mocking edge to his voice as if implying that Mulholland might be numbered amongst the paupers of the world, and it, possibly as intended, rubbed the constable up the wrong way to a considerable extent.

'For a type like you, there's never enough.'

Mulholland followed that remark with an equally in-judicious addition.

'Greed. The filthy lucre.'

This insult apparently stung Oliver into abandoning the goddess and replying in kind.

'And for a type like you. Jealousy.'

'What?'

'Emily Forbes. You fear that she prefers my company to yours.'

'That's not true!' Mulholland exclaimed hotly.

Garvie smiled, as if he felt sorry for the harsh realities with which he had to acquaint the constable.

'No doubt she finds you amusing enough . . . like a dog strayed in from the street.'

For a second Mulholland could not believe his ears, then he let out an enraged bellow; this of course was hardly the behaviour of an arresting officer.

'You're a liar!' he roared, shaking a bony clenched fist in the direction of Garvie who was not in the least part disturbed by the sight.

'You know it to be true,' he murmured apologetically. 'You are not of her class and because I am, you would seek to destroy my reputation for your own jealous ends.'

The man's effrontery almost robbed Mulholland of speech and though the constable would never dream of acknow-ledging the fact, perhaps there was the smallest trace of truth

160

in Garvie's observation that also contributed to his initial of response.

Finally Mulholland found the words and bit them off bullets.

'I care for Emily and she for me. There is no jealousy her only a man doing his job and by God I'll do it!'

'You care for her, do you?' riposted Garvie with a glint in his eye.

'I do indeed.'

The entrepreneur hooked one thumb into the high pocket of his silk waistcoat and wagged the forefinger of the other hand in the air as if delivering a speech from a courtroom drama.

Indeed it was as if he spoke the words for a larger audience than the constable before him.

'Then consider this before you let loose your vile slanders. The documents and invoices for the cargo have been examined and certified genuine by the very top man. Head of the Provi-dential branch in Edinburgh.'

Adding a rhetorical flourish to proceedings, he whipped the thumb from its moorings and raised both hands in the air to emphasise the next salvo.

'Chief insurance adjuster, Mister Robert Forbes!'

In his rush to judgment Mulholland had pushed that thought to the back of his head but it had been abruptly brought to the forefront now. For the first time, he felt the ground shift under his feet, like a man out of balance hurtling down a slope.

Garvie continued his bombardment.

'The contents of the warehouse have been sifted as well. The tobacco fragments scrupulously and scientifically examined. D'you think I could pull the wool over his eyes? A man of his ability and experience?'

'I don't know,' the constable muttered defensively.

'Indeed,' Garvie hammered home, 'you do!'

Mulholland was mute.

Oliver abandoned the theatrical delivery and spoke, as it

161

'A witness,' murmured Garvie, so far unruffled. 'And who might that be?'

'Reliable enough. Mother of Daniel. A fine upstanding woman.' But Mulholland though he strove for firm and measured tone, was suddenly seeing Mary Rough's far from impressive figure in the witness box, with a defence advocate tearing into her.

'And how, if I may ask, did she acquire these Stinkos as you call them?'

'She was there at the time,' muttered the constable.

'While the son was engaged in firing the place?'

'That is correct.'

'To hold his hand no doubt.'

Mulholland had no answer to offer save shoving the cigar box back into his pocket in case Garvie tried to steal the vital evidence.

The constable wondered if he should throw in the handkerchief stuffed up the sleeve of the man at Devlin's, but, in fact, Garvie was not sporting it in such a fashion at this moment and somehow what had appeared another nail in the coffin of proof at Mary Rough's humble dwelling, lacked evidential penetration in these surroundings.

Oliver stubbed out his own cigar and chuckled to himself as if mightily amused.

'Forgive me. A box of cheap cigars and the word of a thieving old woman. I don't see that unleashing the full weight of the law upon my sinful head. Do you?'

'The whole investigation will begin again,' the constable replied sternly, sticking to his guns. 'Piece by piece. All your affairs gone into. Piece by piece.'

'I have nothing to hide.'

'Then you have nothing to fear.'

Garvie rubbed his fingers together to rid them of the shreds of tobacco, then levered himself out of the chair with a certain animal grace and began to walk around the room much in the manner of an advocate.

'And what is my motive in all this?' he flung over his shoulder as he admired the voluptuous goddess who still had not attained and therefore munched upon the apple of love.

'Greed,' came the response.

'I have plenty of money. Unlike so many.'

There was a mocking edge to his voice as if implying that Mulholland might be numbered amongst the paupers of the world, and it, possibly as intended, rubbed the constable up the wrong way to a considerable extent.

'For a type like you, there's never enough.'

Mulholland followed that remark with an equally in-judicious addition.

'Greed. The filthy lucre.'

This insult apparently stung Oliver into abandoning the goddess and replying in kind.

'And for a type like you. Jealousy.'

'What?'

'Emily Forbes. You fear that she prefers my company to yours.'

'That's not true!' Mulholland exclaimed hotly.

Garvie smiled, as if he felt sorry for the harsh realities with which he had to acquaint the constable.

'No doubt she finds you amusing enough . . . like a dog strayed in from the street.'

For a second Mulholland could not believe his ears, then he let out an enraged bellow; this of course was hardly the behaviour of an arresting officer.

'You're a liar!' he roared, shaking a bony clenched fist in the direction of Garvie who was not in the least part disturbed by the sight.

'You know it to be true,' he murmured apologetically. 'You are not of her class and because I am, you would seek to destroy my reputation for your own jealous ends.'

The man's effrontery almost robbed Mulholland of speech and though the constable would never dream of acknow-ledging the fact, perhaps there was the smallest trace of truth

160

in Garvie's observation that also contributed to his initial lack of response.

Finally Mulholland found the words and bit them off like bullets.

'I care for Emily and she for me. There is no jealousy here, only a man doing his job and by God I'll do it!'

'You care for her, do you?' riposted Garvie with a glint in his eye.

'I do indeed.'

The entrepreneur hooked one thumb into the high pocket of his silk waistcoat and wagged the forefinger of the other hand in the air as if delivering a speech from a courtroom drama.

Indeed it was as if he spoke the words for a larger audience than the constable before him.

'Then consider this before you let loose your vile slanders. The documents and invoices for the cargo have been examined and certified genuine by the very top man. Head of the Providential branch in Edinburgh.'

Adding a rhetorical flourish to proceedings, he whipped the thumb from its moorings and raised both hands in the air to emphasise the next salvo.

'Chief insurance adjuster, Mister Robert Forbes!'

In his rush to judgment Mulholland had pushed that thought to the back of his head but it had been abruptly brought to the forefront now. For the first time, he felt the ground shift under his feet, like a man out of balance hurtling down a slope.

Garvie continued his bombardment.

'The contents of the warehouse have been sifted as well. The tobacco fragments scrupulously and scientifically examined. D'you think I could pull the wool over his eyes? A man of his ability and experience?'

'I don't know,' the constable muttered defensively.

'Indeed,' Garvie hammered home, 'you do!'

Mulholland was mute.

Oliver abandoned the theatrical delivery and spoke, as it

were, more in sorrow than in anger, which imbued the words with a sobering formality.

'It is not possible my friend. And if I am to be slandered with this accusation, then so must he. With, at worst, collusion and, at best, downright incompetence. Throw the mud and it will stick to both.'

Again Mulholland made no answer. He was wedged in a cleft stick of his own making.

Garvie turned away from him, looked into the glowing coals and added another load from the ornate brass scuttle; he picked up a heavy iron poker and thrust it in so that the flames leapt upwards; fire was a natural element that would burn anybody. It made no distinction.

'If I am to be accused then so is he,' Oliver said softly. 'His reputation ruined and that of his daughter in society quite shamefully defiled.'

He turned back to face the constable, poker hanging loosely in his hand.

'Are you willing to put Emily through such an ordeal in order to satisfy what I regret to describe as your own petty jealousy?'

The words were said almost under his breath but Mulholland flushed as they struck home.

'I will do my job,' he finally retorted.

Garvie nodded as if they had reached agreement.

'Then do it,' he replied, gathering energy as he spoke. 'Go to the house of Robert Forbes, lay before him your suspicions, evaluate his response and then?' Oliver shook his head as if the enormity of what Mulholland contemplated was beyond belief. 'Charge two innocent men if that is your decision, but for Emily's sake and your own, talk first with Robert Forbes.'

Mulholland made an impulsive movement as if to leave then hesitated.

It provoked a wry smile from the other who knew what was passing through the constable's mind.

'Don't perturb yourself, I shall be here whenever you return, but for now, I must ask you to give me leave to retire to my bed, I have a long day of business tomorrow.'

The alternative was cuff the man and haul him to the station and Mulholland realised the impossibility of that; Lieutenant Roach would have a major fit at what he would perceive as a respectable merchant being treated worse than a common criminal. For a moment he wished that he had McLevy here to advise him then realised that, as well as his other dubious motives, he wanted, for once, to solve a case without the hot breath of the inspector on the back of his neck. The constable's head was in a spin; what had he hoped for here anyway, that Garvie would break down and confess?

In one thing the fellow was correct, for Emily's sake he must talk to her father. Robert Forbes was the man.

'I will be back in the before long,' he threatened.

'And I shall be waiting,' was the calm response.

And so having already made one wrong decision, the constable compounded his error and departed.

Garvie took a deep breath and held it until he heard the front door slam safely shut.

He slowly then replaced the poker; if necessary he would have felled the constable where he stood, but the bluff had worked.

Not many had this past year; the cards had treated him unkindly, however thank God for the blindness of love, which could always be exploited by the sly man.

He had little time to waste.

All their plans were in ruins but something might yet be retrieved.

He would send word by messenger.

It all depended upon his cunning little vixen.

24

But, children, you should never let
Such angry passions rise;
Your little hands were never made
To tear each other's eyes.

ISAAC WATTS, *Divine Songs for Children*

Jean Brash slipped in at the back door of the Just Land to find her bawdy-hoose in a state of chaos.

Screams and vituperations rent the air coming from the direction of the main salon while two farmers from Dumfries, the only clientele of the night so far, but indicative of many more to come since the cattle show at Market Place had not long finished, stood uncertainly in the mirrored hall where they had been abruptly abandoned by big Annie Drummond who had opened the front entrance to admit them.

Jean flashed the Dumfries men a reassuring smile as she shot past and in through the salon door.

There were more high-pitched squeals and one of the farmers shook his head at the other.

'Like pigs wi' their throats cut, eh?'

A solemn agreement was nodded, but both men knew the value of patience, they had endured many storms and rough weather together and at least here they were indoors.

So they waited and tried not to look at their reflection, lest someone stare back that they did not recognise.

The Satyrs of Dumfries. Transformed by lustful opportunity.

Rachel Bryden observed them from upstairs. She had emerged from Jean's boudoir, dressed for outdoors, with a small travelling bag in her hand and some of the words from a note, delivered by hand not long ago, running through her mind.

We are discovered. Grab what you can and run.

That is precisely what she had done and was about to do, taking advantage of the heaven-sent diversion from the salon. The sight of Jean Brash below had sent a shaft of fear through her belly but luckily the woman had been distracted by the altercation.

It was said Jean Brash had killed a man and once she found out what Rachel had been accomplice to, there would be no more favourites played. It would be a hard vengeance; the traditional punishment for a whore who betrayed and broke the rules of a bawdy-hoose, was to be tarred and feathered; head shaved, pitch poured over, a cushion of feathers cut open then shaken out to add in the mix and after all that, the miscreant dumped on a tramp ship to be kicked off at the first port of call.

Not only had she betrayed both bawdy-hoose and mistress, she had robbed as well and Rachel did not intend to experience the due process of punishment for either.

She slipped quietly down the stairs, nodded politely to the two men as if she wished them a pleasant evening, bull to cow, and, on closing the front door, was lost to sight.

One of the farmers pursed his lips disparagingly at the slim body previously presented.

'No' for me,' he pronounced sagely. 'I want something I can find in the dark.'

The other nodded.

'The nights are drawin' in, right enough,' he replied.

So they stood. And waited.

Outside indeed, the aforesaid night had drawn in a cloak of blackness heavy clouds obscuring the moon, as Rachel walked swiftly, footsteps crunching on the gravel path that led to the wrought-iron front gates.

With any luck, as her lover had promised in the note, he would be waiting inside the grounds concealed by the bushes.

But it was quite another figure that stepped out from the rhododendrons.

'Where are ye going, girlie?' said Hannah Semple.

The old woman, the place being as quiet as a morgue, had left Annie Drummond in charge while she went out ostensibly to take the air but, in fact, too restless to stay inside and wondering where in God's name Jean Brash had landed up that she had not yet returned.

Common sense dictates that no one will arrive any earlier back home, if a body goes out on the streets searching for a sight of them, but Hannah had persuaded herself to walk half-way down the hill before, in fact, the returning carriage had swept past.

Neither Jean who was lost in thought, or Angus the coachman who stared straight ahead, had noticed the searcher and, to tell truth, Hannah had not particularly advertised herself, fearful of appearing like some auld granny out looking for the children.

So, under her breath, she had cursed herself for a fool, Jean Brash for a hippertie-skippertie creature, then stomped her way back up the steep brae.

It was a long haul, neither gravity nor virtue being on her side.

Jean would go round the back as usual, Hannah thought as she puffed laboriously up to the front gate, her breath fogging up in the freezing night air.

She rehearsed in her mind severe words of exprobation to her mistress that she doubted she would ever quite utter but then, on entering and moving up the path, noticed the figure of a woman departing the door of the Just Land.

This was not usual and so Hannah had ducked out of sight to observe the approaching mystery, and then nipped back out to confront the recognised identity.

And if there was one person out of the mouth of hell that Rachel Bryden did not want to see, it was the spectre before her. She had been delighted to note the old woman's absence from the bawdy-hoose after the message was delivered at the front door, but had not reckoned on the possibility of an inopportune return.

'Where are ye going, girlie?'

The question echoed in the still, cold night, the fracas in the Just Land being contained within solid walls.

'I received a note,' said Rachel, improvising round some of the truth. 'My mother. My mother has suffered an attack of some pestilence. I must go to her at once.'

'I didnae know ye had a mother,' replied Hannah who was not inclined to believe a word of this. 'I thought ye just arrived out of the blue.'

'I must go to her.'

Rachel made as if to step past but Hannah moved sideways to block the movement, her hand going to the inside pocket of the large, herringbone tweed coat she wore for outdoors. A man's cut, it had belonged to a client who left in a hurry one night, called back to his ship, captain of a whaling boat, Norwegian, never came back, maybe the whale got him.

But the coat was roomy and had a convenient pouch for her razor, the handle of which she held at this moment.

'Where abides this poor auld bugger?'

'Aberdeen,' blurted Rachel picking the furthest away city that came to mind.

'How will you get there this hour? Are ye a besom rider?'

Indeed the idea of being a sorceress and swooping off on a broom would have appealed to Rachel, anything to get her out of here, but she bit into her lip and made sensible response.

'Waverley Station. The night train.'

Hannah nodded slowly as if this made sense and then stood aside, but as a relieved Rachel moved to get past, Hannah checked her by the sleeve for one more question.

'Did the mistress give permission?'

'I did not see her.'

A calculated risk, but a wrong calculation.

'You're a liar,' Hannah retorted.

'She's been out all night, you know that to be so!' was the haughty response.

Hannah smiled bleakly.

'The mistress passed me on the hill not ten minutes afore, and she would be back. You saw but you did not speak to her.'

The truth of that registered for a brief moment in the other's eyes and Hannah noted that Rachel lifted the travel case and pressed it tightly against her body as if it were a bulwark between her and rough seas.

'Now why would that be?' the old woman mused. 'We'll just go back and ask her, shall we not? And maybe hae a wee keek inside that fine valise you carry, eh?'

'Let me past ye auld bitch!'

Rachel losing temper and accent tried to hurtle her way through, but a flash of steel she remembered only too well stopped her momentum as the razor blade landed unerringly on the same spot just beside the eye.

'This time I'll draw blood girlie,' said Hannah softly. 'Now turn yourself round and save that pretty face.'

Little did Hannah guess that these words might well be the last she spoke; a clenched fist hammered down on the back of her neck to send the old woman face first down on to the gravel.

The razor blade spilled out of flaccid fingers and Oliver Garvie looked down in some dismay at his handiwork.

'Is she dead?' he remarked in some concern; smashing Mulholland over the head with a poker would have been fair play, and he could look with equanimity upon a putrid burnt body, but felling old women was perhaps not a gentlemanly act.

In response, Rachel drew back her foot and kicked Hannah hard in the ribs. A low moan came in reply.

'Not yet,' said Rachel Bryden.

For a moment they looked at each other, then the animal attraction that bound and deluded each into thinking they were the only two in the world truly alive, swept them into a carnivorous embrace, lips, tongue and teeth, as if they could eat each other like a plate of liver.

'You took your time,' she panted.

He, in fact, had been skulking in the undergrowth and about to step out and greet her when Hannah beat him to the punch

'It was the very devil creeping in those damned bushes. I am not a Navaho.'

She giggled. He looked at the case she held.

'How much did you get?'

'Everything I could. And you?'

Hannah groaned again and Rachel considered another kick, but perhaps one was enough. She contented herself with putting a foot on the back of the woman's head and shoving her face harder into the gravel.

Garvie thought to protest the action but then what if this old crone had sliced through the precious skin? That sweet countenance was both their fortunes.

'And you?' she repeated, when he did not answer.

Oliver shrugged apologetically.

'I have the cash I carry and that is all.'

'You are certain we are discovered?'

'Yes. And now doubly so.'

For a moment a cold hard reality hovered in the air between the two and then the insanity of mutual obsession claimed them once more.

One more kiss.

Such is love in all its guises.

To escape discovery, they pulled Hannah off the path and hid her under some nearby bushes; the old woman made no sound. Rhododendrons cover a multitude of sins.

For just a second, Oliver Garvie had a pang of conscience over the fate of the crumpled heap of herringbone but it vanished for want of support.

As Rachel hurled the razor into the bushes and then gave a last shove with her foot to bury Hannah even deeper in the underbrush, he spoke thus.

'There is a place we can go. I have made a plan. No one will find us.'

This assurance brought a smile to her face and she pressed briefly against him loin and breast, while Hannah lay like a dead thing at their feet.

'Then my darling boy,' she breathed softly, 'we had best run for our lives.'

As they moved off he warned her, 'But after that, we will have to pay for passage.'

'I can pay the price.'

This grandiose statement provoked her into a reckless peal of laughter and she shook the travel case so that the contents rattled and clinked together.

'We both will,' she affirmed as they disappeared into the darkness. 'We shall both pay the price.'

Hannah Semple was not spared a backwards glance. She had already paid a considerable cost in the defence of her mistress and whether it was to be an ultimate one, might be a matter of conjecture. It was a cold night and getting colder.

25

For what's a play without a woman in it?

THOMAS KYD, *The Spanish Tragedy*

It was more flesher's shop than bawdy-hoose when Jean Brash entered in through the salon door.

The girls were also screaming blue murder and with good reason.

Big Isabel Tasker, who was as tall as Annie Drummond but lacked the latter's colossal width and *avoirdupois*, stood in the middle of the room with a bloody cloth pressed to her contorted face.

Drips of the precious fluid were escaping to run in rivulets down her neck on to the favourite pink gown that Isabel thought most becoming but in Jean's private opinion did nothing for her face or figure.

Like a boiled dumpling.

Isabel had Italian looks, dark auburn curly locks, a rather

blousy dissolute air and it is possible the later years would not be kind to her; but though Jean had a few times read Isabel the riot act, because the girl was a bit of a bully and somewhat predatory as regards the younger magpies, she was more than useful in her ability to take the lead in whatever jinks and capers were requested by a certain tranche of clients who relished a deal of buffeting and horseplay; some of them in fact taking the role of that animal on all fours with a bareback – in all senses – rider to hand. However, though enjoying a drummed heel in the ribs and a firm bit between the teeth, they drew the line at profound and experienced agony.

Which led to the woman standing opposite Isabel, a stiletto yet clutched in her fist.

Francine the Frenchwoman; her dungeon in the cellars was well stocked with instruments for inflicting the desired suffering on those who worshipped at the altar of Odyne.

The goddess of pain.

An artiste to Isabel's rough and tumble, specialist in erotic flagellation and the craft of hook and pulley, Francine was rarely seen above ground at this time of night but, as has been noted, business was on the slack side.

The Frenchwoman had a slim sinewy body, often clothed in black leather, self-designed apparel that she based upon the temple vestments of an Egyptian goddess, enabling both thighs to be revealed and active; her skin was usually white as alabaster though two hectic spots of red rage now burned in the high cheekbones.

She had black hair, cropped short in a mannish fashion, and cut a dramatic figure in the frankly voluptuous colours and furnishings of the salon.

Francine had also obviously cut Big Isabel, but not to the bone Jean hoped. Not too deep.

All this she had taken in at the moment of entry before stilling the injured party who was leading the chorus of howls, by smacking her across the already anguished face.

Isabel let out an astonished yelp then shut up abruptly as

did everyone else except for Francine who already maintained an icy silence, eyes focused on her target.

The other silent person was Francine's lover, and good right hand when dishing out the stripe and squeeze of inflicted pain and pleasure, little Lily Baxter.

Lily was a deaf mute, a cheerful sweet-natured bundle of curves, blue-eyed, snub-nosed, normally a smile never far from her face, in fact the complete opposite of any common held perception of a mistress of castigation.

But now there was little cheer on her countenance; she was huddled on one of the plush divans so beloved by men of the cloth by dint of its Cardinal-red colour, and sniffed dolefully as the tears ran down her face.

In the hush, Big Annie Drummond stepped forward; all this had happened on her watch and plump graceful fingers, more used to stroking chords from the nearby piano, waved in the air as she attempted to explain.

'Whit happened, Mistress Brash, Isabel was cuddling up to Lily, and Lily was enjoying it, everybody likes a wee change now and again – '

Annie stopped when Francine let out a vicious hiss and up came the knife hand.

'Put that away,' said Jean calmly, 'or I'll stick it in your heart.'

She turned back to Annie not even waiting to see Francine slowly replace the knife in the sheath near the top of her white thigh, and, with a look invited continuation of a story already discerned.

But while Annie blethered on it would give Jean time to dwell upon events and find a solution.

And where the hell was Hannah Semple?

'It's been quiet as the grave mistress, and the devil finds work for idle hands, eh?'

Annie's large genial face was creased with unaccustomed thought as she ploughed onwards.

'Anyway, it's cauld as buggery in that cellar and Francine came up to get a wee warm and find Lily.'

'And what was Lily supposed to be doing?' Jean asked.

'She was to bring me down some hot chocolate!' Francine proclaimed, shooting a malevolent glance at the snuffling figure on the divan.

It always intrigued Jean how the mundane inserted itself into moments of high drama; a betrayed love, flashing blade and now hot chocolate.

But does not love lend itself to betrayal?

Any kind of love.

Annie continued, puffing out her cheeks.

'So Francine finds Lily in a wee room wi' Isabel, chases the both in here, cuts the one and swears in French at the other.'

'How would you know the imprecation?'

'*Putin,* she called her,' replied Annie stolidly. 'That's French for whoor.'

Jean shook her head but inwardly she was cursing herself for this state of affairs; Hannah had warned her things were sliding but she had not paid enough heed, too concerned with her own pleasure.

Forgetting she was a whoremistress and whores do not cleave to pleasure. Supply and demand is their trade.

'Is all this true, Lily?' she questioned, moving her lips slowly so the girl could understand. She received an ashamed nod in answer.

All the magpies watched Jean as she closed her eyes in apparent thought, then she reached forward and twitched the cloth away from Isabel's face.

She took out a fine linen handkerchief from her coat pocket, and with care, like a man of medicine, wiped at the cut.

Obviously the stiletto was a fine-quality blade, it had left a thin line clean as a whistle, from the back of the cheekbone, down past the front of the ear, to the jaw.

This had drawn blood, but it would heal quickly and Isabel's thick hair would hide the slender scar till then.

'You'll live,' she said to Isabel, then turned to Annie who was waiting with some trepidation for a heavy reprimand, but

Jean could not blame the woman and where the hell was Hannah Semple?

However, it was not the moment for that question to be asked aloud because it might lead to justified accusations about neglect of duty.

'You deserved this,' she flung over her shoulder to Isabel, and then winked at Annie Drummond and threw her the bloody cloth. 'Take this creature away, Annie, put on some ointment, patch her up and get her back here. She's a working girl.'

'But mistress!' wailed the wounded woman. 'Whit about my catastrophe?'

'As I said. You deserved it,' replied Jean crisply. 'We're headed for a busy night and who knows, one of the clients might prefer a treacherous scratched hizzie; now on your way, Isabel Tasker.'

There was some laughter as the grumbling Isabel was led out of the salon but a measure of tension remained.

Jean turned to the tightly strung Francine and carefully folded up the linen handkerchief, which was spotted with Isabel's blood.

'One of you other two will have to go,' she pronounced. 'And I am afraid that I have too much money invested in you, Francine, those whips have cost me a fortune.'

She walked past the stunned Frenchwoman and confronted the little figure on the divan.

Above Lily Baxter was Jean's favourite painting in the Just Land, 'The Woman with the Octopus'; she had personally hung that work on the wall of every bawdy-hoose she had ever owned; it was a depiction of a woman being dragged under to the depths by a big slimy sea monster, most of the clothes ripped off her and a horrible fate in store.

As well as gingering the clients, it normally and perversely cheered Jean up no end, but not apparently this evening as she gazed with regret at Lily.

Again she mouthed the words slowly.

174

'Lily Baxter, you must leave this fine house. I will give you enough money to last a few weeks and after that, you are on your lonesome.'

A cry of anguish came in answer but not, of course, from Lily. It was Francine who rushed forward to clasp the other protectively to her leather bosom.

'No, the fault is mine!' she declared to the octopus above. 'I have been evil in my nature because it is so cold in that bastard of a cellar.'

'You have a stove,' Jean pointed out. 'In your side room.'

'It lacks impetus,' was the proud reply as Francine hugged Lily all the more tightly. 'But I drive Lily from me because of my bad words and she has gone to have comfort in another place. It is all my fault.'

A tearful Lily had watched Francine's lips and put up a single finger to touch upon them at the end of all this; whether in agreement or sharing the blame was not clear to Jean but she had, as anticipated when the threat was made, got exactly what she wanted.

Authority established, now follows clemency.

'Get back to your hidey-hole the pair of you, before I change my mind and sell you on to the slavers.'

This flat statement sent Lily scrambling to the door though Francine had, as she followed, a touch more *sang-froid*.

As Lily shot down the stairs like a hare, Francine turned to survey the company of frail sisterhood. Any smiles were hastily hidden but then Jean Brash pinned her with a hard look.

'This ends now Francine. No vengeance taken.'

The Frenchwoman nodded.

'Isabel is not worth my candle,' she responded.

That mixed message gave Jean an idea.

'When he's done with the horses, I'll get Angus to bring you down a brazier and some coals. It will provide additional heat and, who knows, you may find other uses for it.'

Francine's eyes narrowed thoughtfully, then she nodded and left.

Jean turned to her girls, on the lookout for any trace of rebellion or insolence, but they were all as good as gold.

A strangled noise from the hall as one of the Dumfries men blew his nose into a flannel hankie reminded her that these two outside were but forerunners of the stampeding herd.

'Best get yourselves ready, ladies,' she murmured. 'A busy night, one market over, the other begins.'

There was some laughter, indeed the farmers were wont to prod and pressure as if sizing up a heifer but they were in the main a good-natured lot, generous with their money and, if you ignored the odd barnyard odour, easy to satisfy.

Perhaps not much in the way of trade for Francine, for men of earth and animals had no great need to be whipped up into a froth, but she and Lily would be falling in love all over again in the side room with the stove.

Love is the very devil.

Then Jean noticed the absence of one other.

'Where is Rachel Bryden?' she asked.

No one knew, no one had seen the pale creature for a while, but the Dalrymple twins, Maggie and Mary, remembered jointly that a note had been delivered to Rachel not long ago at the door.

Jean, for some reason, felt a prickling at the back of her neck but she ignored it, promised herself to ask Annie Drummond about Hannah as soon as they had a quiet moment apart, went to the salon entrance and, before opening, looked back around the room.

It was a sight for sore eyes. Exotic, almost Persian carpets, which thank god were mostly red so that any blood spilt went undetected, plush armchairs, velvet curtains scarlet as sin, the polished piano in the corner, paintings on the wall of nymphs and shepherds in pastoral abandon, the harsh reality of the nearly naked Octopus Woman, and last but not least, the girls in tasteful *décolletage*, raring to have at you.

She opened the door and smiled at the two men who stood patient as cows in a bare November field just before milking time.

'Come away in, gentlemen,' Jean said winningly. 'The ladies are waiting.'

Both men removed their hats, asked not a question about the previous caterwauling, and entered the portals of sin.

All was back to normal, well as normal as a bawdy-hoose ever gets.

Jean Brash had rescued a hazardous situation caused by her own carelessness. That would not happen again; lover or no lover, business was business.

All was well with the world, save for the prickling at the back of her neck.

All was well.

Some hours later, the place was heaving.

An impromptu ceilidh was in progress.

No sooner had the Dumfries men entered into the salon than the rest of the cattlemen arrived, breath puffing in the night, like a herd of bullocks.

There were two shepherds come with the well-to-do farmers, one of them, a wee border man with leathery skin, bow legs and bright blue eyes, had produced a fiddle.

The other was a tall cadaverous specimen with a hooked nose and big eyes that near popped out of their sockets at the sight of the girls in all their glory.

He had disclosed a Jew's harp.

Neither had ever drunk champagne in their life and, after a few glasses courtesy of the house, launched into a fierce jig which set feet a' tapping.

Big Annie Drummond's eyes lit up and she sat down at the piano to show them what city folk could bring to the fair.

As the notes winged their way back and forth, the wild exultation that such music brings began to stir in various female breasts for melody trembles women in the blood more than men and, at an approving nod from Jean, the carpets were rolled back, the furniture pulled to the wall, and then the dance began.

And what a dance it was; perhaps a release of tension after the incident of the drawn stiletto, perhaps a farmer's celebration of a prize bull bought, manhood swinging between its legs at the thought of cows to cover, perhaps flashing glances between Annie Drummond and the wee shepherd, perhaps the beating heart of a primitive ancient monster sacrificed on the altar of civilisation an eternity before; but for whatever reason, boots crashed down upon the floorboards like meteors, while naked feet and legs slid like serpents in a whirling fury as the spirit of the dance took possession of one and all.

Had the great poet Robert Burns been on hand, he would no doubt have found a perfect illustration of his words from the epic *Tam O' Shanter,*

> The piper loud and louder blew;
> The dancers quick and quicker flew;
> They reel'd, they set, they cross'd, they cleekit,
> Till ilka carlin swat and reekit,
> And coost her duddies tae the wark,
> And linket at it in her sark.

Of course Burns was describing a coven of witches rather than a healthy bunch of bawdy-hoose heifers but his eye would have been entertained and delighted at the amount of bare flesh revealed as the girls indeed, like the witches in the poem, sweated up a storm, did not reek however, but threw their coverings aside and went hell for leather at it in petticoats, sark-chemises, or less.

Even the farmers removed their jackets. Hot work.

The hook man twanged the Jew's harp, his digit a blur of motion. More than one of the magpies made note of that fact. A fast finger may please the sugar almond.

Down in the cellar chamber, the unemployed whips, canes birches and battledores, juddered on their hooks in the wall. The tall thistles which provided a more natural source of scourging, rustled together impotently in the water of the long white vase that held and nourished them; even the Berkley Horse, a solid device of wood and leather upon which the rider would be lashed in all senses, shifted slightly on its moorings.

In the side room, Francine and Lily lay in each other's arms, looking up at the ceiling, which shook in sympathy with events upstairs.

The fiddler had moved to 'Lord Eglintoun's Auld Man', a Strathspey to give the company a breather, but with a wink to Annie he shifted pace again to another noble house, 'Lord George Gordon's Reel', and off the dancers flew once more.

Isabel Tasker, wound forgotten, was a blur of motion as she hooked arms and spun, occasionally letting out a loud screech while a brawny cattleman from Stirling eyed her up and wondered what the possibilities of a different dance might be; he liked big noisy women, his own wife was silent as the grave, hardly reached the shoulder and ruled him with a rod of iron.

The Dalrymple twins, whose father Angus was absent on other business, were in the arms of the two Dumfries men and, by the looks of things, about to retire to another pursuit that fired the blood.

Jean watched it all with an indulgent eye but the prickling she had felt at the back of her neck was with her still.

She had questioned Annie and been informed that Hannah having muttered something about fresh air had donned her coat and marched off into the night.

This was not like the woman, Hannah was a fiend for airing the sheets but as regards personal intake, was not noted for poking her head out of the Just Land unless there was good reason; such as grumbling her way across the grass to bring a tray of coffee and sugar biscuits over to Jean where she sat, often with McLevy to hand.

It was her pleasure to then insult the inspector as roundly as possible then disappear back into the safety of the bawdy-hoose.

For her to quit the place and not to return within the hour was, to put it mildly, out of character.

Hannah would not think the place could function without her watchful presence.

Had she done this to punish Jean for her neglect?

To show her what dereliction of duty might bring home to roost?

No. That was not Hannah's way; she would stick her face into yours and give it both barrels.

And indeed Jean merited both barrels.

Once more her lover had informed her that he had business on hand, once more he had waved her a fond farewell but Jean instead of returning at once to the Just Land, in which case all of this trouble would have been averted, had instructed Angus to drive out along the Leith shoreline until they came upon a bleak outcrop where she had alighted, walked to the edge, gazed at the angry waves as they broke over the rocks below, and brooded over the tumult in her heart.

Despite her brave words, it was still there.

Like a knife in the gut.

She had to give this man up. He was bad for business. But the fault was hers. She was not in control.

What in God's name was she going to do?

And where was Rachel Bryden?

And Hannah Semple?

Jean had sent Angus Dalrymple out to search the gardens but it was black as pitch outside and even with a flaming torch, there was a forbidding amount of ground to cover.

Of course, Hannah could be sitting in a tavern by the docks, cackling with glee over the trouble she was causing Jean, and if that was the case by God she would make the woman pay for the worms that were gnawing away at her insides. Make her pay.

The mistress of the Just Land shook her head; these were unprofitable thoughts and she prided herself that the confusion she observed in other minds was not ever part of her reasoning.

Straight. Clear. Clean.

That was Jean Brash.

Except for love.

Love was the very devil.

She had not even had the time to go up to her boudoir and

change outfits, so her clothes were still charged from the aftermath of passion.

The very devil.

The Jew's harp throbbed agreement as the fiddler brought the reel to an end with a mighty scrape of his bow, grinned at Annie Drummond and in the silence while the company took a gulp of air before the advent of more champagne and lust, Jean thought to hear a thump at the front door.

She slipped out into the hall and listened.

Again something thudded against the wood like a dead weight. Or a foot kicking.

The fiddler started another air, 'Tam Lucas o' the Feast', a tune Jean remembered being played at a thieves' wedding which had been rudely interrupted when McLevy came to arrest the bride, Catherine Bruce, for shoplifting.

Catherine and old Mary Rough had been the queens of that trade but that was a fair time ago.

This was now.

Why was she in such dread to open the damned door?

She did so to disclose the giant figure of Angus, a stricken look upon his face, holding the limp body of Hannah Semple in his arms.

This was now.

26

And he that strives to touch the stars,
Oft stumbles at a straw.

EDMUND SPENSER, *The Shepherd's Calendar*

The woman in the framed photograph looked at Mulholland with a severe exacting gaze. She wore dark sombre clothes as would befit the about to be dead wife of an insurance adjuster. A ribbon of black crepe hung round the frame to confirm continued mourning, the death in Victorian terms being comparatively recent, that is three years before.

Martha Forbes, mother of the beloved Emily, and could he see the daughter in the mother?

It was not an unpleasant face, just a touch . . . lifeless, though alive enough when the picture was taken because she was sitting in a chair with the window behind, surely they wouldn't have stuck the corpse up and propped the eyes open, surely not?

But it was a solemn countenance: life a burden to be carried to the grave.

Perhaps the daughter was a fairy child?

His Emily has darting mischievous eyes, white, even teeth, (the mother's mouth was firm shut lest a morbiferous deadly infection enter), straight nut-brown hair, a clear skin, cherry-red lips and a little pink tongue that had licked its way round many a meringue as Mulholland watched indulgently on, a slab of Dundee cake sat solidly before him on the plate.

She was also fond of chocolate confections in the French style although like any well-bred young lady, she frowned upon many other things French.

But that little pink tongue knew its way around the intricate edifices of spun sugar that made up the mysteries of the Edinburgh tearooms.

The voice of Robert Forbes broke the icy silence during which the constable had, to escape the present predicament, allowed his mind to wander.

Forbes was sitting at the other side of a large desk in his study; above and behind a stag's head protruded from the wall, possibly the beast had lacked sufficient cover; the books on his shelves, unlike Oliver Garvie's, were worn with much use, maritime tides and currents, timetables of death and destruction, statistics relating to longevity or the lack of it, natural catastrophes, accidents and acts of God, all grist to the mill.

The frozen silence had been caused by the speculation that the constable had laid before the insurance adjuster.

It was also very cold in the room due to one of the windows being left open, but the older man seemed impervious.

'Are you suggesting,' said Forbes in clipped precise tones, 'that I have made a mistake?'

Mulholland tore himself away from tearooms and tongues.

'No, sir, not at all,' he replied, meeting the baleful stare of Emily's father with candid demeanour. 'But in light of what has come to light, as it were. It may be as well for you to re-evaluate your findings. As it were.'

Forbes' eyes hardened.

'It strikes me, constable, that you are the one in need of re-evaluation.'

'I beg pardon, sir?'

The insurance adjuster took a deep breath as if trying to contain mounting exasperation.

'What you have put before me is slight, riddled with hearsay, and circumstantial. Is this all you possess?'

'At the moment,' Mulholland retorted. He was in truth somewhat nettled himself, not unlike little Nelly, having presented his case hoping for a grave appreciation, and after that, the two men, soon to be related by marriage, fellow investigators together, poring over details, nodding solemn agreement and then nailing Oliver Garvie to the wall.

But, Robert Forbes seemed to be taking this personally.

'The word of a thieving woman, you would place above mine?'

'It's Mister Garvie in the dock.'

'I am implicated!'

This sharp response delivered, Forbes sat back in his chair and tapped his finger twice upon the inlaid surface of the desk. It was a sober charcoal colour and matched the suit of the adjuster, who closed his eyes for a moment in thought and then pronounced his judgment.

'All this seems hardly worth the bother, constable.'

'Bother?' Mulholland almost squeaked the word.

'Examine it, sir.' The small intent eyes bored in as Forbes leant across the desk. 'Who knows where these so-called Stinking D'Oros came from? And this mysterious fleshy gentleman that you surmise to be Mister Garvie? A figment. You have only her word.'

Mulholland opened his mouth but nothing came forth and the stag's glassy eyes above offered little encouragement.

The box of cheap cigars lay between them on the desk, opened to display its wares. Robert Forbes flicked the lid shut with one fastidious finger, and then shoved it back to the constable who pocketed the thing once more.

'The son is dead, the guilty party. The mother, despite her low breeding, is desperate in grief and punished enough. In my opinion, you should forget the whole thing.'

At this point Mulholland would have liked nothing better than to forget the whole thing, to nod his head and hopefully watch a wintry smile spread across the Forbes face with perhaps the merest unspoken indication that his suit for Emily might stand a cat in hell's chance; but he had been too long in McLevy's company and, though he resented walking in the shadow cast by the man, he had absorbed the inspector's brand of justice down to the very molecules.

So, he could not let it go.

Not yet.

Perhaps not ever.

For what said his Aunt Katie? 'Only death can stop the badger's grip.'

Was that a noise outside the study door?

'May I ask you, sir,' he began carefully, softly does it, not a hint that this might be evidential scrutiny, 'at the warehouse, you must have found fragments of tobacco?'

'I did indeed.'

'And the quality. You found nothing awry?'

Forbes pursed his lips and hesitated for a brief moment as if recalling his examination.

'They were burnt to a crisp. But I had no suspicion. The quality was clear.'

'And the cargo documents? The invoices, all the papers from abroad, they were genuine?'

There was a silence and then flat response.

'In my opinion. They were. Without fault.'

'And you have sent confirmation of all this to your head office?'

'Indeed so. As I am bound to do.'

That was that, then.

Mulholland sighed. Life was free and easy when all you had to do was push other folk down the slope.

'I have come to a decision, sir.'

'And what is that?'

The pure and simple fact of it all is that he was an idiot, the constable had realised. Cupid had led him by the appendage. He should have known better when he saw the boy on that branch with the goddess.

Too many irons in the fire.

'I shall do what I should have done in the first place, Mister Forbes,' said the constable firmly. 'I shall go back to my superiors this very night, lay everything I have found before them, and let them come to whatever conclusion the evidence merits.'

He got to his feet with a strange sense of relief, as if he had suddenly come to his senses.

'I should have followed the proper procedure and I apologise for disturbing you at your home. I wish you good night and that's me out of here.'

'Constable, wait!'

The call stopped him at the door.

Forbes had also risen to his feet, hand resting unconsciously on the photo of his dead wife.

'Do you insist upon this course of conduct?'

'I am afraid I have no option, sir.'

The older man shook his head in seeming disbelief and his eyes registered unexpected depth of feeling.

'Then I must ask you to wait until the morning,' he declared.

Now it was the constable's turn to shake his head.

'I have delayed long enough,' he muttered.

The hand of Forbes came up and slammed down on the desk.

'It will give time for me to *absolutely* examine all my findings, to make sure there is not the slightest hint of irregularity. Then I shall present myself at the station in the morning, along with Mister Garvie, and I am certain the whole matter can be cleared up without setting any loose slander afoot.'

There was a penetrative intensity of both word and gaze; Mulholland was taken somewhat aback.

'My reputation is at stake here, constable. Hard-earned. Reputation is everything.'

The little man held himself erect, as if an iron rod had been inserted in his spine.

'I realise that, sir,' replied Mulholland, 'but – '

'For the sake of my daughter, if for *nothing* else. She must be protected!'

A fierce appeal in the father's eyes and the constable had a flash of Emily nibbling innocently at a chocolate cake.

That little pink tongue.

His resolution turned to jelly.

'Very well,' he mumbled. 'For Emily's sake.'

'I have your word?'

'You have my word. Till the morning.'

Forbes nodded his acknowledgement of the pledge.

He stood there, the very embodiment of prideful dignity and inclined his head in farewell.

'Good night, constable.'

'Good night, sir.'

The constable left and, as the door closed behind him, Robert Forbes lifted up the photo of his wife and stared at her. The black crepe rustled round the frame as a draught of cold air from the open window blew across the room.

The stag above him was a twelve pointer, though Forbes had not shot it himself. Fixed fast to the wall high above; the head was strong and powerful.

But, as has been remarked before, the beast had not been insured.

Insurance is everything.

There were two receptacles in Mulholland's possession. One was the cigar case, banging against his leg as he made his way down the dark staircase; his hand closed tightly once more around the other, the sharp edge of the small jewellery box cutting into his palm.

The engagement ring would be safe inside no doubt, snug and upright in its appointed slot.

He had not lost hope; love will conquer all.

Perhaps it could yet be so.

He stumbled on the treads and muttered under his breath; the dumpy maid who had admitted him had not been summoned by Forbes to show him out again, there was but one miserable light by the front portal and a long dim corridor towards it.

A gloomy prospect . . . but from the shadows a white arm reached out from a partly opened door and he was hauled from the corridor unceremoniously out of sight.

Darkness has its uses.

On the other side of that door Mulholland found himself at close quarters with his heart's desire, as a fragrant female form insinuated itself into his vicinity.

Emily Forbes giggled at her own boldness and whispered low to Martin Mulholland.

'I had retired, then I heard a knock upon the street door, then I asked Sarah and she rolled her eyes at me.'

'Sarah?'

Mulholland's voice had achieved a high pitch, aware that as far as he could see in the half-light because the room was in near darkness, the only source of illumination coming from a small desk lamp in the far corner, but as far as he could see, Emily was attired in a frilly *peignoir* of sorts, cream in colour, and though it covered a fair amount, the white of her throat glowed like a beacon in the dark.

'The maid,' she answered, taking a deep breath of excitement, causing the *peignoir* to part a little and reveal an equally frilly white nightgown above the neckline of which was a hollow curve of collar bone and below that same neckline a seductive mound that mercifully was more of a hint than a declaration.

'Rolled her eyes?' he replied, tearing his from this inflammatory scene.

'She said a tall handsome man had been conducted to my father, then I knew it was you, then I sneaked up the stairs to listen at the door.'

'You were listening?'

'Naturally!' she responded with a flash of temper showing in her eyes. 'It would concern me and why should I not take part?'

'And what did you hear?' Mulholland asked with a deal of concern.

'Mumbles. Nothing but mumbles.'

Emily made a little moue of disappointment, breathed in somewhat deeper and moved closer.

He could discern her fragrance clearer now, it would be cologne, women often used such or it might just be natural.

Mulholland hadn't been in such close proximity to Emily before, except in his dreams and then they were married so she could lie on the sheets with dilated eyes and no one would think the worse of him, but he suddenly realised with a jolt of panic that they were in her bedroom and if Robert Forbes found him here then he could kiss goodbye to the fair Emily plus possibly his job as well.

Certainly his prospects of promotion.

Constables on a case were not to be discovered in the sleeping quarters of the daughter of the house.

'I better be on my way,' he muttered. 'I have crimes to unravel, Emily.'

She giggled and looked around the room that, as far as he could make out, was draped with all sorts of femininity.

'But it's cosy in here,' she murmured.

'I'm not all that sure about cosy.'

She leant forward so that her head almost rested on his manly bosom, her hair flowing unpinned and loose.

And there's another warning signal.

'So,' she queried softly, 'what were you talking to father about?'

Arson and cigars were not obviously a response that would fit the bill.

'I can't tell you.'

Was it his imagination or had something rustled up against his kneecap?

'I think I know.'

Her mouth parted slightly and the faintest odour of oil of cloves reached his flared nostrils.

'Do you?' he sniffed.

'And I think I know his answer.'

'You do?'

If she got any closer she'd feel the engagement box bumping up against her or something of that sort.

'He said,' breathed Emily, 'you must wait.'

'He did say that. His very words.'

Mulholland suddenly felt more in command of the situation but that could be undone at any moment.

'And will you?'

'Till the morning.'

She laughed, took a step back and he let out a long shuddering breath of relief. Dilation is all very well in dreams and that applied to swelling also, but in reality they were dangerous as hell.

'You're very droll, sir.'

'That's me,' he muttered.

She moved in close again.

'You mustn't lose heart. My father thinks I am a creature of whims, but I am more than that.'

'I'm sure you're not less,' replied the constable, hoping that this made sense.

'Everything comes to he who waits.'

'Does it now?'

'Everything.'

There was a soft pressure against his arm and he didn't dare look down to see what was causing such, all he knew is that if he had his restrainers to hand he would have slapped them on her.

'Is this a whim?' he questioned.

'What does it feel like?'

Something was caught in his gullet but he couldn't cough it up, not at this juncture.

There was a thud from upstairs as the study door opened and closed. They both tensed, but the steps crossed over the landing above and then another door opened and shut.

However that was sufficient for Emily; like many a young girl she gloried in her power to bewitch the opposite sex but a father's footfall broke the spell.

'You had better leave,' she remarked primly.

'The wisest course,' came the croaky response.

He opened the bedroom door and peered cautiously out before setting off down the corridor; the last thing Mulholland desired to meet was the dumpy maid with the rolling eyes.

As he prepared to slip out of the front door, she called softly after; a little annoyed that he had not paused for a last lingering glance back at her glowing form.

'Martin?'

'What is it?' he hissed; this girl would have him boiled in oil if she didn't keep her silence.

'If the worst happens,' Emily whispered, striking a telling pose, 'we can always sing duets together.'

'I'll have to clear my throat first,' was the terse retort and with that he disappeared into the night.

27

The Minstrel Boy to the war is gone,
In the ranks of death you'll find him

THOMAS MOORE, *The Minstrel Boy*

Dundee, 28 December 1879

The tall gaunt figure was wreathed in the spirals of tobacco smoke, like a mountaintop showing above the mist. He prepared to open his mouth and let rip, Sabbath or not a man had to work. God would understand as he did all things.

This public house down by the waterfront was of the lowest sort, in fact more of a drinking den to which the authorities turned a blind eye since it gathered most of the riff-raff from the city under the one roof and left more respectable places free from their unwanted presence.

Of course the fact that the mill and foundry workers had been forced, after a strike of protest, to accept a cut of 5 per cent in wages and a simultaneous increase of working hours, then, when the strike was broken, many of them being laid off for their pains, might possibly have had some hand in swelling the ranks of destitution and poverty but it had at least brought the working practices into line with England.

That must have been of great comfort to the Scots.

And so aided by the cheapest beer and rough spirit men drowned their sorrows, and watched with glazed eyes while the self-styled Premier Poet of Dundee, William McGonagall, thrust a bony right leg forward and launched into verse.

Ironically the subject matter was 'The Railway Bridge of the Silvery Tay', which though a source of great pride had also attendant grief, since many of its creators had been rewarded on its completion by the news from Alan Telfer that their services were no longer required.

So it was with mixed feelings but strange courtesy that they fell silent and prepared to hear their exploits praised by this outlandish chronicler, hair lank and greasy to the shoulders under a wide-brimmed hat, a long frock coat which flapped around his ankles, a lean structure of face which more than hinted of the skull beneath, a thin slash of a mouth justifiably turned down at the corners, and eyes deep in their sockets, black and piercing fuelled by his obsession with a treacherous Muse.

The din in the place stilled as he raised one hand to signal declamation. His voice rang like a clarion call to arms for it had been honed at first in the penny gaffs of Dundee then village and city halls, by surmounting catcalls, penny whistles, crawmills, and howls of derision from young hooligans and university students alike.

But these here in this tavern were his own folk for he had once been a loom weaver before the Muse struck at his vitals; these in front of him shared in the tradition of the singer and the song.

And so, there was silence as he raised the stout stick he always carried for protection against the Philistines, to signal commencement.

These, the words of his own making. Self-crafted.

'Beautiful Railway Bridge of the Silvery Tay,
With your numerous arches and pillars in so grand array,
And your central girders which seem to the eye
To be almost towering to the sky.
The greatest wonder of the day,
And a great beautification to the River Tay,
Most beautiful to be seen,
Near by Dundee and the Magdalen Green.'

It was truly the worst poetry one particular listener had ever heard but the misguided intensity of the delivery, grandiose belief in the destiny of fame, and the implausible admiration of McGonagall towards the poetic worth of his own genius, might almost persuade the ear to attend part of a following versification.

> 'Beautiful Railway Bridge of the Silvery Tay,
> That has caused the Emperor of Brazil to leave
> His home far away, incognito in his dress,
> And view thee ere he passed along en route for Inverness.'

For James McLevy the second stanza confirmed that the one before was indeed no accident and he withdrew himself into a state of contemplation that he had stumbled upon as a child, when first viewing his own mother's dead body.

Nothing like a lacerated throat to teach the value of strategic withdrawal.

It was as if he saw the vista before him through a long glass and his gaze passed from face to face, scene to scene like a sharp lens. At the same time a buzzing noise hung in the air that modified all other sounds to a soft background so that the total focus of concentration was in the vision.

He witnessed faces scarred by labour and the lack of it, alcohol firing into the features of the men a spurious sparkle, some animation that to the profit of the publican would need frequent replenishing, then also amongst the crowd a few brightly dressed women with gaudy shawls and hot desperate eyes. Old women huddled in corners, jealously guarding the dregs in their glass, shrinkie-faced, thrawn and gash-mouthed; an appearance that told of life survived but not relished.

All this he observed yet he did not see the face he was searching for, and so his gaze swept round again to the round 'O' of the poet's mouth as he brought his masterpiece near a proclaimed conclusion.

> 'Beautiful Railway Bridge of the Silvery Tay,
> I hope that God will protect all passengers
> By night and by day,
> And that no accident will befall them while crossing
> The Bridge of the Silvery Tay,
> For that would be most awful to be seen
> Near by Dundee and the Magdalen Green.'

McGonagall screwed up his face mournfully to indicate a heartfelt concern at that grim possibility before launching into a last verse that praised amongst others a certain Thomas Bouch and then ended with the last lines, inevitable in rhyme, hidebound in rhythm, bawled out to the rafters in artistic crescendo.

> 'Which stands unequalled to be seen,
> Near by Dundee and the Magdalen Green!'

There was a genial if drunken roar of approval and the poet removed his hat to take a very small collection inside the hollow crown before throwing the stick over his shoulder and launching into a boisterous ditty called 'The Rattling Boy from Dublin'. This song brought even more approbation from the many Irish present who seemed to know the words as well as its author did, and McLevy resumed more inward contemplation.

The inspector had come across the Tay Bridge by an early-morning train and not remotely enjoyed the experience; as well as a morbid dislike of being immersed in water, he was not drawn either to heights, earth being his preferred element. And, though it was a flat calm day, the river below like a glass reflecting the image as if the bridge reached down into the very depths, the inspector could have sworn that as the train picked up to a considerable speed there was an uneasy shifting movement under his backside.

It might well also have been an optical illusion, caused by momentary vertigo when he was unwise enough to poke his head out of the window and experience the feeling of being pulled down towards the profound deep beneath, but to his shaky eyes there appeared a vertical oscillation in the High Girders as the train flew past.

However none of the other passengers, who included a fair quota of women and children, seemed in the least perturbed, and so the inspector quit the carriage at the other side, scolded himself for a faint-heart and then spent all day in the city of Dundee, out of his parish and on his lonesome.

Anything beyond Leith was, in his opinion, foreign soil; the rest of Edinburgh he could just about thole but Dundee, in terms of psyche and personality, might well have been darkest Africa.

The natives spoke the same language, that much was true, but they seemed kind-natured and lacked the flinty unstated disapproval with which the Edinburgh citizens regarded their fellow man.

Also they did not give with one hand and take back with the other.

Furthermore the Dundonians lacked malice, the sine qua non of the sentient Celt and, rather than holding a grudge against their obviously superior rival across the water, seemed to derive a deal of humour from the opposite camp.

They placed McLevy as belonging there by his accent and commiserated his unfortunate fate to be landed amongst such a tight-arsed community.

That was that, then.

However, though pleasant enough, the natives were also wary, volunteered no more than the recipient deserved and could smell the police a mile off . . . Which meant that all his inquiries about Hercules Dunbar came to absolutely nothing.

The same result as had manifested in Edinburgh after the jail breakout. The man had vanished and it was McLevy's hunch that he may have headed back to his old haunts here to secrete himself amongst the exiled bridge workers, perhaps pick up the odd piece of labour and be safe from the strong arm of the law.

In the person of James McLevy, inspector of police . . . who had trailed about the place since mid-morning till his feet ached from the hard pavements, cursing himself for a fool who would use his only day off on a wild goose chase.

It being a Sunday, Roach and Mulholland would be safely ensconced in the house of God, while he traipsed from tavern to tavern and one disreputable lodging house to another; starting off near to the Wormit Foundry where Dunbar had once been employed, then sniffing his way like a mongrel dog towards the docks. At least this was familiar territory, not nearly as large as the Leith equivalent but the scurry of rats chittering under the piers seemed familiar and the run-down waterside taverns had the same depressing similarity.

This was where he was happiest. This is where he belonged. With the dregs of humanity.

On this somewhat sour thought, the inspector watched as McGonagall brought his remarkably cheerful lament for Dublin's Biddy Brown, the lost love of the Rattling Boy, to an end and assumed a heroic pose as the cheers rang forth.

The inspector had heard of the poet and the sublime horror of his verse, but this was his first live experience of the man and he would be happy enough if it were the last.

It was too late now to return to Edinburgh. The evening was upon them, a heavy wind rattling the thick windows of the tavern; he would have to register in some cheap flea-bitten hotel and take the earliest train back.

Empty-handed. But at least now he knew the composition of Beaumont Egg. The voices slurred that told the tale but enough of them agreed, after a bought drink or two, that it consisted of beeswax, fiddler's rosin, the finest iron borings, all mixed together with a little lamp black and then used to cure any holes in the iron castings by being melted in with a red-hot bar.

It became hard as a rock and would not melt in the sun but it was not iron. It was grafted on and therefore might be picked out by keen point or shaken loose by great force.

This was from the foundry men but one of the painters of the bridge, a man still in work, daubed with red lead like a savage, boasted of finding at least one hundredweight of fallen iron bolts inside the lower booms of the bridge.

However it was all drunken hearsay. He could just see the contemptuous smile on Alan Telfer's face if it was brought before the man's attention.

There was a sudden outburst of noise and McLevy was hit in the face by a shower of hard dried peas.

It wrenched him out of a black study to see that the publican had grown tired of the fact that Poet McGonagall, who had just announced grandly that due to public demand he would repeat 'The Rattling Boy' in its entirety, had monopolised the audience's attention to the extent that they had rapidly slowed down their consumption of drink.

Therefore they were not filling the publican's coffers to the brim, so he had instructed one of his barmen to throw a wet dirty beer-slopped towel into William's countenance.

While the poet was still reeling from this insult to his honour, the publican and some of the other barmen had picked up handfuls of dried green peas and were hurling them with malign gusto at the Bard of

Bonny Dundee, some of which had sailed past him to sting the inspector.

The poet stood his ground proudly. His sallow well-kippered skin had suffered such painful assaults before and he uttered an immortal couplet in response.

'Gentlemen if you please,
Stop throwing peas!'

Unfortunately this provoked a howl of laughter from the audience who had cruelly shifted sides; it is ever thus for a creative soul amongst the barbarian hordes.

The publican and his men redoubled their efforts and the supply of missiles seemed never ending because they drove the poet, who was trying to bat the peas away with his stick, backwards towards the door out into the street.

McLevy thought idly to interfere but then froze as a door to a private side room opened and four men emerged to see what was causing the hullabaloo.

One of the men was Hercules Dunbar.

Changed in some ways, but not quite enough.

28

I am poured out like water, and all my
bones are out of joint: my heart also in the
midst of my body is even like melting wax.

BOOK OF COMMON PRAYER, Psalm 22, v14

From a dead calm and eerie stillness, the heavy gale had roared up like an animal from ambush and was battering at the whole length of the Tay-side. The devout worshippers returning from their Sabbath meditations were assailed by flying slates and roof tiles as if the devil himself had decided to punish their piety by a demonstration of what happened when Pandora took the lid off the box.

The elemental force of wind and rain ripped the tiles, laths and plaster from attic roofs exposing the good holy people of the house as if they had been stripped bare of decency, naked to the howling laughter of Satan.

Chimney cairns capered and danced like witches in the road, while a shower of masonry fell like giant hailstones and smashed into the pavements below, splitting into shards so sharp they would have drawn blood had the faithful not clung to the shelter of the walls and edged their way towards the refuge of respectability.

Along the shore, bathing huts were ripped asunder, the roofs departing bodily to join in the dance or fly out into the darkness of the raging river.

Surely evil was abroad? Surely the Storm Fiend had risen from his dark lair in the deep and erupted into a frenzy of farts and belches to shake the holy where they knelt in prayer? Was not that heavy blinding rain the sign of a monster lifting its leg from on high to pass its water, marking out the territory below?

None of these thoughts occurred to Hercules Dunbar as he laughed wildly in the chaos, crossing over a small public park near the Magdalen Green. Having bade goodbye to his friends and watched them stagger off towards the poorer billets of the city, he had turned in the direction of more salubrious quarters. Which is where he now belonged.

He was hurled off his feet by the force of the blast and rolled over in the grass like a scrap of paper, but good whisky had rendered him immortal.

And his luck had turned in the shape of a widow woman, a fine lusty specimen towards whose domicile his footsteps were now directed.

Jenny Wilson, an Inverness lassie, come to the city as a maid of all work, had married above her to an older man, Tom Cathcart, a bank teller from Dundee who keeled over one day face first into the money he was counting. She inherited a fine wee pension from the bank and a small house at the other end of the Green.

And she was greatly enamoured of Hercules Dunbar.

God bless the human heart, which in the banker's case had completely failed him.

Jenny could put on some airs and graces, enough to get by, however in reality she craved rough usage in her bedtime activities, something the banker was not equipped to deliver but Hercules had in abundance.

In fact the first time she had essayed a far from maidenly glance at his rampant manhood, it had, as she confided later, fair taken her breath away.

They had met in this selfsame park; her small Cairn terrier had got itself into difficulties with a swan who had grabbed the dog by the neck when the stupid beast had got too damned close in a waterside encounter, barking fit to burst.

The swan then went swimming out to the middle of the pond and proceeded to thrust with combination of graceful neck plus vice-like beak, the yelping animal under the water with the obvious intention of drowning this ill-matched skittery opponent.

Hercules had been sitting on a nearby park bench nursing a sore head from excess of the night before but washed, clean and neat enough attired since he was hoping to gain employment with a small foundry under an assumed name.

He had grown the beginnings of a fine moustache to further disguise himself and it bristled manfully as he, having seen that the wifie was, while shrieking her distress, a well-endowed buxom-looking creature, waded out some distance, swam the rest, and then hammered the swan a blow between the eyes that caused the powerful neck to cease its murderous activities.

Then he had returned with the bedraggled terrier, the hero of the hour, and his wet garments, which she insisted on washing and drying at her home, once discreetly removed, never quite resumed their former station.

In fact, the banker, though lacking the graithlike girth and vigour of Hercules, was of a reasonable match in height and size so not only did he inherit the wife he got some decent clothes as well.

For the first time in his life he lacked for nothing; the woman hauled away under the sheets like a trawler but she did not lack common sense and allowed him a daily sum to have a drink and treat with his friends but not too much that he might get boastful.

Of course the idea was that he would eventually find gainful employment but nothing that would tire him out too much as regards his other duties.

So no wonder Hercules Dunbar was roaring as he rolled over in the grass like a happy child.

The howling wind redoubled its efforts, a westerly gale of up to eighty miles an hour that in other places tore off the shutters and cracked the very windows, but the widow woman's house would be safe enough.

It was in a secluded street, the neighbours were not nosy and if questions were asked, he was a respectable working man who lodged there.

And in a strange way he had become a modified figure in his new fine clothes though the uneasy fear of being stripped down to the bone and made to view himself like a naked animal, never left his split disposition.

His father's fist had seen to that. One blow had cut him in half.

Hercules hauled himself up against a creaking tree, shook himself like a dog to rid his hair of the dripping raindrops and then saw the figure of James McLevy standing before him, like a terrible ghost of retribution.

The inspector had jammed his bowler into the side pocket of his coat and his hands swung loose in the whipping wind.

'Aye, Herkie,' he said. 'A grim night, eh?'

Dunbar nodded, all happiness fled.

The inspector could have explained how he had watched the quarry and his companions laugh at the pea-spattered poet's untimely exit then, after an affable word with the publican, the bill settled, off they went into the wild darkness.

How he had followed on and waited patiently till the group parted company, the numbers being too heavy for the one man.

How he had observed Dunbar roll in the grass like a child and been affected by the strange recollection of when, as young Jamie McLevy, he had crawled through the rushes to steal a pair of boots that had kicked him once too often.

But he said nothing of this save the following.

'You hammered my young constable and caused him grievous injury. You dunged upon the honour of my station.'

'That's good,' was the response. 'As for the constable, he'll know better now.'

'You left a message that we would meet in hell. This night seems as close as we can get in life.'

A gust of wind howled its agreement and one of the young slender trees in the park simply snapped into two pieces as if hacked down by an axe.

McLevy braced himself against the squall and moved forward slowly to where Dunbar was wedged back against the tree; the man's eyes gleaming in the darkness like those of a hunted animal.

Both men were saturated from the rain but it ran down their faces to no avail. They had other business on hand.

'You remember now, Herkie,' the inspector shouted above the distorted clamour of enraged nature, 'the last time we got to grips, you suffered the worst of the exchange. I believe my fist and your belly made strong acquaintance.'

'I have it in my mind,' Dunbar called back. 'But things can change, I am a changed man now.'

'Aye, you have more hair and are better dressed but I doubt the beast remains the same under your skin.'

The inspector was now almost within touching distance and for a brief moment the wind abated, so that he spoke quietly to the desperate figure crouched before him.

'I would advise you to slip the restrainers on and come to the fold of justice like a wee lamb. Is that possible for you to entertain?'

Dunbar nodded his head in the weird stillness.

'That is possible,' he replied, then as the wind broke into another furious tantrum, he used the force of it at the back of him plus the propelled impetus from a foot which he had placed behind him on the trunk of the tree, to shoot forward like a bullet and take McLevy by surprise, bringing them both crashing to the ground.

Close quarters had always been an advantage to Hercules Dunbar for his bones were hard as cold chisel.

He wedged a steely forearm under McLevy's throat and began to press up into the soft flesh. The aim was simple, to crush the windpipe until a lack of breath separated the victim from a conscious state and left him with a neck like a wrung chicken.

The taller man was on top, his full weight pressing down, one arm busy at its chosen employment, the other pinning McLevy's right hand so that only the weaker left was free to flap uselessly at the side.

The policeman's eyes were bulging with effort as he tried to break loose but as the pressure intensified on his windpipe, he began to gasp for air though God knows there was enough of it flying around.

The inspector's skin took on a bluish tinge and Hercules bared his teeth in a savage grin.

'Things change, eh?'

Another jolt with the forearm brought a shuddering retch from McLevy as he fought to get some air into his lungs; the inspector could feel his senses slipping, a darkness behind the eyes.

'Your Auntie Jean will no' help you now,' Dunbar taunted. 'Another mad auld bitch.'

It is possible that had Hercules reflected on such a remark he may have considered that to insult the only woman McLevy had ever truly loved might not have been the best way to induce subjugation but he had blood in his eyes and, at these moments, the primitive emerges club in hand.

However, one caveman deserves another.

McLevy's left hand scrabbled desperately in the loose earth with renewed force and came upon a by-product of his favourite element in the shape of a flat heavy stone which he raised up to smash into the side of the other's face.

The terrible crushing pressure relaxed for a moment as Dunbar's head absorbed the force of the blow. He blinked his eyes in an almost comical fashion as McLevy smashed at him again and then, while the man reeled back, the inspector dropped the stone and rolled away from underneath to land on all fours drawing great gulps of air into his tortured lungs and throat.

The two men slowly then lumbered to their feet and while the storm howled above them in the night sky, lurched and grappled at each other like two prehistoric beasts in the primeval sludge.

But despite Dunbar's animal nature he lacked McLevy's recourse to applied madness under severe stress, a ferocious lupine glare indicating the demonic possession within.

Hercules was driven back towards the tree and one final scything blow to an area somewhere between the belly button and groin laid him writhing to the ground.

'As you say, Herkie,' McLevy gasped, wiping a smear of blood from his nose with one hand while he brought out the restrainers with the other. 'Things change.'

But Fate was not finished with them yet; there would be other acts of violence to play out before these two enemies from birth could truly say the game was over.

The growth that had aided Hercules to launch his attack had creaked and groaned in sympathy while its champion had engaged in combat. It was an old walnut tree and the roots had been weakened by incessant downpour then stretched beyond their strength by the westerly gale. They snapped, and downwards it fell with a writhing motion as if in a death throe.

Like a bolt from the blue.

The trunk and heavy branches missed Dunbar by very little but crashed down upon the vengeful McLevy, pinning him underneath as if crucified to earth.

He could not move, breath driven from his body and a sharp stabbing pain indicating that a few ribs were either cracked or broken and the back of his head aching mightily where the tree had first struck.

One of the wizened fruits of the branches fell off and pinged on to his exposed forehead.

He'd never liked walnuts; they always stuck in the gaps of his teeth.

Again there was a curious still interlude as if the storm was gathering its strength for a final burst of destruction and in the silence, broken only by the heavy rain, came the sound of laughter.

Hercules Dunbar staggered to his feet and looked down at his enemy.

'Ye have tae admit, inspector,' he said with delighted malevolence, 'either God or the devil is on my side.'

'I would venture, the devil,' grunted McLevy, the pain in his crushed ribs jolting him as he tried to move.

But he could not. He was helpless.

He watched as Dunbar put his hand up to the side of his bruised face, swollen and blotched from the stone that McLevy had clattered against the side of his head.

The inspector's body and limbs were entangled and pinioned by the heavy branches that pressed him ever deeper into the earth but his head, by a quirk of chance, was clear, framed by the poor broken boughs like a portrait.

Therefore he could observe as Hercules Dunbar searched out the flat stone, hefted it judiciously and then came back to kneel by the side of the spread-eagled form.

Dunbar lifted up the stone.

'Like for like,' he muttered. 'The storm will take the blame.'

Some of the dark clouds above began to fragment and a ray from the revealed full moon glinted on the stone, as it poised in the air.

McLevy's eyes were steady upon the other's face.

'Can you kill in cold blood, Herkie?' he asked; then it was his turn to laugh ignoring the shafts of agony in his ribcage as he gazed up at Dunbar's puzzled face.

'I am prepared to die. Are you prepared to end my life? Do you have the gumption for such deliverance?'

This was his only hope, the inspector had calculated; he in fact had no desire whatsoever to shuffle off this mortal coil without at least one more pot of coffee and a plate of sugar biscuits with Jean Brash, but his chances of avoiding the grim reaper were somewhat limited.

Pity from Dunbar was out of the question. If he begged for mercy or showed the least fear, it would inflame the man to a primitive lust for the killing blow. The balance must be altered and risk was the key.

McLevy began to sing softly. A song that Dunbar had heard before in the interrogation room when the inspector was King of the Castle.

> 'Charlie is my darling, my darling, my darling.
> Charlie is my darling, the young Chevalier.'

Chanted like an incantation, it caused Hercules to jerk back, nostrils flaring.

'That's Jacobite!' he accused. 'Ye dirty wee Papish porker!'

'Then bash in my brains, because I'm going to sing it any fashion.'

McLevy began again but stopped abruptly and roared with laughter at the look on the face of his mortal foe.

Hercules Dunbar's head was in a spin as the gale suddenly lashed in on them again and he was taken backwards.

His thoughts were whirling like the wind. If he killed this demon he would be safe, no man would follow him; but while McLevy lived, Dunbar would always be looking over his shoulder, always in fear of discovery; he could persuade Jenny to sell the house, move North to her relatives he would be more secure there but even then, even then?

Kill the bastard and be done with it.

But how can you kill a man who laughs in your face?

Hot laughter.

In cold blood.

The song began again and it drove him near mad to the point when he lifted up the stone with a snarl and hurled it downwards.

But if with murderous intent his aim was sadly awry, for the missile crashed beside McLevy's head and bounced harmlessly aside.

The Jacobite air halted its jaunty progress. The wind howled and the rain beat down on McLevy's unprotected face as the two men gazed at each other.

'With any luck ye'll drown tae buggery,' Dunbar remarked soberly. 'Nature will do the job.'

'True enough,' replied McLevy. 'Water will one day be the death of me.'

Hercules suddenly smiled and he moved forward to stand, legs astride, over the recumbent form.

He fished in his trouser flap, produced his not inconsiderable member and a stream of urine joined the rain gushing down on the inspector's countenance.

McLevy froze in disbelief but he should have remembered that there were many facets to the story of the boots.

The pupils of his eyes narrowed to a grey slit flecked with yellow, and for a second he strained up against the weight of wood that held him fast.

Had he succeeded in wrenching free it is doubtful whether Hercules would have survived to refasten his trouser flap and kneel down once more to grin savagely as he looked into the cold lethal eyes of the deeply insulted wolf.

'You and me are the same, McLevy. Under the skin. Jist the same animal. Now we are equal. Like for like.'

Dunbar levered himself to his feet and was about to leave when a command from the depths of the tree stopped him in his tracks.

'Hold it there!'

Covered in pish or not, survive the night in doubt; in spite of ribs cracked, the inspector glimpsed a chance here.

Questions must be asked. If the man thought McLevy to die in this place, he might reveal the truth.

'The auld butler. Did you cause his death?'

Dunbar shook his head in disbelief at the effrontery of the man but answered anyway.

'I did not. I left him where I said.'

'Then who killed the man?'

'I wouldnae know.'

From his disadvantaged position, McLevy probed further.

'When you came to the house that Sunday, you threatened blackmail to Alan Telfer did you not?'

This was not such a wild stab as it seemed; the inspector had been long mulling over Dunbar's veiled allusions from the interrogation.

The man made no response but with an insolent smile invited further deduction.

'The blind eye, you turned. The Beaumont Egg. They would be connected?' continued the policeman.

For a moment Dunbar considered not responding but then a gust of wind blew some muddy leaves over McLevy's face and the effort he had to make to blow them off, jerking the breath from one side of his mouth to the other, brought home how helpless and puny was the questioner.

And Hercules was a boaster. The appreciation he possessed as regards his own clever ploys was boundless. He could not resist this moment.

Dunbar adopted a mysterious air.

'The bridge must open on time,' he opined. 'The cost must not be exceeded. The ore was poor quality, the iron produced shot through wi' holes.'

'So you filled them up?'

'We were ordered so and thus provided.'

'By whom?'

'Alan Telfer.'

'He brought you the Beaumont Egg?'

'Whenever necessary. Had it made up special.'

'Yet you had no written proof. Nothing. So when you went to see him he laughed in your face.'

'But I got my own back.'

'A candlestick only. He's still laughing.'

This blunt assessment brought a scowl to Dunbar but then a sly dirty smile spread across his countenance.

'I had the last laugh. I saw them.'

'Saw what?'

'I'll throw it in their face one day. In front of everybody. In their face!'

This must have been the strangest interrogation in the annals of crime; urine-soaked police inspector, poleaxed by a walnut tree, asks questions of a suspect who might yet change his mind and kill him at any moment.

Yet it did not impinge on McLevy's state for one moment. He had a sixth sense when a fact that might help unlock a mystery was about to be revealed, no matter the circumstances or whether the discloser realised the importance of same.

He also realised the source of the guilt he had sensed in Dunbar as regards the death of his only friend, the riveter, Tommy Loughran, but this was not the time to bring it home; guilt causes anger and that emotion could wait until another day.

Now it was his turn for silence; he stuck out his lower lip and shook his dripping head as if to imply, 'What could the likes of you know? What secret could you hug close that could possibly discomfit the great Sir Thomas Bouch and Alan Telfer?'

Hercules took up the invitation.

'Before I robbed the stick, on the way through, I keeked in the bedroom, maybe a purse lying free. I saw them. Thegither. Telfer was lying on the bed in his shirt and trousers. Sir Thomas was in his nightgown, under the sheets. His head was on Telfer's chest. They were both asleep. Babes in the wood. Dirty bastards.'

Dunbar sniggered then looked down at McLevy to see the effect of his words.

'So,' said the inspector slowly, 'you closed the door, went to the study, thieved your due, were about to leave and then that was when the auld fellow came in?'

'That was when.'

An ice-cold blast of wind hit Dunbar full in the face and froze the disappointment on his features.

McLevy seemed unimpressed. To hell with him then.

'A long night,' said Hercules. 'And cold as the grave. I doubt you will not survive. I'll be sitting by a warm fire wi' a good woman dishing out the hot meal. Black pudding, chappit tatties and kale. Every mouthful I'll think of ye. And I'll wish for your death.'

Then he was gone into the darkness without another word, leaving the inspector soaked in urine and burning with a fierce indignation.

There would be a reckoning for this. Only nature may pass water on inspectors of crime.

But at least he was alive to smell the piddle.

His mind was racing with what Dunbar had told him; if he got out of this alive, the shape of what was forming in his head would have its day.

If he got out of this alive.

29

Who sees with equal eye, as God of all,
A hero perish or a sparrow fall,
Atoms or systems into ruin hurled,
And now a bubble burst, and now a world.

ALEXANDER POPE, An Essay on Man, Epistle 1

The rat had been flushed from its den by the rushing water and scuttled along the side of the park pond, which was like a miniature version of the writhing distant river.

The rodent had no fear of water; its sleek coat repelled the hail of rain as it scurried across the grass towards the underbrush where it might find a ratty haven.

In the tangle of broken branches it glimpsed white flesh and thought, like a good policeman, to investigate, but the flesh moved, a low growl emitted from direction of the white mass and so the rat passed on.

It could always come back later.

McLevy watched it depart with a fierce eye and wondered for the umpteenth occasion how he might remove himself from these desperate straits.

Time had passed and the rain beaten down, with the storm, if anything, increasing in ferocity.

The inspector was part protected by the foliage but it also might conceal him from any passers-by though, as far as he could observe, they were non-existent.

No one but a mad person would be out in such a night.

He averted his face as much as possible but large drips from the broken branches spattered and ran down his skin so that he had to keep his eyes shut, blow out his nostrils like a hog, and keep his mouth tight closed because his head was over an indent in the ground and if he leant it back, water coursed into every orifice.

And yet to keep it upright was a hellish strain, the difficulty compounded by his aching ribs. In addition a sharp pain cut like a knife at the back of his head.

It was a most unpleasant sensation and growing worse by the minute in a darkness that seemed without relief; perhaps Hercules Dunbar had postulated correctly when he thought that nature might do the job.

The inspector's own thoughts were of a grim cast; this was a slow torture and might last till, consciousness lost, the process could proceed unchecked.

If he didn't freeze to death, he would drown. A fine prospect.

Then he heard a voice shouting above the percussive beat of the wind. It had an oddly familiar ring and he strained to discern the figure and make out the words.

'Strong drink will cause the gambler to rob and kill his brother,
Aye! Also his father and his mother,
All for the sake of getting money to gamble,
Likewise to drink, cheat and wrangle.'

Only one person in the universe could write such execrable drivel but it was music to McLevy's ears as the full moon made an opportune appearance to disclose the poet McGonagall in full flow, long coat flapping like the wings of a bat as he bawled out a rhyming diatribe against the evils of alcohol.

McLevy tried to call forth but received an inopportune mouthful of wind and rain and as he coughed this out, further inflaming the jagged pain in his ribcage, the poet continued his bellowing lay.

'And when the burglar wants to do his work very handy,
He plies himself with a glass of Whisky, Rum or Brandy,
To give himself courage to rob and kill,
And innocent people's blood to spill!'

Finally McLevy managed to croak out the man's name, before he passed by and was gone into the night.

'William McGonagall!'

The poet stopped abruptly and a look of fear came on his face; was that Satan on the prowl?

Again the call.

'McGonagall!'

'Who summons me?' he cried, taking up a defiant stance, his stick raised high to combat evil.

'I am an Edinburgh policeman,' came the response. 'And I am under this fallen walnut tree.'

McGonagall cautiously approached the source of this assertion and found at least part of it to be so. The man was definitely under a tree.

'How do I know you are a police officer?' he asked, lest the fellow be a footpad in disguise.

McLevy bit back a vitriolic rejoinder; this numskull was all he had.

'My restrainers will be lying near,' he grunted.

Luckily William found them where they had fallen when the tree made its entrance in the drama, held them up in the blowy moonlight to verify McLevy's profession, then produced his next inquiry.

'Are you in pain, good sir?'

'What does it look like?' was the aggrieved retort.

These things established, the poet proved surprisingly adept and practical at prising the inspector from under the heavy branches of his captor.

He found a broken but still strong enough part of the trunk from the slender tree that had snapped earlier, jammed it under and bore down upon the lever with sufficient force to raise the dead weight so that McLevy could roll painfully free.

It took no time at all. One moment a man looks death in the face, then a second later he is free as a bird.

Until the next occasion.

As the inspector got slowly to his feet he noticed that McGonagall's wide-brimmed hat was, despite the vicious wind, still fixed upon his head.

How did he manage that?

'I am Inspector James McLevy and I thank you, Poet McGonagall,' he uttered formally.

The man's face lit up and he struck a pose, leg extended before, and his walking stick over the shoulder.

'You know of me, sir? My fame has spread to many parts, I believe this cannot be contradicted.'

'I saw you in the tavern. With the peas.'

'I am a Good Templar,' came the oblique rejoinder. 'Only circumstance forces the Muse into such sorrowful surroundings. I have a family to feed.'

McLevy winced at the pain from his ribs and, as he gazed into his rescuer's solemn eyes, felt an obscure pity that would not be denied.

Did the man not know how absurd was the versification he produced?

Obviously not, for William gestured around at the whirling elements as if they were boon companions in the search for truth and purity of vision.

'It is your good fortune sir, that I came this way to seek out inspiration. I am composing a poem against the snares and pitfalls of the demon drink.'

'I heard you,' muttered McLevy. 'The sentiments were to be applauded.'

McGonagall suddenly put a dramatic hand up to his forehead as another shaft from the Muse struck home.

'I have the last verse,' he cried. 'And you shall be the first to hear it, sir.'

And so with aching ribs, a blinding pain at the base of his skull, a murderous bastard fled, and stinking of pee, which the poet seemed not to notice, dying for a coffee or a hooker of whisky to cheer him up, a head full of crime, his heart boiling with vengeance, James McLevy endured these lines of Temperance and goodwill to all men.

> 'I beseech ye all to kneel down and pray
> And implore God to take the demon drink away,
> Then this world would be a heaven, whereas it is a hell,
> And the people would have more peace in it to dwell.'

McLevy had closed his eyes to shield himself as far as possible from this maladjusted poetic onslaught but when he opened them again, McGonagall was still there, still the worst poet McLevy had ever heard and still the man who had liberated him from a bone-crushing walnut tree.

McGonagall waited expectantly. McLevy searched for something to contribute.

'Words fail me,' he finally managed.

He held out his hand to signal appreciation and incidentally bring a conclusion to this torture by verse.

The poet gripped it fast, once more their eyes met, and for a moment the inspector could have sworn that there was the shadow of a sad self-consciousness in the man's face as if he truly suffered from the terrible knowledge that what he proclaimed as genius, was in fact dross of the lowest quality. But then the instant passed, though the man's next words might have intimated such.

'The Muse is cruel,' said McGonagall sombrely. 'She will not let me rest. Night or day, I must put my shoulder to the wheel of creation. And I have a family to feed.'

A hint of a different kind and McLevy took it gratefully, withdrawing from the handshake to find a coin or two in his pocket, which he pressed into the poet's palm.

'I would have given this in the tavern,' he asserted solemnly, 'were we not interrupted by the peas.'

The coins disappeared magically into the McGonagall pocket and he turned to stride off, aided mightily by the buffet of a following wind.

At the margin of moonlight, he twisted round to raise his stick in farewell.

'I thank you, James McLevy. Perhaps one day we shall meet again,' he shouted.

'I look forward to that,' was the response of a man lying through his teeth.

A further thought struck the poet.

'My house is in Paton's Lane, a far cry from here and a humble dwelling but you are welcome to hunker down for the night upon the floor.'

The thought of rhyming couplets with a bowl of thin gruel in the morning sent a shiver through McLevy's aching bones.

'A kind offer but I'll find my own passage,' he called back. 'Yet tell me one thing. In this violent tempest, how do you keep the hat upon your head?'

'Dignity,' was the enigmatic answer. 'A poet is ruined if he is not dignified.'

With that McGonagall departed into the night leaving McLevy to turn and make his way towards the esplanade, that being the general course he imagined Dunbar to have taken.

Though he knew it was a hopeless quest. Who knows how long he had lain there in such sorry circumstance?

The man would be miles away and could have set off in any direction. He could be anywhere in the city.

The part of the esplanade opposite the park was deserted, the rows of houses starting further along, and as McLevy bent over double, part to ease the pain of his ribs part to present a lesser target for the storm wind, the sand and pebbles were blown in a stinging hail from the shore to blend in with the rain and further add to his discomfort.

After struggling into the teeth of the gale for a fair while and finally realising the pointlessness of his effort, McLevy found refuge where a sturdy brick shelter had been erected so that promenaders might, in better climes, view the River Tay in all its glory.

The inspector sank gratefully down upon the hard stone bench.

In the confines of the shelter, the sour odour of the undesired inflicted micturation rose to greet his nostrils. And now that he had no longer the distraction of battling the elements, the throbbing ache from the back of his head was like a hammer beating on his brain.

To distract himself from this predicament he looked out over the violent river, which was hurling waves against the shore like cannon-balls, the clouds scudding across the sky above as if fleeing for their lives.

For a moment the moon was uncovered and by its pale light he could see dimly in the far distance the outline of the Tay Bridge.

The light of a train showed equally dimly as it entered the bridge and crawled across the rails like a child's toy and McLevy was put in mind of when his Aunt Jean had taken him to a fair on the Leith Links.

In a darkened room he had watched a model engine climb a steep gradient towing carriages behind, find its way along an overpass with a tunnel underneath, shoot down the other side, then wind its way back by snakelike curves of track, through the tunnel and doubling back until it found its course returned to the gradient.

He was fascinated how the wheels of the train clung to the narrow ribbon of track, especially as it inched along the overpass and then hurtled down the gradient.

Each time the descent seemed faster and the audience gasps louder.

Then the young boy realised that the root of their fascination was in the anticipation of disaster; the desire to see the tightrope walker fall, the artist on trapeze miss his grip and plummet to the ground, the lion tamer gripped in the beast's bloody mouth, all these in some dark way desired by the watcher.

Jamie McLevy observed the little engine make one more steep and safe plunge then let out a wail and dragged his Aunt Jean to safety before calamity struck.

And now the grown man strained his eyes to discern the distant glimmering lights from a train over two hundred feet in length, the willing squat little tank engine pulling five passenger carriages and a brake van.

Had he been near at hand, he would have seen the tank engine to be olive green in colour, number 224, weighing close to thirty-five tons.

A fine proud beast of burden with each passenger coach lit by brass and iron lanterns where men, women and children were to be disclosed, perhaps lost in thought, lost in love, perhaps asleep on a father's shoulder or looking out with excitement at the violence of the storm.

Safely cradled by the North British line.

But at distance, still a toy train on a toy bridge.

The full moon played hide and seek with the clouds, and the scene flickered before McLevy's eyes while the engine approached the High Girders.

As it entered the iron fretwork, a heavy cloud caught the moon and abruptly obscured all vision like an ominous dark curtain.

The inspector felt a panic build up inside him as if the darkness would swallow him, as if he were in another universe, a separate reality where shadows ruled and his own black thoughts tormented him.

He had uncovered the secret of the bridge, found its weakness, undermined its integrity. Now he carried that knowledge like a diseased person who contaminated all that he touched.

The Masque of the Red Death . . .

McLevy shook his head like an animal trying to rid itself from a plague of flies, but still the thoughts came.

What was his desire? In this empty darkness did he not truly wish for extinction? His own and all known things?

As if in answer, in the pitch black, came three separate and terrible flashes of light from the direction of the bridge, and then as the moon began to struggle free once more, McLevy saw by the emerging pallid light a column of steam and spray rise from the distant river as if some giant had picked up a mountain and hurled it into the waters.

He further strained his eyes; his long vision was excellent but the picture it brought to him provoked a craving for the most profound blindness.

The lunar light had grown stronger to reveal that where the High Girders had once stood so proudly, were now stumps like rotting teeth.

The bridge was down.

The unlooked-for wish had been granted.

Had the train also fallen?

James McLevy fell from the stone bench to his knees and bowed his head in prayer for the lost souls.

Because if the train had plunged deep like a diver, no one could survive that fall.

No one did.

These were not toys.

215

30

For secrets are edged tools,
And must be kept from children and from fools.

JOHN DRYDEN, St Martin Mar-All

Lieutenant Roach looked at the calendar on his desk and
sighed: 9 November 1880. He had the whole of the winter
yet to endure, his blood sluggish already at seasonable ebb,
and on such mornings considered his office to be little more
than a railway station.

No sooner had Constable Mulholland requested an audience
with his superior and the young man hardly sat down, twisting
his fingers together but mercifully making no mention of
impending suits of love, the potential failure of which Roach was
not looking forward to divulging from his Masonic converse with
Robert Forbes, than the door was rapped upon in peremptory
fashion and McLevy came bounding in like a dog after a bone.

To regard the inspector, overcoat damp with the morning
mist, wiry hair on end indeed giving him the appearance of a
vibrant canine, it could never have been suspected that he had
spent the night in broken sleep to awaken with a severe stitch
in his side plus a head full of bad memories.

Thus the past afflicts the present like an uninvited guest, a
spectre at the masked ball.

Job had his plague of boils and McLevy had the Bouch case.
That treacherous pissful slippery bastard Hercules Dunbar was
still at large and it was doubtful if he would ever be recovered;
everyone else was dead except Margaret Bouch who was far too
actively alive and kicking.

The dreadful picture of the spray rising from the wild river
to mark the death plunge of that train almost a year past, had
seared its way into his brain and would be with him always.

But, out of the void, comes action.

The empty feeling in the pit of his stomach had been filled with two strong cups of coffee; he had then made early rendezvous with his omniscient provider of financial lore and his inquiries had borne lustrous fruit.

Ripe enough to sink his teeth into, and if juice dribbles down the chin, so much the better.

As he walked by Great Junction Street towards the Leith station, the morning sun made an unexpected appearance thus dispelling the mist and, to the alarm of some passers-by, the inspector raised his arms towards it, closed his eyes and bathed delightedly in the weak November rays.

'Hallelujah!' he announced to the sky above.

It was often thus with McLevy. A state of inertia as if the very blood had been sucked from his veins was followed by a frenetic burst of activity and high spirits, tending towards the manic and hard to resist.

He stood in the doorway as if an electric charge had been shot through him and winked at Mulholland who, now that the inspector had arrived on the scene, was searching for an altered formulation on how to break his own news.

Roach merely dug his backside deeper into the padding of the chair like a man would ground his feet before a shot out of a deep trap.

He could recognise the signs. Time to anchor down.

Queen Victoria from her position on the wall clasped her plump hands together a trifle anxiously as McLevy almost hopped in the air with satisfaction.

'Our friend Mister Oliver Garvie is facing financial ruin.'

This statement produced a muted response. Mulholland, who would previously have cheered this to the echo, had his own possible ruin to face and Roach had learned that when McLevy was running wild, to be sanguine was to be sagacious.

'How so?' he asked, jerking his jaw to the side.

The inspector hopped again, undismayed by such dull audience.

'He has been hammered at the gaming tables. Gambled the stock exchange and lost. Plunged heavily to recoup. Lost once again with a vengeance. And now?'

McLevy raised a heavy eyebrow like an actor in a melodrama.

'He has nothing left to gamble.'

The inspector looked to Mulholland but received pallid response which annoyed him: the man should be full of beans at the prospect of a rival unravelled, but looked like John the Baptist just after Salome cut loose.

'So says my banking confidant,' he ended tersely.

'Is he reliable?' Roach questioned.

'He runs the bank.'

That was that, then.

Mulholland took a deep breath but McLevy severed, like Salome, the intended contribution.

'I think I may be able – ' began the constable.

'Hold yet, Mulholland,' was the grandiose response. 'The lieutenant and I are in communication.'

'So, what is your thinking, McLevy?'

The inspector smacked his lips like a man dining out on crime and strode around the office, almost skipping at times.

'Twenty thousand pounds insurance money!' he exclaimed. 'My banker friend assures me that no amount approaching that sum has gone abroad from Garvie's account to pay out for this supposed cargo.'

'He may have had the money in other forms,' Roach threw in. 'Securities, bonds, liquid cash, who knows what business-men get up to?'

'Who knows indeed?' the inspector answered back, a wicked gleam in his eye. 'Who knows what swindles they may perpetrate?'

Mulholland winced and opened his mouth again but this time it was the lieutenant beat him to the punch.

'All very circumstantial, inspector. To move against a man of Garvie's standing, I need hard evidence.'

Mulholland thought of the cigar box nestling in his coat

pocket where it hung on a hook in the station cubby-hole, and blurted out, 'I may have some of that.'

There was a silence then both of his superiors turned round as if seeing him for the first time.

This was not quite how Mulholland had imagined it; he had hoped for a quiet word with his lieutenant, a gentle rap on the knuckles plus unspoken appreciation of his investigative talents, then McLevy apprised of the facts in a manner to let the inspector know that although a breach of etiquette might have occurred, talented youth must be given its head.

'Some of what?' the inspector asked finally.

'Hard evidence.'

The McLevy jaw dropped a considerable distance.

'Eh?'

A smile spread across the saurian features of Roach; this was a rare moment.

'Has the constable been to the well before you, McLevy?' he asked benignly.

'He said nothing to me!' was the indignant retort.

'I couldn't get a word in,' muttered Mulholland.

'Well you have now! What evidence? What are you talking about, man?'

The unhappy constable stood to his feet like a schoolboy in class and related the events of the night before, Stinky D'Oros et al.; at times as regards frilly *peignoirs*, swelling and dilation the detail was somewhat truncated but other than that Mulholland stuck to the facts and the facts stuck to him.

At the end of his recitation there was silence. The inspector's face was like thunder and Roach placed a prudent hand over his long snout of a chin as if deep in thought.

Mulholland had a brief devious moment of hope; was that a forgiving glint in the lieutenant's's eye? Had Roach come down on the side of young love?

Inspector McLevy came down differently.

'You withheld evidence!' was his accusation.

'More like delayed, sir.'

'Withheld!! From your superior officer.'

'Most improper,' agreed Roach urbanely. 'I only know of one other man who would do that.'

This snide observation brought McLevy's head whipping round.

'In my case it is strategic,' he allowed. 'Constable Mulholland has permitted his personal affairs to hinder the investigation of a case. We have lost valuable time, and time is always of the essence.'

'It was the previous night only,' ventured Mulholland.

'Of the essence!'

This roar brought the exchange to an end and though McLevy was often guilty of such behaviour as regards his lieutenant, one of the prime reasons was Roach inevitably dragged his feet, scratched around for the rule book, pored over evidence as if it were a tricky putt on a treacherous green, and took forever in granting permission to accomplish what could be effected in one hour of unsupervised action.

Every investigation had its own rhythm, like a symphony, and there was room for only one conductor.

Second fiddles must remain so.

It was too late now to say whether the inspector would have handled events differently; Mulholland had denied him the choice.

So though there was an egoic element to the outrage experienced as regards his subordinate's sleekit, behind the back, round the corner, slimy, ungrateful, underhand, despicable, belly-crawling activities, McLevy also had a sense of genuine betrayal.

He fixed his constable with a cold eye and Mulholland hung his head in apparent shame.

But the young man was calculating the odds. He might yet survive; if nothing untoward transpired, the wrath of the inspector would hopefully pass, especially if they topped and tailed Oliver Garvie.

Of more concern was an official reprimand from his

lieutenant, though McLevy collected them like a child did daisies in the spring. That would go on record and affect the constable's hopes of promotion.

Roach said nothing.

McLevy seethed.

Mulholland calculated.

The silence stretched like a yawning tiger and three little taps upon the already open door signalled the arrival of fate in the form of Constable Ballantyne, the white half of his face peering in, shoulders hunched.

'Come in Ballantyne,' said Roach wearily. 'Join the throng. Perhaps we may all find partners and dance the quadrille.'

This passed the constable by; he had two left feet to go with the other hazards inflicted by a bountiful nature.

Also he had other things on his mind, the weather had turned unexpectedly mild and the station was crawling with bluebottles.

He fixed his eyes earnestly upon McLevy; the inspector, unlike Ballantyne, had no liking for flies and had been known to wreak havoc with a rolled-up *Leith Herald*.

'A report jist in, sir,' he announced gravely. 'The sergeant has it at the desk. He wishes your presence.'

McLevy nodded curtly, Ballantyne departed and before the inspector followed he stuck out a stiff finger at the still figure of his constable.

'Don't you go anywhere Mulholland, I haven't finished with you yet.'

The door slammed behind him. Roach shook his head.

'You've been a fool, constable.'

'I meant well, sir.'

'The road to hell is paved with such intentions,' the lieutenant remarked with some asperity.

Roach stood abruptly and flexed his cramped limbs; he seemed to have been sitting at that desk for an eternity and to alleviate the tightness began to practise golf shots, narrowing his eyes as the imaginary balls split the fairway time and time again.

It is always thus with golfers, the real world being such an unwelcome intrusion into the great game.

With a regretful sigh, Roach returned to actuality. He had still to inform the constable about his failed suit, but there was no need to pile it on here.

The lieutenant adopted a formal tone.

'Let us hope whatever is the case with Garvie, that Mister Forbes may yet provide an innocent explanation and, in that case, there is no harm done. I see no need for official reprimand.'

Mulholland's heart skipped a beat; had Cupid abandoned that voluptuous goddess with the wispy bits and returned to his rightful owner?

For what could stand in the way of young love?

The door opened and McLevy came back in without knocking. He ignored Roach's reproving look as regards protocol flouted, took a deep breath and spoke grimly, no trace of satisfaction in his delivery.

'Robert Forbes has hanged himself. In his study. The body was found by his daughter.'

'Oh dear,' said Roach.

Mulholland let out a low moan in the terrible silence.

Love is the very devil.

'I have sent men to Oliver Garvie's home and offices,' continued the inspector. 'But I doubt our bird will have flown. I was correct. Time *was* of the essence.'

The constable brought his head up to meet the merciless gaze of his inspector.

'There was a measure of arrogance in what you did, Mulholland,' pronounced McLevy in a detached tone that made his words all the more lethal. 'The Scots have a name for someone who rises in arrogance and falls flat on his face.'

Outside in the station, Ballantyne heard the murmur of voices behind the lieutenant's door and wondered somewhat wistfully if he would ever, one day, be admitted to that inner sanctum. Rescuing bluebottles could take a man only so far and no further.

'A puddock,' said McLevy flatly. 'You have made a puddock of yourself.'

'Unfortunately so,' agreed Roach. 'Puddock is the word.'

Scylla and Charybdis were the monstrous guards of the Straits of Messina in ancient times who crushed many an unwary ship between them. Avoid the one and you were impaled upon the other.

Thus wrecked between the condemnation of his betters, Martin Mulholland wished in vain for calm seas and a soft wind. What he received instead was a cannonball amidships.

'Ah well,' remarked a suddenly cheerful McLevy. 'We'd better repair to the scene of the crime, constable.'

'Crime?' came a cry from the shipwreck.

'Suicide is against the law.'

The thought of having to face the accusing eyes of his beloved Emily once it became revealed that his visit had been, at the very least, a contributory factor in her father's demise, sent Mulholland into a guilt-ridden panic.

'Oh, no – I can't – I can't go – sir.'

'Part of the job,' was the stolid response.

'Have pity, sir,' the constable almost wailed, out of the blue coming over very Irish. 'Pity is a grand thing.'

'What's the problem that needs this pity?' grunted McLevy, who was anxious to be on his way; the insurance adjuster was not a game bird that would improve the longer he hung there and the man could not be lowered till a senior investigating officer was on the scene.

'How can I face my Emily? How can I look her in the eyes?'

'Love conquers all,' was the unsympathetic reply. 'Now get your helmet and your cape.'

Mulholland looked to his lieutenant who nodded in bleak concordance with his inspector.

The young man realised for the first time that these two men, so far apart in temperament, shared the same unremitting attitude towards the shorn lamb.

Pity was in short supply.

And so, also realising that if he refused to perform his duty he might as well walk out of the station and kiss the Leith police goodbye, Mulholland screwed up his eyes an instant, opened them again, and then strode out to find his uniform and face the eventual music.

Roach and McLevy looked at each other; suicide was always such a messy business.

'It'll be the making of him,' the inspector remarked somewhat obscurely.

In response, Roach moved to take his heavy frock coat from a stand in the corner.

'I shall come as well,' he announced. 'I feel part way responsible for this débâcle in any case.'

'You and Mister Cupid,' said McLevy.

Roach refused to rise to the bait; the inspector obviously knew that he had acted as love's emissary but he would not grant him the satisfaction of the gory details.

'Perhaps,' he remarked dryly, 'I can be of comfort to the young lady, whilst you and Mulholland examine fibres on the carpet, McLevy.'

'A fair division of labour,' was the equally dry response.

As Roach shrugged into the immaculate frock coat and plucked down a tall hat of imposing proportions, something that looked like the ghost of Mulholland appeared in the doorway.

'Shall we gentlemen?' said Roach.

The other two nodded and off they went to meet the hanging man.

31

Anything awful makes me laugh.

CHARLES LAMB, *Letter to Robert Southey*

The household of Forbes had been in chaos, Emily howling and shrieking like a lost soul while two maiden aunts, Jessie and Jemima, who had turned up as if from nowhere, did their level best to console her.

The maid was also in hysterics; she had turned up late for work that morning and seemed somehow to blame herself.

The cook was wailing in the kitchen where the pulley hung askew over the kitchen table and the very walls reverberated with female lamentation.

While Roach dealt with all this below, McLevy looked up at the bare feet of Robert Forbes; for some reason the adjuster had removed his socks and shoes before tying a rope around the head of the stag mounted securely upon his study wall.

The man had subsequently tied the other end round his neck, stood on a chair perched high upon his desk, and then kicked off into oblivion.

A shaken Mulholland who had been sent downstairs to assist his lieutenant and come shooting back some moments later as if pursued by Alecto the implacable Fury, was engaged with one other constable in untying the knots from the neck of the monarch of the glen and lowering the body to where three other men waited to receive the altered form of the insurance adjuster.

This was accomplished and the corpse laid inside the evidence sheet to be wrapped up and removed to the cold room at the station for examination.

McLevy noted that, from appearances, the man had used the pulley rope from the kitchen but the weather was decent enough they could dry the linen outside.

He almost shared that comforting thought with Mulholland

who, through gritted teeth, was pulling the sheet over the waxy contorted features of his once-upon-a-time future father-in-law, but decided against it.

The dead man's socks and shoes had been carefully laid out on a newspaper on the floor at the side of the desk. The local *Herald* with a headline that read, 'Leith will lead the world!' The print below was too cramped for McLevy to make out in what exactly Leith took up the vanguard position.

Suicides perhaps . . .

The corpse's face had now disappeared from view, a few bumps in the sheet indicating where a life had dwelt.

But what circumstances had driven Robert Forbes to such a pass? To end his own existence? To lie and deceive? To betray his very calling? All of this was so much against the proven character of the adjuster.

As he pondered these matters, McLevy found himself at the man's bureau, rifling through the contents therein.

Possibly this was slightly against the rules but since the nearest member of the family present was dead as a doornail, the inspector assumed tacit permission and delved.

And as he pulled down the corrugated wooden screen that concealed the multitude of narrow drawers making up the top half of the imposing oak varnished desk, he found, prominent and propped up inside, a long white envelope with the name, JAMES MCLEVY, inscribed on the front.

He opened and read.

Everything began to become clear.

There's no fool like an old fool.

Roach entered through the open door of the study and cast a wary glance at Mulholland where he was helping to manoeuvre the body into a position so that it could be lifted up and taken downstairs to be loaded discreetly into the carry waggon and thence to the station.

The lieutenant crossed over towards McLevy who seemed absorbed in a piece of paper, which he held in hand, and spoke quietly in his inspector's ear.

'I have solved part of the mystery,' he announced.

'Uhuh?' muttered McLevy, scratching at his nose.

'Indeed. Emily noticed that her father this very morning was withdrawn and distraught. When asked the reason, he remarked that it was a great pity the constable could not change his mind.'

'Uhuh?' was the unhelpful response.

'He would say no more about the matter and gave her some money to go shopping,' Roach continued. 'Emily loves to shop.'

'So I have read,' was McLevy's obscure rejoinder but the lieutenant paid no heed and ploughed on.

'Like most women she takes all day to perform that function. That is what Robert Forbes calculated, but he calculated wrongly.'

Roach left these words hanging in the air for he was rather proud of the way he had handled the investigation and waited for his inspector to ask the expected question, but as, at last, McLevy looked up from the piece of paper, his eyes were full of suppressed rage.

'What have we here?' Roach inquired, taking note of the anger and hoping he wasn't going to witness another blast of emotion.

When Mulholland had entered upon the scene downstairs, Emily, who had developed an irrational but intense loathing for the constable as being the bringer of her father's death, had launched, aided by the spinster sisters who chimed in like some Greek Chorus, a vehement almost frenzied attack upon the young man.

Roach had ordered him immediately from the room but the constable was shaken to the core as men often are when women let rip, and though he seemed to be holding himself together at the moment would have probably realised that romance had been somewhat nipped in the bud.

The lieutenant had been a bit shaken himself; tears often came to his wife's eyes over dead sparrows and the like, but full-blown female grief left a man helpless.

All he could do was murmur condolences and leave spinsters, Emily, maid and cook to their collective sorrow.

You cannot bring back the dead; Orpheus had made the best effort so far, but then unfortunately looked back.

Roach certainly did not intend to make the same mistake and, with some sense of relief at misery being in the lower reaches and him on high, regarded the still figure of McLevy who held what Roach now discerned as a letter of sorts in his hand.

'What have we here?' repeated the lieutenant.

'The whole story,' was McLevy's bitter response. 'And what a sad, sorry business it is.'

Roach took the letter and read Robert Forbes' somewhat spidery writing, though that may have been caused by an inner anguish.

James . . . God forgive me for what I am about to do. I know, for certain, that you will not. I have betrayed everything I hold dear in my life, my reputation above all.

In my loneliness, after the death of my wife, I took to visiting a house of ill repute. Not often, but enough. I formed an attachment to one of the young women, Rachel Bryden by name, and was sufficiently foolish to write her some letters of deep affection.

Oliver Garvie came to me and informed me that the girl was going to make the letters public by selling them to the newspapers. They would be my ruin and hold me up to the most savage ridicule.

He could prevent it but in return he must request a small favour. Small! Only this one time and never again. He assured me that the day the insurance money appeared in his account, I would have the letters in my hand.

It was out and out blackmail and to my eternal shame, but for the sake of my daughter, I accepted the bargain.

There's nae foule like an auld foule.

After the constable's visit, I realised that there was no escaping the consequence of my actions and even if Garvie wanted to try to brazen it out, I was finished with lies.

And, so I am.

This is my confession. But I cannot thole the shame of a public prosecution. I have sent Emily out shopping. She loves shopping.

The maid will discover my body. God forgive me.

By the time Emily returns, everything will be tidied up and she will be at least spared the sight of me.

This by my own hand,

Robert Forbes.

Lieutenant Roach glanced over to where the luckless Mulholland sat with the other constables to await orders, a withdrawn disconsolate figure.

A quote from Burns came into his mind.

'The best laid schemes of mice and men, gang aft agley,' he muttered. 'The maid overslept and was late to arrive. Emily came back unexpectedly. Forgotten her purse. On the hall table she found a note directing the maid to go to the police, bring them back, and convey them to the study. It conveyed her instead. A sorry business indeed.'

'I can find little pity in my heart.'

McLevy's face was like stone and Roach was moved to plead the adjuster's case.

'The shame, McLevy. It broke the man.'

A mild remark which provoked its opposite as McLevy erupted into an expression of the anger he felt within; he had once witnessed another suicide as a small boy looking down at a woman who had sliced her throat like an apple and bled regardless of the horror she had left behind.

He, the son.

She, the mother.

His inheritance.

'Shame?' he almost snarled. 'Who cares for shame? He could have stood up, admitted guilt, taken his punishment – who knows what friends may have rallied round?'

Roach was stung by the broadside and answered back.

'Would you?'

McLevy fell silent and the lieutenant warmed to his theme.

'Would even his own daughter?'

'She never got the chance,' was the sombre response. 'All

she saw were her father's bare feet swinging in the air, toenails and all.'

Both men were genuinely exercised now, each seeing something of the other's point of view but driven by an ethos that was a cornerstone in the way they saw life.

'Then what should he have done?' Roach asked. 'How could he break such dreadful tidings?'

'Sat with her, told her the truth, begged her forgiveness,' McLevy responded. 'If she really loved him as a daughter, she would have been his support.'

'I somehow doubt it,' the lieutenant muttered.

'She never got the chance one way or the other,' the inspector growled. 'Her birthright was sacrificed on the altar of his respectability. That is *truly* shameful.'

While this exchange progressed, Constable Ballantyne had made a surprise appearance at the study door and signalled Mulholland out.

He had been sent from the station to break some bad news to his inspector but had enough sense to know that a body blames the messenger.

Ballantyne had long ago distinguished the constable as being the link between lower and higher, much the same as Mercury would wing up from earth to Olympus, and so, not realising Mulholland's agonised personal connection to the affair, delivered the intelligence such as it was, and returned to his bluebottles.

This, indeed, was the final straw for Mulholland, and, the colour fled from his rosy cheeks, he came back to inform his superiors that Oliver Garvie had unfortunately flown the coop.

His offices were empty, his house was empty save for the old retainer, and though a search would be mounted in the immediate area and then throughout Leith, he, Martin Mulholland, was not hopeful of its success.

Neither was McLevy or Roach.

It was the last brush stroke in a very black picture.

The whole room went still as if Jack Frost had laid his icy

fingers upon the company and frozen them to the spot.

Then McLevy sparked into action; the state of stasis was not one of his favourites and anything is better than contemplation of the void.

He sent the stricken Mulholland plus two other constables in the direction of an address in McDonald Road and instructed them to gain entrance by hook or by crook; that accomplished they were to investigate a room at the back of the house where a man of Garvie's description would have been renting and might be found.

The inspector was not optimistic about the finding part but who knows?

In any case, McLevy had quite another venue in mind. He doubted he would catch the man there either but he might uncover a relevant fact or two.

And play merry hell.

The rest of the crew he dispatched with the body of Forbes to the carry waggon and thence the station.

Now, the room was empty save for himself, Roach and the stag's head.

The lieutenant picked up a picture frame from a small table beside the desk and regarded the depiction of the wife of Robert Forbes.

He had met the woman a few times at official functions and exchanged some polite words such as one does. She had seemed a decent sober soul, quite properly dedicated to her husband and taking great pride in his achievements.

What would she think now?

It often perturbed Roach, the idea in some quarters that those in heaven were still able to witness the exploits of those left behind on earth.

If so, it must put quite a damper on the paradisiacal bliss.

And where would Robert Forbes end up?

The word suicide did not even occur in the bible but it was a safe bet that God the Creator who giveth and taketh away, would frown upon his function being pre-empted.

Though if he knew and performed all things, did that not make Him a part of this unfortunate event?

The pulley rope, the stag's head and the bare feet?

All gifts from God.

McLevy had been standing by in silence while Roach was struggling with these unfamiliar notions; the inspector was deliberating on his own behalf and, not for the first time, was caught between the fierce impetus of investigation and the disquiet of what it might uncover.

So be it, however. No mercy.

Roach voiced a thought that had never been far away from his mind since the news had been broken at the station.

'For the moment,' he said quietly, 'there is no need to make this public.'

'Not until Oliver Garvie is caught,' came the obdurate response. 'But I will lay my hands upon him.'

McLevy could see which way the wind was blowing but it wasn't going to whisk anything under the carpet.

Roach changed the subject.

'This girl, Rachel Bryden, would she be one of the magpies of the Just Land?'

'I believe it may be so,' said McLevy.

'Then your friend Jean Brash comes into the picture?'

'I believe she may.'

Roach had long considered that his inspector's relationship with the bawdy-hoose keeper would one day see McLevy compromised beyond his control.

However he contented himself with a sly dig.

'A woman of influence, eh?'

For a moment the inspector's mind flashed back to a lighted window beneath which he sat like Humpty Dumpty while passion raged above.

'Uhuh,' replied McLevy with a hard glint in his eye, 'but as regards that influence, it is a question of how far and how deep it goes.'

Roach nodded, and for a moment the two men stood in the

silence of the room, which was finally broken by another muffled howl of grief from the lower reaches.

'I take it,' said McLevy, who had noticed the shaken state of Mulholland's earlier return, 'that love has not conquered all?'

'I am afraid not,' was the sober reply. 'In fact I fear that it may have gone up the chimney.'

They both looked in the air towards the stag but it was just another victim.

32

Mine is the most plotting heart in the world.

SAMUEL RICHARDSON, *Clarissa*

If Hannah Semple had been conscious, she would have derived a deal of bleak amusement over the undignified squabble in progress next door.

But the old woman lay in Jean Brash's boudoir in the midst of the peach-coloured chiffon and gauze reflecting back and forth from the mirrors, like a character in a fairy tale waiting for the kiss of a prince to jolt her into life.

She was flat on her back, not an unknown position, her hands clasped together over the sheets.

Hannah had not stirred since the giant Angus had lain her gently down on the bed the previous night.

The doctor had come and gone, diagnosed concussion from a blow to the back of the head, cleaned then dressed the wound and prescribed a strong opium-based medication. Then the man of medicine had left, advising rest, prayer and patience.

And so Hannah rested, her breath shallow but regular; unlike the rammy going on in the next room.

Jean Brash and James McLevy; hammer and tongs.

He had arrived with blood in his eyes, been taken aback to

witness the recumbent Hannah, expressed brief but sincere enough sympathy and then asked bluntly what had transpired.

It was to his mind suspicious happenstance that Hannah had been struck to the ground the night before Robert Forbes was about to launch himself off into the air.

One up, one down.

Jean, riven with guilt about her part in Hannah's bad fortune, answered truthfully enough that she did not know.

He then queried the whereabouts of Rachel Bryden.

Jean flinched; could he already have cognition of her humiliating loss of face and property?

She waited for him to drop a further remark to indicate such but he did not; merely stared at her through slate-grey unfriendly eyes.

Again she answered truthfully, she could not help. The girl had disappeared.

What Jean did not add, however, was that her people were searching the nooks and crannies of Edinburgh to track down Rachel Bryden and, once found, there would be hard questions as regards certain missing valuables.

McLevy sensed that she was hiding something and it fuelled his own dark doubts.

He went for the kill, stuck his face into Jean's, related the facts of the insurance swindle, the death of Robert Forbes, blackmail originating from the Just Land, and after naming Rachel's part in it all, hammered her with the name of Oliver Garvie.

For Jean the last was like a kick in the stomach.

Made worse when McLevy more or less accused her of being part, if not author, of this conspiracy.

Thus the rammy began.

'What do I know of Oliver Garvie?' she lashed out.

'Ye were his fancy woman,' was the brusque response.

'Who says?'

'I do.'

'How so?'

McLevy had no wish to bring Humpty Dumpty astride a damp wall into the equation.

'Garvie was put under observation after the warehouse fire; a woman of your description was seen entering his lodgings out of a carriage also identified.'

'From the horses no doubt?'

'From the coachman, Angus Dalrymple.'

'A social visit,' was the response.

'That's a bare-faced lie.' McLevy was hot and bothered; this was getting near the knuckle.

'Says who?'

'Ye were seen from the back window in flagrante!' he bawled, a flush creeping up the back of his neck.

'Flagrante?'

'On the verge of it!'

'Who did all this seeing?' she bawled back, equally embarrassed.

Humpty Dumpty was unavoidably revealed.

'I did,' said Inspector James McLevy.

Jean's mouth fell open and, for a moment she resembled a virgin nymph disturbed at her morning ablutions.

'Ye – ye – dirty old beggar,' she finally gasped.

'I performed my duty,' was the stern rejoinder.

McLevy was certain that he had nothing more than observation and incipient piles on his mind the night in question, pure as a newborn lamb.

However, they were both deeply discomfited as if coming upon each other naked in a biblical situation.

Adam and Eve.

The side room, into which Jean had ushered McLevy, to spare the comatose Hannah from his intrusive presence, had a small dressing table with a three-sided mirror, below which on a smooth white marble surface lay a dainty confection of colognes, sprays and various unguents.

There was another door which no doubt led to a room

where other feminine mysteries were lurking but upon being tugged into this adjoining one, McLevy, after a swift glance round, thanked his lucky stars there was not a commode in sight.

You never can tell.

The inspector was squeamish about matters feminine latrinal; the only regular woman in his life, Bathsheba the cat, did her business on the slates, which suited him fine.

But now he had other things on his mind.

'Never mind all that,' he accused. 'Were you in cahoots with Oliver Garvie, partners in all things?'

'Go to hell, I was not!'

'But you would confirm that Robert Forbes was a client of the Just Land?'

'He had his requirements.'

'And his chosen magpie was Rachel Bryden?'

Jean sniffed and made no answer. McLevy probed further.

'Whit about this Rachel Bryden? She worked here, you must have known the goings on, eh?'

'That bloody girl, I'll wring her neck.'

'How so?'

'She stole from me!'

Jean had been hugging this bitter grievance to her bosom since she made discovery, not able to confide in anyone save Hannah who was unable to respond and Mistress Brash could not now restrain her anger any longer. Bad enough to lose her property without being roped into a blackmailing ring.

'All my jewels, the skinnymalinkie whoor!'

This childlike but heartfelt insult caused McLevy to jerk his head back a little.

'How does that occur?'

Jean caught sight of herself in the dressing table mirror. She had waited up all night by Hannah's bedside, and at least managed to change her clothes and underthings, but the plain grey gown she had thrown on made her appear to be a mortuary attendant.

She had also scrubbed her face, put nothing back on and my God, to her unblinking eyes, she looked her years and many more this November morning.

'It must have been her,' she muttered. 'Rachel. Before she left. All my jewels, my beautiful pearls. Robbed.'

One thing a woman will rarely lie about is the state of her missing jewellery.

McLevy came to the conclusion that Jean might well be innocent of the conspiracy, though it was still possible that she had taken a part and then been double dealt when the plan fell to pieces.

So he fished further in deep waters.

'All this took place under your nose, eh?'

'Right under the very nostril,' was her grim reply.

'How was that possible?'

Was there cruel pleasure in this pursuit? Jealousy getting its own back for a scene in a lighted window?

'That's not like you Jean, the mistress of the Just Land twisted and turned like a fool.'

'I was in love.'

This flat statement silenced the inspector for a moment and Jean, who had spoken to herself as much as to him, chewed a bitter cud, her thoughts lining up to torture their creator.

All this under her nose right enough, betrayed by her own paramour, the two of them laughing at her, ardent lovers themselves no doubt, sporting in the bed, laughing at her.

The older woman.

Twisted and turned. Humiliated.

She became aware of other laughter, the source of which was James McLevy.

'Oh dear,' he spluttered. 'Oh dearie me. Oh dearie, dearie me.'

Now truth to tell, though there may have been an element of malicious enjoyment in this reaction, it was also the product of contradictory emotions. Something had been stirred by these four simple words.

I was in love.

All his life McLevy had defended himself against madness and was not the passion of love a version of that?

Or madness an offshoot of love?

Whatever. In common with most men when faced with feelings that conflict like two boxers in the ring, he took refuge in laughter.

The splutter became a guffaw.

'But you're a bawdy-hoose keeper, love is what you buy and sell. That's your stock in trade!'

'*Lust* is my stock in trade,' she answered, angered and rubbed raw by his apparent hilarity.

'What's the difference?'

'Nothing you could recognise,' she replied scathingly. 'The only love you possess is for yourself and justice.'

McLevy's eyes glistened with merriment; it was an aggravating sight.

'Aye, you might well be correct there. Oh, dearie me.'

Of course incidental to all this was the fact that the inspector had now accepted that Jean was not part of the blackmailing plot.

But she did not feel in the least grateful at this deliverance and came at him savagely, claws unsheathed.

'What woman would want you anyway? She'd have to be desperate and half blind.'

'Only half?'

This caustic observation came from neither but the voice was unmistakable.

Hannah Semple stood in the doorway, hands clasped around the knob to steady her. She was arrayed in one of Jean's nightgowns; big Annie Drummond and the mistress having eased her out of the previous night's damp and dirty clothes into something less soiled.

Hannah also caught sight of herself in the mirror; the nightgown was perhaps more suited for Sleeping Beauty rather than her stocky frame.

'My God,' she said. 'Mutton dressed as lamb.'

'Hannah,' said Jean, all anger forgotten as relief flooded through her very being. 'You've come to life.'

'You two would waken the dead,' replied the old woman with spirit, but then her hand slipped from the doorknob and she fell towards them to be caught up in both their arms.

It was a considerable weight borne mostly by the inspector who was scrabbling for purchase on the smooth slippery material of the nightgown.

'Keep your hands tae yourself, McLevy,' she informed him hoarsely. 'I'm a clean-living girl.'

Jean laughed and she hugged the old woman fiercely to her in spite of Hannah's squawks of protest.

McLevy somehow got caught up in all this and wondered how he always ended up in these straits.

Like three drunks on a Saturday night, they staggered back into the other room and laid the old woman to rest once more upon the bed.

Other than the one jaundiced glance towards McLevy, Hannah's attention had been completely fixed upon Jean who was busy pulling up the sheets to cover the old woman.

'I let ye down, mistress,' she murmured.

Jean shook her head.

'More like the other way round,' she replied softly.

'It was the fault of both,' McLevy butted in, anxious to get on with establishing facts. 'What happened, Hannah?'

Pausing for breath every so often Hannah Semple told the story, as far she knew it, lips twisting wryly towards the conclusion.

'I should have cut her throat the first time she was hanging out the washing. That was my mistake.'

'We'll make it up to you,' remarked Jean sweetly.

'The sleekit bitch. I had her in front of me, but I didnae look behind.'

McLevy and Jean exchanged glances: there could be no doubt as to the hidden assailant's identity.

'Not very gentlemanly,' said the inspector.

'If I get to him before you,' Jean responded with a cold light in her green eyes, 'Oliver Garvie will be a shadow of his former self.'

'He will come to the arms of justice,' said McLevy.

The previous animosity between them began to bubble to the surface and Hannah's eyes glazed over.

'Whit's the matter wi' you two now?' she mumbled. 'Worse than a pair of weans.'

Jean quietened the old woman down, tucked her in and promised to tell her the whole story in all its sordid detail at a later opportunity. As she and McLevy made for the door, and he about to open it for her in a parody of politesse, Hannah called from the bed.

'I've been having some gey queer dreams, mistress.'

'That would be the opium,' Jean replied.

'Opium?' came the muffled retort. 'I've aye fancied that stuff. Whit a way tae get there though.'

As the door closed, Hannah was cackling softly under the covers.

'Opium . . . Well, well. Fancy that now.'

And drifted off into a dream where the Just Land was invaded by white unicorns crashing their hooves upon the stairs and sticking their heads out from every window.

Beyond the door McLevy and Jean witnessed big Annie Drummond bidding an affectionate goodbye below to her wee shepherd, the man's fiddle tucked neatly under his arm, blue eyes agleam with post-coital delight.

Annie was accustomed to her vast form as a barrier to acts of passion but the wee fellow had leapt all over it like a mountain goat.

For a good part of the night. A giddy goat.

The Jew's harp man had long since departed, his owner calling him to heel like a farm dog but the shepherd's master was a kind soul and had left his man with these wise words.

'Enjoy yerself Douglas. It's a lang winter wi' naethin but the sheep for solace.'

It had been, unlike the fate of many others that night, the best time of the shepherd's life.

He closed the door after one tender kiss from Annie, her plump hands framing his face, and as he marched away up the gravel path towards the iron gates, he unslung his fiddle and played a jaunty air; the notes winging their way up into the sky above to give the larks some competition.

Annie Drummond crossed back and disappeared into the main salon where a pile of cream cakes was waiting.

Love's appetite.

James McLevy sang words to the faint tune from the vanishing shepherd.

> 'And wasna he a roguie, a roguie, a roguie.
> And wasna he a roguie, the piper o' Dundee.'

Jean Brash looked at him and said nothing.

'It's a Jacobite air,' he remarked.

'I know what it is,' she replied, her eyes steady on his face.

He jerked his head in the direction of the departed fiddler.

'You're taking in all sorts these days.'

Again she said nothing.

The relationship that existed between them was one that dare not speak its name in case it got arrested, but the ground had shifted underneath their feet and now there was enough unsaid between them to fill a literary volume.

'I don't suppose a modicum of coffee is at hand?'

This remark, aimed at getting back to safe terrain, met with a curt rejoinder.

'This is a bawdy-hoose, not a coffee shop.'

That was that, then.

McLevy nodded acceptance and walked off down the winding staircase but halfway down turned back to address her.

'How did you come across him anyway? Oliver Garvie. Was he a frequenter of your wee nymphs?'

'I met him at a garden exhibition.'

'Oh aye. Ye like flowers.'

He could have departed there and then. She could have remained silent. But neither could leave it be.

'Was it daffodils?' he asked.

'Roses,' she answered.

'And was he an expert?'

Jean's mind flashed back to the moment in the garden when she had been inhaling the delicate fragrance of a yellow rose when Garvie had appeared beside her.

She had been struck at first by his absolute confidence in the physical self; he had made no attempt to engage her by the usual channels of flirtation or impress her with his importance or wealth, merely talked about the flowers with knowledge and appreciation.

She responded like a lady of quality but all the time she was aware of how easily he lived in his skin. Like an animal.

Almost diffidently he had suggested tea in the pavilion and it had all led on from there.

Of course he had been primed by Rachel Bryden to know her tastes and predilections and she had been seduced like a fool. Played like a fish. A foolish stupid fish.

And she should have remembered that the yellow rose is a symbol of infidelity.

Yes, he was an expert. An expert in many things.

Jean became aware that the inspector was waiting for an audible response, a strange, oddly vulnerable look upon his face.

'He appeared to be,' she said finally.

For a moment McLevy blinked like a disappointed child and opened his mouth as if to say something, but then he sniffed as if something had become lodged in one of his nasal passages, hauled out a large white handkerchief and blew noisily upon the unsuspecting square of cloth.

Jean closed her eyes; she recognised signs of the man going into one of his uncouth phases.

The inspector peered into the hankie with some interest, glanced up as if suddenly remembering that she was still present and adopted pompous delivery.

'If by any lucky accident that web of informers and street keelies that you have in your employ for matters nefarious, happen to chance upon Oliver Garvie and Rachel Bryden before the forces of law and order, you will deliver these miscreants into my hands.'

'I will do what I see fit,' was the retort.

This stung McLevy into further raising his voice like Moses on the mountain.

'You will do what I tell you Jean Brash, the law is above all things.'

'Then the law can find them.'

'Forget your foolish pride, you're not the first woman to make an idiot of herself over a younger man.'

If Jean had possessed something close to hand she would have hurled it into his great pudding of a face.

'Well if I ever take another lover, I hope not to find you keeking in through the curtains!'

This remark, so below the belt in implication and inaccuracy, brought a gasp of indignation from the target.

'You flatter yourself that I give a damn about what you do with a body nurtured on the common wages of sin!'

'A lot of words for such a lack of interest.'

McLevy jammed the bowler on his head and clattered down the stairs, hurling a backward stricture over his shoulder.

'If you interfere in the due process of justice then I will bring the law down on you like the Hand of God!'

Such was his impetus off the bottom of the stairs that he skidded on the polished floorboards of the hall, almost crashing into Francine the Frenchwoman as she emerged from the cellar steps to find out the cause of this commotion. Her sinewy arm shot out, fingers splayed like talons to catch him before he fell.

'Careful M'sieu Inspecteur,' she said quietly, her face serious and intent. 'At your time of life, pain is to be avoided unless paid for and supervised.'

McLevy drew himself up with dignity, marched to the door

and turned round to deliver a final caution to Jean who stood at the top of the stairs glaring down at him.

'I warn you Jean Brash, cross me in this affair and I will close your bawdy-hoose down.'

'Ye havenae got the power,' Jean asserted, 'half the city council take their pleasure here.'

The door slammed in answer and he was gone.

Francine shrugged up at her mistress and disappeared back down into the cellar. The General Synod was due to gather in the city soon, so she and Lily, now restored in harmony, were due a busy time of it. Churchmen, unlike farmers, enjoyed the scourge of sin and punishment.

Jean found herself alone, an isolated figure in a plain grey gown.

For a moment she felt once more the sharp knife of humiliation twisting in her gut.

Oliver Garvie and Rachel Bryden.

They had robbed and deceived her, struck Hannah Semple to the ground. They had taken her beautiful black pearls that she loved above all things.

If she got to them first, they'd never see the light of day.

33

Full fathom five thy father lies;
Of his bones are coral made:
Those are pearls that were his eyes:
Nothing of him that doth fade,
But doth suffer a sea-change
Into something rich and strange.

WILLIAM SHAKESPEARE, *The Tempest*

Leith, 29 December 1879

The Tay Bridge had been miraculously translated back to its former glory. The High Girders were no longer snapped off like matchsticks and stood proudly against the skyline; the men, women and children so dismally drowned, had been sucked back out of the water and carefully returned into place in their carriages as a mother would tuck her child safely in the bed at night.

The train itself, a cheerful puff of smoke from its stack signalling a busy stoker, was in position on the rails high above a calm river, the sky above almost cloudless and the whole aspect depicted a harmony between nature and the machinery of men.

All was peace and stillness.

It was a photograph however, and Alan Telfer looked from it to the baleful figure of James McLevy.

The secretary had answered a loud midnight knock upon the door in the vain hope that it was Sir Thomas Bouch returned from Dundee to relate that the whole thing had been grossly exaggerated, there was no disaster, no deaths, and so everything could return to normal and once more they might incline their heads over the sacred drawings.

But Sir Thomas was in the Royal Hotel in Dundee avoiding the other occupants, mostly comprising the English and Scottish journalists who were at this moment filing telegraph reports to their own papers and the world press, informing them that the first body had been found.

A woman dressed in black, her face white and the skirts floating round her as if she was some sort of sea creature, a jellyfish perhaps.

The name was not yet known but a mussel-dredger had discovered her sliding on her back between two sandbanks in the water.

He had only a long hook to pull her into his rowing boat and, despite being a man who was hardened by the cruel ways of the sea, sobbed and cursed like a madman as he hauled the sodden corpse aboard.

She was the first of sixty eventually found. Another fifteen were never recovered, only the fish knew their whereabouts.

Therefore when the secretary, who had remained behind to hold the fort to deal with the expected deluge of inquiries, opened the street door, it was James McLevy he beheld.

Like a spectre on the doorstep . . . risen from the deep.

The man had pushed silently past and made directly for the study and Telfer had no option but to follow up the stairs and carefully close the study door behind them – the wife of Sir Thomas was also in the house and he had no wish for her to stick her pointy nose into this; since the death of the old servant she had taken up camp in the place and when the news had arrived, had offered to accompany Sir Thomas to Dundee. But the great man had shaken his head; she was too fragile for such affairs.

This refusal had delighted Telfer; the woman could retire to her quarters and sew her eyelids together as far as he was concerned.

He was trusted to hold the fort. Above all people.

A single draughtsman's lamp illuminated the sloping desk, where the drawings were tidily assembled, and reflected as far as the standing McLevy, giving his features a sinister cast like a villain in the footlights.

He had looked at Alan Telfer and still said nothing. Telfer had looked at the photograph of the bridge.

The silence grew.

McLevy finally spoke.

'You are guilty of present death,' he said.

Telfer attempted to twist his mouth into a dismissive smile but under McLevy's implacable regard it froze as if his lips had been pressed against a block of ice.

'I assume you refer to the terrible accident?' he murmured, edging towards a narrow drawer in the filing cabinet where he kept a small revolver; it was a dainty piece, silver-handled, which he had bought in Paris as a curiosity but it could fire and was already loaded.

'No accident,' replied McLevy. 'It was slaughter.'

Telfer was near enough the drawer now that he could wrench it open and open fire in case the man threatened him physically; the inspector was obviously labouring under some powerful delusion and had a dangerous glint in his eye.

The policeman was unkempt, his clothes bearing traces of mud and dirt, a strange feral stink to him as well, eyes bloodshot, chin unshaven; in fact he resembled a wild man of the woods more than an officer of the law. In truth McLevy was close to the point of utter exhaustion.

Word had spread through the city of Dundee like wildfire and the inspector had found himself swept like a cork in a raging torrent of people who gathered at South Union Street, heaving like an animal, filling the road from side to side; women and children were crying not yet sure of a reason but there would be reason soon enough, the men angry and close to violence because the staff of the Tay Bridge Station had prudently barricaded themselves in, not knowing any more than the crowd but, like them, fearing the worst.

A woman lost hold of her child and the throng swallowed it up; she let out a piercing scream of loss and that was enough to start a scuffling panic, fists and voices raised as the crowd swayed to and fro, out of control.

McLevy scooped up the child, a little girl, under his arm and fought his way through to the mother but as he handed the girl over there was a crash of breaking glass as someone in what was now a boiling mob hurtled up against the main door of the station and burst it inwards.

It was an ugly situation; some of the crowd had arrived to meet relatives and loved ones off the train and though the cry that the bridge was down had split the night and window after window had flickered into life as if the city were aflame, not one person knew what was going on.

The bridge was down but where was the train?

For a moment it looked as if the mob was going to break into the station and run amok, but then another cry went up that a boat was going to leave from the harbour to approach the bridge and, like an ebbing flood, the throng melted away heading down towards the harbour and esplanade.

McLevy did not go with them; he had already been on the esplanade and seen enough.

Some other folk had not followed the main crowd, these were the ones who had relatives and loved ones on the train.

They stared at the station door; its structure had been shattered and a great shard of glass pointed up like a finger of ice.

They stared at that door in the dumb suffering hope that it would open and one after the other the passengers would file through, a little shaken by the experience but with tales to tell of how the engine had shuddered to a halt as the bridge fell behind them, then inched its way along to safety while they sang hymns of redemption to raise their spirits.

One after another . . .

But no one came through the door.

The wind still whistled in the street but quieter now as if satisfied with the night's work and McLevy whose head had drooped wearily where he was propped up against the station wall, found a sticky sweet being pressed into his hand.

He raised his head to see the child that he had rescued earlier, the donor, her mother smiling anxiously at the inspector as if he held the fate of the world in his hands.

The inspector nodded grave thanks to the little girl and popped the sweet in his mouth. Barley sugar, not one of his favourites and in places covered with the fluff and grit from her coat pocket, but it tasted like manna from heaven.

The strong winds had blown the odour of urine from his clothes and skin but he could still sniff it, and the sweet was fine compensation.

The mother looked across at him where he sucked at the offering with evident relish and felt hope rising irrationally in her breast.

Surely a God who provides barley sugar would have mercy on them all?

The woman smiled and indicated the child who was staring at the inspector to make sure he masticated at the proper time because there was a moment when barley sugar needed to be crunched otherwise it was only half a delight.

'She's waiting for her brothers,' the mother remarked, nodding her head in approval. 'My husband as well. He's a schoolmaster. We have friends in Kirkcaldy. Two boys all day, the poor man will be stone tired. Still, all's well that ends well, eh?'

But her eyes were fearful and the child, looking up at McLevy for confirmation, found something else in his face that suddenly provoked a loud wail of abandonment.

She ran back to her mother and buried her head in the woman's skirts.

All at once the barley sugar tasted like ashes in his mouth and he spat it out on to the ground.

The mother gazed across at him, tears in her eyes, but McLevy closed his eyelids at the twist of pain in his guts.

He had nothing to offer save contamination.

The others waiting in the street fell silent; the only sound was of the whistling wind and a child's sobbing.

The station door swung open, but it was only the wind.

No one filled the space.

No one came home.

Somehow the inspector had returned to Edinburgh the next day, sent word to the police station that he was incapacitated by dint of high fever and wandered the streets like one stricken by such, unable to rest or sleep, haunted by the stark images of the previous night, himself like a phantom, without substance as if the very marrow had been sucked from his bones.

He could not eat but managed a series of strong coffees at various stops, which propelled him further on a journey to nowhere.

The ache in his ribs lessened but the pain at the base of his skull, accelerated by the caffeine, intensified till it became like a spike driven upwards through his brain.

The faces he saw on the streets were like grotesques, the features twisted out of shape; sly malignant goblins, witches and warlocks stalked the city, eyes sliding sideways as they passed him by.

A street vendor selling hot chestnuts had, to drum up trade, a small female monkey dressed in a gingham gown chained to a stand beside the brazier.

Children were encouraged to throw nuts at the animal, ostensibly to feed it but it seemed to McLevy that, with evil intent, they hurled the missiles so that the poor beast was struck time and time again.

The monkey chattered its teeth together lethargically, the yellow eyes with strangely slit pupils looking out at a world inescapably alien and terrifying.

It screeched forlornly and the children began to imitate the sound, the high-pitched shrieks drilling into McLevy's head till he could stand it no longer and quit the scene leaving the animal to its simian fate.

What after all could he have done to save the beast?

Bought the monkey?

How could an investigating officer arrive at the scene of a crime with a monkey on his shoulder?

Lieutenant Roach was of crocodile persuasion; he would want to eat the prey. Ballantyne would feed it bluebottles and Mulholland would wish to marry the poor beast. Jean Brash would have it labour in the Just Land. Perhaps Margaret Bouch could care for the lost soul; she would take it to the docks where they might watch the ships together and dream of freedom.

Night had fallen long since as he wandered plagued and haunted, driven to distraction by thoughts that hung before him like flies swarming round the liquid amber eyes of a cow in high summer.

But a cow was not a monkey.

That way madness lies.

As midnight chimed from the nearby church tower of Saint Thomas, James McLevy found himself before a door that seemed familiar.

He knocked upon it and when he saw the face of the man within, he knew why he had come and what his mission was on earth.

Retribution.

Now, in this study with the cold pale eyes of Alan Telfer upon him, McLevy was about to deliver it.

Retribution.

'You cut corners in the making of that bridge,' he said.

'Who tells you that?' Telfer responded calmly though there was the slightest twitch at the side of his mouth.

'Hercules Dunbar.'

Telfer laughed, but there was no humour in his cold intent eyes.

'As I have said before, a drunkard, a thief and a murderer.'

'I shall grant you the first two but not necessarily the last,' the inspector replied.

Telfer's hand rested on top of the filing cabinet and he drummed his fingers upon the surface as if impatient to be done with the tiresome subject of homicide.

'Then who was responsible for Mister Gourlay's demise?'

'That arrives later,' was McLevy's flat retort. 'Let us stick to present death.'

His tongue felt thick and heavy in the mouth, the orifice dry and clogged as if cotton wool had been stuffed inside; the pain was like a knife in his head as he struggled to find the words.

He wondered if eels were feasting on the body of the schoolmaster, the little boys still holding to his hands.

Where to begin, eh?

Retribution.

He also looked at the photo of the Tay Bridge. Never guess it was shot full of holes.

'Did Sir Thomas know?'

'Know?'

'What went on at the Wormit Foundry?'

Alan Telfer's eyes shifted to where a portrait of the great man gazed down like some biblical patriarch, the wings of hair at each side of the dome of his balding head a mischievous contrast to the full solemnity of his beard and moustache. The face as always was impassive, the eyes deep and brooding.

The secretary had to be careful here; the man before him was swaying slightly and closed his eyes as if some inner pain or conflict was pulling him apart, but what and how much did he comprehend?

'Sir Thomas soars above the petty details. His work is on a scale that few may recognise. High above.'

'Like Icarus?'

Alan Telfer chanced a thin smile and McLevy moved to wipe it off the man's face.

'The bridge has fallen. The train. Present death.'

Telfer bowed his head.

251

'A terrible tragedy,' he murmured.

'When I questioned you some time ago about Beaumont's Egg, you affected to know little of such material and yet you delivered regular shipments to the Wormit Foundry.'

The secretary shook his head as if this whole affair was beyond his comprehension and made no answer.

'It was used to cover up faults in the construction of the iron girders, the very girders that fell last night and took innocent people to meet their maker.'

McLevy took a step towards Telfer and the secretary's hand inched open the drawer.

'Men, women and children. Drowned deep. The divers will find some, others may float to the surface and the river will keep some for itself.'

Telfer took in a lungful of air; it was as if this man had brought the very stink of fleshly corruption with him, as if the atmosphere had contracted so that there was nothing left to breathe, a contagion of mist and guilt.

'I cannot be held responsible for an act of God,' he declared.

'God has nothing to do with it!'

For a moment it seemed as if McLevy was about to strike him and Telfer nerved himself to grab for the gun, but the inspector stopped and put his hand up to the back of his neck as if some inhibitor had been clamped in place.

While the man was thus rooted to the spot, Telfer recovered himself somewhat.

'I made many visits to the Wormit Foundry but only to check the progress of the work, inspector. Anyone who says otherwise is advancing a vile defamation.'

McLevy said nothing and Telfer was emboldened enough to elaborate further.

'You have only the word of Hercules Dunbar. A violent man of malicious temperament. How can you accept his word over mine?'

'There will be others,' was the muttered response. 'I have spoken with them. And they told me of other faults. Bolts and ties shaken free and found scattered like dead rats. There will be an official inquiry. The truth will emerge and you will be brought down, Sir Thomas as well.'

'He knows nothing!' Telfer cried.

'He was responsible for that bridge. He designed and built it. It is his creation.'

Alan Telfer saw suddenly a bleak and terrible future staring him in the face. His actions would destroy the only person he had ever loved.

There would be an inquiry. Everything would be revealed. Everything.

And if there was the smallest shred of hope existing, McLevy wrecked it with his next words.

'And now we come to past murder,' he said.

On that nightmare walk through the city, his brain had teemed with strange visions, hallucinations almost, as his unconscious mind put together the events of the night when Archibald Gourlay had died.

And now it was laid out before him like a map of destruction.

'Dunbar saw you that night,' he said hoarsely, swallowing hard to get enough saliva to form the words.

Words are slippery creatures.

Telfer sensed a killer blow and felt like spitting in the man's face. How dare he come here with his slime and dirt, how dare he bring death to the Lords of Creation?

'In the bed together,' McLevy continued. 'You were both asleep, you cradling Sir Thomas in your arms.'

The secretary opened his mouth to deny this, and then closed it again. There was more to come.

'This is how it happened,' said McLevy, putting out one hand against the edge of the desk to steady himself. 'Dunbar pushed the old man to the floor as he related and then made his escape with the candlestick. Gourlay was confused, all at sea, a good servant though, whose first thought would be to acquaint his master of these dastardly deeds.'

The inspector laughed suddenly at his choice of words.

'Dastardly deeds!'

The laughter turned into a gasp as a shaft of pain near split his skull and Telfer, observing the sudden appearance of agony on McLevy's face, could only hope for more of the same. From whatever cause perhaps the man would die, the secretary thought; perhaps his head would explode into a thousand pieces and no one would put them together again.

But McLevy did put them back together. He was a policeman after all. That was his job.

'So in the dark, frightened out of his wits, the poor old bugger throws open the bedroom door without knocking and there before his very eyes is what Hercules Dunbar had previously witnessed.

'Perhaps he called out, "Maister, Maister, thieves abroad!" or some such thing as he rushed into the room. Sir Thomas slept on like the dead but it woke you up from your slumbers and you remarked on Gourlay's face the knowledge of what he had that moment observed.

'Bedfellows. A flagrant breach of custom. Brethren of the Fly as they are known in some circles.

'Before his very eyes.

'And Archibald Gourlay was a terrible old sweetie wife who loved to gossip, he would not be able to keep this to himself, he might even tell the mistress of the house.

'That could not be allowed.

'So you got out of bed and talked softly, calmly, moving towards him as he retreated, his eyes popping as he told you about the theft, perhaps even that he had recognised the man as Dunbar, eh?'

A tired smile spread across McLevy's face as Telfer's reaction betrayed the accuracy of that remark.

'Then you saw your chance. Behind the old man a steep flight of stairs with stone flags below. One push. Blame it on the burglar. One push and you were safe.'

Although the other's face gave nothing away, it was uncanny how close to the truth McLevy had come, as if he had somehow wormed his way inside Telfer's mind.

Indeed that is what the secretary had done, stretched his hand forward, hardly touched the terrified old man who lurched back and fell to crack his skull open like an egg, the blood spilling out like soft yolk.

Telfer had watched the body twitch like a person under sufferance of a nightmare, and then grow ominously still.

Satisfied then, that all was protected once more, the secretary had returned to look at Sir Thomas as he lay securely stupefied upon the bed: the great man was addicted to sleeping draughts, which Telfer administered each night.

Without them Sir Thomas could not rest.

And Telfer lay beside him each night, in all innocence, holding him close, protecting his genius, stroking the side of his face as you would a child.

He would lie beside his love till the morning light and then return to his own bed in the attic room.

Innocent. Only an ugly brutal world would see it otherwise or that pigmy of a wife who would arrive out of the blue with her sharp suspicious eyes, prying, eager to destroy the harmony of fellows together.

Each weekend Sir Thomas would depart for the country and Telfer was free to pursue his own predilections in some specially selected taverns by the docks where the sailors all came in.

And thus refreshed, the secretary came back to Bernard Street and harmony.

He had killed to preserve the peace. A peace that now could no longer exist.

Telfer emerged from these thoughts of dark destruction to find McLevy still before him, the man's eyes like glowing cinders in the parchment-white face.

'You have no proof,' he said. 'It is Dunbar's word against mine.'

'After the inquiry,' said McLevy, a savage grin on his face, 'you and Sir Thomas will both be fair game. Disgraced. And the murder trial will follow. The mud will stick.'

He suddenly roared with laughter, a wild berserk note in the sound.

'Your name is mud!'

This phrase had been once thrown at McLevy and it came back into his head with a vengeance.

The sound he produced was more like the snarl of an animal than human laughter; it filled the study with a mocking, gleeful contemptuous wall of noise that quite unhinged any scraps of composure Alan Telfer had managed to retain.

He lunged for the gun but the inspector, despite his fatigue, had earlier noted the secretary to be enamoured of the sliding area of that part of the desk and was across in a fierce swift movement to wrest the revolver from the man's nerveless fingers.

McLevy looked down at the implement with a deal of disdain.

'More like a lady's gun,' he remarked. 'Still, I suppose it might do the trick.'

He laid it on the desk on top of the drawings.

'Jist in case they blow away when the storm winds arrive. I believe they're on the way.'

Alan Telfer stood before him like a man stripped naked and for a moment there appeared on McLevy's face what might almost have passed for a look of compassion.

Then it passed when he remembered the frightened pitiful countenance of Archibald Gourlay and the mother at the Tay Bridge station, terror in her eyes, beseeching him for a certainty he could not provide.

'I'll see you in court,' he said, turned abruptly and made to go. But when he got to the closed door, comically enough, he twisted the handle the wrong way round and had to struggle before wrenching the thing open.

At the doorway he paused for a last word to Telfer.

'Ye look like a ghost,' he remarked, and then was gone.

Telfer waited till he heard the outside door slam shut and then moved to the desk and sat down on one of the high stools. This was his. He always sat here and Sir Thomas on the other. Always.

He reached across to the gun, picked it up and peered into the muzzle.

It was clean, as it should be for he, Alan Telfer, was a meticulous man.

He shot from the gun on a regular basis. There was a spot on the remote Leith shoreline where he would go, place a rusty can or whatever he could find in the washed-up debris upon a rock and sight carefully along the barrel.

And then he would press the trigger.

It was a solitary almost childlike occupation where each hit on target was greeted with a suppressed exclamation of pleasure.

His father had been an army man as well as an enthusiastic sadist. His mother had died in the line of duty. Perhaps it was his father's head he was lining up in his sights.

Now he had a different objective in mind.

Even if Sir Thomas survived the inquiry, and Telfer knew the faults in manufacture and construction that the great man had overlooked in the progress towards grandeur; even if he came out with some reputation intact, his unwitting involvement in a murder trial and the squalid revelations that would be implied in the popular press would completely destroy the name and reputation of Sir Thomas Bouch.

That must not happen.

He, Alan Telfer, would remove the cause.

And a further benefit: people would assume he had committed the act from guilt; the Beaumont's Egg factor would deflect much of the blame on to him.

It was a pity Sir Thomas would not know of his sacrifice but he could not risk leaving any written letter in case it fell into the wrong hands.

Besides he must do this quickly while his nerve held.

All this had flashed through his mind as he turned the revolver and pressed it into his open mouth.

He remembered as a small boy, a tale in the regiment when a captain who had embezzled the mess funds had blown his head to pieces.

But that was with a rifle and a terrible bloody mess.

This would be neat as a cabin boy.

And yet he hesitated. What if the discharge lacked sufficient power? What if the bullet did not reach the brain but lodged somewhere else on the journey?

As a train delayed for a station.

'Do it,' said a voice.

Margaret Bouch stood in the doorway her gypsy eyes filled with cold hatred.

Alan Telfer gazed back at her with the same icy loathing. The bitch must have listened at the door, he thought, and for a moment was tempted to spend a bullet and shoot her where she stood.

But there had been enough damage done and she would not reveal the secret to preserve her own name.

Though when he was gone, she would rule.

However there was one consolation.

The innocent comfort he had provided for her sleeping husband she would turn in her mind into something sordid and with any luck the loathing would lodge there and torture the woman to the end of her days.

With any luck.

Once more he lifted the gun and stuck the barrel hard against the roof of his mouth, his eyes unblinking upon her.

Sir Thomas Bouch looked down upon them both; the third player in a twisted triangle.

'Do it,' she said. 'Do it, or I will.'

Outside in the street James McLevy levered himself away from the street door; he had collapsed back against it after banging the portal shut; the resultant noise rang through his head and near shattered his skull in two.

'Never slam other folk's doors, Jamie McLevy. It shows a lack of good breeding and impresses not one soul!'

That's what Jean Scott had often counselled him and she, as in all things, was correct and proper.

Like a sailor in a heavy swell, he lurched from side to side as he moved away from the door heading for the docks where he knew of a tavern that rarely closed.

He would knock at the rearwards door, be recognised, admitted, a hooker of peat whisky would be laid before him in a small back room with perhaps a slice of black pudding or the poor man's meal of salt herring and potatoes.

And for a moment in his miserable life, he might find some rest.

It was a still night, so the shot when it came from above, sounded like the crack of doom.

McLevy looked up at the lighted window of the study and nodded approval.

Of course he might never find Hercules Dunbar and without the man's testimony there would be no trial for the murder of Archibald Gourlay, the whole thing being surmise on his part.

In fact he doubted, even with Dunbar, that Lieutenant Roach would consider moving to trial against one of his own kind, disgraced or not.

But best not to mention all this to Alan Telfer, just pile on the guilt and leave the gun in plain view.

Retribution.

It made perfect sense.

Said the madman.

This night he had no more thoughts to think, feelings to feel, or death to bring.

Tomorrow he would lay some flowers on Jean Scott's grave. Winter roses. Incarnadine.

As he walked off into the darkness Margaret Bouch watched from a corner of the window, ignoring the smell of cordite and the corpse slumped over the desk behind her.

There had been a little blood but the bullet had performed manfully; the man was dead no doubt about it.

She had gazed into his baleful eyes before closing them with two delicate fingers.

There was no doubt that the man deserved to die. She and the inspector had delivered Telfer from his own evil.

It would be their secret. Never told. Inside their minds, for ever.

And so she sang, as she watched the figure in the street below.

> 'Put him in bed with the captain's daughter,
> Put him in bed with the captain's daughter,
> Put him in bed with the captain's daughter,
> Earl-aye in the morning.'

Of course the captain's daughter was another name for the lash of a cat o' nine tails and the drunken sailor would suffer horribly for his misdeeds but, as she sang, a single tear for some obscure reason, trickled down her face.

Though she was not the crying kind . . .

34

It is one thing to show a man that he is in error,
and another to put him in possession of truth.

JOHN LOCKE, *An Essay Concerning Human Understanding*

McLevy slurped at his coffee and perused what he had just written in his diary.

Some days had passed since that stramash with the mistress of the Just Land but it had got the blood moving that night and, having returned to the station to agree with Lieutenant Roach a certain course of action for curing the love-sickened Constable Mulholland, he had come back to his lodgings to clarify some details in his case notes as regards the warehouse fire.

He had then checked the seagoing time of a certain ship, the *Dorabella* in Leith docks, which was bound for Argentina in a few days' time, and had formulated a plan of campaign.

This involved waiting.

In the meantime both his forces and Jean Brash's spies had fine combed the city for three days and nights to no avail. The fugitives were not to be found.

McLevy had not been surprised.

Tonight the wait was over. A long shot but worth a try.

There was time to spare yet and so he had put pencil to paper. The first in a long time. A good omen.

He peered down; there was no doubt that eyesight was playing tricks upon him and he might have to consider the purchase of reading glasses.

His two latest book purchases, the Arab legends and Poe's short stories were squared neatly at the right-hand corner of the table. The Eastern typeface was generous though slanting but Poe's was crabbed and narrow, and the inspector wondered if this had damaged his optics somewhat, to say nothing of the content as regards his mind.

'The Tell-Tale Heart' for instance . . . a madman kills an old man because of a supposed evil eye, buries him under the floorboards and then is betrayed by the louder and louder beating of the dead man's heart.

The strange fancies of the author's mind stirred McLevy's own uneasy imagination. Sometimes he felt haunted by his own history as it beat louder and louder in the confines of his soul.

He took a deep breath to still this shivering within and muttered his own written words as an incantation against the guilt that followed him like a black dog.

The Diary of James McLevy, 13 November 1880

The past and present collide like two bulls in a field and so it is in my thoughts this evening.

Robert Forbes and Sir Thomas Bouch, two men far apart in temperament and standing yet inextricably linked by their fall.

They had built an image of themselves in their psyche that could not endure the cold blast of reality.

In Forbes' case it was a slippery whore who roused him from his widowhood to an ardent desire that had lain dormant in him, no doubt since birth.

He found himself not what he thought himself to be and as his penis blossomed, so his common sense dwindled.

If we ever find the letters he wrote to Rachel Bryden, I expect they will be filled with protestations of love.

Nae foule like an auld foule.

But are we not all fools in the end?

Over love especial.

And now the other case.

Sir Thomas thought himself to be a giant and in that iron certainty lay the seeds of his own destruction.

According to the late Alan Telfer, the bridge builder towered above us all like a Colossus but there's only one God and he does not take kindly to competition.

Heat did for Icarus, and the howling wind blew Sir Thomas Bouch away like a shrivelled leaf.

On a more practical note, Mulholland, another soaring specimen, has been, some days ago, sent back to Ireland to recompose himself and his Aunt Katie will hopefully fill him with barnyard saws and Irish stew so that he will return to Edinburgh a sadder but wiser man.

But time is a great healer and an engagement ring may fit on many fingers.

After the speedy and very private funeral of her father, Emily has fled to the country with the maiden aunts. I believe somewhere in Stirlingshire, where pulley ropes perform their proper function.

As for myself I have no place to fall and business on hand. So I shall close this ledger and return to it when occasion allows.

While he did so, an indignant scrape upon the window announced the arrival of Bathsheba and McLevy sighed.

He would have to feed the cat and pour out her milk but then there was the rest of the ritual. She had to retire to her little niche by the fireplace and groom herself from head to toe before embarking on to the moonlit slates of Leith.

Still there was yet enough duration.

On the desk beside the diary where it lay, was an oilskin pouch, which McLevy gently parted to reveal the outline of a heavy black revolver.

He crossed to slide the oilskin into the side pocket of his heavy outdoor coat.

Time enough.

While the cat tucked into her provender he walked over to the narrow cupboard where he kept his hidden treasures, opened it up and carefully laid the diary back to its provided place beside a mother-of-pearl box that had been given to him by a dying man more than twenty years ago.

He carefully prised up the lid and looked in. It was somewhat gloomy in the cupboard but sufficient for him to discern amongst other things, a broken grubby scrap of white feather, a lock of golden hair, and a fragment of black material.

Mementoes of past crimes.

One of which he had promised the dying man to solve but had yet to deliver.

He closed the lid again and noticed a rolled-up pamphlet of paper stuck into the corner of the cupboard.

McLevy frowned. An interloper.

He pulled the paper out, closed the cupboard door and walked to the small table by the window where he penned his most profound ruminations.

He spread out the paper to read and the words of Poet McGonagall thus thundered in his mind.

> Oh, ill-fated bridge of the Silv'ry Tay,
> I must now conclude my lay
> By telling the world fearlessly without the least dismay
> That your central girders would not have given way,
> At least many sensible men do say,
> Had they been supported on each side with buttresses,
> At least many sensible men confesses,
> For the stronger we our houses do build
> The less chance we have of being killed.

Bathsheba finished up her milk and with natural grace, jumped up to her appointed spot by the fire. She licked her paw, dabbed daintily at her whiskers and looked over where McLevy stood like a statue, paper in hand.

Then she licked again and began to groom behind her ears, a hive of activity compared to the still figure at the window, marooned in the moonlight.

But animals have not time for memory; they live in the present.

The past is a uniquely human predicament.

35

I can endure my own despair,
But not another's hope.

WILLIAM WALSH, Song, *Of all the torments*

Dundee, 28 February 1880

As the crowd filed into the building that housed the Board of Trade Inquiry, they were regaled by a poem, in its own way almost as disastrous as the event itself.

William McGonagall had begun composition the day after the bridge fell, that is the Monday, and ended with a sorrowful sweep of the pen on the following Tuesday evening.

Even by his standards it plumbed the depths, although the poet might offer as excuse the fact that having rescued an officer of the law that fateful night, he had returned to his home and attempted to pacify with the monetary contents of his collection a long-suffering wife.

The poor woman was driven to distraction by the transformation of what she had thought to be an ordinary weaver catapulted into the grinding jaws of the Muse, then chewed up and spat out to emerge as a fully fledged poet before her very eyes.

McGonagall gave her the coins, went to his bed and slept soundly through till morning.

Thus he missed first-hand experience of the searing catastrophe and the howl of collective grief when it finally became known that the train was lodged at the bottom of the river with survival an impossibility, unless a beneficent God reached down his kindly hand.

But, as the Sabbatarian ministers so piously pointed out later, travelling on a Sunday was a profane act of the North British Railway Company and its passengers, transgressing the Law of God and desecrating the day he had lain aside for drawing breath.

So with his mighty right hand He had thrown a storm to punish the sinners for He was, as they never tired of telling you in the bible, a Jealous God who guarded the Sabbath like a roaring lion.

Therefore rather than bringing deliverance, God might well be a number-one suspect.

As the people hurried past, McGonagall offered the sheets of his poetry in vain except for the one woman, Troll Barbara, a squat powerful figure and the only female welder in Dundee, who pressed a coin into his hand, crunched the paper up in one massive paw and disappeared through the door that led to the Inquiry Court.

The poet wondered about starting all over.

> Beautiful Railway Bridge of the Silv'ry Tay!
> Alas! I am very sorry to say, etc. etc.

But somehow this morning he lacked the strength to launch off once more into the epic lay and merely stood with his arm outstretched like a statue in long coat skirts and a wide-brimmed hat; the folk bustling past were content enough to treat him as such, ignoring the still figure in their rush to find a decent seat to view the spectacle, for it was the third day of proceedings and the revelations were coming thick and fast.

A stocky figure approached the poet who perhaps resembled more a scarecrow than a statue. The man also put forward a coin but this was of some value, in McGonagall's opinion, approaching the worth of the verse inscribed in the pamphlet that he gravely offered forth.

The fellow accepted it equally gravely and stashed it into his pocket.

The light of recognition flashed in the poet's mind.

'You are the man from the walnut tree!' he exclaimed.

'I am Inspector James McLevy,' the officer himself replied, 'and I have to thank you for your labour that night.'

McGonagall struck a proud attitude.

'As well as a poet,' he declared, 'I am also a Tragedian. I have often essayed Othello on stage. It gives a man great strength in crucial predicaments.'

McLevy wasn't sure how smothering Desdemona with a pillow equated to hauling out a sodden officer of the law from under an ancient nut tree, but he contented himself with bowing solemnly to the poet, who replied in kind, and then without another word, both men went their separate ways.

The inspector to the inquiry, and McGonagall to roam the streets with the beginning of another masterpiece beginning to form in his teeming mentality.

He had suffered much on the stage; eggs are wonderful and yolky to eat but not flying through the air towards you, yet nevertheless the fact that the clergy ranted against the theatre had brought his blood to boiling point.

For did not the best plays see vice punished and virtue rewarded?

Some versical fragments began to run in McGonagall's mind as the Muse sped round the wide rim of his hat.

We see in Shakespeare's tragedy of Othello, which is sublime,
Cassio losing his lieutenancy through drinking wine;
And, in delirium and grief, he exclaims – 'Oh, that men should put
an enemy in their mouths to steal away their brains!'

Thus uttering these lines aloud, the last one of which was the best he would ever write, the poet passed out of sight and for this moment left the stage.

At the same time, the inspector stood at the back of the inquiry room behind one of the pillars, watching as the final witnesses from a succession of workers from the Wormit Foundry, faces so pitted with iron dust that it seemed as if they were composed of the element itself, gave evidence in halting bewildered tones as if they had been hauled bodily from their place of work and then bolted into place in front of the examining board, council and gentlemen of the press.

The Wreck Commissioner, Henry Cadogan Rothery treated them gently enough, because these were not fellows who understood the rights and wrongs of the situation; they did what they were told. No more no less than that.

But from their words, and the testimony of the previous, a depressing and calamitous picture had begun to emerge.

Beaumont Egg. That very name which they mentioned time and time again started to assume the magical dimensions of an iron-clad panacea; it had been used to plug faults in the castings, the blown-holes, cracks and fissures of all shapes and sizes, the remedy was always at hand to be melted in, left to harden, smoothed over, painted, then waved goodbye.

Available at all times from the foreman's office.

Black magic.

Unfortunately the purveyor of this sorcery, Hercules Dunbar and the supplier of same, Alan Telfer, were unable to give statements. The former had disappeared from sight and the latter had died by his very own hand.

But other foremen testified that Telfer had brought the substance and its use was common practice.

While all this was in motion, Sir Thomas Bouch sat at the very front so that the audience were treated to a view of his broad back. His son was adjacent to him and on the other side the diminutive figure of his wife.

McLevy had pondered whether to offer evidence to the inquiry but since Dunbar had vanished there seemed little point in offering the testimony of a man who wasn't there.

And as regards the events of the night of Telfer's suicide, he awoke the next morning refreshed, headache miraculously gone, but with a hazy fragmentary memory of what had passed between them.

And he preferred to keep it that way.

At the back.

Meanwhile, at the front, Margaret Bouch glanced sideways at the impassive face of her spouse and wondered what was going through his mind.

The image of her husband and Alan Telfer in embrace whether innocent or lascivious had initially disgusted her but now it merely provoked curiosity.

Had Telfer put a bullet in his brain from guilt or to protect the one he loved?

If the latter then this was love indeed.

The kind that kills.

In the late morning and all through the afternoon, the court, having heard evidence from lesser beings, summoned before them the professional classes who had taken part in the construction of the bridge.

One after another they were revealed to be lacking in the basic require-ments for their proper function, ranging from honestly incompetent as in *the case of Henry Noble the supposed Inspector of the Tay Bridge, an assistant to Sir Thomas whose only practical experience was that of an apprentice bricklayer, to Albert Groethe, Manager of Works, a confident Christian and decent to the core who had to admit nevertheless, 'I am not a practical iron man.'*

Thus the Wormit Foundry had been left unsupervised and the bridge itself neglected and uninspected from May 1878 to December 1879.

Then there was much talk of wind and pressure, though none of the esteemed gentlemen had been on the doomed train to experience the reality of same, but finally Sir Thomas Bouch himself had been brought to the stand.

His blank face hid a growing numbness and the wall he had built round himself for protection proved no stronger than the bridge in contention, as question after question cracked the façade to reveal the bewildered soul behind the great man.

His refrain became, 'I cannot answer that question for my memory does not serve me well.'

Already there had been savage attacks upon the very design of the bridge itself but to that query he shook his head like an animal besieged on all sides by predators.

No, he insisted, the train must have been lifted off the rails by the force of the wind and crashed into the High Girders.

Nothing could withstand that blow.

The fault was not his design but a flying train.

He seemed oblivious of the catalogue of failure that had been laid bare, and the gathering storm of public opinion.

So when he was asked the fatal question by Rothery, the Wreck Commissioner, 'Sir Thomas, did you in designing this bridge make any allowance at all for wind pressure?'

'Not specially,' came the reply that damned him for ever.

Henry Cadogan Rothery blinked for a moment as if someone had smashed a fist in his face.

'You made no allowance?'

Sir Thomas Bouch shook his head as if mystified by the repeated question.

'Not specially.'

'Ye dirty murdering bastard!'

Troll Barbara had drunk three hookers of whisky washed down by the same number of draughts of ram-stam beer that morning early, and though her constitution was not unused to such intake, the mixture swilled around in her brain to fuel a furious anger and resentment at the dry proceedings of the inquiry.

She had worked on the bridge for a short while and had heard the stories of retaining bolts shaken loose by the vibrations from the speeding trains as they exceeded the lawful limit on the bridge while they raced the morning ferry boats across the river.

Although Barbara could testify well and good to the work she had accomplished, a terrible feeling of guilt coursed through her at the thought of all these dead souls, innocent and unavenged.

And that she somehow was a part of it.

So she rose in her anger and howled an accusation at the man she considered responsible for the poor bloated bodies that were still coming to the surface after all this time.

One had even been washed up on the Caithness shore.

It had travelled further than the train.

'Sir Thomas Bouch, I call ye out!' she cried in her grief and fury. 'I name ye as a murderous swine with not a decent bone in your body!'

Uproar ensued as the court officers and attendants tried to haul the berserk woman from her place; others took her part and McLevy noticed amongst them, the wife of the schoolmaster, her face flushed with rage and pain as she joined in the wall of abuse directed at the bridge builder.

Missiles were thrown and Sir Thomas was hustled away to the side for protection; he looked up at his accusers who were now losing momentum as Troll Barbara was manhandled out of the court, his face impassive, head slightly cocked to the one side as if observing from on high.

Not all of the spectators had entered the mêlée and, as order was being restored, McLevy, who had noted with some relief that the little girl who had given him the barley sugar was not accompanying her distraught mother, became aware of another's scrutiny.

Sir Thomas's son had followed after his father so the faithful little wife had been left to fend on her own.

Margaret Bouch, unattended and out of the spotlight, had also turned to observe the chaos, and spotted McLevy standing at the back behind the pillar.

He withdrew slightly at her regard, and then peeked round again like a schoolboy.

The ghost of a smile touched her lips and she raised one gloved hand, forefinger pointed, thumb upright like the raised hammer of a gun and shot him where he stood.

Luckily no one except the inspector saw this gesture of impropriety.

It was not often a woman got the drop upon McLevy and he wondered what it meant.

36

Every man loves what he is good at.

THOMAS SHADWELL, *A True Widow*

Now he watched her in the Old Ship tavern and still wondered about the moment. That and many others.

It might be concluded that he had the advantage now because she was not aware of his regard as she reached forward to lay her hand upon the sleeve of a man sitting opposite her with his back to the inspector.

Naval fellow by the looks of it, a captain's hat on the table beside him, sandy hair tinged with grey, bit of a sea dog perhaps.

McLevy had come to the tavern for a strong dram of whisky before embarking on what might well be a lamentable fool's errand and should he happen to have guessed correctly then he might also lament the fact that Constable Mulholland was nursing a broken heart in the bogs of Ireland and therefore not available to be a good right hand.

He could, of course, have brought other constables for reinforcement or even broken the rule of a lifetime and informed Lieutenant Roach of his proposed action, but somehow it had seemed better to be on his own.

Better the devil you know.

And indeed, in official company, he would never have ventured into the Old Ship, swiftly drained his tumbler, been about to leave, and then heard her unmistakable laughter wafting through the tobacco smoke from the tavern dining room.

There were windows in the shape of portholes in the wooden wall and he gazed through one into the dining room like a sea creature that had somehow squelched its way up on to the timbers of the vessel.

The porthole glass was thick and slightly distorted but he could well enough distinguish Margaret Bouch, widowhood discarded this night to judge by her bright blue dress, as she threw back her head in more laughter to display the white taut skin of her throat, the gypsy eyes now mocking and flirtatious.

Of course the inspector should have felt relieved that he was no longer the target of those dangerous eyes, but he did not.

He felt unworthily betrayed.

Humpty Dumpty.

Sitting on a damp wall. Watching at a porthole.

Margaret lifted up her glass and drained it at a gulp, most unladylike to behold; her companion signalled at one of the waiters.

McLevy watched as the serving man bent his head, took the order and then exited. In order to get to the bar the fellow had to pass the static figure of McLevy who detained him by the arm.

'Whit did he command?' was the question.

'Ye mean like a ship?'

'I mean like the drink!'

'Champagne. Best quality.'

The waiter, Mattie Turpin, was an old birkie who had seen the world come and go; he knew McLevy from long since and assumed that the inspector was lurking with intent.

'The man,' asked McLevy with a nasty gleam in his eye. 'What is he?'

'Norwegian,' replied Mattie and shot off towards the bar

because it had entered his mind that if McLevy were on the point of arresting someone, it would be best to get the champagne down and money paid.

A grandfather clock that had pride of place in the dining room struck the full hour. It chimed quarters and half as well: a prudent and practical measure to remind any seaman or passenger therein that the tide waited for no man.

It now announced the hour of eight and as McLevy heard the muffled tones through the wall, he realised that duty was a' calling.

He took one last look to see Margaret raise the large hand of her companion in both of hers, and hold it tenderly as Mattie brought the champagne. The waiter twisted off the cork, the bubbles fizzed and the drink was poured. It was enough to make a man want to spit.

One of the tarry-breeks in the rough quarters of the Old Ship, in fact the bar where McLevy himself drank, had indulged himself beyond common measure due to the fact that his handsome sailor laddie was about to leave the port of Leith for the New World and it would be a long haul leaving the man minus able-bodied comforts, his own boat heading for Holland tomorrow morn.

The tar's voice was hoarse and rough as he lifted it in song, and he gave a melancholy lilt to the normally jaunty tune as if he could already observe the sea stretching like a prison sentence before him.

McLevy left on that air and Margaret Bouch stilled the glass of champagne on the way to her lips as she remembered the moment when Alan Telfer, his cold eyes upon her, pulled the trigger of his silver-plated revolver.

> *Bang him in the head, 'til his brains are busted,*
> *Bang him in the head, 'til his brains are busted,*
> *Bang him in the head, 'til his brains are busted,*
> *Earl-aye in the morning.*

A lone seagull perched atop the foremast of the good ship

the *Dorabella*, bound this night for sea and eventually the port of Buenos Aires in Argentina, hunched into itself moodily and emitted a mournful unmelodic screech.

It might well have been the same bird that had observed McLevy and Mulholland these five days past after the warehouse fire, though one gull looks very much like another.

A dank November sea mist had covered the Old Docks like a funeral pall, and neutralised the bird's keen eyesight upon which it relied for various titbits dropped or thrown carelessly away by embarking passengers.

Or perhaps a tearful relative having waved goodbye might find they had no appetite for the farewell cake and hurl it, with its white wrapping, into the sea; that was when the gull made its move, swooping down to grab the sweet concoction just before it hit the water and alerted some lesser of the species that the game was on.

But this night they could drop a whale in the water and the bird would be none the wiser.

Indeed, there was a mighty splash but it was just some young boys running wild in the harbour, who had made use of the general obscurement to heave up a large piece of broken timber and hurl it into the water. As it floated off into the darkness, a watchman cursed and chased the boys for their lives; the gull spread its wings and glided silently off to join the other spectres wheeling in the mist.

One of which was James McLevy who slipped quietly aboard the *Dorabella*, his revolver resting in hand within the side pocket of his coat.

This case had been saturated with dampness since the beginning and now it seemed as if his very pores were falling victim.

However the fog makes useful ghosts of us all; he had used the play of light and dark as the warning lamps of the ships shone fitfully in the gloom, to cloak his maritime pursuits.

The boat was a bustle of activity, preparations for departure getting under way, sailors busy at their appointed tasks, cargo being made fast in the hold below and some passengers already on the quay gathering to bid farewell to loved ones because though primarily a cargo ship, the *Dorabella* had some berths free for those folk bound for South America.

The following was McLevy's reasoning.

Oliver Garvie had used this ship to bring in his dubious consignment of cigars, and no doubt had more than a passing acquaintance with captain and crew.

Even if the couple had so far managed, these three days, to hide in Edinburgh away from Jean Brash's battalion of street keelies and spies, they would eventually need to make a break for what they considered freedom.

What better transport than the *Dorabella*?

Of course, after brutally beating Hannah Semple to earth they could have taken an early-morning train to London or such because Scotland would be too hot for them with the twin forces of Sin and Justice breathing down their necks, but no one of their description had been seen at any of the main stations.

No. And in fact the ship itself might even have been a safer place to hide out before fleeing the country because it was an encapsulated world safe from prying eyes.

Whatever the case, the best chance of catching the buggers was to board the vessel a touch before departure and it also justified his solitary expedition. If he arrived with a flotilla of constables, the malefactors would be spirited away and hidden while he was still arguing the toss about boarding the ship.

As McLevy inched his way on the slippery deck past the bustle and motion in the gathering murk, he caught a glimpse of what must be the captain under one of the ship's lights.

The man was rapping out staccato commands in what the inspector presumed to be some sort of Spanish lingo; he was a short swarthy fellow, heavy eyebrows, drooping moustache, gold tooth agleam, and resembled a pirate rather than some trustworthy mariner.

To McLevy's prejudiced eye the whole crew might as well be

travelling under skull and crossbones, so he resolved not to get wrongsides of them.

He inadvertently clanged his foot into an empty iron bucket, cursed it under his breath for a betrayer then praised it as a guide because it caused him to swing round and see a doorway, red lamp above, where the strong light from within held its own with the fog.

Hopefully this was intended to show the arriving wayfarers passage to their cabins and McLevy, trusting that if seen he would be mistaken for such, ducked inside and was lost from sight.

He descended a narrow flight of steps to an equally narrow corridor, which split in two directions.

From the left passage came the far mumble of voices, and, as he strained his ears, the inspector could make out unmistakable cadences of Lingo España.

Better swing right then.

There was a tightness in his gut and he found it difficult to breathe; he was now in the bowels of the ship, or if not the bowels then one of the large intestines, and McLevy experienced an unpleasant claustrophobic frisson; like a piece of waste product passing through.

Also he could feel a movement under his feet as if he were walking on the skin of some prehistoric monster.

That would be the sea.

He was a creature of dry land.

The corridor took a sharp left and there was his destination, a row of cabin doors each already open to await occupation.

Except for the one at the end where the portal was firmly closed.

A sudden yowl behind startled him near out of his wits but it was only the ship's cat come from nowhere, a large ginger tom with one ear flattened by feline warfare.

'Bugger off,' the inspector hissed. 'Bathsheba wouldnae give you a second glance!'

The cat strolled back down the corridor, tail stiffly aloft at the perceived insult and McLevy made his way to the closed door.

He tried the handle but it held.

McLevy put his eye to the keyhole, looked through and saw that luckily the key had not been left in the lock; in addition to that, the aperture also provided the sight of a naked female backside in motion with the ship.

He averted his eyes and produced a set of lockpicks he had once confiscated from a premier exponent of their craft but mysteriously forgotten to hand in at the station.

As McLevy inserted the delicate instruments, one after another to manipulate the perfect fit, his ear pressed against the door and witnessed the voices within.

A man and woman. Tones subdued but sharp.

'For God's sake put some clothes on.'

'Why should I? I have nothing to wear.'

'You have your gown.'

'It is creased and filthy, as are my underthings.'

'Wash them. As I did mine.'

'Liar. You borrowed from the sailors. I cannot do that.'

'You'd be surprised what sailors wear.'

The sweat ran down McLevy's face as he felt, at last, one of the lockpicks click softly into place. He did not enjoy confined space, it brought back memories of when he was a wee boy in a locked room and, as his mother lay dead in a recess, the walls had begun to press in upon him.

He had howled like a wolf and Jean Scott, their neighbour and his salvation, had knocked upon the door and called through, 'Jamie, I cannae get in if you cannae get out.' He had found the key, unlocked the door and she had held him close while the hot scalding tears ran down his face till he thought he would drown in them.

Another click. Not long now. Just as well, his ear was getting sore.

That bastard captain, he took my jewels.

Not all. You wear a pretty necklace.

You gave them like a coward!

We had to pay for passage.

What if he wants the rest? What if he cuts our throats and throws us in the sea?

This question was never answered because at that moment McLevy sprung the lock, the door flew open and he was upon them, revolver levelled.

Rachel Bryden and Oliver Garvie, one naked the other not but both the worse for wear, love's dream transformed into bickering cabin fever.

He was in crumpled shirt and trousers, unshaven, she in her skin, which fitted well enough.

Rachel's face, a sight that McLevy found it best to concentrate on, was blotched and sulky; the enclosed cabin where they had obviously been holed up for days judging by the mess, remnants of food and litter of bedclothes, stank of various stale odours some of which it was better not to identify.

Both of their mouths were open but thankfully as yet no sound emerged as he swiftly closed the door.

He spoke quietly, no need to frighten the horses.

'Miss Bryden, Mister Garvie; a pleasure to meet you once more.'

He inclined his head solemnly towards Rachel.

'I would be obliged if you could dress yourself ma'am. We have an appointment with justice.'

Garvie was looking at him as if he could not believe his eyes.

'How did you know?' he muttered finally.

'I am an inspector of crime,' replied McLevy. 'It is my speciality.'

Rachel still had not moved and McLevy, whose eyes had not strayed below the collar bone, noted a pearl necklace round her neck that he had seen many a time nestling at the throat of Jean Brash.

To his eyes it had never been much to look at, the small pearls a sort of greenish black colour but the display brought him to a curious anger.

Hannah Semple had been felled to the ground for such baubles and it looked a damn sight better on Jean.

He held out his hand, the other steady as a rock aiming the revolver at Garvie's chest.

'I'll take the trinket,' he announced. 'It belongs to another, though I don't doubt she thieved it like your braw self. Whoors thegither.'

For a moment it appeared that Rachel was going to refuse this elegant request, then she caught a flicker of a glance from Garvie and nodded obediently.

But as she raised her arms to undo the clasp at the back of her neck, her breasts leapt into prominence, the nipples pointing at McLevy like two sentries on duty.

No man, unless the blood is completely frozen in his veins, can ignore the mating signal of erectile tissue and the inspector, though defended like the Castle itself, was also a biological specimen.

His eyes wavered momentarily and that was enough for Garvie to launch himself at the policeman, with Rachel diving in low from years of practice.

But another part of McLevy's biological conditioning was reflex. He smacked Garvie a sharp blow on the side of his head with the revolver to leave the man dazed on his hands and knees, then spun Rachel round, planted his foot on her equally distracting buttocks and shoved her head first on to the lower bunk bed.

Jean Scott had always thus advised him, 'You must never raise your hand to a woman, Jamie, but that disnae mean you cannot deliver a good kick tae the backside.'

He quickly cuffed Garvie's hands behind the man's back, shoved him with his foot into a corner and when Rachel finally disentangled herself from the grubby sheets, she found herself face to face with the wolf.

He took the pearl necklace from her and carefully stashed it into a secure inside pocket of his coat, then buttoned the flap over for insurance.

'Make yourself decent,' McLevy growled. 'Or I'll run ye stark naked through the streets of Leith.'

Rachel played a last card, lip trembling, surrender her area of expertise. She bowed her head meekly and then looked up, the pale blue eyes promising sweet acquiescence.

'You are a strong man, inspector,' she whispered. 'I'll do anything you wish. Anything.'

A yellow light came into McLevy's eyes and he reached out his hand but instead of the expected caress, his fingers took hold at the base of a throat so recently denuded of the pearl necklace.

The fingers tightened, cutting off the supply of seductive breath.

'I've already told you what I want, girlie. Obey such before I knock you unconscious and dress you myself.'

She clothed quickly, her own hands shaking, and when that was accomplished, the policeman cuffed her likewise behind the back, hauled Garvie to his feet and lined them up together as if for parade inspection.

'You're lucky it's me,' he remarked softly. 'If Jean Brash had found you first, Mister Garvie would be watching his means of procreation bouncing down the road in front of him, and you, Miss Bryden, would be left with a face only a mother could love.'

For the first time truly, the lovers realised that they were no longer children of fortune in a wild game against the world. This was real. The fairy tale was over.

The look upon McLevy's face chilled them to the bone; it had no pity, no anger, just the detachment of a hangman.

He ripped the bed sheets into strips, which he placed over their mouths and tied behind, knotting them firmly into place.

The inspector had a fine calculation to make. The easy bit was over, now he had somehow to get them on deck at the same time as the other passengers arrived because in public view the crew and captain would not dare interfere. However if he was intercepted before that, he would be forced to use the revolver and shooting Argentineans by and large was frowned upon, especially on their own boats.

Once more he cursed the fact that Mulholland was not on hand; the Irishman took to violence like a duck does to water and that hornbeam stick of his was worth a thousand threats.

One massive piece of good fortune was that, when he pulled the small curtain away, the porthole of the cabin looked on to the harbour side of the ship.

The vessel itself was riding high on the sea, the tide just about to turn and from this vantage he could peer upwards to see the outlines of the folk beginning to mass by the gangplank. Women were no doubt weeping, men chewing on their pipe stems, children unaware of parting sorrow sliding on the wet wooden planks of the pier, hoping to grab a piece of the leaving cake in its white wrapping.

All grist to the mill.

But when they made their move, so would McLevy.

He turned back to address the rigid, gagged figures.

'Hannah Semple survived that vicious dunt to the back of her head. I am sure that will please you?'

He waited till both nodded. They already seemed to have lost identity and character. Peas in a pod.

'Unfortunately,' he added genially, 'Robert Forbes hung himself from the head of a stag. He left a letter that incriminates the pair of you. A voice from the grave, eh?'

This time there was no response, save for a choked sob from Rachel though that may have been gathering mucus.

The inspector glanced back through the porthole to calculate the odds once more and then his own blood froze.

Fleetingly the fog had lifted and the lamps outlined the shapes of a man and woman passing by heading further up the pier to where another ship, at a later hour, was preparing to depart for the New World. The woman was a buxom type, waddling a little as she clung on to the arm of her escort, a tall bearded fellow, who walked solemnly beside her, his head inclined a little to the side, looking downwards as if to guard against a slip and fall.

His face was turned towards the *Dorabella* and McLevy would have known it in the grave.

The sea mist returned, the man and woman lost to sight.

For a moment McLevy was almost paralysed by shock, and then his heart started pounding like a steam shovel. His mind was likewise throbbing; what the hell was going on? Was Fate intending to make a monkey out of him? What happened to that pitiable monkey anyway?

Never again would he grant Mulholland leave of absence; not even if the father of every female he cast his glaikit Irish eyes upon, hung themselves like a row of Christmas decorations, not even then!

He pulled himself together and glanced at his timepiece. Thirty minutes till the ship sailed. He could do it. Just. Was he not James McLevy inspector of crime? Or was he just a monkey on a stick?

In for a penny, in for a pound.

McLevy dragged the couple over to a slim iron stanchion that acted as a support in the cabin, running from floor to ceiling; he unlocked their restrainers for a second then refastened them so that the pair were pinioned arms behind, with the stanchion as jailer. Their eyes were fearful and bewildered which was only right and proper.

'I'll return shortly,' promised the inspector. 'Meantime behave yourselves or I'll dump you at the Just Land for the benefit of Jean Brash.'

Then he was gone, the door locked behind.

Oliver and Rachel shuffled round so that they could gaze into each other's eyes.

Tears and pain.

Love is the very devil.

The ginger tomcat thought the same as it was rudely shoved aside by McLevy's foot while the inspector made his way swiftly back up the corridor. The cat had taken a perverse liking to this strange human and yowled plaintively as it followed the policeman.

His decision to maroon the fugitives in their cabin was more than justified when he encountered two of the crew before ascending the stairs to the deck.

They mistook him for a passenger but if he had been propelling bound and gagged prisoners, he doubted they would have come to the same conclusion.

Up on deck, ghost once more to the gangplank, leave the bloody cat yowling on ship, and then?

In for a penny, in for a pound.

37

Mine eyes have seen the glory of the coming of the Lord:
He is trampling out the vintage where the grapes of wrath
are stored

JULIA WARDE HOWE, *Battle Hymn of the Republic*

The bearded man stood at the very edge of the pier and gazed back eastwards where he imagined Edinburgh to be as a lone seagull screeched overhead; another hungry bird.

Typical of his native city that it would be hiding at the very moment he was about to depart.

The place had done him few favours and left many scars but he would miss the harsh beat of that stony Midlothian hammer, pounding him into shape from birth. It was good his companion had gone on board and left him to have this last moment of fogbound privacy.

She was a good woman, and he would do his best to grapple with her for ever.

He lifted one bony big-knuckled hand in farewell to his native land. Good riddance. A New World beckoned.

But the Old World was not finished with him yet.

A soft tune was whistled from westwards behind him and the bearded man froze at the fragment of melody.

'Charlie is my darling, the young Chevalier.'

He turned to find James McLevy in the mist.

'Well Herkie,' said the inspector quietly. 'It's been a long journey.'

McLevy held his revolver loosely at the side and in his other hand carried a length of rope he had picked up from the deck of the ship.

His plan was to stun Dunbar if necessary, bind the man then drag him back to the *Dorabella*, leave him dockside with the two strongest men he could find amongst the respectable throng, deputise others as special constables and retrieve his fugitives from the stanchion of justice.

With witnesses to hand, the captain would not dare interfere.

That was his calculation, but first things first.

Of course he could have sneaked up on the man and felled him where he stood but somehow that did not seem fitting for his old enemy.

So, he preferred to whistle instead. And now they were face to face.

Hercules Dunbar had lowered his head at the sight of his nemesis but now raised it again to speak.

'I am a changed man, McLevy.'

Indeed his eyes and voice were level and considered but that cut no ice with the law.

'Your past actions cannot change,' was the inexorable response. 'And they have caused many deaths.'

The inspector moved slowly towards his quarry, and as he did so, pronounced judgment.

'I absolve you from the butler's demise though you are more than implicated, but what of your only friend, Tommy Loughran?'

The guilt McLevy had intuited in the man was uncovered like a nest of maggots and Dunbar flinched as if he had been struck in the face.

'He died in the February storm when three High Girders fell; it was believed the cause was that they had not been securely moored in place. But in your heart, you suspected that it was due to the bad practice in your foundry.'

There was now hardly an arm's length between them and McLevy was intent on pressing home bleak advantage.

'The wee riveter. Your best pal. He died. Of your neglect. Of your transgression.'

A look of fear passed over Dunbar's face as if he was being drawn back into a terrifying past.

'I sent money tae his wife, out of my own wages!'

'I am sure that compensated her mightily,' was the ironic rejoinder. 'But for three years after that, you continued. Knowing that you were sinning against both God and Tommy Loughran. On and on you went.'

'I did what I was told,' Dunbar muttered.

'That's not good enough,' replied the inspector who was suddenly brought to mind of the little girl who gifted him barley sugar and then saw the death of her father in McLevy's face. 'Not remotely.'

He brought the revolver up to point at Dunbar.

'I cannot prosecute you for the poor bastards who died that night the bridge destroyed itself, but I have you in the frame for robbery, violent and duplicitous assault of a police constable, breaking out of Lieutenant Roach's jail and pishing in my face.'

'Ye deserved that,' was the rejoinder.

'Turn round, Herkie,' said McLevy. 'Put your hands behind your back. The game is over now.'

As Dunbar slowly did so, he threw a plaintive remark over his shoulder.

'I could've taken the boat from Glasgow, but I wanted to see Edinburgh for a last time.'

'You can watch it on the way to the penitentiary.'

'Can ye not let me go McLevy? I have a good woman on hand. We will get married in the New World.'

'She'll have to find another class of criminal. Now clasp your paws together and stick them straight out!'

Dunbar did so, arms extended backwards, and McLevy approached cautiously; he had fashioned a slip knot in the rope and planned to drop it over the man's hands, pull it tight, then make it fast possibly round the fellow's neck.

From Hercules' point of view, although he had pitched his voice to pleading, he knew that to be a waste of time; however he had too much to lose. Indeed he was changed, this woman had been the making of him; they had hidden out in the country with her relatives who owned a farm, and he had found a peace and harmony that he never believed could ever have been possible in his life.

She had sold the house in Magdalen Green and they had money to spare.

In the New World, as he had promised her, they would get married and then have their own farm.

He would kill for that dream.

In a strange way, he had not been surprised to see McLevy; the two of them were linked like birth and death.

And so though he presented an abject figure, his every sense was tuned to the moment when McLevy's balance shifted, and then he would make his strike.

The inspector, in turn, perceived the coiled tension of the other and, sleeve riding back to expose an expanse of white cuff, lifted his revolver in warning to lay it right behind the man's ear.

'Softly does it, Herkie. If she loves you, she'll be waiting when you emerge from the Perth Penitentiary thirty odd years from now.'

Who knows what might have happened at that moment, perhaps Dunbar would have swung desperately round, McLevy forced to shoot him where he stood, or the rope pulled tight upon the defeated wrists, then Hercules dragged off like a captive, who knows?

In fact, Fate once more intervened.

First it had been in the guise of a walnut tree, and now it struck in the form of a ravenous seagull.

The bird had been circling above after an unsuccessful effort to wrest a piece of stale bread from the beak of a razorbill only to find that its heavy-bodied opponent was surprisingly stubborn and had a whole flock of relatives who descended upon the bigger bird and chased it for dear life.

Thus the gull was hungry, chastened and desperate; so when it glimpsed below the white of McLevy's cuff as he lifted the revolver, that colour only because his landlady Mrs MacPherson had bleached, washed and ironed his shirts before they yellowed beyond measure, the bird, through the tendrils of mist mistakenly thought it saw the white paper of a leaving cake.

Conditioned reflex did the rest.

It dived straight as an arrow, through the fog, neck extended, to jab a lethally sharp beak into the inspector's outstretched hand.

McLevy howled in pain and the revolver flew out of his grasp to skitter along the wet planking until it was lost from view.

He hammered the bird on the head with his free hand till it pulled the beak away then dropped at his feet but, in the meantime, Hercules Dunbar had spun round, and seen the form of the inspector outlined against the faint lights of the ships in the far distance.

Dunbar dropped his shoulder and rushed at McLevy, driving him backwards so that they both fell off the end of the pier into the dark waters below with a muffled splash.

All that remained behind was a dropped revolver, a piece of rope with a fashioned slip knot and a bedraggled semi-conscious seagull.

In the distance, from the West Pier, the fog-bell tolled like an intimation of mortality.

Meanwhile James McLevy was about to make peace with his maker –though the situation was far from tranquil.

In fact it more resembled a nightmare from which the

sleeper struggles to awake, where every breath jolts the heart with a premonition of impending doom.

When they had hit the water, the coldness had shot through his body and shocked him like a lightning bolt.

The inspector was enveloped in darkness near infernal, immersed in an element he had always feared would be the death of him, and locked in combat with a man who seemed intent on giving him an undesired and fatal baptism.

The two men were clasped together in a deadly embrace, McLevy clinging like a limpet round Dunbar's neck because it was the only way to keep afloat. He also knew that if Dunbar were granted any space to exercise those powerful forearms, he would be drowned like a rat.

Which was happening in any case, as Hercules took a deep breath then dived under the water taking McLevy with him. The policeman managed to grab a gulp of air before the sea claimed them both but his lungs were being stretched to breaking point and his whole being thrashed in dreadful panic as the most primitive fear overwhelmed him.

His mouth was shut but the water coursed up the nostrils, into his eyes, the salt blinding and the desperate need for inhalation building up into a silent scream.

The weight of his heavy overcoat threatened to drag him even deeper as he tried to hold on to his adversary because if he let go he would drown like a dog. Then Dunbar drove his fist into McLevy's distended solar plexus.

The last remnants of air whooshed out in a trail of bubbles and McLevy spluttered as water rushed in to replace the other element.

Then just when he thought he could bear it no longer, Dunbar drove up to the surface again, the inspector still clinging on like a limpet.

They were locked together face to face, both breathing heavily but Hercules had enough to spare for last rites.

'I am sorry James McLevy,' he wheezed a trifle painfully. 'As you say. A long journey. Take my secret with you.'

With this remark, Hercules Dunbar drew in another deep breath and plunged them once more into the cold deadly sea.

This was the final act. McLevy felt his whole body freeze as it recognised imminent annihilation.

Again the water swirled around him, drowning the world in a clammy dank embrace and he was sinking deeper into the flood, his consciousness failing, darkness at the back of his eyes, ready to welcome extinction.

What had saved him would now be his death. Dunbar would hold him under till his lungs collapsed.

As a dying man is supposed to experience his life flashing before his eyes, so McLevy had a vivid picture of the moment Dunbar and the other boys had held his head under the Water of Leith, then released him to lie gasping on the bank, howling with laughter as they ran away to leave him alive and swearing vengeance.

Vengeance. And he had wreaked it. With two kicks of his tackety boots.

And suddenly there was another howling. The wolf would fight for its existence, consciousness be damned.

McLevy let out a bloodcurdling scream regardless of the water that rushed in, prised himself away from Dunbar and kicked the man just below the kneecap with all the force he could muster.

Dunbar's grip slackened. One more kick. The other knee.

Now, whether the cartilage tissue at that spot had its own historical memory of pain and humiliation or it had been grievously weakened by the blows from all these years ago, in truth mattered very little, but the end result was that Dunbar loosed his hold from the terrible agony incurred.

The inspector grasped the man by his waterlogged hair, pulled the head back to expose the throat and hammered a series of devastating blows into the soft flesh. Dunbar reached out to try a catch at McLevy's eyes with his hooked fingers, but they found no purchase.

Another few blows and suddenly Hercules Dunbar had

gone, down into the depths of the sea and McLevy was heading in the opposite direction like a cork out of a bottle.

He broke the surface of the calm water, gasping and retching for breath, then began to sink immediately, for as has been previously related McLevy could not swim a stroke and he had just destroyed his only means of flotation.

The inspector tried to shout but his voice had been strangled by the salt of the sea, and the darkness before him lay unbroken like a waiting shroud.

The heavy coat was yet again dragging him under and though he thrashed around desperately, it was a losing battle.

As if to emphasise this, something thudded painfully into the back of his head. He grabbed at it in the darkness and his fingers made contact with the splintered rough surface of the large piece of timber that the wild young boys had thrown into the sea.

A blessing on the wild boys.

McLevy hoisted himself on to the spar, the upper part of his body sprawled across while his legs dangled in the sea.

It was deathly cold and he felt his senses slipping but he wedged himself as best he could and thus drifted off into the misty darkness.

However the tide had now turned and Inspector James McLevy was heading out to sea, where he might join with the shipwrecks and ghastly mariners who inhabit the edges of the watery main.

Once more the fog-bell sounded in the night.

38

Methought I saw a thousand fearful wracks;
A thousand men that fishes gnawed upon;
Wedges of gold, great anchors, heaps of pearl,
Inestimable stones, unvalued jewels,
All scattered in the bottom of the sea.

WILLIAM SHAKESPEARE, *Richard III*

The woman's body was facing away. Her black hair streamed behind like sea snakes in the water of the deep.

His mother, Maria McLevy, hand still clutching the shearing scissors used to cut her throat.

The little boy floated towards her. Jamie McLevy, he would save her, everything would be fine, they would be happy and she would smile and hold him close.

Except that his mother had rarely smiled and never held him close.

No matter. Jamie would save her anyway.

He was no longer afraid of the water. See? He could move, breathe, his body was weightless and he twirled round like a seal for the sheer joy of motion.

She was vertical, standing on the bottom of the sea, as he approached and gently touched her shoulder to let her know that the saviour was at hand.

The contact from the tip of his finger spun her round and he looked into her countenance.

The red bloodline was still etched across her throat but other than that her face was peaceful.

Except for the eyes. The sockets were empty and, as he watched, a small black eel slipped out of one, with another wormy creature following.

They chased each other, in and out of both sockets and the

290

horrified little boy realised that the eels were playing hide and seek.

Life and death.

Hide and seek.

James McLevy let out a fearsome roar, opened his eyes and found himself looking up at Lieutenant Roach.

The inspector was somewhat reassured. Roach might bear a passing resemblance to various sea monsters but his eyes, though bloodshot, were firmly in their sockets.

The lieutenant suddenly whipped out a handkerchief to let loose an explosive sneeze.

'I hope I'm not catching a cold from you, McLevy,' he admonished the still figure in the hospital bed. 'Proximity to dampness is a dangerous pastime.'

The inspector nodded. It was about all he could manage.

Roach accepted such as a signal of health.

'I have passed this time composing a funeral oration just in case,' he announced. 'Would you like to hear it?'

'No thank you,' McLevy croaked faintly.

Roach walked away from the bed and winced as stiff joints cracked accompaniment; he had been sitting in a chair for more hours than he cared to bring to mind, until the inspector's muffled yelps had brought him to the bedside.

There was a high window in the room and the officer peered out through it on to the street below. He sniffed at some flowers in a vase on the windowsill, scratched a fingernail upon the glass, and threw some words over his shoulder.

'A fishing boat came upon an object floating in the sea. Dragged you aboard like a beached whale.'

McLevy said nothing in reply; other than lingering facets of the dream, his thoughts were lucid enough as he recollected the events aboard the ship and on the pier but the rest of his animal functions seemed to be in some state of suspension.

'The boat had been out all night for a poor harvest,' Roach continued. 'Then they found you. A prize catch, eh?'

The lieutenant's dry laughter hung in the air like a line of washing and McLevy discovered a raging thirst.

'Could I have some water, please?'

'Have you not had sufficient of that substance?' Roach muttered as he walked back to pour into a tumbler from the jug, which lay on a small table beside the bed.

McLevy levered himself up, jammed a pillow behind for support then took the tumbler and slowly sipped at what had nearly killed him.

'Like a beached whale,' said Roach with satisfaction.

'When did they find me?'

'First light.'

'What hour is it now?'

'Middle afternoon.'

That meant the *Dorabella* was long gone.

'Of the second day,' the lieutenant added.

Long, long gone.

'Second day?'

'You have been lost to the world for more than thirty hours. A relief for many.'

McLevy's eyes were beginning to focus and for the first time he noted that his normally immaculate lieutenant had grown some stubble on his long chin and the stiff white collar was somewhat crumpled.

'How long have you been here, sir?'

'Too long for my comfort.'

The idea that McLevy might glean a smidgeon of solace from his concern and possibly use it one day to advantage sent Roach into total disavowal of any affection.

He straightened up into official posture and blew his nose reprovingly.

'I am assuming inspector,' he said with another sideways twitch of the jaw, 'that you have an explanation for this maritime farrago?'

McLevy closed his eyes somewhat wearily.

'I have indeed, sir. But it's nothing that cannot wait until tomorrow.'

'That is a decision for me to make not you. By the way a passenger has been reported missing from a boat bound for the New World, his wife is in a terrible state. Would this have anything to do with yourself by any chance?'

'She is not his wife,' McLevy answered obliquely.

'How would you know?'

'It's a long story, sir.'

McLevy's head drooped on to his chest and Roach grunted at the sight.

'You were making a terrible noise before you honoured us with your waking presence.'

'I was dreaming.'

'About what precisely?'

'Hide and seek.'

Roach shook his head, strangely relieved that things were getting back to normal.

'I shall hear the tale tomorrow, inspector. It had better be good.'

Hercules Dunbar was at the bottom of the ocean; the lovers would no doubt be discovered, freed, and then sail on for Argentina where there was no treaty of extradition and all policemen have moustaches and gold teeth.

Would this make a good tale? McLevy wondered.

The lieutenant would not be best pleased but a mitigating factor might be that the Forbes case would not therefore have to be reopened and the man's reputation could remain intact and free from shame.

After all, like Dunbar, he had paid for his sins with his life, the insurance company was not out of pocket and the only person who had lost materially was a certain bawdy-hoose keeper.

Unless, of course, you count Mulholland's loss of his one true love.

Is love material?

The suicide was already hushed up due to the deft hand of the Masonic Brotherhood and now the whole mess could be swept under the carpet.

Respectable houses are full of such cover.

McLevy became aware that Roach was still there, though he had moved to the door and opened it.

'You were lucky to survive, James. A guardian angel must have been flying on the waves.'

The lieutenant looked across, a wry, baffled twist to his long snout.

For a moment McLevy met his gaze, then both men looked away in some embarrassment.

'Close your eyes and it might be she will appear,' said Roach in a rare burst of poetic imagination.

'Who will?'

'Your guardian angel. Goodbye,' was the cryptic response as the lieutenant shut the door to dream of his own heavenly guide who might cure a vicious slice that had appeared lately on the course to plague him.

It might be connected to the fact that Mrs Roach was talking of taking in lodgers. Young men, preferably.

The lieutenant stopped and swung his arms slowly.

A slice was the very devil.

He walked through a swing door; nodded to someone he knew and departed the scene.

McLevy as instructed replaced the tumbler and closed his eyes.

He dozed off into a fragile, broken slumber but mercifully without images thrown up from the deep and later he could have sworn to hear the door click open again.

Surely Lieutenant Roach had not returned to vex him further over protocol?

As he struggled once more back to consciousness he sniffed a vaguely recognised fragrance.

Rosewater maybe?

Did guardian angels use such?

He risked a squint hoping perhaps to see a resplendent being with golden wings, radiance manifesting from every orifice, but instead he saw a woman in a long black coat with what looked like a peacock feather sprouting from her head. It turned out to be stuck upon a fashionable hat.

'You look a sight,' said Jean Brash.

McLevy stuck out his lower lip like a little boy.

'Whit are you doing here?' he muttered.

'Lieutenant Roach sent word you were at death's door. I came to help you through.'

He wasn't quite sure how to interpret that, but nodded as if it made sense.

Then he remembered something that might take the sour look off her face because they had parted on bad terms last meeting, and Jean, like most women, could hold a grudge till hell froze over.

Behind her, McLevy had just noted, hung up to dry on a stand in the corner, was his greatcoat.

'Were ye ever a pocket delver?' he asked.

'A girl has to live,' she answered tersely.

He had just about enough strength to raise his arm and point a finger at the coat.

'Try your skill.'

Jean Brash crossed to the coat and slipped an adroit hand into both outer pockets.

She came up blank but on running her hands like a caress down each side, found a promising bulge, slid her fingers inside, undid the securing flap and the digits emerged holding the pearl necklace; more than a little damp from its ordeal but once carefully dried and lightly caressed with the finest cloth, the delicate greeny black would glow like a panther's eyes.

Jean's own green eyes sparkled with delight. This was her treasure beyond all riches; Tahitian pearls she had paid a king's ransom to own, the seller being a villainous South Sea smuggler who had landed up in Edinburgh because of the number of throats he had cut in exotic climes.

She'd had them certified genuine by no less that the Royal jewellers themselves, cashed in everything she possessed to buy them and sent the smuggler sailing to cut more throats.

The French Empress Eugenie had once owned such a necklace, though the pearls were twice as numerous and twice as big but then she'd had to sell them when the Empire fell.

Twice as big.

But then Eugenie had been an Empress.

Jean was merely a bawdy-hoose keeper.

She had relished wearing the necklace at the Just Land, holding to herself its great value, the subtle unassuming beauty of the gems nuzzling next to her skin.

Her heart had near broken at their loss and now she had them back thanks to this awkward bugger on the bed.

'Oh James McLevy!' she exclaimed. 'You are a wonder of the world!'

He blinked. Women, in his opinion, were often simple creatures. A few wee pearls cheered them up no end.

The peacock plume dipped approvingly as Jean fastened the necklace once more round her neck, safer there than any-where. Then she came over and sat on the bed facing the inspector who tried to look as if this happened every day.

'Tell me the story, James?' she inquired tenderly.

And he did. Keeping it brief for his strength was not great. The salient points, naked backsides glossed over.

She was silent when he concluded but her mind was racing like a blood-horse. Rachel Bryden had obviously worn the necklace because she aped her mistress but luckily the tawdry bitch had not realised the true value or she would have hidden it up the leg of her drawers.

That was to Jean's good fortune but not quite enough com-pensation; there was the small matter of Hannah Semple's injury, now mercifully healed, and Jean's own humiliation, not healed remotely.

McLevy meanwhile was dying for a cup of coffee but hospitals were not noted for such a remedy.

'Buenos Aires?' Jean murmured.

'Uhuh.'

'I have a friend there,' said Jean. 'She keeps a bordello.'

'That's a surprise.'

'It is a low-class establishment down by the docks, my friend has always enjoyed the rougher end of trade.'

'Unlike your braw self.'

The inspector must be recovering because he was beginning to look grumpy, but Jean paid it no mind. She would write to her friend who was also in cahoots with some of the most nefarious cut-throats of that lawless community.

The lovers would be found, if not the rest of her jewels. And after that?

'I shall see about getting Rachel some employment. It is the least I can do.'

Miss Bryden could ply her willowy trade with the scum of the harbour, lascars, pirates, plus the odd slave dealer thrown in.

We'd see how long she kept her looks.

McLevy, exhausted or no, had not been fooled in the slightest by Jean's apparent philanthropy. There was an evil glint in those green eyes.

'What about Oliver Garvie, your demon lover?'

'My friend has another establishment, equally squalid.'

'For restless women?'

'For hungry men.'

'Oh, dear.'

It would seem love's destination was fraught with woe, and Cupid might count himself lucky not to be in Buenos Aires.

McLevy felt a tide of weariness sweep over him, what was it the bible said?

Sufficient unto the day is the evil thereof.

'I lost my revolver at the harbour,' he remembered.

'I'll find it for you,' promised Jean.

He nodded, then slid under the clean crisp sheets and brought them up to his nose.

'I'm off to the Land of Nod,' he announced, and promptly fell unconscious.

After a few moments he began to snore, another sign that he was returning to himself.

Jean hesitated for a second then bent down and kissed him gently on the brow.

'Sleep well, James.'

On these words Jean Brash left, checking before she opened the door that her pearls were in place. A girl can't be too careful.

McLevy slept like a child, a profound and dreamless slumber where his soul travelled to far-flung shores of the psyche and found there, rest and contentment.

For one brief instant, there may have been the merest flicker of Icarus in his mind but it was harmless, promptly banished, and did not reappear.

He was shaken into consciousness some six hours later to perceive not a guardian angel but a small starched figure, uniformed, ramrod straight, who then proceeded to light the lamp beside his bed.

'I am Nurse Sheekey,' she announced. 'Are ye awake?'

'I am now,' he muttered.

'Folk sleep their life away,' she remarked cuttingly.

The woman bustled to the door and threw a command back just as she exited.

'Pull yourself up, Mister McLevy. I have something on hand for you.'

Then she was gone and he, hoping that she had not been referring to a purge of some sort, groggily levered himself once more, stuck the pillow behind and sat there like a dog in a kennel, waiting for its bone.

And it duly arrived in the form of a tray with a steaming coffee pot, innumerable lumps of sugar in a bowl, a fine china cup and saucer with a plate of sugar biscuits on the side.

The tray was placed on astounded McLevy's lap where he sat, then Nurse Sheekey stood back to admire her handiwork.

'Don't thank me,' she declared before he could open his mouth. 'The nice lady came back and arranged all this. I just heated up the coffee.'

The inspector sniffed at the spout of the pot. It was a Lebanese grinding. Jean Brash.

'She paid for this single room as well,' Nurse Sheekey further vouchsafed grimly.

McLevy had puzzled over this previously because he had been sufficiently *compos mentis* to notice that the room was well appointed, even a vase of flowers at the window.

He had wondered about that because he did not see either Lieutenant Roach or the police authority rising to such generous heights.

Probably why the lieutenant had informed Jean, to spare himself the expense.

'I was wondering about that,' he said.

'Well now ye know.'

With this pithy rejoinder, Nurse Sheekey marched to the door where she turned to address him.

'Are you James McLevy the thieftaker?' she asked.

'I am indeed.'

'You're a lucky man.'

On that remark she shut the door and was gone.

Maybe he was a lucky man. He should have known better than try to save his mother, she was dead and gone. Though it was a wound that would never heal.

Leave that be.

He had enjoyed, however, the feeling of freedom as he floated in the water.

Perhaps he would learn how to swim.

Leave that be, also.

James McLevy reached out and with trembling hand, poured the black and sacred liquor into the cup. Four lumps of sugar, a wee nibble on a biscuit to tantalise the taste buds and then?

He raised his cup to Jean Brash, and drank.

And it came to pass that nearly an hour later, the patients of the Leith Hospital, suffering under a variety of ailments, heard, drifting faintly from one of the upper rooms, fragments of a Jacobite melody.

James McLevy danced around the hospital room in his bare feet, nightgown billowing at his calves, fuelled no doubt by three strong draughts of the finest Lebanese, but also a weird elation as if a great weight had been lifted from his shoulders.

And as he danced he sang accordingly, lifting a dainty corner of the nightgown to allow the making of a leg.

> ' 'Twas on a Monday morning,
> Right early in the year,
> When Charlie came to our town
> The Young Chevalier.
> Charlie is my darling, my darling, my darling,
> Charlie is my darling, the Young Chevalier.'

Through the high window where the vase of flowers looked out into the dark, the night sky was clear and as he capered joyfully within, a shooting star fell from heaven to the earth below.

What goes up must come down. That is the nature of things. But McLevy didn't give a damn. The case was over.